Destination Waterloo

Destination Waterloo

A Pennywhistle novel

by

John Danielski

www.penmorepress.com

Destination Waterloo John M. Danielski
Copyright © 2023 John M. Danielski

ISBN: 978-1-957851-23-5 (EBOOK)
ISBN: 978-1-957851-24-2 (Paperback)
BISAC Subject Headings:
    FIC014000FICTION / Historical
    FIC032000FICTION / War & Military

Editor: Chris Wozney
 Cover design:
EMILIJA RAKIĆ PR EMILYS WORLD OF DESIGN
Please send all correspondence to:

Penmore Press LLC
920 N Javelina Pl
Tucson AZ 85748

Dedication

To Hans Koenig, a great teacher and an even better friend.

And in memory of Professor Bernard Bachrach at the University of Minnesota, who taught me that the essence of history is story-telling.

Acknowledgments

Special thanks to my editor Chris Wozney for making our weekly conferences so much fun. To paraphrase Frank Loesser, "She has the cool, clear eyes of a seeker of wisdom and truth, yet with the slam, bang, tang reminiscent of gin and vermouth."

Special thanks to James S. Danielski for his advice on the characters of Maxwell and the two Gagnes.

Special thanks to Joe Hopkins for his patient policing of the many iterations of this work.

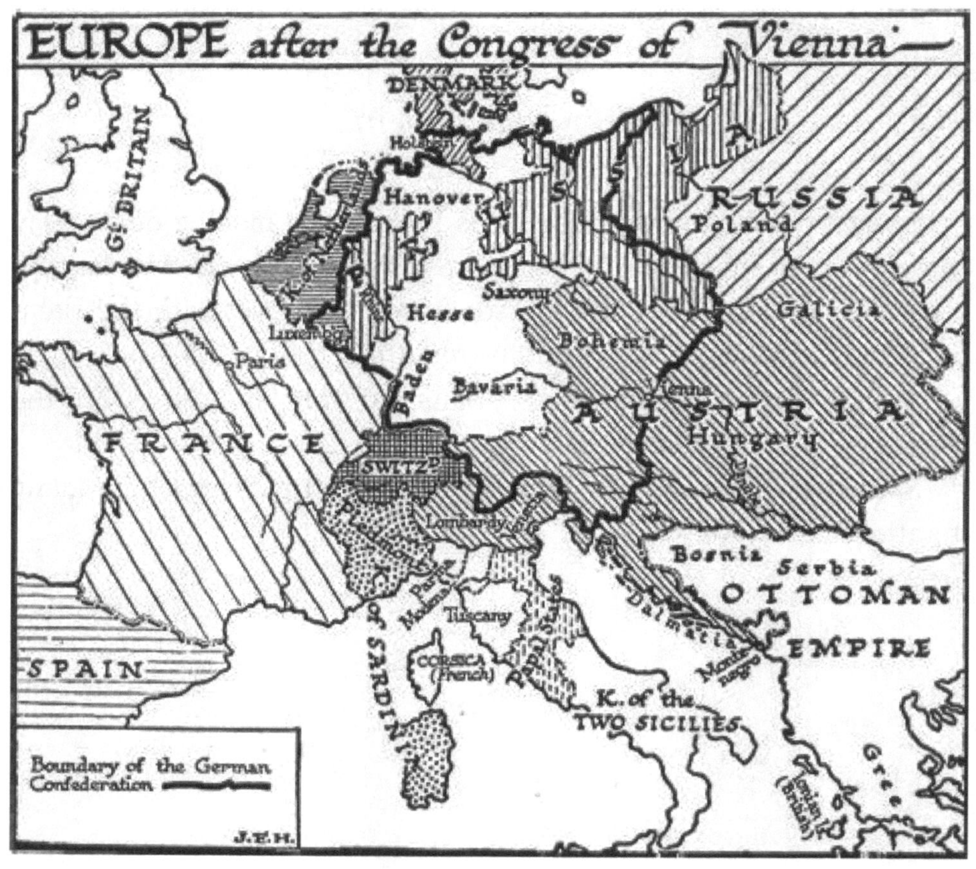

EUROPE after the Congress of Vienna
Gt BRITAIN
DENMARK
Holstein
Hanover
Saxony
Hesse
Luxemburg
Paris
Baden
Bavaria
FRANCE
SWITZ.
Lombardy
Bohemia
Vienna
AUSTRIA
Hungary
RUSSIA
Poland
Galicia
Tuscany
CORSICA
(French)
K. of SARDINIA
Bosnia
Serbia
Dalmatia
Montenegro
OTTOMAN
EMPIRE
K. of the
TWO SICILIES
Ionian Is
(British)
Greece
SPAIN
Boundary of the German
Confederation
J.F.H.

Destination Waterloo

"In war, everything is simple but even the simplest thing is difficult."
— Karl von Clausewitz

Chapter 1

Maiden Voyage

12 June 1815

Waves of fog rolled into Boulogne Harbor like sheets of delicate silk. A slight wind put misty crests on the surf lapping against the harbor breakwater. 20 anchored vessels bobbed gently with the incoming tide and patchy, slow moving clouds took turns blotting out the full moon. The harbor front was deserted, save for a flock of gulls sheltering beneath exposed dock pylons and two assistants of the harbormaster ringing loud fog bells every thirty seconds. It was a good night to stay indoors but an even better one for sabotage.

Atop a mist-cloaked hill overlooking the harbor, the melancholy cries of the bells camouflaged the sounds of Thomas Pennywhistle dashing from the pine woods. Coming up directly behind the patrolling sentry, his right leg lashed out in a vicious stomp of the man's left calf and his fist crashed hard into the base of his skull. The guard collapsed without a sound but still drew breath. He should have used a knife instead of a fist, but Pennywhistle saw no point in inflicting unnecessary death: the guard would be out for long enough for his expedition to accomplish its purpose. He looked to be an older man, probably an unemployed veteran only recently returned to the colors. That tracked with what he had observed of the rest of the 80-man garrison. It was probably a *corps de reserve*: a "Dad's Army" composed of men who were unfit for field work but could adequately perform garrison duty. Bonaparte need every fit man for active campaigning.

Only a high stone wall separated Pennywhistle from the Port du Plaisance Dockyard. The Dockyard occupied a spear-shaped spit of land that stood at right angles to the main channel of Boulogne Harbor. Eighteen 12-pound garrison guns defended the seaward side-a belated response to the 1806 Congreve Rocket attack that had burned much of the port to the ground. The land walls were strong but showed the ravages of age and neglected maintenance.

He inserted a grappling hook into the barrel of a specially modified Giradoni air rifle, aimed carefully above the summit of the 12-foot-high wall, and fired. There was no flash and the only sound was a quiet *phut*. The hook soared through the air and dropped on the other side of the wall. He jerked hard and felt strong resistance: the hook had bitten hard onto the wall's surface.

The rest of his team emerged from the shelter of the pines. Lieutenant Balthazar Barton of the Royal Engineers was a scholarly man who was an expert in constructing, operating, or dissecting anything mechanical. Lieutenant Barclay Cochrane of the Royal Navy was an impulsive man bursting with the passions inspired by his many enthusiasms. He was also a superb pilot and helmsman with an encyclopedic memory for the local shoals and sandbars of Boulogne Harbor. Their expertise would be useful in helping him figure out the fate of the prize they sought.

The trio was dressed in the everyday attire of common French sailors: white shirts with black kerchiefs, short blue jackets, loose peppermint-striped trousers, and black leather round hats. They had practiced the rolling gait of sailors on land and had sprinkled drops of whiskey on their jackets to give the impression of just returning from a night of jollification. Rather than traversing the shadows, they would hide in plain sight. If captured, they would be summarily shot as spies.

Two other teams of three dressed similarly were approaching the dockyard, one from the East by land, armed with the expedition's weapons, and one from the West by boat, armed with the expedition's explosives. The teams were dispersed because smaller groups were less likely to be noticed. Unencumbered by heavy accoutrements, Pennywhistle's men could move the fastest and could serve as a rally point for the other two.

Pennywhistle loaded a second grappling hook into the Giradoni then pulled the rope tight and began to climb. When he reached the summit of the wall, he lay on his belly, and fired the air rifle a second time, this time at a 45-degree angle. The second grappling hook lodged in the lintel of a door to an equipment shed. He took a piton and small hammer from his haversack and drilled the piton into the stone between the trigger and trigger guard, turning the gun into an anchor. He pulled the line taut, then removed a greased iron contrivance that resembled the Greek letter omega. It had handholds at its sides. Pennywhistle draped it over the rope, then gripped its handholds. He gave a quick shove with his shoes and found himself sailing over a smelly swamp that acted as a second line of defense. Ten seconds later he dropped three feet to dry ground.

His team followed a minute later, and he conversed with them briefly. "Stick to the plan and stay close to me. You all know the layout of the dockyard and our objective is the rope walk building. If the fog becomes too thick to see well, let the Rhyme of Signs guide you. They are the markers of the small wine kiosks used by civilian contractors and will serve as our waypoints:

"Past the swamp and two streets west, tread
to the sign of a Gamecock's Head.
Round the corner, two streets north, then follow
until you come to the tidal hollow.
Incline to the left and count paces ten
to the sign of the Fox's Den.
Incline right and ten paces more
to the Sign of the Toreador.
One street East, straight as a scope,
will lead you to the House of Rope.

"If a guard sees you, bluff it out. Don't retreat, sing; loudly and off key, as if you wish him to join in your celebrating. '*Ah! Les Crocodiles*' is certainly bawdy enough and you all know the words. The craft we seek will be moored to the leeward dock. Once we rendezvous with other teams, we will determine a course of action. *HMS Amphion* is standing by to supply a tow, but I am not sure if we can figure out how to pilot her in the few minutes we shall have available. In that case, we scuttle her."

Pennywhistle sensed the men's curiosity. While his own interest in the weapon was considerable, his main desire was to get the job done so he could be reunited with his wife.

Napoleon's escape from Elba changed everything for Pennywhistle. He simmered with a smoldering rage born of frustrated plans. He had been serving as the British Naval Attaché at the Congress of Vienna and had been pleased at the contributions he had made to a lasting peace-something of an atonement for the lives he had taken during his 12 years as a seagoing soldier. His plans to resume civilian life had exploded on March 7, when the Congress received word that Bonaparte had escaped his island prison. Bonaparte was declared an international outlaw by the Congress and plans were swiftly laid to assemble military forces to bring him to justice. The Duke of Wellington, who was serving as the British Minister Plenipotentiary, was designated to command the Allied Forces defending the Low Countries; the place where the returned tyrant would likely strike first.

Pennywhistle reflected that Wellington, as a young man, had been an accomplished violinist, but had burned his violin when he decided to shed the mantle of the dilettante officer and adopt that of the serious soldier. Pennywhistle felt that returning to war was his metaphorical equivalent of playing a burned-up violin. He could have declined Wellington's request to serve as naval aide, but his wife knew his sense of duty even better than he did.

"Wellington is the greatest commander of the age except for Bonaparte, and you have earned his trust, something he does not give lightly," his wife, Sammie Jo, had told him. She was a blunt spoken American who wore the mantle of an English lady uneasily.

"He prizes discretion, and Castlereagh has undoubtedly told him of how you cleverly solved a thorny problem for the Prince Regent without bringing any unwanted attention to the Crown. Besides, you would be impossible to live with if you said no to the Duke. Oh, you'd be fine for a week or so, would put on a brave front and pretend that family mattered more than duty, but deep down you'd know that you could not give your full attention to me and your child because you hated yourself for choosing the safe, easy path. You've worn duty like the hair shirt of a monk, and try as I might, I have never been able to persuade you to take it off for more than a few days at a time. To miss history in the making would gnaw at you, and you'd eventually spend your days pining for action. Vienna would become a prison... and you might even come to resent me. Admit it, you want to be there when Bonaparte is finished for good. Don't worry about me, I will manage just fine. Margaret will help me through the birth and make sure the best midwives in Vienna are at my side. When you get settled in

Brussels and fully understand your duties, send word and I will come as fast as I can."

"But I so want to be present when our child is born! Leaving you when you are close to term seems the action of... well... a cad."

Sammie Jo had smiled at him. "Not marrying me would have been the action of a cad. Carrying on with other ladies would make you a cad. I know what you are, and I know where you need to be. I ain't no fragile thing who faints at the sight of blood, not even my own, and I can handle pain. Besides, midwives generally keep men out of the birthing bedroom. After everything we've been though, why should I be afeared of a little thing like labor?"

That conversation had occurred two and a half months ago. The period in between had been one of chaos and confusion as Wellington hastily assembled an army, many of the men raw levies, and worked hard to whip them into fighting trim. To further complicate matters, it was a multinational army composed not just of British, but Dutch, Belgian, Hanoverian, Brunswick, Nassau, Saxon, and Westphalian allies.

His own duties as the naval aide-de-camp had to be learned on the job. He was supposed to be a staff officer but often functioned as a free roving intelligence gatherer who needed the experience of a line officer to fix a myriad of problems. His recent promotion to lieutenant colonel of the Royal Marines gave him sufficient authority that his official requests were taken seriously, and his knighthood gave him enough social cachet that he was invited to high toned parties where deadly serious business was transacted over games of billiards.

His chief duty was to ensure that Wellington's naval supply line was protected. That line ran from England across the Channel to the port of Ostend, Belgium, then seventy miles to Antwerp, then another forty miles to headquarters in Brussels. The Royal Navy was usually more than adequate for policing sea lanes, but the threat Pennywhistle faced this night was unique because it was based on an unknown technology that everyone thought had failed years ago. Emil du Picq, however, had thought otherwise, and like a modern Prometheus, he had brought a new kind of fire to mankind.

Pennywhistle operated an informal network of spies in the Channel Ports, and over the past two weeks had received reports of a deadly ship that was being readied for sea trials. Rumors had filtered into Wellington's headquarters that Bonaparte's newly constituted *L' armée du Nord* was about to move, so it made sense that Bonaparte might contrive a naval annoyance that could be synchronized with the army's advance.

At first Pennywhistle had thought his agents' reports exaggerations, but when one brought a partial set of design plans for the contrivance, his skepticism had vanished. He'd studied the design carefully over several nights, marveling at the complexity of the machine but frustrated at not having the complete specifications; like a novel with a beginning and end but no middle.

The machine was a ship built of copper plates around iron ribs. It was named *Nautilus* and could tow a mine called a carcass: a cigar shaped copper cylinder containing two hundred pounds of gunpowder. The mine contained a spike that could penetrate an enemy hull, and contact triggered a gunlock mechanism that ignited the gunpowder. The mine was attached to a long line that unspooled as *Nautilus* guided it toward a target. The Americans had devised a similar weapon during the War of Independence and called it a torpedo, after the *torpedo nobilianus:* a cylindrical species of fish whose body generated an electric shock when touched. This weapon had blown up a forty-foot sloop provided by the Ministry of Marine, or so one of his agents had insisted.

Plans for the dockyard were not difficult to obtain, but it had taken a week to assemble a team, formulate a tactical deployment, and clandestinely cover the 78 miles between Ostend and Boulogne. An entire day and night had been expended conducting a covert reconnaissance to get an idea of defenses and sentry routines. The Royal Navy had cooperated, assigning a frigate to the use of his expedition. He would alert the ship with a blue signal rocket. HMS *Amphion* was already in position, with the wind fair for a close approach to Boulogne Harbor.

Angry words were being exchanged in the Dockyard Superintendents' Office as Pennywhistle's infiltration began.

"I can't believe it!" exclaimed *Capitaine de Vasseu* Marius Ducasse. Ducasse was a tall, sharp-featured teetotaler of thirty years who radiated the intellect, zeal and vigor of the True Believer as well as a contempt for anyone who did not meet his lofty ideals of abstention from alcohol. His impeccably tailored captain's uniform of blue broadcloth reeked of Parisian hauteur and was a complete contrast to the dirty, rumpled uniform of the middle-aged man he faced. "Nautilus' sea trials begin tomorrow morning and instead of doubling security patrols and leading them *yourself*,-which is the correct conduct for an officer, I find you tucked away in your office, sprawled on a cot! With a bottle of brandy in one hand and a whore in the other! What manner of soldier are you? The Emperor is counting on you to protect the ship I am to command!"

"Don't you go pickin' on my Rene! He's a good man!" slurred the young redhead cradled in the Chef-de-Brigade's arm.

"Silence, woman!"

"Manners, Ducasse! I thought you aristos prided yourself on them. I may have come up through the ranks, but I have shown courtesy to women since childhood." boasted the Dockyard's commander in a gravelly voice suffused with rum. Rene Paradis was a squat man who was the temperamental opposite of Ducasse: cynical, greedy, and unenterprising. He looked the sort who had been given his present job by a relative and had accepted it only on the promise that he could extort kickbacks from the dockyard contractors.

"I have two three-man patrols out presently and that is more than adequate. You demand miracles from a command of old men, Ducasse, but I have more realistic expectations. If you have something brittle, you use it carefully, not push it hard. I remind you that I have been fighting the enemies of France for fifteen years while you have been fighting them for... oh that's right... you've never been shot at."

"You have been 'fighting' from behind a desk! It is only bad luck, Paradis, that has kept me from confronting the enemies of the Emperor. The success of *Nautilus* will give me a chance to remedy that situation in a way that will alter the course of history! You must understand what is at stake here! Command of the entire English Channel! I have trained my crews and support personnel meticulously, and tomorrow they will show the world just how effective is good training! You, on the other hand, have fobbed off the supervision of your men onto that old relic, Cadieux, who is an even worse sot than you are!"

"Enough!" barked Paradis. "I have better things to do than listen to an arrogant young pup tell me how to do my job and rant about phantom future events. Go back and tuck your babies into their bunks and give them the benefit of..." he sneered... "your *wisdom* in a bedtime story."

"I shall send word to the Emperor of this outrage! You will be sorry you did not listen to me!"

"I am already sorry that I have listened to you. Intriguing behind your superior's back is exactly what I would expect of you, Ducasse, but you will find I have friends in high places."

Ducasse looked as if he would explode. He opened his mouth to speak then realized he was confronting a brick wall. Red faced, he spun on his heel and exited the room with an angry step.

"More brandy, my dear?"

"Thank you, Rene. You are so civilized. Unlike that horrid young man who just left."

Pennywhistle's team advanced through the dockyard boldly but it was largely deserted. They passed one patrol and waved merrily to the men as they staggered drunkenly. The guards shook their heads in amusement at the antics of the young out for a carouse; it was the time of night when men like themselves preferred to be sound asleep.

Twice they nearly got lost when the fog thickened but the rhyme saved them. Then a strong wind sprang up and dissipated the fog entirely.

When Pennywhistle rounded the corner of the large ropewalk building, the leeward dock came into view. Absent the fog, the bright full moon illuminated *Nautilus* at anchor. She rode low in the water, with two-thirds of her bulk below the surface. Her 6.5-meter copper hull resembled a horizontal teardrop with a tall metal dome atop the vessel's forecastle. She was half as tall as she was long, had a beam of just under two meters, and a draft of 2.5 meters. The three portholes in the dome covered 300 degrees of vision and made it a functional conning tower. The top of a double-bladed wooden screw at her stern protruded above the waterline. Pennywhistle knew from his stolen set of plans that it was used for propulsion. Two adjustable horizontal diving planes were attached to her rudder and an extendable snorkel tube to ingest air lay just behind the dome. Beneath the hull were twin iron ballast tanks that could be filled with water. This craft was a true submarine vessel, capable of delivering a torpedo while submerged.

It had a furled, ribbed sail just astern of the dome. The sail seemed to be a secondary method of propulsion. Pennywhistle knew from the blueprints that propulsion was supplied by an interior hand crank that turned a long shaft that in turn rotated the exterior screw. It would not be a fast vessel, but it nevertheless could move when a lack of wind becalmed sailing vessels — an invaluable asset.

Proximity to the intriguing invention had an effect on Pennywhistle; his original intention to destroy it quickly melted in the forge of his curiosity. He resolved to capture it instead.

The three guards on the dock in front were sitting, not standing. They were conversing quietly, in between taking puffs of their pipes. They looked anything but menacing.

Pennywhistle knew that the best way to allay suspicion was to ask for someone's help. He pasted a drunken smile on his face and lurched forward. "Say, friends, could you help me and my mates out? We want to smoke our own pipes but seem to have forgotten our lucifers."

The first guard looked up at the happily inebriated trio and saw no harm in honoring the requests of sailors. "Certainly, glad to oblige," chuckled a sentry with a large paunch. "But with all the rum you've had, are you sure you want to ignite anything? Ha! Ha! Ha!"

"We like to live dangerously," laughed Pennywhistle in response. He ambled toward the one who held out a match.

Three kicks and three punches later, Pennywhistle had rendered the sentries unconscious. Cochrane bound them with stray bits of rope careless workers had left lying on the dock. Then the men surveyed the invention in the water.

"What a remarkable craft!"," exclaimed Cochrane. "I had heard rumors of a wonder ship's existence, but when I made inquiries I was told it had been deemed unreliable. Wasn't the inventor Robert Fulton? The American famous for his steamboats."

"He abandoned this project and sold the prototype for scrap," replied Pennywhistle. "The buyer was a wealthy eccentric named Emil du Picq, who lavished mountains of francs on fixing the problems that had plagued its designer. Unfortunately for us, du Picq still intends for it to serve Bonaparte. Now it seems to me that Bonaparte's return to power has an air of desperation to it. He needs every advantage he can muster, and if this invention enjoys even indifferent success, such a vessel prowling the Channel could wreak havoc on British commerce, and the British Navy."

"Ahoy, there!" A voice in English drifted across the dock as the *swish swish* of oars quickly increased in volume.

An 18-foot launch containing Team B pulled alongside the dock and its commander lashed it to a mooring post. "Ahoy, there, Colonel," called out Lieutenant James Masters of the Royal Artillery, a combative man fascinated by the power of explosives. "We have been lying here in the channel for the last twenty minutes, observing. Those guards you subdued look to be the only watchmen. I have the charges ready with pressure activated gunlocks and adhesive backs. Just give the word and I will attach them to the hull as limpet mines and blow this ungodly craft sky high."

"Hold on, Lieutenant. We need to give *Nautilus* a full inspection first. It may be possible to seize her. She is clearly an advanced craft that our own naval architects should have the opportunity to study."

Team C cockily sauntered up: the happy drunk act had clearly worked for them. They concealed their Baker Rifles in circular bags of sailcloth. They could have them ready at a moment's notice to provide a protective cordon of firepower while the inspection proceeded. Royal Marine 1st Lieutenant Carhart snapped to attention and gave a crisp salute that Pennywhistle returned smartly.

"Carhart," commanded Pennywhistle, "I want you and your men to set up observation posts using the cover of those buildings over yonder: ambush positions. The garrison looks to be composed of reactivated retirees and men of science masquerading as sailors. Should either group get too close, three or four rounds should be enough to either keep them occupied or drive them off. Once that is done, dash for the launch. Your actions will give us time to set the charges. Alternatively," Pennywhistle surveyed *Nautilus*, "while it will be a tight fit, this vessel looks big enough to take all nine of us, and I should prefer to depart as her passengers."

"Aye, aye, sir. I will make it so."

A blue rocket pierced the sky from the sea a mile and a half distant. *Amphion* was in position and the wind was fair for a close approach to Boulogne Harbor.

Pennywhistle's team leaped from the dock onto the strange vessel's hull, then ascended a small stairway that led to an entry hatch in front of the metal dome. Pennywhistle examined the heavy glass in the dome's portholes and decided they allowed enough light to make candles unnecessary during the daytime. A metal rectangle attached to the base of the dome stored reserve air brought in via the snorkel.

The interior of the vessel was narrow and constricted; Pennywhistle felt as if he had just entered a giant beehive. "Ow!" he muttered as he banged his head. The interior was designed for an average-sized Frenchmen, not a man of 6 feet, 2 inches. The smell reminded him of a mixture of oil, charcoal, and old raisins. There were two large candleholders attached to the hull, with candles that were probably made of spermaceti to give maximum illumination as well as minimum smoke. Pennywhistle lit the candles; in addition to providing illumination, they would also be useful for gauging the amount of oxygen.

Barton examined the adjustable slide that could be used to raise and lower the snorkel and thought it was a masterly piece of engineering. He read the expression on his superior's face and gave an engineer's judgement. "I would say we could manage four hours submerged before breathable air became a problem."

Pennywhistle examined the long bench occupied the center of the deck, above which ran a long crank connected to the screw. There were handholds for nine men, though the crank could be turned by as few as two. There was a wheel at the bench's edge to steer the craft. Pennywhistle, Barton, and Cochrane sat down and began to slowly turn the crank. Their actions continued for several minutes until Cochrane gave an assessment. "She might make two, three knots with the crank fully manned and favorable currents. More if the sail is engaged and the wind is strong. The helmsman would have to be guided by instructions from a man peering out the conning tower."

Ducasse's anger with Paradis had not dissipated. Indeed, it had increased in intensity. The anger not only quickened his steps back to the barracks, it sharpened his resolve to act. Time to take matters into his own hands! Paradis had told him to tell his men a bedtime story. By God, he would, but this tale would rouse the men to action! *Esprit de corps* was high in his command of forty men — an elite unit utterly unlike Paradis' casual and ineffectual guards.

He had chosen his men through a rigorous selection process, seeking out ambitious spirits distinguished by their intelligence, active natures, and facility with things mechanical. They had the traditional contempt of sailors for the army, and that went double for incompetent reservists. They would be more than willing to patrol the docks tonight. They had all been issued muskets and though they had practiced little with them, as they were engineers, not butchers; but Ducasse was certain their zeal would ensure they gave a good account of themselves should any intruders materialize.

Pennywhistle surveyed the multiple sealed gauges on the control panel and realized that he had seen them identified in the blueprints of the vessel. The were a compass, clock, barometer, ballast tank fill, vent, and close, heading, speed, distance traveled, depth, pitch, yaw, and diving plane angle. An inclinometer indicated whether the diving planes were pointed up or down and used small bubbles to indicate angles; the bubbles were pressurized carbonated water in mercury. It astonished him that the depth gauge went to twenty meters.

The seven colored toggle switches represented a complete mystery: their functions must have been covered in the part of the plans that he had never seen. He gathered that each color stood for a specific function.

"I know what some of these are, and I can make guesses about the others," contributed Cochrane.

"We may just have to use trial and error: post observers outside to see what happens when we hit a switch. That's assuming our French friends allow us the time to make a systematic examination. We may have to depart in haste and hope for the best."

"Shouldn't we just blow up this contraption?" suggested Masters.

"That would be the safest course, Lieutenant, but this vessel represents something that may change the future of naval warfare."

Next to the panel were two small wheels that opened and closed the doors of the ballast tanks to either admit water or expel it. On the right were two large hand pumps that were used to force out water and make the vessel rise. A rectangular gauge resembling a barometer indicated some kind of drogue was attached to the vessel, perhaps a supply craft.

A foot high galvanic pile lay at the base of the panel, two naked wires protruding from its positive and negative terminals. Galvanic batteries were alternating piles of copper and zinc discs separated by cloth panels. The pile appeared fully charged and designed to deliver a substantial electrical jolt, but looked to be a work in progress that presently served no useful function. Then a memory of Samuel Bentham's dry dock in Portsmouth hit him. Bentham's was the world's first dry dock that flushed the water using steam pumps. Once hooked up, the pile probably would do the same for the ballast tanks, substituting electricity for steam. Mr. Fulton was indeed a clever man.

Crack! Crack! Crack! The shots from Carhart's rifles caught all three Frenchmen in the chest. Carhart hated killing the old men of the patrol, but they had seen something and had been on a direct course to the dock. For now, the coast was clear, and he fervently hoped no one had heard the shots.

But a block away Ducasse and his column of forty men had heard the shots. He had roused them from their bunks, given them a fiery speech, and was quick marching them to guard *Nautilus*. "I was right! I was right!" Ducasse shouted. "There is no time to lose. *Vive l' Empereur! Vive l' Empeureur!*"

Several choruses of *"Vive l' Empereur"* erupted. The sailor's enthusiasm thrilled Ducasse. *They will be unstoppable,* he thought. The pages of the drill manual that he had memorized turned slowly in his mind's eye.

Carhart heard the choruses and found it strange that his opponents had no interest in a cautious, stealthy approach. But then, some commanders believed that shouts and slogans inspire men. Carhart deemed them silly and ridiculous.

Carhart and his assistants, 2nd Lieutenants Kemp and Hodge, sheltered behind salt pork barrels and waited. All were experienced marksmen, and the moon would illuminate their targets. Carhart would dispatch a warning to Pennywhistle as soon as he was sure of how many men he faced.

Pennywhistle had completed his examination of *Nautilus* and had a general idea of how it was operated; nevertheless, he expected contingencies would materialize that required fast improvisation. It was time to test the toggle switches. He was confident that he could get *Nautilus* to sea if she ran on the surface, but a dive would be risky: with his limited knowledge, they might go down but never come up.

Crack! Carhart's first shot wounded Ducasse in the shoulder, but instead of disabling him it increased his anger and determination. The shots of Kemp and Hodge were more effective, killing the men beside him and shocking his sailors, who really were more technicians than military men. They had been rushing forward in a column, the fastest way to move men, but a bad formation for a fight. Ducasse realized he faced trained riflemen and gave the sensible order: fall back and regroup behind the shelter of a long warehouse. A man lacking his zeal would have paused, sent a runner to alert the army, and waited until real soldiers arrived to fight alongside his un-blooded sailors. But he hated Paradis and was determined not to share any credit with him. He therefore decided to attack immediately.

He soothed their alarm with calm words and reminded the men of their patriotic duty to defend "the great experiment" to which they had given months of thought, toil, and tribulation. He formed his sailors into two ranks of twenty men each, made sure muskets were loaded, bayonets fixed, and alignments straight and true. He unfurled his glass and poked it round the corner of the warehouse to survey the area ahead. Though he could see no sign of the enemy, he knew they were out there: waiting, wary, and bent on all sorts of mischief. He had to get them to show themselves, and the best way to do that was by muzzle flashes. Carhart waited patiently, willing to let lambs march to the lion's den.

Ducasse decided to risk a conventional advance, shoulder to shoulder and all in a line. When you were a military sorcerer's apprentice, you went with simple spells. His men had not drilled much, because getting an experimental craft ready had presented a myriad of problems that proved voracious consumers of time, allowing little for parade ground evolutions. Volley fire had two advantages; it compensated for a lack of individual marksmanship and bolstered the confidence of neophytes by promoting a sense of group solidarity.

He gave the command to perform a right wheel, which brought them out from behind the warehouse. He then ordered the sailors to halt, dress ranks, and prepare to advance with bayonets leveled. Ducasse was doing things strictly according to the 1791 standard manual, *Reglement Concernant et les Manoeuvres de Infantrie;* he even recalled the illustration that showed what an advancing line should look like.

A shot rang out and a man collapsed with a cry of surprise and pain. The men murmured, and a few flinched. "Forward, march, at the quick step!" bellowed Ducasse. The line began to move, and he pointed it in the direction of the shot.

A second shot rang out and another man dropped to the ground, writhing and groaning. The line kept moving toward the muzzle flashes, but he could feel the fear rising. It would have been so much easier if his men had a visible enemy to advance against! His men were itching to stab someone, but right now they were fighting shadows.

The line advanced a further ten paces, when a third man fell dead. A mixture of fear and anger flowed through his men. Ducasse wished he knew something about skirmish tactics, but he had only a limited schooling in conventional ones. He thought about ordering a fast dash at the muzzle flashes but that could easily degenerate into chaos. No, it was better to keep group integrity intact with a methodical advance.

When a fourth man fell after another ten paces, Ducasse realized his enemy was waging a calculated war of nerves to sow fear and uncertainty, striking down random soldiers with precisely aimed shots at odd intervals. He had to do something to give his men a way to strike back at their unseen opponents.

He ordered his sailors to halt, then gave the commands to shoulder arms, make ready, present, and fire. A volley blasted out, aimed in the general direction of the enemy shots. He heard splinters fly from some barrels, but there was no enemy response. His men reloaded and fired a second time. More splinters flew, but there was still no enemy response. The men reloaded but this time he told them to wait while he listened. A full minute passed without a shot fired. Then another and another.

Murmurs of satisfaction reached his ears. His men seemed to believe their show of resolve had frightened off the enemy. He wanted to believe that too, but that was probably unlikely. He wondered if he had been lured into playing the role of Braddock at the Monongahela, where a much smaller force of French and Indians firing from the cover of a forest had nearly wiped out a British force relying on European parade ground tactics.

He gave the order to advance, but this time at the regular rate of 76 paces a minute, not the quick step. The men proceeded twenty paces with no sign of an enemy presence and their confidence spiked. Suddenly, three shots rang out, three men collapsed, and all illusions were shattered. The sailors halted in confusion. One man started to shake, one retched, and one stood frozen like a statue. Once panic gained a foothold it spread quickly; a cohesive line could degenerate into a rabble in seconds.

A fifth shot only wounded its recipient but proved a tipping point. The men in the rear ranks broke first, backing away slowly, then pivoting quickly and breaking into a run. They were swiftly followed by the men of the first rank. The one thing the sailors did not do that was common to panicked men was to drop their muskets to gain greater speed.

Carhart had done his job and knew it was time to go. Then he heard a loud rumbling of horse hooves, six working as a team. "Bollocks!" he muttered. It wasn't the horses that worried him but what they likely pulled: six-pounder field pieces.

Pennywhistle heard the gunfire and knew he was out of time. "Masters, tell Carhart to get his men aboard, then lay the charges on the dock. Rig them with tripwires. I noticed rope oddments lying on the dock. String enough rope around so our pursuers will not see the trip wires. Then get back here on the double."

"Aye, aye, sir! But what about the mooring lines?"

"Leave them to me."

"Come back! Come back! Remember your duty!" Ducasse shed tears as he shouted helplessly at the backsides of his fleeing men. *How could they have forgotten their duty to our Emperor?* he wondered. *By God, I am not finished yet. I will chase them down and rally them.*

Ducasse's sailors had slowed their run to a walk half a block later; evidence that the panic was superficial and redeemable. The startled sailors jumped out of the way of the thundering horses towing limbered field pieces and realized that the army had somehow been alerted. They looked at each other in embarrassment and shame that they were being outdone by an army of old men. To rub salt in the wound, a column of forty soldiers passed by and sneered at them.

"T'as pas de couilles!" "Fils de pute!" "Connard!" were among the mildest taunts that the passing old soldiers hurled at Ducasse's sailors. Those translated respectively as *you have no balls, you are the son of a whore,* and *arsehole.*

It was at that moment that an out-of-breath Ducasse arrived. Rather than berate his men, he offered redemption. "Sailors of France, it is not too late to reclaim your honor! Even the best runners stumble. But they pick themselves up and finish their run with glorious sprints! I call upon you now to follow me in a dash of glory and honor. Let us return to the dockyard and nobly finish what we have started. I have a plan to employ you in a way that will make sure the victory belongs to us, not the army!"

"Yes! I want my honor back!" bellowed Matelot Allard.

"So do I," proclaimed Matelot Faucher.

"Let us not waste another second!" urged Matelot Darroze. "Let us all wipe away the stains on our souls."

"Then shoulder your muskets and follow me!" Ducasse thundered. *"Vive l' Empereur!"*

"Vive l'Empereur" shouted the sailors with wild abandon as they clenched their muskets and formed themselves for marching.

"Nothing can stop us now!" roared Ducasse with a martial smile on his face and a dream of immortal renown in his head. He had learned from his mistakes, as had his men, and they deserved a second chance.

Carhart had provided a good assessment of the dockside situation, but Pennywhistle remembered Wellington remarking that a personal survey of a potential battlefield was always better than a secondhand report, no matter how astute and observant the reconnoitering officer. He popped open the hatch, stuck his head into the humid night air, unfurled his Ramsden, and panned it over the area. Thanks to the bright moonlight and his elevated position, he could see three threats approaching from two different directions.

The three field pieces posed the biggest problem. Judging from their distance and speed he had about five minutes before they unlimbered and opened fire. An eighth of a mile behind the guns was a column of marching soldiers. He estimated he had six minutes before they could deploy. These men would be veterans who knew the terrain, and though past their prime, they would be seasoned, savvy, and experienced: much harder to break than newly minted troops.

The same column of sailors that Carhart had run off had reformed and was advancing rapidly. They would be in firing range at about the same time as the six-pounders.

His handful against 100 men and three guns were poor odds. His best chance of success lay in a speedy escape in *Nautilus*. A complete set of blueprints might have made this possible, but in war one generally had to act on woefully incomplete information.

His knowledge of the optimal readings of the gauges was informed speculation, his estimation of the functions of the toggle switches little better than guesswork. He was reckoned a clever man, but trying to puzzle out the workings of an eccentric inventor's mind was a challenge best undertaken in a mechanic's laboratory, not the cramped confines of a vessel under fire.

The hull was a problem. *Nautilus* might be an ingenious craft, but she was fragile. She relied on stealth rather than stout timbers for her defense, on being invisible; tonight her location was known and she was the focus of everyone's attention. Even musket balls could penetrate the hull's copper plates at close range, and it was anyone's guess how much damage she could absorb from solid shot before she lost her watertight integrity.

Pennywhistle clambered out of the hatch and down the stairs, clutching a signal rocket in his right hand. He pointed it at the sky, lit the fuse, and watched it soar into the heavens. *Amphion* would see the flare and move closer to shore. He had never met *Amphion's* captain, James Stewart, but the man had a professional reputation for gifted improvisation.

He surveyed the charges Masters had laid; he had done a masterly job of concealment. It was unlikely that any of the approaching men would see anything but masses of tangled rope. Pennywhistle severed the two mooring ropes with his cutlass and *Nautilus* began to drift, ever so slightly, on the tide. He dashed up the stairs, entered the craft, and slammed the iron hatch cover shut, rotating the small circular wheel on its underside to make a watertight seal.

Once inside, he was gratified to see all three teams had taken up positions. Cochrane manned the wheel and diving plane controls, Barton monitored the gauges and toggle switches, and the rest stood ready to rotate the crank.

His men looked at him with confidence and expectancy, expecting of him a magical intuition that he knew he did not ordinarily possess. His nickname of "Bombproofed" was doing its unwonted work again, persuading men that he was close to unkillable. He wondered if they believed the heavenly protection they thought he enjoyed would shield them as well, or if it was enough for them that the mission itself succeeded.

For a brief second, he thought of the trust that a newborn had for its parents and wondered what his infant son looked like. Sammie Jo had sent him a sketch, but drawings paled in comparison to holding the genuine article in your arms.

"Gentlemen, prepare for departure." He suppressed his rising excitement at the prospect of danger and spoke with a studied calm that suggested confidence in a good outcome. "Mr. Cochrane, how is the helm?" The helm was a miniature of a standard ship's wheel.

"Answering, Skipper, but she is sluggish."

It pleased Pennywhistle to be addressed by the informal term for captain.

"Mr. Barton, do the gauges seem to be operating?"

"I think so, Colonel. It's hard to tell. I wish I was certain about each of their functions."

"I will accept your best guess. Do I have it?"

"You do..., Skipper."

Pennywhistle smiled.

"Masters, can you and your men maintain a steady pace with the crank? Forty minutes should get us to the *Amphion.*"

"We can, sir."

"Good.

"The channel zigzags, Skipper," cautioned Cochrane, "so we must be careful. I recommend our initial course be one-six-zero degrees."

"Zigzags make steering complicated, Mr. Cochrane."

"True, but I have the sand bars and shoals mapped out in my mind's eye."

Ping! Ping! Ping! Ping!

"Mr. Barton, any changes in your gauges?" barked Pennywhistle.

"Just one gauge, Skipper. The hands on it are rotating wildly."

"Bullet impacts?"

"My conclusion, Skipper."

Pennywhistle stepped up into the conning tower and realized that he had miscalculated the timetables. The sailors had already begun firing. Their volleys were ragged but steady.

He heard a pounding on the hatch cover and started as a pair of angry French eyes glared at him from the other side of the porthole. One sailor had apparently raced ahead of the rest and designated himself as a one-man Forlorn Hope. He had somehow avoided the charges on the dock and held aloft a smoking double-barreled pistol. The hatch cover was much stronger than the hull, so his bullets must have ricocheted.

Pennywhistle played a hunch. He climbed down, grabbed the wires from the galvanic pile, and touched them to the hatch cover. The electricity triggered a loud scream and the pounding stopped.

"Mr. Masters, start turning the crank. You and your men must give it everything you've got!"

"Aye, aye, Sir. All we lack is a horatator," said Masters. His grin was crooked. The horatator was the man on a Roman galley who beat the rhythm for the rowers.

The crank began to turn, and Nautilus began to move.

"Keep firing! Keep firing. *Nautilus* must not be allowed to escape!" yelled Ducasse. His men were firing at will, and since the enemy soldiers had vanished from view, they were shooting at *Nautilus* itself. Musket fire is never accurate; nevertheless, rounds struck *Nautilus'* hull at irregular intervals. Ducasse hated to damage this masterpiece of engineering, but anything was better than allowing her to be seized by these *espèces de con.*

Soldiers added their volleys to the sailors'. Their training and experience ensured that their volleys were more accurate. Bullets slammed into *Nautilus* with greater frequency.

Ducasse thought it ironic that his sailors must now damage the vessel they had worked so hard to get ready for sea. But he also realized musket fire would never stop *Nautilus*, which had already entered the main channel. He had considered ordering a headlong charge while the vessel was still in dock, but one man had tried that and failed. Besides, the hull would be slippery, and prying open the sealed hatch cover would be difficult. Then he remembered the launch he had been issued when he took the command. He had dismissed it as unnecessary, but now it might be just the thing. It contained a six-pounder cannon on a slide: solid shot could disable or sink the *Nautilus*.

Pennywhistle observed the three cannons unlimbering through his Ramsden. His stomach lurched, and the erratic *ping ping* of musket balls added to his alarm as he realized he was about to find out the true strength or fragility of *Nautilus*. It was a sea trial of a kind, although considerably different from the ones the French had intended to carry out on the morrow.

"Mr. Barton, what is our speed and course heading?"

"Speed is three knots, Skipper. We'd be making four, but tide and current are against us. The sail is jammed and won't unfurl. The course is zero one zero. I estimate twenty minutes before we reach the open sea."

"Mr. Cochrane, how is she handling?"

"Sluggish but steerable. It's as if we are towing something."

Pennywhistle started and blinked. "My God! I know what we are towing."

"What is it, Skipper?" inquired Masters.

"A torpedo!" He saw looks of puzzlement. " It's a cylindrical mine. *Nautilus'* sea trials were to begin tomorrow, but I had no idea they intended to test her weapon during her first run." Pennywhistle described to his crew the situation on the dock.

"The torpedo gives us a way to fight back!" exclaimed Barton. "But how do we release it?"

"That's the problem. I don't know. I think it might be one of the toggle switches.

"Which one?" asked Masters.

"We hit all of them and hope for the best. But we have a more pressing problem."

"What is that?"

"A well-placed shot from those three cannons could cripple us. At our present speed, we will be in range for at least five minutes."

Ping, ping, ping. More musket rounds found the hull.

"Anyone notice any leaks?" inquired Pennywhistle.

Each man surveyed the section of hull nearest him. The cumulative verdict returned was none... so far.

"What do we do?" worried Cochrane.

"Only one thing we can do. We dive. Open the ballast tanks, Mr. Barton, and cross your fingers."

Alarm had roused Paradis from his comfortable office. He galloped up to Ducasse, bellowing, "You damn fool! Your sailors will never stop them!"

"You're the bloody fool! If you'd posted more guards and sent out more patrols this would never have happened! The only reason you are here now is because you heard my men's gunfire!"

"Bah! Well, I am here now, and I take command. I order you to—"

"Wait, I have a plan!" Ducasse's face lit with a wolf's smile. "Hear me out. This will work."

Paradis disliked Ducasse, but he knew the idiot was clever in a way he himself was not. "Very well, but be quick."

"There is a launch with a cannon over yonder. My men will man it and attack *Nautilus* by sea from the rear. We will aim to disable her rudder and her screw. Your guns can open fire from land. We will have her in a crossfire!"

Paradis scowled at having to give Ducasse any credit. "Then what are you standing here for? Get your men to the launch."

"Yes, sir!"

The twin ballast tanks filled quickly, and *Nautilus* began to descend. Pennywhistle watched the gages as well as checking for any leaks caused by the increasing water pressure. Watertight integrity was holding, and there were no significant fluctuations in the gauges. She was descending faster than he'd expected, but it was still far too slow for his liking.

Ducasse and his men got the launch into the channel and loaded the cannon. His men were rowing hard, but it was against the current and progress was slow. They could see the outline of *Nautilus* ahead, just at the outside range of his six-pounder. He was debating when to open fire when he noticed her outline was shrinking. She was submerging! "*Merde!*" He sighted the cannon carefully. "Fire!" A sailor jerked the lanyard and the cannon shot backward on its slide.

Destination Waterloo

"Merde! Merde!" shouted Paradis as he noticed the vanishing hull. His battery was loaded, and the gun captains had just finished sighting the cannons, supervised by an NCO who had earned Napoleon's personal thanks for the conduct of his guns at Austerlitz. The sergeant said a silent prayer and shouted, "Fire!" The cannons bucked, roared, and spouted flames as three cannon balls flew into the night.

Pennywhistle observed the muzzle flashes while a meter of the conning tower remained above the surface. One ball barely missed the conning tower, one landed two meters astern of the rudder, and one struck the craft amidships. It was good night shooting from a *corps de reserve*, and if they readjusted their aim the next salvo might be fatal.

The question was whether or not *Nautilus* could fully submerge before they could fire again.

From the slightness of the impact amidships, Pennywhistle judged the ball had clipped the hull's edge rather than landing a solid blow. Nevertheless, it popped a rivet, which went shooting across the cabin, barely missing Cochrane's head. Pennywhistle held his breath as he pressed his hand on the hull where he guessed the round had struck. His hand remained dry.

The churning screw made soft *swoosh swoosh* sounds, and the revolving crankshaft emitted a humming noise that reminded Pennywhistle of locusts on the fly.

"How is she handling, Mr. Cochrane?"

"Taking the dive well, Skipper. Diving planes set at 3 degrees, descending at 2 meters per minute."

"How deep is the channel here?"

"Twelve point five meters."

"Set depth to one zero meters."

"One zero meters, aye."

The conning tower slipped beneath the surface just as the cannons fired a second time. One round landed where the tower had been a moment before, causing turbulence but no apparent damage.

Pennywhistle explained his plan. "The torpedo should rise to the surface once released, and the current that has worked against us will speed its passage. I want the torpedo to detonate the explosives that Masters laid out on the docks; that should take out the cannon crews. But there needs to be plenty of distance between us and the torpedo when it goes off."

"A sound plan, Skipper," commented Barton.

"Far from it, but it will have to do. And now, gentlemen, let us discover if we are geniuses or fools."

Pennywhistle took out his pocket watch, guessing that five minutes would put *Nautilus* at a safe distance from the docks. The cramped cabin suddenly felt incredibly stuffy as the sweat quotient jumped. When that interval had elapsed, he hit all seven switches.

There was a jolt, a lurch, a creak, a squeak, and a hissing sound. He had no idea what had just happened, but the vessel appeared to be moving faster and descending more quickly. He had been supremely lucky: one switch adjusted the trim on the port side, and a second that of the starboard, so their actions canceled out. A third switch extended an additional diving plane on the port side, while a fourth did the same on the starboard side. A fifth switch increased the speed of the driveshaft's revolutions, and the sixth fired the torpedo. As for the seventh...

"We not only detached the torpedo but the towing cable as well," reported Barton.

"Helm is responding better," remarked Cochrane a minute later. "And we have gained a knot in speed."

Everyone grew quiet, waiting for the deep rumble of a detonation. Pennywhistle took out his Blancpain watch so he could mark the time for his report. The explosion came at 01:10 hours and shook the boat hard. The hull groaned like a walrus in labor. The strength of the pressure wave prompted Pennywhistle to examine the interior hull, but the cabin had sprung no leaks. The violence of the wave was proof that the torpedo had indeed detonated the explosives on the docks. He wondered what damage he had caused.

Ducasse's boat capsized from the shockwave, but all of the sailors along with himself made it to shore. They were shaken and bruised but intact. He felt personally disgraced, but he thanked God that one of the requirements he had made for his command was that every sailor be able to swim. Most sailors in both the French and Royal Navies could not; officers did not mind because this inability cut down on desertions.

Paradis was crushed by a flying cannon barrel. Most of his gun crews died as well, and those who survived were horribly mangled. The old soldiers who had provided volley support for the guns had already begun marching back to their barracks when the blast hit. Sergeant Beaumere, their commander, "Old Rough and Ready," had ignored Paradis' drunken orders to remain in place once *Nautilus* submerged. His body ached with arthritis, and he looked forward to a comfortable chair and a mug of hot rum.

"We've cleared the harbor, Skipper. Now we hope *Amphion* is in position to give us a tow," said Cochrane with a note of triumph in his voice.

"That's assuming we are able to surface," cautioned Pennywhistle. "*Nautilus* is an experiment, after all. Let's give her a little sea room before we try. I want to make sure she is beyond the range of any shore batteries."

Running blind and deaf and only being able to guess your position was as frustrating as it was nerve-wracking. The air grew fetid with fear and sweat as the minutes dragged by like boulders pushed uphill. No words were spoken, but the expressions on the men's faces made Pennywhistle realize they were worried their vessel of deliverance might turn out to be a copper coffin.

Pennywhistle felt an unwelcome wetness at his feet and looked down to see a layer of water an quarter of an inch deep.

Cochrane noticed the same thing a moment later. His eyebrows arched in alarm. "We have a leak, Skipper."

Pennywhistle watched the water level rise a quarter inch in sixty seconds, which he counted mentally. "We probably have multiple leaks from musket ball punctures which have widened from the water pressure."

"How long before the problem becomes critical?" asked Cochrane.

"Your guess is as good as mine, but given time it will be fatal. We must surface."

Lieutenant Kemp looked up from his wet shoes and started to shake, emitting low whimpering tones that sounded like an animal in distress. Pennywhistle surmised he had been fighting claustrophobia the entire time, and the leak had proved the last straw.

"Mr. Barton," said Pennywhistle with all the pretended calmness he could muster, "open the ballast doors. Mr. Cochrane, set diving planes for three degrees up."

He bent down and applied the positive and negative wires of galvanic pile to a pair of terminals next to the ballast door indicator. He hit the switch on the pile's base, but all that happened were two tiny sparks of blue. The man he electrocuted must have absorbed its entire charge. They would have to do things the old-fashioned way.

"Mr. Kemp! Pull yourself together and help Mr. Hodge pump out the ballast tanks."

A hissing sound and a jet of air caused Pennywhistle to look up at the oxygen storage tank. It had been punctured as well.

"Colonel!" exclaimed Barton with alarm. "The ballast door lever does not seem to be working. The doors may be jammed."

Pennywhistle tried the lever himself. Barton was right. But perhaps the problem was not the doors but the lever that controlled them. "Barton, do you have anything like a scalpel in that engineer's tool kit you keep on your person?"

"I do, Colonel, and a wad of surveyor's grease to assist, if I read your intentions correctly."

"You do." Barton quickly produced the scalpel and grease. "I understand you once studied to be a doctor, Colonel. This will be your chance to perform a form of surgery. "

The water was rising faster; four inches now covering the deck.

Pennywhistle greased the area round the lever, inserted the scalpel, and began to twist gingerly, searching for some blockage. He felt like an untrained cracksman trying to open a safe in the dark. *Slosh, slosh.* The water lapped at the top of his shoes. Each musket ball had acted like a small dose of poison: not immediately detectable, but fatal once a critical mass had been reached. The scalpel finally hit something. He gave a sharp twist, and a tiny shard of metal flew skyward. He removed the scalpel, held his breath, then toggled the switch. It was free and clear. The gauge for the ballast doors indicated they were opening.

Kemp and Hodge set to work pumping vigorously the moment the doors were fully opened. They were winded when they finished five minutes later. The water now came to just below their knees.

"Ballast Tanks read empty," fretted Barton; nothing appeared to be happening.

The candles began flickering. *Nautilus* was bleeding oxygen even faster than she was taking on water. Pennywhistle noticed he was having trouble breathing. The air stank like an old shoe that had spent a week in a latrine.

Thirty seconds of terror passed before *Nautilus* lurched, made a *glurg glurg* sound, and began to move upward.

"Let me out, let me out!" Kemp screamed as he made mad clawing motions on the hull.

Barton silenced him with a slap to the face. "Waste of oxygen."

"Rising at three meters per minute," observed Cochrane with relief.

The water in the cabin continued to rise as well, its accumulating volume of water slowing *Nautilus'* rate of ascent almost to the point of stopping it. By the time she reached the surface, water had reached the waists of Pennywhistle's men.

On the deck of *Amphion,* Captain James Stewart gasped as a large copper dome burst the surface, barely two hundred yards from *Amphion's* port side. He had not been apprised as to what *Nautilus* looked like and could not have been more shocked if Neptune himself had appeared.

The candles inside Nautilus died the moment before her hatch cover popped and Pennywhistle's head emerged. He coughed twice, then sucked in lungfuls of fresh sea air. He blinked in relief at how close *Nautilus* was to *Amphion.* "Ahoy, Captain Stewart," he shouted. "My vessel is sinking. Could I trouble you for a launch?"

"Yes... ah... certainly," replied an astonished Stewart, who immediately shouted commands for a boat to be lowered.

Pennywhistle's men climbed slowly out of *Nautilus,* their movements clumsy because they had been breathing air heavy with carbon dioxide. Pennywhistle found his thinking muddled, but trusted it would clear as the sea air worked its purifying magic. Save for Kemp, his men wore expressions that were mixtures of fear, confusion, and gratitude: condemned men granted last-minute reprieves from punishments that they did not understand. The bulging, darting eyes of Kemp made him look like he had lost his mind, and it was entirely possible that he had. Pennywhistle's men gripped *Nautilus'* hull for dear life, bobbing up and down as they struggled to resume normal breathing. By the time they were hauled into the launch, only the top third of the vessel was visible.

Nautilus disappeared beneath the waves just as the launch reached *Amphion. Damn shame,* thought Pennywhistle. *She deserved better than Davy Jones' locker.* His mission of denying *Nautilus* to the enemy had succeeded, yet the feeling that a technological treasure had been lost persisted, destroying any sense of satisfaction. The dockyard defenders had accomplished their mission to the same degree as he had: denying his countrymen the chance to explore the mysteries of a remarkable craft far ahead of its time.

Pennywhistle saluted Captain Stewart. "Request permission to come aboard, Captain."

"Granted, Colonel, and in turn I request that you dine with me and furnish a full account of your acquaintance with that strange craft."

"I barely knew her, Captain, but I feel a great lady has passed far too soon."

Chapter 2

Baptism of Fire

15 June 1815, 3 am, 8 miles from The Belgian Frontier

Churruh! Churruh! Churruh! The bewitching song of the European Nightjar pierced the silence of the dark and carried for a good mile. Like the men marching on the road beneath them, the flock of birds was on a journey: a yearly migration from the Sahara to Great Britain. Jean-Paul Gagne, *sergent* in the French 92nd *Regiment Ligne*, found their songs pleasing, and they helped to keep his tired men awake. Missteps, jostling, and collisions occurred frequently during advances in darkness, but he marched with the wide, easy stride of the experienced campaigner. Tonight's march was a blessed relief to Gagne; the previous day's advance of Napoleon's *L' armée du Nord* from Maubeuge to the edge of Belgium had been cursed by 25 miles of hot roads, high humidity, and surly peasants who did not welcome the Empereur's return.

"War makes even the best man stumble, but as long as you are stumbling do your best to stumble forward." Gagne gave a Gallic shrug as the words of a former commanding officer popped unbidden into his mind. That officer had frozen to death at the crossing of the ice-choked Berezina River, but not before he had exhorted Gagne to dig deep into himself and discover the hidden strength of will to keep going. Gagne was one of only 30,000 French survivors of Napoleon's

600,000-man invasion of Russia, a scrappy stalwart who had endured the bloodiest day of the Napoleonic Wars at Borodino, typhus, dysentery, Cossacks, starvation, and worst of all, General Winter. Small, square, and sturdy, given to short, economical gestures, his bald head, furrowed cheeks, and badly reset nose gave him an air of inviolable authority. His alert grey eyes reflected the guarded pessimism of the skeptical soldier, and though his face looked considerably older than his 35 years, his body possessed the fitness of a young man in his prime.

"Merde, merde, merde! No, no, no!" growled Gagne. "How many times do I have to tell you, Le Duc, to march with the barrel of your musket down, not up! A rain shower is on its way and will turn your powder to sludge. Start using those ears for something more than jug handles!" Gagne's raspy voice matched his temper and tongue of hot peppers; he could swear until the leaves shook on the trees, yet he never held grudges. His rough speech forged a bond with recruits; unvarnished truths were better received than the *La Gloire* exhortations of officers. His boiling earnestness was fueled by a seemingly inexhaustible store of energy.

Gagne had been mustered out of the army upon the return of Louis XVIII. The mass discharge of veterans had flooded an already depressed job market, and a lack of civilian skills had prevented him from finding steady work. He had been taken in by his family as an act of reluctant charity, but had chafed under their Quaker pacifism and efforts to reform him. When the Emperor returned, he'd jumped at the chance to answer the call of the colors.

The partly overcast sky obscured a three-quarter moon; few stars were visible. A night march cloaked an army, but the swift pace demanded by their emperor punished the man doing the marching, as Gagne's sore feet, aching joints, and tired eyes attested. Still, the discomfort was familiar, and traversing a paved road was far easier than transiting the trackless steppes of Russia. He focused his sight on the packs of the men marching to his side and limited his thoughts to simply putting one foot in front of the other. He felt he was exactly where God intended him to be; his conception of God was more like a stern sergeant major than a benevolent grandfather.

Gagne's 24-man platoon marched four abreast at reverse slope arms; musket butts up and barrels down, the weapon draped casually at a 45-degree angle over the left shoulder. A pace was reckoned at .508 meters; the ranks advanced at two paces apart, six ranks deep, and proceeded at 76 paces per minute or 3.5 kilometers per hour. His small command was part of the 1st battalion, 92nd Regiment Ligne under Colonel Etienne Tussot: 22 officers and 550 men. Tussot's chief task was to protect the artillery train following the column's rear. Gagne's men had been trained as *voltigeurs*, light infantry, and it would be their job to skirmish with any Prussians who presented themselves.

"Close it up, close it up, close it up, boys," commanded Gagne with quiet authority. "Button things up tight and true and keep your pace steady." Straggling was always a problem with new recruits.

Gagne considered the cool of early morning as a gift; it came with empty roads, an absence of insects, and a somnolent enemy. The humid air carried the scents of poppies, begonias, and tulips grown in nearby gardens. The price of a night advance was the loss of sleep: no soldier had snatched more than three hours prior to the beating of assembly at 2 am.

"God damn army! God damn army," muttered a drowsy Private Tremblay, who had never met a situation that he could not complain about.

"Shut your bloody trap," growled Gagne.

Tremblay stopped until Gagne moved on. "God damn army," he whispered.

Gagne was used to chronic sleep deprivation, but the platoon under his charge was showing its effects. Fatigue and sixty pounds of equipment turned soldiers just out of training depots into clumsy marchers who were little better than uniformed zombies. It was not that the recruits lacked zeal, just seasoning.

It annoyed Gagne that he did not know his men well. The army had been hastily assembled and he had barely learned their names. In Gagne's opinion, it required six months to make a passable soldier, but the men dumped on him had but three weeks of instruction. They were good on the manual of arms but hazy on the more complex maneuvers of light infantry. The campaign itself would have to be provide the rest of their training.

Their secondhand uniforms had been scavenged from thrift shops or sold by poor widows. They were showy, featuring bold colors that could be recognized through the billowing clouds of battle smoke: double breasted blue tailcoats cinched at the waist with brass buttons and white facings that formed a "V" shape; red epaulettes, collars, and cuffs, bone-colored breeches, and white gaiters completed the outfit. Their headgear consisted of a tall, unwieldy cylindrical hat called a shako, designed to increase the illusion of height. Black and red, made of heavy felt and leather, with a wide black bill that shaded the eyes, held in place by twin brass chinstraps, each shako had a brass plate in the center that depicted an Imperial Eagle perched atop a half shield, with a circular cockade of white, red, and blue above and a 152-millimeter-high crimson plume.

Their .69 caliber Year IX Charleville muskets were 58 inches long and weighed ten pounds. Most had seen plenty of use before being issued to Gagne's men, and many had enlarged touch holes, reducing the impact power of each round.

"Take it back! Take it back! She ain't no whore!"

"Maybe she didn't charge you, but she charged me! That makes her a whore in my book."

Private Messier punched Private Laurier hard in the temple, knocking him to the ground. He leaped upon his prostrate tent mate and began to industriously pummel him. "Take it back, Take it back."

Gagne grabbed Messier by the collar and jerked him to his feet, then slapped him hard. "What's the matter with you, you bloody fool?" The question was rhetorical since Gagne knew the answer. Extreme fatigue often caused tempers to fray and brought hidden grievances to the surface. "We've got a war to fight and you're fussing over a God-damned woman! Consider yourself on report. I will deal with you later. Now get marching," Gagne said roughly as he shoved Messier forward, then he helped Laurier to his feet.

Gagne's command of teens and grandfathers had been thrust upon him because he was good at transforming disparate individuals into a military unit. His youngest charge was a tall thirteen-year-old who had lied about his age; the oldest was a man who claimed to be sixty, though he had likely subtracted a decade from his actual age. Most of them appeared to be nineteen or twenty. The training depot had eliminated the entirely unfit, but even so, many were indifferent physical specimens, and Gagne was unsure how many would survive the rigors of an extended campaign. Still, the Emperor promoted on merit and had once boasted that every recruit potentially carried a marshal's baton in his knapsack. Many of the most successful soldiers had come from unpromising backgrounds, odd ducks like himself.

Three-fourths of his men were volunteers, the rest were conscripts. He called them "the leftovers" because they were castoffs from the margins of society. Most had been itinerant urban or agricultural workers, though six were household servants let go without recommendations — not a good indication of character. A substantial number were orphans, and most had been on the public dole at some point in their lives.

He noticed the unsteady, halting steps of Private Legrand and recognized the symptoms: the man was walking in his sleep. He clapped Legrand's head smartly. "Wake up! Wake up!" He hissed the words just above a whisper, but there was an undercurrent of sympathy in his voice. The man snapped awake from what appeared to be a pleasant dream. "Suzette? Suzette?"

"I am not your girl, dammit! Now keep moving, LeGrand. Not far to the border. It will be light soon. Trust your Emperor."

The dazed man resumed his progress, but looked downcast that Suzette was only a dream.

Gagne's encouragements were overheard by others in the column and several recruits responded with tired exclamations of "*Vive l'Empereur! Vive l'Empereur!*"

"Silence there," Gagne growled. He appreciated that morale was good, but the only people permitted to speak on night marches were officers and NCOs like himself.

"Get that musket back on your shoulder, now, you damn fool, or you will wish you'd never been born!" The half-awake Private LeDuc was dragging his musket behind him — an unpardonable sin for an infantryman.

"Just half a league until the next halt. You can make it." A column generally stopped for ten minutes each hour to allow stragglers to catch up. It gave soldiers a chance to rest and replenish their canteens.

Private Martin whispered to Gagne, "Sergeant, my big toe just poked through my shoe."

"What do you expect me to do about it? I'm a sergeant, not a cobbler, damn it. You're no worse off than the rest of this lot, so stop complaining."

Private Dubois had detached a long baguette from its string attachment to his knapsack and was chomping as he marched. Each man carried one as a ration, but it was not considered proper to eat on the march. Gagne ignored the infraction; he himself had been reduced to skin and bones in Russia. Gagne also knew that Dubois would always remain a civilian at heart.

Private Dumas was the best of the lot. He marched confidently, learned quickly, and was a man the other recruits instinctively trusted and relied upon.

Gagne kept his eye on Private Tremblay. He was the kind of man who pulled a unit apart: an unrepentant thief who was just as likely to prey on his fellow soldiers as outsiders.

Private Rochfort had the hawk eye of a true marksman, and with a bit more seasoning, could be a real menace to enemy officers.

Private Du Bois was a short, reedy little man who amused the platoon with his jokes and stories.

Private Fontenoy made no impression on anyone: a bland, colorless man who would probably always remain a cypher.

Private Martin was the hardest to figure. A dreamy lad who wrote poetry, he did well enough at drill but did not relate well to others, seeming to live in a universe of his own.

Enough illumination touched the sky for Gagne to see the hands on his pocket watch. Full dawn, the ability to distinguish objects clearly at the quarter mile, would manifest in another hour.

Gagne had confidence in his corps commander, General Comte Reille, who had been with Napoleon since The Siege of Toulon in 1793. Although Gagne had only been given orders pertaining to his platoon,

NCOs had established informal networks with other NCOs that often gave them access to surprising amounts of confidential information. Gagne had good strategic instincts and read maps well. He was also a voracious reader of newspapers. The press in Belgium was indiscreet, so the dispositions of the enemy were no secret. He had puzzled out that Reille's 2nd Corps of 25,000 men, 38 cannon, and 1,200 horses was headed toward the town of *Marchienne du Pont*, on the Belgian side of the River Sambre. That would place 2nd Corps behind the right flank of General Hans von Zieten's Prussian 1st Corps, forcing the Prussians to fight or flee.

"Looks like you guessed our destination correctly," remarked Sergeant Poivre, Gagne's best friend from the platoon marching in front of his own. He had dropped back to compare notes. "When we took that last fork in the road, well... let's just say your intuition has not deserted you."

Gagne smiled, "Deduction, not intuition. The *sur les derrieries* strategy works every time, and Marchienne was the logical place for Reille's part of the plan. How are your men holding up?"

"As well as can be expected. Many complain; they don't call them *les grognards* for nothing, but they march reasonably well for rookies. I wouldn't say they are itching for a fight, but they will push hard against any force that stands in their way. Several are proving resourceful foragers." Poivre flashed a sly grin. French armies were to civilians what the locusts of Egypt were to crops. "How about yours?"

"Morale is good, though I have had better troops. That is to be expected. The *Empereur* really had to scrape the bottom of the manpower barrel for his new recruits. I take comfort in that most of the army is composed of veterans like us who have seen plenty of action. But at least my men are of better quality than the horses. I can't remember when I have seen such a collection of sorry nags: too old, too young, or just skin and bones."

"That's no surprise. 187,000 horses went into Russia, but only 1,600 returned."

Gagne winced as memories of the horrors of Russia stabbed his brain. "*Mon Dieu.* Watching horses die is unbearable. Their pleading eyes and terrified whinnies show that they have no understanding of what is happening to them. They are innocents." Uncustomary tears rose in his eyes but did not fall, and the darkness hid them.

"What time do you expect we will reach Marchienne?"

"About 4:30, assuming there are no 'distractions'."

Poivre smiled wryly. "About as likely as a battle plan surviving the first five minutes of fighting."

Poivre understood that the *sur les derrieres* strategy necessitated that the Army of the North march as three separate wings, executing wide sweeps that would penetrate the enemy rear and eventually encircle him. One part of the army would act as an anvil while the rest reassembled to form the hammer. The Anglo-Allied Army of the Duke of Wellington and the Prussian Army under Prince Blucher had a combined strength of 242,000, more than double that of Napoleon's forces; but supply issues meant that their units were scattered in detachments over a wide area of Belgium, while Napoleon's forces were concentrated and mobile. The *Empereur* planned to move fast, beat the two armies in detail, and capture Brussels. Coordination between Wellington's staff and Blucher's was haphazard at best, and it was common knowledge that the British high command doubted the allegiance of their Prussian allies; the *Empereur* was an expert in exploiting the disunity of command.

Gagne also knew the *Empereur* prized luck, and tonight his luck was in. Reille's six columns occupied four miles of road, but so far had not encountered a single Prussian picket or cavalry patrol. The Prussians ahead were untested, like his men: two thirds of them were *Landwehr*, glorified militia, lacking combat experience.

Thud. Private Collette collapsed and started to snore.

"Help him out or straighten him out, Sergeant?" inquired Du Bois.

Gagne debated whether to hoist Collette to his feet or kick him, but decided Collette's body had rendered a verdict that no amount of threats could contradict.

"No, let him sleep. Dragging him along will just slow us down."

Colette would be part of the inevitable winnowing of a marching column. He might rejoin the army, once his sleep debt had been paid.

Collette reminded Gagne of his nephew, physically at least. He regretted that the 16-year-old lad had decided to follow in his footsteps — much to the irritation of his annoyingly pious brother. The family orchard produced some of the best apples in Normandy, and young Jacques Gagne was destined to manage it, but his soldier-uncle's war stories had accidentally lit a fire in Jacques' imagination. Gagne had warned Jacques that war was cruel, harsh, and not for the faint of heart, but his warnings had instead served as a grand challenge. Jacques had volunteered, and by a curious stroke of fate had been assigned to Reille's corps. He was not more than half a kilometer away.

"You might want to tighten the straps on your pack. Yours is sagging a bit and that increases the strain on the back."

"Thanks, Faveau," whispered Jacques Gagne. "I will remember that."

Jacques Gagne wondered why his column had stopped. The *thud thud* of massed feet, the *clip clop* of horses, and the *crack-crackle* of iron-rimmed cannon wheels had been replaced by a low rumbling of voices. The sounds of a great army moving were music to his ears, and it he felt bereft that the melody had vanished. He checked the pocket watch that had been a dying gift from a recruit who had succumbed to dysentery: 3:40 am. The sky had already acquired the pewter hues of first light. This was one of his favorite times of year: the long-lighted days of June. Midsummer was barely a week away.

Two-and-a-half months before, he had been wearing a farmer's smock with sackcloth leggings, and had never been more than ten miles from home. Now he was a *bombardier de deuxième classe* of the *deuxième Compaignie, deuxième Regiment d' Artillerie a la Pied*: Gunner Second Class of the 2nd Company, 2nd Regiment of Foot Artillery. His job was that of a ventsman: responsible for closing the venthole with a leather thumbscrew when the piece was being wormed, sponged, or loaded. Failure to perform that action could result in an explosion, from compression igniting stray bits of cloth or powder. Anyone could be a footslogger, but being an artillerist demanded attentiveness and skill. He kept his uniform well brushed because he took pride in being a member of an elite corps. It resembled that of the infantry save for having breeches of blue and the addition of a waistcoat of the same color.

"Hey, Gagne, have you any tobacco, on you? I've got some gold jewelry I picked up in the last village to make it worth your while." *Caporal* Jelune was widely recognized as a man who was always one step ahead of the provost marshal.

Gagne looked at him sternly; his mother's Quaker beliefs informed his words. "My mother made me swear on a Bible to abjure tobacco and alcohol."

Jelune laughed. "How precious! And how stupid! You're a soldier now, why should you listen to what an old woman thinks? The men like you; you could make deals with folk who would not have anything to do with me. We could be a team," he said persuasively.

Destination Waterloo

"My mother cautioned me about people like you and I intend to follow her warning."

"Prig!"

Gagne stood an even six feet tall and possessed a lean, muscled frame that was the product of hard farm work. Muscles came in handy in the artillery: a 6 pounder's recoil pushed it backwards the same number of feet, and 540 kilograms had to be manhandled back to the original position after every shot. A mop of straw-colored hair sat atop an oval face with heavy eyebrows, generous lips, and a pronounced cleft in the chin. It was a friendly face and a trusting one. Yet those who looked deeper into the lively blue eyes would have detected a deep determination to be a Gallic Dick Whittington. His hands were often remarked upon. They were the size of small skillets, yet with long, graceful fingers that possessed a remarkable dexterity. Coupled with an intuitive mechanical acumen, he could repair any farm tool with speed and dexterity. That skill came in handy in the artillery, which employed many specialized accoutrements. His company sergeant, Etienne Goulet, had marked him as a candidate for rapid promotion.

Gagne's unit was not just a military organization, but a moving village. *Capitaine* Julien Fivel commanded 88 men: 4 officers, 9 NCOs, 20 gunners of the first class, 48 gunners of the second, and 7 other ranks including 2 drummers, a furrier, a blacksmith, a wood worker, a metal worker, and a clerk. It was also a mobile industrial enterprise that was able to create, repair, and service everything necessary to get the unit into combat and then recover from the damage incurred after the battle was done.

Armament consisted of four 6-pounder cannons and two 5.5 inch howitzers: long barreled cannon that fired solid shot and canister in a straight line; stubby barreled howitzers fired explosive shells in arcs. Guns were attached to two wheeled limbers when they needed to be moved any distance, but in battle aggressive commanders pushed them forward by turning their men into human bullocks. The British and their allies thought of artillery as a defensive weapon; Napoleon had an opposite viewpoint.

Each weapon required two 4-meter-long ammunition caissons to ensure the company had 150 rounds ready for battle. The caissons and limbered guns were towed by 179 horses; 6 mules carried the company baggage.

Gagne squinted hard, trying to see what had caused the 120-meter-long column to grind to a halt. Goulet dashed up and grabbed his forearm. "Need your help, Gagne. A 6-pounder has broken a wheel and is blocking the road. Let's put those magic fingers to good work."

"I've never replaced a cannon wheel, Sergeant, but I have changed a few on farm wagons." Gagne smiled. "I would be honored to assist."

"Good man, Gagne. I like your zeal."

As he and Goulet threaded their way through the crowd, Jacques observed experienced soldiers in action. Or rather, inaction. French soldiers used a marching blockage in one of four ways: sleeping, eating, smoking, or copulating. The first was the easiest and most common; the last was difficult but far from impossible.

A virgin himself, he was shocked to see the act of coitus being casually performed behind a tree just ten feet from the road. He heard rather than saw it; both participants had leather lungs to which they gave vent. It could have been a soldier and his wife; 4 women accompanied each battalion. Each woman had to be certified as either a *blanchisseuse*, a laundress who was also expected to sew and mend clothing, or a *vivandiere,* who sold food, drink, and useful items that were not regular army issue.

More likely the cries of ecstasy came from a *fille de joie*, a local prostitute taking advantage of a golden opportunity. Repeated attempts by officers to send these women packing met with only temporary success, because soldiers welcomed them. Garrison towns had officially recognized brothels, but those were of no use to an army on the march. Enterprising women followed the army and pocketed their fees.

"How about a quick one, dearie?" urged a voice that belonged to a blowzy figure in a calico dress. Her hand descended on Jacques' shoulder and moved deliberately downwards. "You're a handsome spark, so it will only cost you a single sou."

Goulet grabbed her hand and neck, spun her around, and gave her a swift kick in the backside. "Begone! The lad needs a real girl, not an old tart who is half in the bag!"

Jacques was stunned; his mother had taught him to treat all women with respect.

Goulet smiled cynically. "Don't worry. When we reach Brussels, I will take you to the best sporting house in the city. You can have your pick of a whole stable of women."

Privates Dionne and Dupuy focused on eating their three-pound loaves of bread, their ration for two days.

"What do you think?" said Dionne.

"It's a lot better than the shit we got back in Maubeuge," asserted Dupuy. The wheat flour was not particularly tasty, but the bread's golden color indicated that it had not been burnt. The rest of their rations, 8 ounces of salt pork and 2 ounces of rice, could not be eaten until fires were lit.

The highlight of the meal was 2 ounces of brandy, which they sipped between bites of bread. It was usually issued only after a hard forced march, but General Reille had made it available as a show of the confidence he reposed in his men. "Much better than the stream water we filled our canteens with yesterday!" observed Dionne.

Four men behind the eaters smoked their pipes; other men of the ordinary, or mess, of 16 were already sound asleep. A few snored loudly. The ability to fall asleep anywhere, anytime, and at a moment's notice was something all veteran soldiers eventually acquired. Jacques envied that ability. He was dead tired but far too excited to fall asleep. There was so much going on that he did not want to miss a second of it.

He and Goulet brushed past the six members of the company band who were cleaning their oboes, bassoons, and horns. Their services were not needed during a night march, but their music played an important role in inspiring men during battle. "Evening, Gagne," murmured Dupleix, the bassoon player. "Evening, Dupleix," Jacques murmured back. They had struck up a friendship when Jacques had shared a basket of apples that his mother had sent.

A dog padded up next to Jacques and Goulet. Jacques gave him a pat on the head.

"Who's a good boy?"

"Woof! Woof!"

The dog was a full-size poodle, nearly four feet tall at his curly head, smart and trained for hunting. No one knew where he had come from, but most suspected that he had once been the property of a nobleman. When he had first shown up, he had sported the remnants of the traditional cut for poodles who fetched the waterfowl their masters shot: shaved limbs and sides to make swimming easier, with bands of the characteristically woolly fur around joints, to protect them and keep them warm in cold water. The animal had attached himself to the company and proven useful as both a watchdog and a source of comfort. The men had adopted him as their mascot and named him Rifle, because the markings on his forehead resembled the lands and grooves of a rifle barrel.

A few paces beyond the musicians, Jacques spotted the cause of the column's discomfiture: a six-pounder with a badly damaged left wheel. The heavy piece had been uncoupled from the towing horses; the wheels were propped four inches off the ground by two steel tripods that had been inserted under the main axle. A spare wheel had been rolled up, but the linchpin that held the broken wheel to the axle was stuck as tightly as if had been frozen in glacial ice. The thick iron linchpin weighed 2 kilograms, was nearly a meter long, and was shaped like an inverted question mark. Three gunners took turns pulling at it, but it refused to budge.

"*Merde! Merde! Merde!*" shouted *Caporal* Grandchamp.

"Slap some more grease on the pin," suggested *Sergent* Ledoux.

"Mix in a quarter liter of vinegar with the grease," suggested *Capitaine* Fivel, "then add a little tallow."

Two bombardiers took Fivel's suggestion as an order and within five minutes had assembled and mixed the requisite ingredients. One applied the muck to the pin, slathering a coating half an inch thick. Stray daubs and clots made a mess of his blue uniform.

"Get Le Mans up here!" shouted Fivel. *Caporal* Le Mans stood six feet six, not only the strongest member of the company but the one with the biggest sense of self-importance. If anyone could free the linchpin, he was the man. Le Mans appeared and immediately apprehended why he had been summoned. "*Mon Capitaine*, it will be child's play to extract the pin," he bragged.

"Do it, Le Mans!"

For the next two minutes Le Mans pulled and pulled, working up a mighty sweat as he huffed and puffed. He tried several different angles and grips, but nothing worked. Finally, he shoved himself back from the wheel proclaiming in disgust, "There is no power on heaven or earth that can remove that thing."

The small crowd that had gathered groaned collectively. At that moment Jacques stepped forward. "*Mon Capitaine*, might I offer a suggestion?"

Fivel eyed him skeptically. "It's Gagne, isn't it? Do you have some country boy wisdom that has eluded the rest of us?"

"Not sure if it is wisdom, *mon capitaine,* but it's something my father taught me. Do you have some whale oil handy? A quarter liter added to the grease might do the trick."

Whale oil was expensive, used for lighting, and the province of officers, not enlisted men.

"I have a supply, Gagne, but the quantity you suggest would use it all up."

"I am sorry about that, *mon capitaine,* but I think you will agree it is urgent the road be cleared."

"That is true," growled Fivel. "Very well, but this had better work."

Fivel trudged off to the pack horse that carried his belongings. He rummaged through his portmanteau and plucked up a vial filled with a grey liquid. He marched back to the cannon and was about to hand the vial to Le Mans when Jacques intercepted it. "Let me handle this, sir, and back up my words with actions."

Fivel eyed him. "Very well, Gagne. I respect a man who has the courage to stand on his words." He gestured toward the cannon.

Gagne took a deep breath, aware that all eyes were on him. A novice telling veterans what to do risked public ridicule and even punishment; he saw many mouths set in cynical sneers. But you either believed in yourself or you did not.

He approached the cannon with deliberate steps. His uncle had told him that in the army, even if you were not quite sure what you were doing, act like you did. Moving too fast would send a message of panic; moving too slow would send one of dread. He stopped six inches from the linchpin and surveyed it carefully. He moved closer, then emptied the vial onto the linchpin and massaged the contents over the greasy surface. Geometry played a large part in being an artilleryman, so he calculated angles with special care before deciding where to place his hands for maximum purchase. Once his fingers curled round the pin, he closed his eyes and took a deep breath. He allowed his fingers to explore, trusting the intuition that resided in their tips. He slowly adjusted his grip as he found the pin's key pressure point.

He took another deep breath and mouthed a quick prayer. He never spoke much about his faith, but it formed a large part of who he was.

He gritted his teeth and pulled with all his might. The pin slid down and out. He held the linchpin up for all to view.

Murmurs of surprise and approval rippled through the assemblage that had expected him to fail. French soldiers did not give endorsements easily, but when they did, it was enthusiastic and whole-hearted.

Le Mans did not join in. He hated being shown up by a child. Then and there he resolved to visit his revenge on Gagne when it was least expected. Perhaps during battle; you never knew when friendly fire might strike. That is, if the Prussians didn't kill the boy for him.

Fivel clapped Jacques on the shoulders. "Well done. Keep this up and you'll make *caporal* before the campaign is concluded." He turned away and bellowed to those watching. "Don't stand their gawking! Get that wheel off, now!"

Jacques pitched in, too. In five minutes, the cannon had a new wheel; in ten, the column resumed forward progress.

It was now just after 4 a.m. and light enough in this northern latitude for Jacques to see clearly. The hamlet of Lobbes would have furnished a fine subject for a painting by the Flemish Master Peter Paul Rubens. Its gentle charm came from neat red brick cottages, white windmills, blackthorn hedgerows, golden brown fields of wheat and rye, and thousands of crimson and yellow tulips. Women were already hanging up their washing to dry, and a cattle herd traversed a narrow lane, guided by two shepherds and three dogs.

Le Mans eyed it greedily. It was a rich, fat country, untouched by war and brimming with good things he regarded as plunder. To him, campaigns were all about enrichment, not glory.

Two hundred yards away, *Herr* Gunther Grosse, Prussian *Oberstabfeldwebel,* and his commanding officer, *Hauptman* von Gillhausen, watched from behind a hedgerow the passage of enemy French troops.

"I know what you are thinking, *Herr Hauptman*," murmured Grosse, "but to attack now would be folly. Our task is to observe and report. That is best done if we remain in the shadows. We've let five French columns pass in order to count their numbers and identify individual units. Our concealment is so good that even their cavalry *vedettes* have missed us. Let's not push our luck. It's time to go."

Oberstabfeldwebel Grosse of the 2nd Company, 1st Battalion, 1st Westphalian *Landwehr* was not a religiously observant man, but now he prayed that his officer would listen to him. Grosse was the Prussian equivalent of a sergeant major. A veteran of six campaigns, 26 of his 52 years had been spent in the army.

The *hauptman* whom Grosse was doing his best to advise, Heinrich von Gilhausen, was an intelligent, earnest officer who led from the front, and the men liked his enthusiasm. But he was only 19, and his only campaigns had been against the virtues of well-bred ladies. Grosse had seen the same fervid sparkle in the eyes of half a dozen dashing young officers, and they were all dead. Here was another young aristocrat determined to uphold the family reputation by winning renown. Such quests usually ended badly for enlisted men.

"On the contrary, Grosse, we need to exploit our luck." Von Gilhausen looked at Grosse with the earnest gaze of a lord who respected his chief game keeper yet considered his judgement compromised by the onset of senility. "Information is good, but glory is better." His eyes gleamed. "We have 200 men who are in position with every advantage of cover, preparation, and surprise, so why not use them? Is it not an officer's duty to show initiative, Grosse?"

"Well, yes, but an officer also needs to understand that restraint in the service of strategy sometimes serves his mission better than an immediate tactical victory."

"Is it not an officer's duty to harass, confound, and weaken the enemy?"

"It is, however—'

"Should we not do everything in our power to soften up the enemy and reduce the burden upon our compatriots to the rear?

"True enough, and yet—"

'And is not surprise an officer's best ally?"

"Granted, but—"

"Are we not at right angles to the enemy, the perfect position to launch a flank attack?

Grosse sighed in exasperation. This annoying Socratic dialectic was dangerous with the enemy so near, and Grosse doubted he had any chance of persuading an officer consumed with proving his manhood. "We do have a good position, *Herr Hauptman*."

"What is the greatest threat to our infantry ahead?"

God, this is getting tiresome, thought Grosse. "Grape and canister from their artillery. Their guns are efficient, which is another reason why we should decamp before they unlimber."

"And if we disable their gunners, would that not confer a great advantage upon our infantry to the rear?"

"It would, but the range is extreme and most of our men are new."

"Three volleys fired from cover. That's all. Disrupt and dash. The confusion should make our withdrawal easy."

"As you wish, *Herr Hauptman,*" Grosse said bleakly, "but I warn you, this is a very bad idea."

"You are thinking like an old man, Grosse."

"Perhaps, but due caution is why I am still alive."

The dog Rifle *woof*ed warningly; seconds later, Jacques heard zipping noises and felt several rushes of air speed past his face. He stopped and craned his head about, more curious than frightened. The shots were coming from behind a thick hedgerow, though no shakos nor uniforms were visible. Jacques realized that he had just been shot at. Things seemed to be moving in slow motion, and life had taken on the unreality of a dream.

"Get down, you damn fool!" shouted Goulet, as he shoved Jacques to the ground. There was only a flash of uniform as a sniper ducked behind the hedgerow, but the black shakos, dark grey coats and light grey trousers indicated they were Prussian *Landwehr.* "Prussians!" the whisper spread quickly through the grounded company, all hugging the earth tightly, seeking to make themselves the smallest targets possible.

Jacques unshouldered his musket and silently advanced it upon the sandy soil. Eager to strike back, he hoped he would be commanded to kneel and fire. Artillerists were issued shorter versions of the five-foot infantry Charleville but seldom had occasion to use them. More shots flew, increasing in volume and sounding like the buzzing of bees. The net effect caused Jacques' blood to race and demanded his feet propel him forward.

Goulet put his hand on Jacques' arm, forcing down his musket. "Not our job, Gagne. Stay put. My ears are good judges. The range is too great for them to do much damage. They are too weak to capture the guns, so they are trying to kill the gunners. The *voltigeurs* will flush them out and the hussars will drive them off."

"But, but, but... we have to do... something!" Jacques hissed.

Goulet shot him a cynical glance. "We are doing something. By staying put, we occupy the enemy's focus. Now keep quiet and be patient."

Jacques swallowed his protests and resolved to watch and learn.

Von Gilhausen's first volley wounded only six French soldiers, but his men cheered anyway. Grosse shook his head dolefully. The French *voltigeurs* were headed straight for a field of six-foot-tall rye that would give them cover. A close quarter fight would not end well for the Prussians.

"*Herr Hauptman*, we must withdraw."

"No! Just a few more volleys!"

"Then have the men aim for bigger targets: the horses. Without them the cannons can't move."

Von Gilhausen frowned. "Rather a shame. I like horses."

Blue-coated French *voltigeurs* flowed by silently on Jacques' right, arrayed in loose skirmish order: three feet between each man. Rather than firing conventional volleys in three ranks from a fixed position, *voltigeurs* were the essence of mobility, advancing in short, quick rushes, now stopping every ten seconds to kneel and fire. The enemy could not see them, only the swaying of the rye stalks when they moved. Moving in clumps of eight, each man had a partner who covered him while he reloaded.

"Stay down, Jacques," cautioned a familiar voice. "My men and I will protect you." Jacques looked up to see the face of his uncle, who winked as he passed by.

Sergent Jean Paul Gagne's' *voltigeur* rookies performed with varying degrees of skill. Dumas shouted as he fired, encouraging the others. He felt a sharp punch to his ribs and his next breath came in a gasp, but the excitement of the moment cancelled out the pain and he kept firing. The sound of gunfire had roused Collette from the sleep of the dead and he had run full speed into the fray, laughing and capering like a madman between shots. Du Bois looked terrified but kept up a steady fire. Rochefort was taking very careful aim at the puffs of smoke; his rounds were the likeliest of all to find a target. Despite Le Duc's dragging his musket earlier, he now handled it efficiently. Du Bois did everything right, but in slow motion. Tremblay performed well, but the dreamy-eyed Martin simply froze. Tremblay kicked him hard in the rump, which brought him out of his trance. Legrand panicked, threw down his musket and ran for the rear, only to be felled by a bullet that penetrated the base of his skull.

Private Fontenoy's reaction was the strangest of all, though Gagne knew it was more common than most NCOs cared to admit. Fontenoy loaded fast and efficiently but discharged every shot at the sky, as if shooting at invisible birds. Some men, even when their life was in threat, simply refused to kill; and no amount of threats or training could compel them to act otherwise.

Most of the men on both sides fired too high, a common effect of excitement and inexperience. It was the baptism of fire for many. Gagne recalled the terrors of his own first fight: profuse sweating, knotted stomach, dry lips, a compelling urge to vomit and flee, but underneath all this, a compulsion to find out if he was a warrior or a weakling.

Firing at targets who were well concealed while enduring fire from enemies who also could not see their opponents meant that few shots struck anyone. Yet the zipping rounds prevented a Prussian advance and gave time for a French flanking column to approach from the left.

Sergent Gagne saw a flash of blue in the distance and knew the flanking trap was ready to be sprung. Colonel Tussot bellowed, "Charge!" and Gagne's men joined 250 others in a mad, pell-mell dash, bayonets thrust outward and hungry, nearly every man screaming like a demon. The 92nd burst out of the rye and closed the remaining hundred yards. The rest of Tussot's command launched an attack from the opposite direction.

"Oh, shit!" exclaimed *Oberstabfeldwebel* Grosse. "They have us flanked! We need to get the men out of here!"

Pale as a sheet, von Gilhausen froze. Grosse shook him hard, and he blinked. "Yes, yes, yes. Give the order, Grosse." But before Grosse could say a word, a red hole appeared in his forehead, and he was flung backward. Von Gilhausen grunted in surprise, then stared at the crumpled body as if he had just lost his best friend. From a professional point of view, he had. *I should have listened to him.* With the glue that held the outfit together gone, discipline evaporated and panic began to spread.

"First platoon, face left! Second Platoon, face right! Fix bayonets and prepare to receive attack!" Von Gilhausen shouted the right commands, but his thin voice carried poorly and his men were not disposed to listen. Nothing induces pure terror like two lines of bayonets forming a rapidly closing vice. The hedgerow had limited Prussian casualties, but now they were out in the open. Prussians transformed from soldiers to rabble; they broke and ran.

The French saw only their backsides, and they were running so fast that French bayonets never pierced a single Prussian uniform. The infantry was herding rather than killing, but that was just fine with the French, because the *coup de grace* had just arrived in the form of thundering horses ridden by fearless riders.

"Form on me! yelled von Gilhausen helplessly as the last two men of his company raced by. "Form, on…" Von Gilhausen's words died as a cavalry saber sliced across his shoulders. He had been so focused on the infantry, that he had missed the approach of French cavalry. *An ambush!* he realized belatedly. *Must have been sheltering behind a grove of trees to the rear. Shakespeare was right, 'Hell is empty. All the devils are here.'* His thoughts ceased as his heart stopped.

Colonel Marcellin Marbot relished the precision of his stroke that had felled the enemy commander. He knew he had destroyed the last hope of a Prussian rally, but his blood was up and it demanded that the outcome of the present contest be annihilation. His 7th Hussar Regiment had first gained fame in 1795, charging across a frozen sea to capture an entire Dutch fleet. Cutting down broken men would not add to the regiment's laurels, but it was still satisfying to hone your skills with live targets.

His 460 French hussars spurred their sleek horses to the gallop and their sabers slashed with an extravagance that matched their elaborate uniforms. Designed to awe and impress, the uniforms were well suited to men famous for their outsize dash and daring. They wore circular hats of bear fur, close-fitted jackets of hunter green with gold piping, fur trimmed pelisses thrown rakishly over right shoulders, skintight crimson breeches, and highly polished black boots whose tops covered the knee. The curved blade of each Year IX saber could sever a neck with a single swipe, and many did so now. There were six basic slashes prescribed in the sword's manual, and the rampaging hussars used all of them. A favorite maneuver was to gallop ahead of a target and slash backward at the neck, circumventing the protection offered by high, stiff collars.

Jacques Gagne watched the bloody conclusion with the rest of his company. The horsemen were like mounted guillotines, and Jacques gasped as heads parted from necks and shrieks of pain and despair filled the air. The ground shook from plunging hooves and macabre bouncing objects. One man's face was cleft in two by a wide diagonal slash that ran from his hairline to his jaw. A second was felled by a blow that took off the top of his head, leaving the brain exposed. A third was raked across the eyes in a stroke that blinded but did not kill. He collapsed, mewling and puking. An entire platoon was cut to pieces running through a field of tulips: splashes of blood overwhelmed the blossoms and turned a garden into a slaughterhouse.

When the soldiers were finished off, the hussars set upon the local cattle. Fresh steaks were a far better reward than any medals, and slashing running bullocks was great sport; the hussars laughed with a glee as they cut and thrust. What remained after the hussars cooked and ate their fill would be gobbled up when the slower-moving infantry passed through.

Viktor and Ethan Janssen, the two young shepherds who had been herding the cattle, cowered behind a stone wall. They quietly cursed and cried as their family's fortune vanished, but counted themselves fortunate that the chaos of battle and a knowledge of local geography had saved their lives. Hussars had a reputation for slaughtering anything that moved once a battle was joined.

Private Karl Schmidt, the sole Prussian survivor, sheltered beside the lads and wondered what to do. His mind was fuddled with shock and grief, and he dimly understood that he was not thinking clearly. The Prussian Army actively discouraged initiative on the part of recruits, which made determining a course of action even harder. All he could think to do was shelter in place until the danger was past, then cautiously make his way to headquarters, a kilometer and a half to the rear. General von Steinmetz, the brigade commander, would know what to do.

Gazing at the corpses on the ground, Jacques Gagne realized that the dead Prussians were not more than four or five years older than he was. They did not look like the devils or demons he had been warned about, but perfectly ordinary young men, such as you might encounter at a market. He was glad they had been beaten, but rather than feeling triumph he felt sadness at the waste. They might be mistaken in their allegiance, but it was just possible they believed in their cause as ardently as he believed in his.

"Vive l'Empereur! Vive l'Empereur!" shouted his childhood friend, Jean-Luc Boulet, a few paces away, voicing an enthusiasm that Jacques found curiously absent in himself. Jean-Luc jumped up, placed his shako atop his musket and commenced waving it extravagantly. *"Vive l' Emper—"*

His shout was caught off by a musket ball, the product of the last spasm of a dying *landwehr*'s trigger finger. The round entered through his mouth and exited the back of his head. He pitched forward and collapsed without making a sound.

Jacques dashed over and tried to raise his friend. As the dead weight sagged in his arms, tears started to his eyes. He could not decide if Boulet's death was a random act of senseless violence or an act of retribution from a God who differed from the benevolent entity his Catholic friends had told to him to trust. A memory flooded his mind, of their breakfast on the day they had enlisted. The hot cider, warm baguettes, fresh butter, and his mother's preserves had tasted particularly delicious once they decided to translate their patriotism into action, each boy inspiring the other to do something that he would not have done on his own. The smell of fresh bread, apples, and strawberries returned, and for a few moments he was back in Normandy.

He dropped to his knees and began mindlessly stroking his friend's hair, as if that somehow might bring him back to life. Rifle joined him, emitting low moans of sympathy. Gagne noted idly that a rising wind no longer carried the smell of tulips but the iron scent of blood. He felt that he had lived an entire lifetime in fifteen minutes. Staring blankly into space, he lost all track of time.

Le Mans observed Jacques' mourning with contempt. The boy's sentimentality was a show of weakness, and La Man's hatred for Jacques deepened.

A little way off, Martin was enviously eyeing the shoes of a dead soldier.

"Go ahead, he won't be needing them," urged Tremblay, noticing. "Take them, or else I will."

"But isn't that defiling the dead?"

"His feet don't hurt, but yours do. Nothing sacred about pain."

Martin bent down, removed the shoes from the corpse, and substituted them for his own. They were a size too large but in excellent repair.

"Now you're learning. The dead are a lot more reliable source of supply than the commissariat," Tremblay added cynically.

Jacques felt a comforting hand on his shoulder and looked up to see his uncle's face. "Heartbreaking to lose a lifelong friend, isn't it? I am sorry it happened, and you will lose more mates before peace returns. Cherish their memories and cry if you must, but grieving too much will burn the heart out of you." His uncle reached into his knapsack and extracted a small flask. He handed it to his nephew. "Best pain killer around. A couple of snorts does wonders."

Jacques took a sip and wheezed. Whatever the stuff was, it was potent!

"A first fight is never what you expect, Jacques, but you may take pride that you followed orders and exhibited a temperament as steady as a rock." He paused, gazing down at the upturned face of his favorite nephew. 'You just left your childhood behind. You are a man now, and must demand the respect that attends on that."

The men of the platoon who heard this address were surprised by the compassion in their sergeant's normally flint-hard eyes. For a brief moment, he seemed almost human.

Sergent Jean-Paul Gagne glowered at the men gathered about him and bellowed, "Stop your damn lollygagging and get back into ranks. We march in ten minutes." He relented slightly but kept a stern expression on his face. "For a bunch of leftovers, you did... an adequate job."

Gagne's flash of humanity, his backhanded compliment, and the bestowing of a nickname kindled something the sergeant had been hoping for since the start of the march: a sense of family. The men jumped at his words and reformed into a column. Dumas appeared unsteady, odd for the best man in his platoon. Then Gagne noticed blood dribbling from the tails of his coat. That dribble changed to a gush and Dumas collapsed, never to rise again. *Damn shame*, thought Gagne. *War takes the best ones.*

Jacques felt hollow and empty, not at all manly. He looked up and caught sight of a camp follower walking aimlessly and wailing. She carried a baby in a tiny blanket, but its eyes were closed, and it was unmoving, likely stillborn. An army on the march was the worst place imaginable to give birth, yet it happened from time to time. His mother's words came back to him: "No matter how miserable you think you are, there are always others who have a far greater reason to be."

He took a long pull from the whiskey flask and thought back to the trollop who had propositioned him. He hoisted himself to his feet and wondered where she was just now. She suddenly seemed the most beautiful woman in the world.

Chapter 3

The Haunted Inn

15 June, 3 a.m., on the Belgian Frontier.

"I must ask you sir, what business you and your people are about at this late hour of the night." The youthful Prussian Hussar was polite yet firm. The three other members of his mounted patrol had drawn their carbines as a precaution. Their job was to scout the gap between Wellington's and Blucher's armies, report any French incursions on the *Chausse de Charleroi,* and detain any suspicious persons.

A breeze stirred the humid air and parted the low hanging clouds. The three-quarter moon gave sufficient illumination that the hussar could see that the man with whom he was speaking wore clothing that was expensive yet unostentatious. His mount looked expensive as well.

The Earl Grosvenor, a stately man in his mid-sixties, summoned every ounce of his considerable dignity, rose in his saddle, and replied in perfect German, "We are British subjects, *Herr Rittmeister,* and I am the Earl Grosvenor. We are on our way to Wellington's headquarters. I am a good friend of The Duke of Richmond, one of Wellington's closest associates, and inside the carriage are two women: my wife and Lady Pennywhistle, the wife of Sir Thomas Pennywhistle, Wellington's Naval Aide. While I cannot claim we are on official business, I nonetheless bear confidential letters from Lord Clancarty, the acting British Ambassador in Vienna. They contain information that the Duke will want to see. We are only on the road because we wish to reach Brussels at the earliest possible moment. I should also mention my coach carries Sir Thomas' infant son."

The *Rittmeister* started in his saddle. "*Bombproofed* Pennywhistle?"

"The same," replied Grosvenor.

"I have heard of this man," declared the hussar. "The gentleman who tested death itself."

"The story has been exaggerated, but in a manner of speaking, yes, he has. Might I know whom I am addressing?"

"Baron Justus von Gruner, *Rittmeister* of the 2nd Schlesian Hussars, at your service."

Grosvenor searched his memory. "You would not happen to be from Torgau, would you?"

"I would."

"Would Wolfgang von Gruner be your father?"

"Yes. But how could you know that?"

"Your resemblance to your father is pronounced. We met at the Court of Frederick just before the king died. We shared an enjoyment of the music of Bach and the writings of Voltaire."

Von Gruner's tone changed from imperious to friendly. "Forgive me, my lord, for stopping your caravan, but arms runners have been using all manner of conveyances to smuggle guns to Bonaparte's army." He shook his head in disgust. "I should also point out it is quite possible that French cavalry scouts may have crossed the Belgian frontier and could pose a danger to your party. They may take an altogether unhealthy interest in any documents you carry, and they have keen noses for sniffing out plunder. Might I suggest that you and your party seek shelter until daylight? Your horses look tired and a few hours rest would do them good."

"Your point is well taken, *Herr Rittmeister*. We have four soldiers with us who are experienced in the use of weaponry, but if there is a place that you could recommend, we might indeed take a few hours of rest."

Von Gruner considered. "I know of a place a mile distant, the *Auberge d'Argent*. It is the only inn for many miles. It might serve. But..."

"I sense problems, *Herr Rittmeister.*"

"Oh, the inn is well maintained, and the food is good, but the locals will not go there. It caters only to distant travelers who do not know its reputation."

"And what is that?"

"That it is haunted, and the spirits are active and unfriendly. Demons are reported to prowl the caverns that underlie its foundations. Those go back to a Roman barracks that once existed on the site."

Grosvenor's eyebrows arched in skepticism.

"I don't believe in ghosts and demons," von Gruner hastened to add, "but the locals do. The inn is managed by a family for whom the appellation "odd" would be polite. And it is true that three deaths have occurred at the site: prominent men who died under curious circumstances."

"It sounds like the sort of place to avoid, but," the Earl sighed, "beggars can't be choosers. I thank you for your information, *Herr Rittmeister*. Give my regards to your father."

"He passed two years ago."

Grosvenor touched his hat in respect. "A pity. The world is a poorer place for his absence."

Destination Waterloo

"I wish you a safe and swift journey." Von Gruner snapped a salute, barked a command to his subordinates, whirled his sleek horse about, and galloped away.

The Earl frowned; he knew that a council of war would have to be called. He was used to directing matters by fiat, but Sammie Jo's stubborn belief in American style democracy demanded that all the people on the present expedition have a voice if a major change to their itinerary was contemplated. It was outrageous that the opinions of servants and children should matter in any way, but Sammie Jo always solicited their opinions.

The caravan's members were 15 in all: Sammie Jo; her baby, Nicholas, and his nanny, Mrs. George; the Earl and Countess of Grosvenor; Lord Steven Thynne and his bride, Sarah; the Earl's man, Peg Leg Grimsby, who doubled as the coachman; the countess' maid, Beasley; Sergeant Major (retired) Dale; his wife, Deborah; their son Andrew; the orphan Johnny; and Sergeant Major Owens. Sergeant Rhys Owens, a fireplug of cynical Welsh combativeness, rode next to Dale. He was a fit, dark-complexioned man who had started a side business of selling war souvenirs to aristocrats; he'd joined the expedition because he felt sure a battle was shaping up between Wellington and Bonaparte that would leave plenty of relics for an enterprising man of business to scoop up. Thynne's cousin, Coronet the Honourable Hoylet Huntley, 10th Hussars, rounded out the expedition. He had served as Lady Sarah's escort to Vienna. Huntley was 28, proud and brave, but sometimes spoke in odd ways about strange subjects and later had no memory of his discourse; it was almost as if two people inhabited the same body. Thynne had often covered for his cousin when the younger man had gotten into trouble at family gatherings.

The discussion that ensued resembled a tiny Parliament. The Earl related his talk with the hussar to the group, then Sammie Jo assumed the role of Speaker of the Commons. "I don't think we should stop at that inn. It sounds dodgy. And I'm only 35 miles from reuniting with my husband, who's been gone for what seems to me three lifetimes. I aim to get reach him as soon as possible and introduce him to his son." She smiled fondly down at the baby in her arms, then one hand stole away to pat the gun beside her. Sammie Jo regarded her trusted .44 caliber long rifle, The Widowmaker, as an important part of the expedition. Rather than an inanimate object, she reckoned it a living entity.

Thynne spoke up. "But a French cavalry patrol could disrupt those plans, perhaps permanently. I recommend we sleep for a few hours at the inn, then push on at first light."

Huntley gave his viewpoint. "The horses are nearly spent. They need rest and food even more than we do." He looked thoughtful and added, apropos of nothing, "If all the horses in all the world were lined up end to end… there would be a mountain of dung."

"My map says there is a livery stable ten miles south of Nivelles; that's only six miles. We can grab a few hours sleep there then swap out the horses for a new team," argued Sammie Jo. "With a fresh team and a little pushing, we could be in Brussels in four hours!" Her eyes glowed with carnal longing for her husband.

"I agree with Lord Steven," advised Dale, formerly her husband's most trusted subordinate. "We should bivouac for the night at the inn. Exhausted people make dangerous mistakes."

"Sammie Jo, you are not thinking clearly," remonstrated Margaret, Countess Grosvenor. She had been Countess Leith until her marriage to the Earl, and she was Pennywhistle's godmother. "You are thinking like a newlywed. I understand, but you need to think as a mother. Since you refuse to use a wet nurse, you must consider the quality of your milk. The less sleep you get, the poorer its nurturing value. Trying to sleep inside a coach is no substitute for a bed."

"You should listen to her," interjected Sarah. "She has the child's best interests at heart. Isn't that what your husband would prefer?"

Sammie Jo pulled a face. At that moment, the infant awoke and burst into tears. She rocked him gently and cooed to him until he quieted. "I guess Nicholas just weighed in with the most important vote of all. How many of you here agree with him? Raise your hand if your vote matches his."

Everyone raised their hands.

"So be it. We stop at the inn."

"Good! Good!" squawked Plymouth, a blue and green parrot perched on Sammie Jo's right shoulder.

A collective sigh of relief rippled through the others. Sammie Jo possessed an incredible strength of will that often blinded her to the virtues of moderation. Her core toughness sometimes caused her to demand actions of others which were second nature to her but trying to lesser mortals.

"But no more than six hours!"

The other adults nodded their assent, and the caravan of a coach and two baggage wagons resumed its progress. They came to a crossroads that featured two gibbets swinging slowly in the wind. Only one was occupied, but the corpse had been there quite a while, judging by the state of decay. A swamp to the right of the gibbets gave off the miasma of rotting vegetation. A ruined church lay behind the swamp. Bats flittered in and out from the decrepit belfry tower.

Two hundred yards further along the road was the inn: a rambling, half-timbered, wattle and daub edifice of black and white that would have been at home in Tudor England. The sign that depended from an iron hook over the door depicted a silver dragon.

Grosvenor thought a dragon was an odd choice, hardly a symbol of hospitality. As he approached the inn's front veranda, a feeling of dread rippled over him, though he could determine no rational reason for its touch. He believed in God and an afterlife, but belief in ghosts was not allowed in the Enlightenment Club of which he was a charter member. As he moved closer to the inn, he had the sensation that he was being watched.

He was indeed being watched, but not by a specter or shadow. None the less, many reckoned Jerome Le Guin the very essence of a human devil. He was a malefactor who wore many criminal masks, and always stayed two steps ahead of the authorities.

Grosvenor mounted the loudly creaking stairs to the inn's porch and rang the bell several times. An owl hooted from an oak tree several yards away and swooped upon a hapless mouse. A black cat dashed past his feet. Water dripped slowly from a small well pump at the base of the oak, a rising wind whistled through horizontal cracks in the inn's wattle, and an unlatched shutter banged loudly against a window. He noticed a small kitchen garden to the right of the porch filled with deadly nightshade: a plant with many medicinal uses, but highly toxic if given in the wrong doses. A broomstick lay propped against the garden gate. An increase in humidity had generated a mist that now swirled around his feet.

After a minute or so, he heard loud, lumbering footsteps. The door rasped on its hinges and opened slowly. A seven-foot-tall man stepped through. His cadaverous face resembled the theatre mask for tragedy. "You rang? How may I help you, sir?" The manner of address was polite, but the low, rumbling voice carried a threatening quality.

For a second, Grosvenor stood paralyzed and thought that he was dreaming. He recovered himself and assumed his most formal manner. "I am the Earl Grosvenor and have a party of quality with me. We require beds for the night. I trust you can accommodate us."

"I am Eugen La Rue, and we can indeed accommodate you. We are usually very busy, but Bonaparte's imminent return to Belgium has resulted in a dearth of travelers."

The man's mouth smiled but his eyes radiated tension. Grosvenor wondered why the prospect of a profitable night's work would cause anxiety.

La Rue would have been happy to have Grosvenor and company on any night save this one. The vast cavern beneath the inn concealed hard men about a dangerous business. A large wagon and an armed escort would be arriving soon to convey the fruits of their labor across the border. Those men paid him well and would want him to turn these potential guests away, which was why they had been industriously circulating ghost stories about three murders that had happened a century ago.

A gaunt woman with a frog-like face joined La Rue and smiled a smile without front teeth. "I am Marie La Rue, my lord. I presume you have a lot of baggage," she gushed in an annoying sing-song voice.

"We do."

"I have 10 children who will carry your luggage, my lord. I shall rouse them straightaway."

Grosvenor wondered if the children would look as strange as their parents. "Very good, madam. Now if you will excuse me, I shall alert my party."

Le Guin had heard the entire conversation through a speaking tube he had secretly installed under the floorboards. It was always useful to monitor the comings and goings at the inn, for the very authorities he wanted to evade sometimes stayed at the inn. He was angry that la Rue was taking unnecessary risks, but he also understood that the Earl would pay well. And la Rue would demand payment in advance, so he would have no objections if his guests left in a hurry. It was time to stage a haunting.

His assistant, a stoop-shouldered man named Du Bois, tapped him on the shoulder. "The men are almost done with the inspections. They will start crating shortly. I thought you might wish to hear their verdicts on the weapons."

"I do."

Le Guin accompanied Du Bois to a large cavern built of Roman brick that had once been used as a granary. Seventeen men were in the process of reassembling muskets after carefully inspecting them. Each specimen was a .75 caliber British New Land Pattern Musket that was known colloquially as a Brown Bess. Next to each man was a case marked with a broad arrow and the letters B and O, indicating they were the property of the British Board of Ordinance — or had been until they were stolen from a factory in Liege. The British government sometimes subcontracted the manufacture of Brown Besses to Liege gunsmiths, and these weapons had been intended to arm the Hanoverian allies of the British. Once reassembled, the guns would be transferred to unmarked cases.

"Well, Rebeque, what do you think?" Le Guin asked the best of his inspectors.

"Ahh, monsieur Le Guin! Every one of these guns is a prime specimen; not a defective spring, screw, lock, barrel, or stock in the lot of them. The French are desperate for weapons and will pay us in gold! 102 muskets are enough to equip an entire company, and that will put a fortune in gold in our hands."

"I had in mind two gold Napoleons for each musket," chuckled Le Guin.

"That's extortion," laughed Rebeque. "The standard price is one."

"Extortion is my business, or at any rate, one of them. We do have a problem, though. Unwanted visitors upstairs."

"Is it time for bedsheets, chains, and moaning?"

"It is the perfect time for a ghost story. This lot may be less gullible than most, so your men will have to put on a truly haunting performance."

Sammie Jo watched the parade of luggage-carrying children with astonishment. Their methodical back and forth movements reminded her of bees entering and exiting a hive. She had never seen such a strange looking assemblage of misshapen forms, and they excited her pity. From the thinness of their limbs and the bowed shapes of their bones, she figured they suffered from varying degrees of rickets. Their odd faces made them seem descended from bullfrogs, and she would not have been surprised if they'd started croaking *ribbet, ribbet.* Sammie Jo knew the pain of perpetually being regarded as the outsider who did not fit in anywhere; she would make sure all the children received generous tips. And perhaps she could find something nourishing in the hampers to share.

One gnome-like youngster of ten tugged at her sleeve. "*S'il vous plaît*, will you tell the coachman to follow me? My brother and I will water and feed the horses."

"Of course, ..."

"Pierre, milady." He ducked his head. Even in the dark Sammie Jo could see his hair was unbrushed, dirty and unkempt.

He was rail thin and looked like he needed food and water far more than the horses did. She had the impression that there wasn't enough love at the inn to fill a saltshaker. She reached into her pocket and handed him a half crown. "Don't tell your folks, or they will confiscate it. When you get time, go into the village, and buy a decent meal."

Pierre's sad face lit like a Christmas moon. "I can buy many meals for this much!"

"I don't like the idea of staying in a place that's haunted. I saw a ghost once, and it was terrifying," whimpered Maude Beasley, the Countess' dressing maid.

"How did you know it was a ghost?" inquired Mrs. George.

"Because I could see through him!"

"Really?"

"Well, mostly. I melted from fright!"

"You look solid enough."

"I got better."

At the same moment, the men were discussing security arrangements. "My Lord," said Thynne to Grosvenor, "I am going to scout this place and I would like Owens to assist me. Why don't you and the others escort the ladies inside and get settled."

"I will do so, but I think we should first settle the issue of standing watch. I don't believe this supernatural rubbish, but our baggage and horses need protection. There is something off about our hosts, and it is just possible some French scouts might pay us a visit. Rather than have one man lose four hours sleep, I propose we split the watch among us: 48 minutes each."

All the others signaled approval, except Dale. "I must demur. You know how protective Lady Pennywhistle is of her baby. She has asked me to stand watch over him while she sleeps."

"Not surprising," observed Grosvenor, "since he is frail. His life was despaired of in the week after birth."

"He has borne the journey well," offered Huntley. "His complexion has improved, and he seems to be gaining weight.

"He is a remarkably easygoing child and cries very little," added Dale.

"This is our best bedroom, Lady Pennywhistle," the innkeeper's wife said proudly.

The room contained a gigantic bed of black oak that left little room for anything else. The square canopy was held aloft by four massive columns, and the headboard was graced with square panels that featured intricate carvings. Sammie Jo blinked in astonishment. "Well slap my head and call me silly! Just how big is that bed?"

"In English measurements, it's 8 feet, 9 inches tall; 10 feet, 8 inches wide- and 11 feet long. It's a copy of the Great Bed of Ware back in England. Your Shakespeare mentions it in the play *Twelfth Night*. A hundred years ago, the owner of the inn a was a devotee of Shakespeare and had it built. It's very popular for wedding nights."

"It looks like it could hold four couples! Wedding nights usually only involve one pair."

"It comes in very handy when we are busy."

Sammie Jo knew bed-sharing was a common practice in country inns. Even sharing such a bed, more a work of art than a piece of furniture, would be a night to remember.

"It can certainly accommodate the gentle folk in your party. I can put the servants in another room down the hall. You're welcome to carve your name in the posts. Lots of guests have."

"What do you think, Margaret?" asked Sammie Jo.

"It's not often that you get to sleep in something out of Shakespeare," replied the Countess. "I fear that I shall become so absorbed in studying it's carvings that I may not get any sleep at all."

What neither knew was that the massive bed was not flush with the wall because it shielded a small door in the wall that was virtually invisible: it had no latch and was opened by pressure at its top. That door led to the cavern beneath.

"Are you sure we shouldn't just kill them while they sleep?" asked Du Bois.

"I prefer employing guile to violence," replied Le Guin, "and I don't want to worry about disposing of their bodies. Besides, the disappearance of important people might raise questions we do not want asked. Are your men almost ready for ghost box theatre?"

"Curtain goes up in five minutes. We will start with the inn children. Their hysterics will add to the confusion. Just in case, I will have each man bring a weapon. To be used only if the whole thing goes to hell."

"But the children have seen this act before."

"Doesn't matter. They believe the place is haunted. Their cries will be authentically fearful."

"I think any danger tonight is going to come up that road," stated Thynne, pointing to the road that led to the Sambre and the frontier.

"That's your opinion," commented Owens, "I rule nothing out. That barn over yonder will make a good observation point. You can also keep an eye on the horses. There is a door on the second floor that could be kept open for the aiming and discharge your firelock."

"Exactly what I was thinking. If I spot anything suspicious, I will fire a warning shot."

Beasley and Mrs. George's dislike of each other sprang from sharing the same domineering nature, and neither relished the idea of sharing a bed. Both women were fretful.

"I hope you don't snore."

"I don't. What's that you're holding in your hand?"

"A Celtic Cross from my Irish grandmother. Blessed with holy water, 'tis, and has within a fragment of bone from St. Patrick himself. 'Tis an absolute terror to ghosts."

"I thought crosses only worked on vampires."

"Oh, vampires it's sure to destroy! Ghosts it just scares."

"Lucky I have you to protect me," declared Mrs.'s George with heavy sarcasm.

Two kilometers away, a wagon pulled by sturdy farm horses was approaching the inn.

"We are ahead of schedule," gloated Emil Fournaux, a professional smuggler who regularly ran expensive goods across the Belgian frontier. "Do you think the guns will be ready for us?"

"I know Le Guin," responded his brother Julien, sitting next to him in the wagon's drivebox and clutching a blunderbuss. "He always allows more time for a task than he really needs. That way, when he completes it early, he seems exceptionally industrious and clever. I expect the crates are already packed and ready."

"Do you think we really need a cavalry escort?"

"I do not, but the French insisted. It will be four men, and they will be wearing civilian clothing. They may already be at the rendezvous."

"This will be our last run, Emil. With things heating up along the frontier, gun running is getting too damned dangerous. No point in making money if you are not alive to enjoy it."

"I agree. After tonight's run, let's pop open a bottle of champagne and celebrate our retirement."

Ten miles west of the Silver Dragon, one of Von Gruner's Hussar scouts, Trooper Kleist, trotted up to report to his commander. The other two men of the patrol had already returned and had found the neighboring roads clear of any traffic. Kleist showed initiative uncommon in the Prussian army, seeking places of concealment that other scouts missed. Von Gruner welcomed a man who thought for himself and operated effectively without supervision. If only the entire Prussian cavalry corps was made up of Kleists!

"Well, Kleist, is your report as mundane as that of your friends?" grumbled von Gruner, annoyed that the Belgium countryside seemed to be a picture of peace. He had never seen action and was eager to prove himself.

"I am not sure, sir. I spotted four men, ten minutes ago, headed toward Nivelles."

Von Gruner's eyebrows arched in enquiry.

"I sheltered in a grove of trees and watched them pass. There was something was odd about them."

Von Gruner's breath quickened. "How so?"

"They were dressed in the riding coats of aristocrats, but instead of being clean shaven, they all sported mustaches of the sort favored by hussars. I could swear their saddles were those of French cavalry. They rode like hussars too, not civilians. Very erect postures, and the canter of their horses kept a military cadence."

Von Gruner slapped his fist into his palm in satisfaction. "I congratulate you on your powers of observation. I think they may be French scouts, though I wonder why they would adopt a disguise, since that makes them liable to be shot as spies if captured." He scratched his head in thought. "They must be on some special errand. Perhaps they are connected to these gun runners we have heard so much about. Whatever it is, we shall investigate. You will guide us to their last position, then we will shadow them and pounce when the moment is right."

"Might I offer a suggestion, sir?"

"Ordinarily I am not keen on suggestions from those without the king's commission, but you have shown yourself uncommonly perceptive, so I will listen to what you have to say.

"I think they might be headed to the *Auberge d'Argent*. It has a peculiar reputation."

"I am familiar with its notoriety, Kleist."

"I wonder if that reputation is being used to cloak a gun running operation, *Herr Rittmeister*."

"H'mmm. I had not thought of that connection. We must investigate." Von Gruner's face glowed with excitement at the prospect of action. "There is no time to be lost. Lead on, Kleist."

Kleist saluted. "It will be my honor, *Herr Rittmeister*." He put the spurs to his horse and galloped off, followed closely by von Gruner and the other troopers.

A trap door opened in the room of Mrs. George and Beasley. Two men emerged quietly, clad in bedsheets dripping with blood, with gobbets of gore applied to various parts of their costume. One had a small set of chains in his hands. The bedsheets had eyeholes and covered them from head to toe.

The two men nodded at each other, then bent low over the women. "Ooch! Oooh ! Oooh!" They moaned and groaned with voices of melancholy and malevolence. The second one rattled his chains loudly. Each dumped a small vial of blood on the sleeping women.

"Ahhh! Ahhh! Ahh!" Beasley screamed as she shot up in bed. She reacted on instinct and thrust the Celtic Cross into the face of the nearest specter. She was astonished when the ghost didn't flee or dissolve but let out a long "Owww!" and staggered backwards. The heavy cross had struck the faux specter squarely in his right eye.

Beasley shook Mrs. George awake. "We must flee," quavered Beasley. "The portals of Hell have opened." She jumped from the bed, grabbed Mrs. George's wrist, and jerked her to her feet. Mrs. George was still half awake and saw the ghosts through a gauze of sleepy winkers. She kicked at one bedsheet from anger at being roused from a sound sleep and connected with something solid instead of ectoplasm. The bedsheet yowled and commenced moving up and down in a hopping motion.

The two women dashed into the hall bent on warning others. Mrs. George was certain that their visitors were human, but they were nevertheless bad men bent on mischief.

Six children of the innkeepers ran screaming down the hall and bumped into Beasley and Mrs. George. They clutched at them in terror and pointed to the end of the hall. Two more ghosts were advancing: moaning, groaning, and rattling chains.

The rising wind chased away the clouds cloaking the bright moon and gave Thynne a good view of the Nivelles Road. He spotted a large wagon coming toward the inn, accompanied by four men on horseback. The horsemen were dressed as civilians, but Thynne was a cavalryman and recognized professional troopers by their horsemanship.

The only pickups or deliveries that were done in the dead of night were illegal ones; the inn must contain something the French Army wanted badly.

Destination Waterloo

Disguise might also mean that the troopers would not consider themselves bound by the usual laws of war and might deal harshly with any civilians who got in their way. As a serving officer in the 1st Lifeguards, it was his duty to oppose the French wherever he found them, whether in uniform or not. He had two loaded Baker rifles at hand to stop the advance and alert his party to danger.

He waited patiently for the wagon and riders to close the distance. A lurching figure stumbled out of the woods carrying a stone jug and singing merrily: likely a local peasant out on a bender. He bobbed and weaved toward the cavalrymen. A shot rang out and the ambling figure collapsed. The rider's willingness to kill a harmless drunk told him all he needed to know about their intentions.

He heard a creaking noise coming from what appeared to be a large haymow, a hundred yards behind his position. The haymow parted into two halves, as if each half had been bolted to a platform. Two doors opened. The bright lights of many torches revealed the entrance to a large cavern lined with an ancient brickwork pattern that told him this had once been a grain storage depot for the Romans. The road leading downward was wide enough to accommodate the wagon.

The commotion in the hall put Dale on his guard. "Awk! Awk! Bad! Bad" squawked Plymouth as he flapped his wings in alarm. He had been perched on the giant headboard of the Belgian Bed of Ware and had spotted the opening of the small door to its rear. Two specters had emerged and peeked out from around the giant headboard. Dale heard his alarm and spotted the intruders. He fired his Baker, and one "ghost" flew backward and spurted blood. Sammie Jo jerked awake, grabbed the Widowmaker next to her, rolled sideways both to aim and protect her baby, and fired the rifle at the second specter. The round caught the wraith in the back of the head, and he collapsed with a thud that ectoplasm would never have made.

Grosvenor, the Countess, and Huntley, sharing the huge bed with Sammie Jo and her child, snapped awake. The gun smoke told them all they needed to know, and they leaped out of the bed. Since they slept fully dressed, they were ready to depart immediately. The question was: where?

"For ghosts, they sure do a heap of bleedin'," jeered Sammie Jo. "Someone wants to frighten us out of here pretty bad, but they will have to do better than that."

"We need to get everyone back to the coach and wagons," cautioned Dale, "and I need to see to my family."

"Wait just a damn minute, Andrew, I ain't gonna be run off like a no-account, lily-livered squatter. These damn spooks threatened us, and I sure as hell aim to find who sent them. I aim to give them all a dose of frontier justice."

"You can't do that all by yourself," warned Grosvenor.

"I ain't goin alone. The Widowmaker's coming with. You can join me, Robert, if you bring your pistols and sword. Margaret can watch Nicholas. She won't let no harm come to him."

Margaret had moved behind the bed and felt the rush of air through the open door. "They came in through this rabbit hole, but it would be foolish to follow the stairs back to their source."

"Maybe, but my dander is up and I ain't backing down."

"I shall accompany you," proclaimed Huntley. "I pledge my pistols, sword, and honor to your cause, Lady Pennywhistle.

"That's right handsome of you, Mr. Huntley. I accept."

His eyes flickered as he gazed at the pooling blood, and his cheek twitched. "Blood and revenge are hammering in my head."

Grosvenor thought it an odd time to quote Shakespeare.

"I wonder if this is all a distraction," argued Dale. "Create fear and chaos inside the inn so we pay no attention to what is happening outside of the inn. Send us fleeing in one direction while something wicked approaches from the opposite side. Lord Steven needs reinforcements. I will send Owens. After I get my family and the servants to safety, I will join him."

Johnny and Andrew Junior raced into the hall, followed by Deborah and Sarah, who had been in the room next door. Children were running and screaming in the hallways, but eleven-year-old Johnny was not frightened at all. He had seen real battle, and the two bedsheets approaching were poor imitations of ghosts. He raised the pistol given to him by Pennywhistle and shot one in the chest.

Andrew Junior gasped. "You shot him! You shot him!" He had never fired the pistol his father had given him in anger.

The second ghost stared down at his fallen companion, cursed, then abandoned all pretense of being supernatural. A very human hand holding a pistol emerged from under the bedsheet.

"Fire, Andy, fire!" Johnny yelled.

Andrew closed his eyes and fired in the general direction of the specter. The ghost was only five feet away, so his unaimed round found a home in its chest. The ghost crumpled.

Andrew opened his eyes and gasped at what he had done. He looked about to vomit.

"Don't take it so hard, Andy," consoled Johnny. "He had a gun. Would you rather it was you lying dead, or me?"

"You did right, Andrew," soothed his mother as she hugged him tight

"I just want to be a newspaper editor like you, Ma," gulped Andrew.

"I know you want to fight your battles with words, not firearms, but consider this: what is happening now will make a fine story for the newspapers back in London. I will get all the details when this is done and write it up. And you will help me."

This prospect consoled Andrew, and his sobs abated to snuffles. "Aren't you scared, Ma?"

"Certainly, but a good reporter knows danger and a good story are often inseparable."

"This," mused Sarah, "is a Gothic novel come to life."

"Except that no one here is wringing their hands or fainting," Deborah retorted.

Thynne was just about to open fire when Owens appeared at his side and quickly explained the situation at the inn. Thynne explained his surmise about gun running.

"I brought two weapons, mi lord. Thought you could use the help."

"You take the drivers, Owens, and I will take the horsemen."

"Done." Both men raised their rifles, carefully tracked their targets, then fired. The wagon's driver looked puzzled as he saw a spreading stain on his chest, dropped the reins, and slumped backward.

The lead cavalryman looked toward the source of the sound, but his horse was hit a moment later. The horse reared and plunged, taking the cavalryman down and pinning his leg under the weight of its bulk.

Emil shook his brother. "Julien, Julien, speak to me. Speak to me —" his sentence was cut short by Owen's second bullet.

Thynne targeted a second cavalryman and aimed at a flash of moonlight glancing off the man's polished saddle pommel. His round jerked the rider from his horse.

Thynne and Owens reloaded with the speed of which only veterans were capable.

Destination Waterloo

A quarter kilometer away, von Gruner's hussars heard the shots. They had been on the trail of the French for the last half hour. They'd observed the rendezvous with the wagon, but wanted to discover the caravan's ultimate destination before acting. Now Von Gruner debated whether to approach cautiously, close, dismount, then fight on foot with their carbines, or ride hard to close the distance. He decided on the latter; risk was their business after all. Rather than having his men draw their sabers immediately, as a novice officer might have, he would wait until they were right on top of their quarry, maximizing the shock of sabers drawn quickly in unison.

Sammie Jo, Grosvenor, and Huntley eased themselves through the small door on all fours, then stood up. Headroom was only five and half feet, so all had to bend low. The passage connected to a network of tunnels that were dimly lit by a distant source of light that seemed brighter at the top of a flight of stairs that led downward. Sammie Jo, Widowmaker in readiness, cautiously advanced. Grosvenor and Huntley followed, each with two pistols at the ready. Grosvenor had tried to argue her out of leading, but she would not hear of it.

There was a rustling noise and two ghosts emerged from a side tunnel ahead of them, muttering unintelligible words to each other. Their postures suggested that they were discouraged. They reached the staircase and swiftly descended.

In the cavern, Le Guin heard the gunfire and began shouting at his men, panic edging into his voice. "Are all the guns crated?"

A chorus of ayes answered his inquiry. "Then get the crates on the carts and push them out to the wagon as fast as you can."

"But it sounds like the wagon is under fire," objected one portly older man. "You said we would not have to risk our hides."

"Things change," retorted Le Guin scornfully. "Now shut up and get moving."

At that moment, two dispirited men emerged from the tunnel leading to the surface, holding their ghost costumes in their hands.

Le Guin glared at them.

"They fought back instead of scarpering! One shot me in the rump and it hurts like hell!" The short, dumpy man pointed to the wound.

"Two of my friends are dead!" bellowed his companion.

Sammie Jo's ears perked up as she heard the faint echoes of angry voices. She motioned her companions to draw closer and whispered, "Let's follow and eavesdrop. Once we know what is going on, we hit them hard and fast. Guns, then steel."

"Take no prisoners?" whispered a strangely gleeful Huntley.

"Anyone who threatens children gets no mercy," she snarled coldly. "I brought my own steel insurance." She pulled a knife from the long blue duster she wore when traveling and flourished it. Both men started; they had not known she carried a knife, let alone one of epic proportions. "Back home, we call this a Maryland Toothpick."

The large knife had a strong cross guard and was 18 inches overall with a blade of 12 inches. It had a razor-sharp double edge, the top edge having a crescent shaped indentation that made it useful for skinning. It could be used to dispatch wounded animals, just as a hunting sword did. But unlike a hunting sword, its size made it a deadly weapon in a close quarter brawl.

The stairs ended in a small balcony that overlooked a massive cavern. It was well lit with torches and a dozen men toiled, loading crates on to small, wheeled carts. The cavern's doors at the top of an uphill road were open.

Grosvenor recognized the markings on the crates that had been discarded. "Gun runners!" he whispered.

"We have to stop them!" hissed Sammie jo. "Those guns could be used against my husband! And Wellington," she added.

The sounds of gunfire erupted at that moment and the men in the cavern looked toward the source on the other side of the open doors.

"Every man grab a firelock from the rack," shouted Le Guin, "then get those carts moving to the entrance, fast. The French are under attack, and unless we go to their rescue, none of us get paid! Now, move, move, you dogs!" The anger in Le Guin's voice snapped everyone into action.

"This is our chance!" whispered Sammie Jo. "We have five shots, and the range is only twenty yards. Anyone left standing gets our blades.

"Shooting men in the back seems unsporting," said Huntley.

Sammie Jo scowled at him. "You're not at Eton, Huntley."

"I didn't like Eton. They gave me the boot because I challenged the headmaster to a duel."

Suddenly, the prospect of violence triggered something deep in Huntley, something he worked hard to keep locked away. His left cheek twitched, and his posture stiffened. His eyes rolled. His face seemed putty for a split second: morphing from his usual expression of kind solicitude to one that reveled in mayhem. His eye color changed from brown to blue; his voice dropped an octave, his lisp disappeared, and his soft voice became aggressive and arrogant. He spoke in short, quick bursts of profanity in stark contrast to his usual genteel speech. "Let's fuck 'e m up! Oh yes! Oh yes! They must pay!" He paused and began chanting, "Fuck 'em up, fuck em up, fuck em up," as if the words were a dark parody of a Gregorian chant.

Sammie Jo stared at the Earl in bafflement. "What is going on?

"I think... he is having some sort of fit."

Sammie Jo noticed Huntley was shaking slightly and moved closer, hoping to calm him. "Huntley, Huntley, are you with us?"

Huntley batted away the hand she placed on his shoulder. "I am not Huntley!" he shouted manically. "I am Beowulf, and those men out there are the minions of Grendel! They must be smashed! Smashed, I tell you! If I fail, the monster they serve will return and destroy all!"

Sammie Jo rocked backwards in shock.

"Stand clear!" Grosvenor warned her.

As Owen readied his next shot, four riders in a line came roaring down the road, shouting in what sounded like German. These riders were uniformed: Prussian hussars by the cut of their jackets. Moonlight flashed off their extended blades. The Frenchmen turned to face them, but before they could draw their swords, the Prussians had severed their sword arms. Each Frenchman endured a whirring farrago of blades in the seconds before they tumbled from their saddles. By the moonlight, Thynne recognized the leader of the Prussians: it was the *Rittmeister* who had inspected their caravan and spoken at length with the Earl.

Just then, shouting men with guns emerged from the long tunnel.

Huntley leaped down the last few steps and ran at the men heading toward the cavern doors. Screaming like a madman, he fired his pistols into the backs of two smugglers. Before they even hit the ground his sword was out, and he was thrusting toward the back of a third. As he pierced the man's heart, he shouted, "You will all die in searing pain!"

Destination Waterloo

"A silent ambush would have worked better!" muttered Sammie Jo.

The men with guns exiting the tunnel stopped in confusion, uncertain whether the greatest threat lay to their front or their rear. The screaming demon armed with a sword inspired more terror than their bedsheets ever had.

Sammie Jo raised Widowmaker to her shoulder and sighted, taking advantage of the illumination provided by the many torches. She held her breath, let it out gently, and squeezed the trigger. Her aim was true; the man dropped the gun in his hands before he hit the ground. She reversed the Widowmaker, intending to swing it like a club, then jumped down and charged. Grosvenor readied his own firearm.

His first shot hit one man at the base of the spine, the second took another between the shoulder blades. He drew his sword and confronted a man who had also drawn a sword. The man was aggressive and skillful. Grosvenor parried four slashes and blocked two cuts and thrusts. His opponent pressed him hard, and he found himself retreating. He was better than his opponent, but age had slowed his ripostes and diminished his energy reserves. He absorbed one cut to the shoulder that was painful but not deep and was breathing hard when his opponent reared back to deliver what he likely intended to be a fatal cut to the head, but his foot slipped on some horse manure. Trying to regain his balance, he dropped his guard and Grosvenor struck: one thrust to the heart. His opponent blinked once, snorted and clutched his chest, then collapsed.

Sammie Jo smashed one man's face with her rifle butt, then whirled it round and bludgeoned another man's kneecap. A third man struck her from behind, knocking her down and sending the Widowmaker skittering away. She instinctively rolled hard to the right, and so avoided being skewered by a plunging butcher knife. She scrambled to her feet and drew her own blade. She confronted a man who held his weapon in a way that indicated this was not his first knife fight.

He cursed as he slashed; "Whore!" was the politest thing he called her. She blocked two upward slashes, then kicked him hard in the shin and slashed a deep gash in his right thigh. He yelped but slashed twice again; so quick was his second cut that it nearly reached her jugular vein before she batted it away. Blue sparks flew as her blade deflected his next cut at her shoulder. She forced his knife down and sideways and stomped on his foot. He yowled in pain. She crashed her nearly six-foot-tall body hard into his, disorienting and unbalancing him. Her eyes met his; hers flamed with hate, his darkened with fear. She kicked him hard in the knee, grabbed his shoulders as he crumpled, and slammed him into the floor. She pounced like a cat on a wounded canary. Twice she stabbed the already wounded thigh, allowing her anger to strengthen each blow. Blood didn't flow, it jetted. While he thrashed violently for a brief time, then stilled, Sammie Jo hastened to retrieve Widowmaker.

Men were running back down the tunnel, pursued by horsemen slashing wildly. She heard rifle shots and saw Thynne and Owens near the cavern's entrance, firing into the mass of smugglers.

Le Guin dropped to his knees and looked up into von Gruner's grim face, begging for something he'd never given to any of his victims: mercy. "Spare me! Treasure beyond your dreams will be yours if—" Von Gruner's blade slashed his face and ended his life.
Seeing their leader so abruptly dispatched cowed the rest of the smugglers, and they surrendered.

The final victim was not a smuggler, but Huntley, felled by friendly fire. A round from Thynne's rifle had killed its intended victim at close range, and the bullet had retained sufficient velocity to exit the smuggler's body and pierce Huntley's chest.

When Huntley fell, Thynne screamed "No!" in horror. He ran forward and dropped to his knees to cradle Huntley's face in his hands. Huntley's eyes flickered open. His irises widened in surprise, then understanding. "Better this way, Cousin. The dragon I hunted was within me all the time." He gripped Thynne's hand hard, then his grip relaxed. His breathing stopped, and his eyes turned fixed and staring.

Thynne began to weep softly. "What have I done? What have I done?"

Sammie Jo walked over, helped him to his feet, and embraced him with sisterly love and kindness. "It's not your fault. It's not your fault! It's mine. If I'd stuck to my original plan and bypassed the inn, this would never have happened!'" Tears coursed down her cheeks.

Grosvenor had also come alongside, and while his voice was kind, his words reflected realism. "The fault is no one's. His death is a fluke of war. I shall make sure his death is listed as killed in action and shall mention that he was instrumental in recovering 102 stolen muskets. And so he was. He did not die for nothing."

"I shall pay for his funeral," whispered Thynne, his voice choked with tears. "He must be given a proper burial in Brussels."

Von Gruner walked over and shook his head. "Your friend died a warrior's death, and a life's worth is never measured by its length but by its deeds. Allow me to assist you and your friends. It is still a few hours before dawn, and you should rest before taking to the road. My men and I will stand guard until you awake and provide an escort to Brussels."

"Thank you," said Grosvenor. "I know some of my countrymen do not trust Prussians, but word of your actions will spread and do much to reconcile our people."

"The British and Prussians must act as the staunchest of allies if we are to defeat Bonaparte."

"Wellington and Blucher are both men who will see this campaign through to the bitter end."

"True, but I fear the end of this campaign will be very bitter indeed."

Owen's mind remained clear despite the maudlin atmosphere. It occurred to him that the Frenchmen had probably been bringing a small fortune in gold coins to pay for the stolen arms. While the avaricious part of his nature wanted the money for himself, his better portion knew that shared danger demanded shared reward.

He walked over to Sammie Jo and quietly whispered his thoughts to her. Her face turned thoughtful. She said nothing for a full minute, then her mouth widened into a smile.

"Gentlemen, may I have your attention. A matter of importance has just been represented to me." She copied the commanding tone of voice her husband used on the parade ground, and it had the desired effect. Every eye and ear in the cavern focused on her.

"Sergeant Major Owens has just told me that if we search the dead Frenchmen's saddle bags, we are likely to find a considerable quantity of gold that was to be used as payment for the guns."

Von Gruner's troopers spoke no English, but the word "gold" needed no translation.

"Now, I know y'all think you deserve a reward," continued Sammie Jo, lapsing into her ordinary way of talking, "and I won't argue that you ain't right, but I suggest that we split whatever gold there is four ways, so that helps out more than just us. I propose one quarter of the funds go to the support of the ten children in the inn. They are in a pitiable state. I know from experience what it's like to go to bed with an empty belly. I will tell the parents that a weekly emissary will be sent to check up on the children, and woe betide them if the young 'uns ain't happy and healthy. The innkeeper and his wife may be bad 'uns, but they are smart enough not to disobey powerful people who could make things tough for them.

"One quarter of the remaining coins will be given to Wellington's fund for military widows and orphans once we reach Brussels, to help those who suffer the most from war." She addressed von Gruner. "Let one quarter be given to you and your men. The remainder can be distributed among my entourage using a prize money formula favored by the Royal Navy."

Von Gruner translated for his men, who looked at each other in uncertainty, mirroring the caution in his voice.

"I believe we can offer an additional inducement," said Grosvenor to von Gruner. "I have carried out a brief inspection of the cavern and discovered the chief smuggler has invested some of his money in tangible goods."

"Other than the guns, I do not see anything valuable," replied von Gruner skeptically.

"Just around the corner is a concealed stable containing a number of fine horses. They look to be Lipizzaners. Concealed under hay at the stable front are ten bottles of Louis XIII de Remy brandy. One of my friends paid five hundred pounds for a single bottle last year. I see no reason why you and your men should not take, say, six of the horses and all the brandy as a reward for your efforts. Since you have vowed to provide us with an escort, I want you to have the best horses available."

Von Gruner translated for his men, and they all cheered up visibly at the prospect of two things every hussar loved: expensive horses and expensive liquor. Von Gruner bowed graciously. "I accept your offer, my lord, and believe we can consider this deal concluded."

"It is good to see some lasting good come of this sordid affair," said Grosvenor.

"I speak for Huntley's conscience and myself," added Thynne. "Let charity and hope triumph."

Sammie Jo smiled with satisfaction.

Chapter 4

A Map and a Bully

15 June, 1815, 3 a.m., British Headquarters, Brussels

The three-story, white Palladian structure that served as Wellington's headquarters was silent. It was a good, central location; the building fronted on the Brussels Royal Park, and British officers occasionally strolled the park's walkways in brief intervals away from their offices. Most of the men who worked there had gone home at 10p.m., after a 15-hour work day.

The small clock on Pennywhistle's office desk struck 3 a.m., jolting him awake. He had intended to close his eyes for only a quick catnap, but realized to his horror that he had been sound asleep for nearly four hours. He raised his head from his desk, blinked twice, and wiped the crusts from his eyes. He ran his fingers through his sandy red hair, which felt in need of washing. He rubbed the stubble on his angular Plantagenet face and longed for a close shave and a hot bath; he had been at work almost 24 hours straight. Leaning back in his chair, he stretched his arms and his legs and let out an extended yawn.

After lighting two new candles, he rose and walked over to the Franklin Stove that occupied a third of his small room. He picked up a large silver pot and poured his fourth mug of coffee. The stove generated unwanted heat, but it kept the coffee warm. He stood by the stove and took a grateful swallow of the blessed nectar. Pennywhistle's fondness for coffee marked him as an eccentric, but he refused to be cajoled into drinking the tea that was the lifeblood of the rest of the staff.

Since his arrival on April 15, he had been overwhelmed with paperwork, so late nights had become commonplace. The Duke of Wellington's staff of 52 included many officers who had only recently arrived and were still learning their duties. In addition to his official obligations as the Duke's naval aide, Pennywhistle was constantly repairing the work of four newly minted subalterns who got things wrong more often than they did right. Since the staff had been hastily assembled, improvisation had become the order of the day.

Wellington's efforts to put his own men in positions of authority had been severely limited by the Duke of York, Commander-in-Chief of the British Army and second son of George III. York disliked Wellington, so he deliberately sent second- and third-rate officers who enjoyed high social status, which made discipline problematic. They had to be accommodated and placed in positions where they could do the least damage they could contrive. That sometimes meant that the nominal commander of an outfit had his duties carried out by an officer of less rank but real competence.

Wellington was respected as a soldier and a diplomat, but his prickly personality made him a difficult man to like. The Duke rose early, worked hard, and no detail was too trivial to escape his attention. His written orders and correspondence were perceptive, direct, and concise. Just as he could size up the defensive possibilities of a piece of terrain in an instant, so too he could quickly cut to the core of any issue under discussion. This approach was appreciated by men for whom time and truth were currencies, but it made Wellington many enemies among the vain and prideful.

Destination Waterloo

He kept his own emotions buttoned up tightly, and he spoke with condescension of those who did not or could not do the same. Sparing with praise, those who did not meet his high standards frequently found themselves on the wrong side of his sharp temper and barbed tongue. He demanded an instant response to any question he asked and savaged any man who was tongue-tied. Little freedom of initiative was granted to subordinates; he often reserved decisions for himself that other generals would have delegated to their staff. Similarly, Wellington acted as his own intelligence chief; he personally reviewed reports instead of relying on summaries prepared by lieutenants and captains.

He was a stickler for maintaining the rules of social rank. Very, very few friends were granted the privilege of addressing him by his Christian name of Arthur. His nickname among officers was "the Peer" or "The Beau"; soldiers referred to him as "Beaky," or "Old Nosey" in reference to the striking Roman nose that protruded from his face.

The eyes on either side of that nose were a frosty blue: perceptive, probing, and judgmental. 46 years old, five feet ten and of a medium build he was in superb physical condition from long hours of riding and moderate meals. His constitution also gave him the ability to get by with very little sleep. He spoke quickly in a tenor voice with a hint of a lisp. Though he possessed a singular wit, he did not laugh often. His laugh was distinctive: halfway between a bark and a whinny.

For all his reserved, aristocratic hauteur, he was a man of Spartan habits, simple tastes, and well-defined routines; there was nothing ostentatious or extravagant about him. In an age famous for larger-than-life heroes and adversaries, he was down-to-earth.

Admiral Nelson had viewed his sailors with affection and felt that most men had promise; Wellington reckoned that most soldiers were crude, unreliable, and volatile, needing the strictest discipline. He punished infractions like looting with a severity that was legendary. At the same time, he never hazarded the lives of his men recklessly, and this won from all but the sulkiest a firm respect. In the camp talks around the evening fires, when foot soldiers swapped stories and compared experiences, many a man was heard to say he'd rather fight under Wellington's command than any other officer.

Wellington had once called his men 'the scum of the earth', but the newspapers reporting this had left off the rest of his statement: "It is wonderful that we have made them the fine fellows that they are." Once, when asked by a friend if he thought he could beat Bonaparte, Wellington had pointed to a British soldier strolling through Brussels Royal Park. "It depends on that article there. Give me enough of it and I am sure."

Now Pennywhistle sat down at his desk and resumed writing his readiness report describing the British garrisons in Ostend and Antwerp, charged with protecting Wellington's supply line. A knock on his open door caused him to look up, to see Wellington regarding him with sympathy. As usual, he was dressed in civilian clothes, which actually made him stand out in a crowd of scarlet uniforms: black boots, white kidskin trousers, a high collared blue frock coat and a cravat of white silk. "Burning the midnight oil again, I see. Work never ends, does it, Sir Thomas? And I am afraid I must call on your services once again. Will you join me in my office in ten minutes?"

"Of course, Your Grace."

Wellington nodded and was gone abruptly. Wellington usually started his own day at 3 a.m., after dining at 7 p.m. and retiring at 9. His habit was to handle correspondences from 3- to 7 a.m., then embark on a series of inspections of various units. He read reports carefully but preferred to see things for himself.

Destination Waterloo

When Pennywhistle entered Wellington's office, the general was examining a large map of southern Belgium spread upon the desk. "Come in, come in, Sir Thomas," directed Wellington, with a brief smile that was uncharacteristic of him. "Draw close, and I will explain what I need."

Pennywhistle had the impression he was about to be favored with something rare: direct insights into the Duke's plan of campaign.

"You have done a satisfactory job protecting my supply line. My problem now is determining where Bonaparte will strike. We know he is on the move, and I see three possible axes of attack." He traced three lines on the map with a finger. "Here, against the Prussians to the East of Charleroi; or a direct assault against Brussels; or... one of his patented flanking maneuvers round my right, in the direction of Hal, to cut me off from Ostend. I think an advance between Mons and Binche most likely. Rumors abound about Bonaparte's intentions, many of them no doubt spread by his agents to sow confusion and distraction, but what I know at present is that he is approaching the Belgian Frontier. I dislike adopting a posture of inaction, but until I receive more reliable information I shall have to do so. I simply do not have the manpower or the supplies to deploy corps to all three zones in numbers that could stand up to Napoleon."

"A difficult situation indeed, Your Grace. How may I help?"

"A year ago, when I was touring the Low Countries, I scouted locations where an English Army could fight a creditable defensive action against a foe as formidable as Bonaparte. I had the Royal Engineers draw detailed topographical maps of three possible battlefields. I have been consulting two of those maps, but the third has gone missing. This map is of a low ridge in front of a small village called Waterloo." Wellington tapped the paper twice. Pennywhistle peered down. He had never heard of the place, and little enough could be discerned on the map's scale.

"The fellow who accompanied you on the submarine mission, Balthazar Barton, was the one who had drawn the missing map and knew where it was stored. I sent him to retrieve it two days ago, but have heard nothing from him. He is a dependable officer, as you know, and I fear he has meant with some accident or misadventure. I need that map as soon as possible. I charge you to retrieve it, and to find out what happened to Barton. All he told me was that it was in the village of Dauphin on the River Zenne, about five miles from here. The Royal Engineers established a depot there in 1814 during the Bergan-op-Zoom Campaign. When the site was evacuated, the map was left behind by mistake."

Pennywhistle just wanted to sleep, but he kept his face neutral and his voice steady. "Of course, sir. I can leave immediately."

"One other thing, Sir Thomas. I have an officer that I would like you to take along. His name is Ensign Maximilian Maxwell, and I am at my wits end trying to figure out what to do with him. He is a walking catalogue of everything that is wrong with the officer corps and has bungled every assignment given him. However, his grandmother is a friend of Queen Charlotte, so I cannot just send him packing. The Queen keeps sending inquiries about his progress and I am tired of lying to her. You have a reputation for salvaging the unsalvageable, and I want you to work your magic on Maxwell. I grant you carte blanche."

"Has this young ne'er-do-well any talents that might prove of value?"

"When sober, he is a good shot and a creditable swordsman. However," Wellington's voice flooded with censure, "he is often drunk, frequently insubordinate, and generally shirks responsibility. He is a great bear of a man and has the temperament of that animal woken prematurely from hibernation. He will fight at the drop of a hat. The counsels of reason have no effect on him. I fear all he understands is violence."

"Since I am the court of last resort, I promise you my best effort, Your Grace." Pennywhistle snapped to attention and saluted, but frowned inwardly. The last thing he needed was to be saddled with a wastrel.

Wellington returned the salute. "Good luck, and report back to me as soon as you have the map. Time is of the essence."

A sergeant informed Pennywhistle that his young charge was in the stables behind headquarters. "At least, that's where he usually disappears to, when he's not underfoot and making a nuisance of himself, sir." Pennywhistle found Maxwell sprawled languidly on a groomsman's bench, snoring loudly. A comely young woman, wearing only a corset, screamed, grabbed her clothes, and fled at Pennywhistle's approach.

Maxwell wore a contented expression on his face, likely basking in post coital bliss. His scarlet uniform was disheveled, with dried blood on the collar, and smelled like it had just been plucked from the inside of a rum barrel. His oval face sported several black and blue marks, and while it was handsome, a two-day growth of beard did not do it any favors. He was indeed massive; Pennywhistle estimated his height at 6 feet 5 inches, and his weight at 280 pounds.

Pennywhistle shook his head at the sorry sight.

Maxwell looked to be about twenty; most ensigns were younger. The lowest commissioned rank was often given to sixteen-year-olds who carried a regiment's colors even though they had not yet begun to shave. Maxwell's red face matched his hair; his puffy cheeks, bloated lips, and profuse sweating all indicated that he was living life greedily. "*Eeeeeruppp*" a long, loud burp erupted from his mouth.

Pennywhistle kicked him smartly in the backside, grabbed his shoulders, jerked him to a sitting position, and shook him violently. "Wake up! Wake up, Ensign Maxwell! Now!"

"Who the hell is kicking me? Go away, you God-damn scoundrel, and let me sleep." His speech was slurred, though his accent suggested an education at Eton or Harrow. His phlegmy eyes struggled to focus on Pennywhistle.

"On your feet! That's an order, not a request, Ensign. I am Lieutenant Colonel Pennywhistle and if you weren't an officer, by God, I'd see you got twenty strokes of the cat."

Mention of flogging spurred Maxwell to full consciousness. He staggered to his feet, took a dirty glove from his pocket, and tried to slap Pennywhistle with it, intending a challenge to a duel.

Pennywhistle intercepted his wrist and twisted it smartly to the right and down, making Maxwell drop the glove. He then delivered a slap across the face, more to pierce the alcoholic fog than out of real anger. He nonetheless put fire in his voice. "Wellington hates dueling, but you already know that. I will forgive your monstrous insubordination only once because your services may prove useful to me. But if you dare challenge me again, I shall not wait for the field of honor but will shoot you dead on the spot. Mutiny is a capital offense. Grow up! I am not your damn babysitter."

Rather than startling Maxwell back into his senses, Pennywhistle's words provoked his anger. "Babysitter? Babysitter! If you weren't wearing that uniform, I'd teach you a lesson with my fists that you'd not soon forget! I swear you shall regret the day you try to tell me what to do. Go back and tell Beaky that I am the wild stallion that cannot be broken." His voice carried the belligerence of a bull speared by a picador. He spat, then belched. "You're not fit to lick my boots, much less be order me about. I'll bet your wife uses her society connections to shield you from real men who could rip you apart." He guffawed.

The idiot is trying to pick a fight! Ordinarily, Pennywhistle would fight fire with water and try to cool passions, but Maxwell was a hard case, so far sunk in the abyss of arrogance that it was time to overcome a smaller fire with a greater one. Wellington's words about this one only understanding violence came back to him. "If your fists have the same force as your insults, I have nothing to fear. You," he sneered, "are only a battle virgin with a big mouth."

Maxwell scowled.

"I hear Dutch courage in your bragging, and I question whether you have any of the real article."

"Are you calling me a coward?" demanded Maxwell with astonished outrage.

"My meaning could not be plainer. You seem stupid as well. As for your threats, let me oblige you. A duel is only between gentlemen and too good for the likes of you." Pennywhistle removed his silk cravat, took off his scarlet coat, and rolled up the sleeves of his white cotton shirt. "I will set my rank aside. It's now just one man against another. I dare you to do your worst, but I give you fair warning: you will not last twenty seconds. So, what's it to be, obey or fight?"

"You warning me? Ha, ha, ha! I have never lost a fight!"

"Then its high time you had that experience." Pennywhistle's voice rippled with disdain. "You're no challenge to me, just my morning exercise."

Pennywhistle turned sideways, crouched slightly, widened his stance, and brought his hands up in front of his face. His palms were open, not closed, as was traditional in Savate, the French art of street fighting.

Maxwell experienced a moment of indecision. He was used to seeing fear in the eyes of his opponents and liked to enjoy it for a few seconds before the pummeling began. Now he saw two cold eyes that made a shark's seem those of a kitten.

"I'm laughing at the big bad bear," chuckled Pennywhistle.

Maxwell growled a curse, then stripped off his coat and shirt, revealing a muscular chest and arms with a layer of fat that obscured their definition. "I was having a nice sleep, but cleaning the smile off one of you perfumed wankers makes an early rise worthwhile."

Maxwell threw a rabbit punch at Pennywhistle's ribs that he easily knocked away. He riposted with a back fist to Maxwell's jaw.

Shocked that his attack had failed, Maxwell retreated a yard. The iron taste of his own blood filled his mouth. He spat and began to circle slowly, searching for an opening: his fuddled mind dimly realizing this was going to be different from the bar brawls he was used to. His opponent had fast reflexes and exuded a dangerous calm. Maxwell's bloodshot eyes flared. He knew the bottle of rum that he had consumed impaired his movements, but he was bigger and stronger than his opponent, and that had always been more than enough to win.

He charged with his arms open, grabbing for Pennywhistle, who snapped a sharp kick to the groin. Though it would have stopped a sober man cold, the rum dulled the pain sufficiently that the kick only slowed Maxwell, who tackled Pennywhistle, his full weight landing on top of him. His powerful rage unleashed, Maxwell laid into him with the fury of a berserker. Pennywhistle locked his arms together in front of his face like a boxer. He was able to block all but one punch, but that connected squarely with his left cheekbone and made his head ring and his vision blur.

In a desperate attempt to stop the onslaught of fists, he clapped the palms of his hands hard on Maxwell's ears to blank out his sense of balance. This bought him the time to launch a palm heel strike that caught his opponent straight in the nose, causing him to snort and propelling him away. Maxwell careened backward as Pennywhistle rolled clear and staggered to his feet.

Maxwell had not quite regained his footing when Pennywhistle's left fist crashed into his chin, and since the oversize drunkard could absorb an insane amount of punishment, he followed that up with a right upper cut. Pennywhistle then slid his left arm behind Maxwell's neck as he gripped his left wrist with his right hand. He thrust his hip out and crouched, jerking Maxwell's wrist downwards. The ensign flew over him and crashed hard. If this had been a fight to the death, Pennywhistle would have finished him by a smart application of his boot to the Adam's Apple. His intention, however, was not to kill Maxwell but to teach him the law of the jungle: no matter how tough you are, there is always somebody tougher. But administering the lesson had cost him. He was breathing hard, his forearms throbbed, and his cheek would soon be black and blue.

Maxwell lay in a heap. His breathing sounded like a damaged bellows, and he teetered on the brink of unconsciousness. When his vision cleared, he beheld Pennywhistle standing over him with an open pocket watch.

"I predicted twenty seconds; you managed to last a full minute. You have more bottom than I expected, but the proverb holds true: the bigger they are, the harder they fall. Perhaps now we can have a productive conversation." Pennywhistle jerked him to his feet, then shoved him back onto the bench.

"Have I your attention, Ensign?" Pennywhistle barked.

"Y-yes," mumbled Maxwell groggily.

"Yes, what?" Pennywhistle bellowed.

"Yes... Colonel," Maxwell hissed back, sticking out his tongue in a gesture that only a rude schoolboy or a foolish drunk would make.

Pennywhistle smacked Maxwell across the mouth with the back of his hand. "If I were less civilized, I should see your tongue cut out and jammed up your rectum. Test me again, and the lesson will be more severe. Now, do I have your attention?"

"Yes, Colonel," mumbled Maxwell in a subdued voice that stopped short of obedience.

"I am overwhelmed by the grandeur of that honor," said Pennywhistle with biting sarcasm. He quickly explained the mission, though he wondered how much Maxwell could absorb through his inebriation. He concluded by saying, "I don't think you will be of much help, but I could be wrong. You can sober up during the ride. Follow my orders and don't get in the way. Keep your eyes open and your mouth shut. It's time to chase Frenchmen, not skirts. Wellington says you have skill with a gun and a blade. Is that true, or mere puffery?"

"Oh, it's true!" Pennywhistle heard a hint of pride in Maxwell's voice, a good sign.

"Forgive me if I am skeptical. You will have to prove it to me."

"Just let me at those froggy bastards, sir!" boasted Maxwell, in the voice of a man who wanted to show a superior predator that the man he had beaten was still dangerous. A strange expression crossed his face. "Lieutenant Colonel Pennywhistle," he mused. "Wait, you wouldn't happen to be Bombproofed Pennywhistle?"

Pennywhistle sighed; his unwanted sobriquet was known here. "It seems I cannot shed that nickname."

"I had a cousin who served with you in America who told me the story. Imagine! Bombproofed Pennywhistle in my presence. Well, ain't that a ray of sunshine in the morning!"

"If your cousin served with me, you should know I am a reasonable man. As such, I am willing to give a fellow a second chance to correct a first impression. Consider yourself on probation."

"Thank you, sir." While Maxwell liked the idea of being an officer who commanded respect, virtue was hard while vice was fun. He hated authority the way a vampire hated the cross, and a part of him was already plotting how he could work round this martinet.

"Don't thank me yet. You will find me a hard taskmaster. But if you make it through today's mission with honor, there is hope that you might someday become something other than a commissioned clown. I will go to great lengths to help a man out if he shows me the character to warrant investing in his future."

Maxwell's eyes flickered with uncertainty. He was almost touched by Pennywhistle's sincerity, and a crack opened in the wall of distrust that he used to keep everyone out. "No one expects me to do well. I'm sure my father hopes I die in battle."

"I know nothing of your past; as far as I am concerned, you have a *tabula rasa*. Perhaps your family sent you to the army for a bad reason, but swords are often two edged. The army may be your chance at redemption."

Maxwell's grin was feral. "I could take on the whole French Empire myself if they'd put me in real combat. Since I have been here all I get to do is argue with stupid captains, fuck the local wenches, and knock the teeth out of their fiancées."

Pennywhistle shook his head. "Spoken like a man who holds the false opinion that each John Bull is worth ten Johnny Crapauds. Consider yourself the cat that has used up eight of its lives and remember that I am your last resort. If you fail me, I see dark times ahead: cashiering, imprisonment, transportation to Botany Bay, even a firing squad are all distinct possibilities."

"I'm ready to fight, Bombproofed! Point me at the French and stand back with your watch to count my dead!" Maxwell imagined himself triumphant over England's enemies, basking in the admiration of fellow officers and his father's approval. It was a lovely vision.

"It's *Colonel* Pennywhistle, is that clear, *Ensign*?" Pennywhistle snapped sharply. *Good Lord, the man never stopped!* "It's time you learned that military courtesies are not suggestions. And regulations only vex a man who lacks the wit to see they are for the betterment of all." The trick would be to enforce discipline strongly enough to break Maxwell's resistance without breaking his spirit. "Now, we have a mission to complete, and it's time to get cracking."

"I will not let you down, Colonel." Maxwell was not lying, but he was unsure of the sincerity of his words. A devil within was whispering, "Are you sure this is what you want?"

Pennywhistle wondered whether he had just adopted a lost lamb or a marauding wolf. He knew that a drunk's promise was unreliable; an emotionally volatile man could change his direction faster than a weathervane in a strong wind. He would have to watch his back.

Chapter 5
Smugglers' Den

15 June 1815, 5 a.m., the road to Brussels

Sammie Jo's eagerness to see her husband was stronger than patience or the need for sleep, and urged her to gallop hard for Brussels. With her good eye for horseflesh she had commandeered the fastest of the Lipizzaners at the inn. Reluctantly, she had accepted *Rittmeister* von Gruner's escort — at the insistence of the Earl. She now set a furious pace. Her instincts told her a big battle was coming, and soon. Tom would want to be in the thick of it, and she dreaded that he might die before she ever had the chance to hold him again.

She hated leaving her baby behind, but little Nicolas would be safer with the Earl and Margaret. Fervently she prayed for all their safety. If the road they traveled washed out, not only would their passage be slowed, there would be a very real risk of their coming to harm. Their luck held; the flashes of lightning and booms of thunder presaged a storm that continued to hold off.

As they got closer to Brussels the number of mounted couriers increased, confirming her suspicions that a showdown between Wellington and Napoleon lay just over the horizon. Wellington's couriers were delivering reports to the general and relaying back his orders; no doubt Napoleon's couriers were similarly busy. These couriers were from the 3ʳᵈ Hussars of the King's German Legion, chosen for their reliability as well as their fluency in English and German. Now von Gruner proved valuable, for he was able to allay any suspicions aroused by their sudden appearance and rapid approach. Sammy Jo had to admit to herself that the Earl had been wise when he'd insisted she not travel to Brussels alone.

The couriers were astonished to see a woman who rode like a man rather than sidesaddle. She wore her honey-blonde hair in a bun under a bolero hat with red beads round the crown. The exotic headgear was as dashing and distinctive as the black Spanish riding habit she wore above the pantaloons that allowed ease of movement. For overworked couriers too busy to socialize with the ladies of Brussels, she was a fantasy on horseback.

Von Gruner himself had never beheld such an athletic woman. Her movements were lithe, quick, and graceful, and she and the horse moved as one. Her cornflower-blue eyes glowed with the thrill of speed, which was of a piece with what he had seen back at the inn. This was a woman who enjoyed living on the edge: challenging danger rather than backing away from it. What he didn't like was how hard she pushed the horse. He did not think her naturally cruel but fanatically single-minded. Still, he admired her strength of will and devotion to her husband, and wished he could meet such a woman.

She finally stopped at *L'Auberge du Grand Marais*, six miles from Brussels, allowing that her horse was about to drop from sheer exhaustion. He pulled up next to her. "Perhaps we should have a brief meal before proceeding further."

"Can't spare the time. I need to hire their fastest horse right quick and be on my way."

"Your horse needs—"

"I know, I know. He is almost blown. I've been bad to him, but I aim to make it up." She patted the horse gently and whispered soothing words to him. "I will instruct the innkeeper to give him special food and care. You can be on your way, *Herr Rittmeister.* While I appreciate your courtesy, we are close enough to the city that my safety is in no doubt. I know you want to return to your scouting; I can see duty is as important to you as it is to my husband."

"I feel it ungentlemanly to leave you here alone and unguarded."

"I have Thynne's sword, two of the Earl's pistols, and Widowmaker, so I won't be alone. Any rascal that tries to cross me will find there ain't no faster quick draw than yours truly."

Von Gruner doffed his hat and made a sweeping gesture. "Lady Pennywhistle, I wish you a safe journey. My respects to your husband and I wish him good fortune in the battles to come. I shall say a prayer for your son and ask the Lord to make his health more robust. For now, I bid you good day, my lady." He pivoted his horse and was gone, at a much slower pace.

Sammie Jo wasted no time. She discovered that Pierre Longchamps, the innkeeper, was a rabid Bonapartist, but he became an ardent monetarist when she flourished several gold coins. He did not like the British but did like that they paid their bills in coin rather than paper scrip of questionable value. Her heavily accented French got the message across that she needed a fast horse, and she needed it now.

The innkeeper's eyebrows arched, and he made a shrugging gesture with his hands. "I have two horses that are docile beasts that might suit your needs..." Sammie Jo frowned, "but they will never break any speed records. On the left... I have another horse that is... well, a special case. I am not sure he is suited to a lady."

Her curiosity piqued, Sammie Jo's eyes sparkled. "Tell me more."

The innkeeper had purchased a stallion for a song from a local breeder, hoping to resell him to an aristocrat who liked a spirited mount. The beast showed promise as a racehorse but had a nasty temper, and the breeder had given up trying to break him.

"I warn you, milady, this stallion is dangerous. You put your life in the hands of *le bon Dieu* if you mount him, but the devil will be in the bit."

"I ain't never met a horse whose got a stronger will than me. Horses ain't smart but they have lots of intuition. They test you and draw conclusions right quick. If he can't buck me off, he's mine. What's his name?"

"Diable."

Sammie Jo chuckled. "Well, some people have called me a very devil, so maybe we are a good match. Bring him out and let me see what he's made of."

"I take no responsibility for your safety, milady."

"I'll look out for myself."

Longchamps and his son got a saddle and bridle on Diable without a problem. The innkeeper knew the beast was cunning, trying to lull any would-be rider into a false sense of optimism. He almost seemed friendly, but the innkeeper knew it was an act. His heart misgave him. Would the beautiful lady be duped into taking a bad fall?

Sammie Jo knew horses and was not fooled. She walked round Diable twice and gave him a careful examination. She looked him straight in the eye and saw his core clearly. His eyes challenged: *You will never beat me.* Hers retorted, *Watch me.*

"Open the gate," she commanded the innkeeper, "then stand back and give me room."

Destination Waterloo

She walked twice more around the horse, trying to create a feeling of uncertainty in Diable. On her third pass, she thrust her boot in the stirrup, leaped into the saddle, and gripped the reins for dear life.

Diable shot out of the stable like a bolt of lightning, then commenced bucking violently in the paddock. Sammie Jo knew the trick was fluidity, not rigidity, to keep her posture loose enough to roll with the horse's motions, like a sailor treading a heavily pitching deck at sea. The horse neighed and snorted defiantly and nearly threw her twice, but she tightened the grip of her muscled thighs. Despite the danger, she was enjoying herself. Eventually Diable's bucking slowed, then gentled to kicks that Sammie Jo rode out effortlessly, then stopped altogether. The horse snorted twice in surrender.

Sammie Jo's voice turned gentle. "Now that you've got the orneriness out of your system, I aim to train you right. I ain't never going to let anything bad happen to you that I can stop, but you've got to trust me." She patted his head and cooed softly, "Trust me, trust me, trust me."

The horse sensed her good intentions and relaxed. She instinctively knew he would cause her no further trouble. "I'll take him," she brusquely informed to the astonished innkeeper. She also paid for a serving of sausage and cheese on a baguette, and downed a few gulps of a golden ale that tasted of peaches.

Five minutes later she was flying down the last six miles to Brussels, letting Diable have his head, wanting to find out just how fast he really was. He was a magnificent animal, and she could make a great deal of money on him as a racehorse. Yet that interested her not at all. She wanted a beast that matched her spirit, and each fast-passing mile confirmed that she had found him.

She halted Diable in front of British headquarters, but not before he showed his spirit by rearing dramatically. The two privates guarding its entrance kept their rigid postures but blinked in surprise. Several officers who had watched Sammie Jo's arrival from their second-floor windows rushed down the stairs to find out the identity of this exotically attired woman atop a powerful stallion.

Captains Lennox and Bartram burst out of the front doors and stopped in front of Sammie Jo, their faces alight in a mixture of awe and curiosity.

Sammie Jo knew the look and took charge. "Gentlemen, I am Lady Samantha Pennywhistle, and I am here to see my husband, Sir Thomas. I need one of you to take charge of Diable and one of you to guide me to his office." She flashed a smile.

The two men exchanged startled glances. They had heard stories that Sir Thomas' wife was both beautiful and a force of nature. "Of course, Lady Pennywhistle," replied Lennox in formal tones. "It would be my honor to serve as your escort." Bartram pulled a face because he wanted that task, but moved forward to take charge of Diable.

Lennox extended his hand and helped Sammie Jo down from the saddle. His hand tingled with the electricity of her personality. He offered his arm, which she accepted. "His office is on the third floor. I shall take you there directly."

"Well, aren't you just the sweetest thing!" She knew her country girl persona had a melting effect on some British aristocrats, especially the male ones. "Lead on, Captain..."

"Lennox, milady. I have worked with your husband and admire him."

"It pleases me to hear that, though it does not surprise me."

Sammie Jo attracted admiring glances as they proceeded to her husband's office. When his knocks went unanswered, Lennox opened the door and was astonished to find the room empty.

Sammie Jo's face fell, then a thundercloud formed on her brow. "What is going on, Captain? My husband is a creature of habit, and I can't think why he is not at his desk."

"Nor can I, Lady Pennywhistle. He consistently works long hours."

"Captain, I want to solve this mystery as fast as possible. I need to talk to the Duke."

Lennox flushed in embarrassment. "He is very busy right now—"

Sammie Jo cut him off with a smile. "Oh, he will see me. Just tell him it's Lady Pennywhistle. Now be off with you."

Lennox saw the determined look in her eye and decided it was best not to argue. "Very well, milady. Make yourself comfortable while I see if he will grant you a brief audience." Lennox departed at a brisk walk that stopped just short of a run.

Sammie Jo had met Wellington at parties in Vienna and knew he was two different individuals. With men he was stern and gruff, but with beautiful women he became expansive and charming. He was a consummate ladies' man, and quite the boudoir swordsman. Rumor had it that he had bedded two of Napoleon's former mistresses while serving as Ambassador to France: Mademoiselle Grassini, a famous opera singer, and Mademoiselle George, a star of the Parisian theatre.

She sat down in her husband's chair and tried to picture Tom performing his duties. The office was spartan; but then, he never cared much for ostentation.

A smiling Lennox soon reappeared. "The Duke will be delighted to receive you. Please follow me."

"Lady Pennywhistle! What an unexpected pleasure." Wellington bowed and kissed her hand the minute she crossed the threshold into his office, then broke into an appreciative smile that his men never saw. "Lennox tells me you must have had a long and tiring journey."

He gestured towards a chair. "Please make yourself comfortable while I order some refreshments. If I recall, you prefer coffee to tea."

"Your memory serves you well as always, Your Grace."

"See to it, Lennox."

"Very good, Your Grace."

"I know your time is valuable, Your Grace, so I will be forthright, even if that means my speech is less than... ladylike. I have not seen my husband for two and a half months, and he has never held his child. Imagine my disappointment when I traveled all this way and found his office empty! I am hoping you might be able to tell me something of his whereabouts."

Wellington looked dubious. "He is on an important mission, and I do not know his whereabouts. But it is my expectation that he will return before nightfall. The Duchess of Richmond is throwing a grand ball tonight. Allow me to say that I am sure you would find the ballroom a much more pleasant place to spend your time than waiting in his office. I know you have never met the Duchess, but she is good friends with the Earl Grosvenor, and I am sure she would make you welcome. When Sir Thomas reappears, my aides will direct him to the ball."

"An excellent suggestion, Your Grace." She flashed her most winning smile. "We will be staying with Lady Densham, a distant cousin of the Earl. I just arrived a bit ahead of the rest of party."

"I will have the Duchess send a written invitation for you to Lady Densham. And I hope you will hold a place for me on your dance card."

"Of course! I know you are an excellent dancer, and I love dancing."

Wellington beamed at the compliment.

Lennox reappeared with two China cups of coffee on a silver platter.

Sammie Jo sipped her coffee daintily, in a ladylike fashion. She wondered where her husband was and how he was faring. Then she rose from her seat, to the surprise of Wellington, who relished an extended round of flirtation. "Forgive me, Your Grace, but if I am to attend a ball then I had best prepare. I certainly could not attend in my present attire. My clothing trunks are unlikely to arrive in time, so I expect I'll have to scramble to find something suitable. I thank you for your hospitality and the invitation, and I look forward to a waltz with you."

She curtsied, and he rose and responded with a bow. "Until tonight!"

She turned gracefully and exited the office with a step that was a tad too quick for a real lady.

"Remarkable woman," observed Lennox.

Sammie Jo didn't care about the ball. She just wanted to find her husband. Wellington had at least told her a location where he might be, and she was a good tracker. She had no idea if Tom was in any peril, but she was armed, dangerous, and had a fast horse.

She thanked Bartram for minding Diable, then asked for directions to the village of Dauphin. Bartram gave her detailed ones. "I was stationed there with the Royal Engineers in 1814. They had a depot there on the River Zenne. Why are you so keen to go there, my lady?"

"Family business," she replied, determined to keep her real purpose to herself and tell a likely story to appease curiosity. "An aunt that I have not seen in a while moved there to..." she feigned an expression of embarrassment, "escape some creditors back in London."

Bartram smiled knowingly. "Half the Britons in Brussels are here for the same reason. The cost of living here is half that of London. I wish you a pleasant journey, Lady Pennywhistle."

"See you at the ball tonight, Captain."

Sammie Jo departed headquarters at a conservative trot, but as soon as she could not be seen from the windows she increased her pace. Once clear of the city, she spurred Diable to a full gallop.

***

15 June, 1815, 7 a.m., the Zenne Compound outside the village of Dauphin

The Royal Engineers had erected a combination headquarters, foundry, cartography workshop and storage depot on the River Zenne in the village of Dauphin. The four buildings were surrounded by a six-foot wall that had two entrances: one from the river and one from the village. It was more a gated compound than a fortress, but in an emergency it was not a bad place to mount a defense.

After Napoleon's abdication on April 11, 1814, the Royal Engineers had abandoned it. The compound had remained empty and neglected until two weeks ago, when a group of forty men had reoccupied it: hard-bitten German ex-soldiers down on their luck, yet they paid for supplies in cash and were well behaved when they came into town. They discouraged both visitors and inquiries. It was unclear to the locals if they were supporters of Bonaparte or the new King of the Netherlands.

First Lieutenant Balthazar Barton of the Royal Engineers was now a prisoner of these men, though he was being treated decently enough. He was fed well, accorded the military courtesy that a British officer would expect, allowed to bathe regularly, and given a feather bed on which to sleep. He simply was not allowed to leave. His captors needed his professional services, and since that required disclosing their real purpose, he would remain their prisoner until their task was complete. That would likely be in a few days, but by then the map he had in his possession would no longer be useful. For the fourth time in two days, he found himself arguing with the leader of the men, *Premierleutnant* Alphonse Adelman.

"You should let me go. You and I need not be friends, but we do not have to be enemies. We both want to see Bonaparte beaten, and the map I have in my possession may well help Wellington accomplish just that!"

"I appreciate your point of view, Lieutenant, but I am taking a long-term perspective. Wellington is an able commander and will succeed or fail regardless of whether he has your map. I am looking to the future of Saxony and the welfare of our King. You are a man of honor, Lieutenant, but you fail to understand how deeply the high-handed actions of *Feldmarschall* Blucher have wounded the honor of my countrymen."

"I will allow that Blucher made a bad decision, but his general goal is still a good one."

"Bad decision? Bad decision?" Adelman's voice was rough with anger. "It was a terrible decision, a disgraceful decision! My men and I fought bravely for the Allies at the Battle of Leipzig and rendered honorable service as part of the Army of occupation of the Netherlands. When the domain of Saxony was reduced *by forty percent* by those idiots at the Congress of Vienna, we grew angry but made no protest. When the Saxon Army of 14,000 was placed under the command of the Prussians, we all gave our strongest efforts to make the best of a bad situation. When we were assigned to the Army of *Feldmarschall* Blucher we tried hard to fit in and impress him with our zeal. But we were treated abysmally. We were given poor food and worse weapons, ordered about like slaves, and placed under the command of officers who hated us. We protested our mistreatment. At first we were ignored, then punished harshly. Finally, a few hotheads simply refused to obey orders. Blucher made no distinction between the troublemakers and honorable soldiers like me and my men. He took his wrath out on all of us. Seven officers were executed by firing squad in front of the army, private soldiers were flogged within an inch of their lives, and 10,000 of us were discharged in disgrace and told to make our way home as best we could."

"I sympathize, yet Bonaparte's sudden reappearance forced everyone to improvise, and hasty scrambling sometimes results in good men being treated badly. Marshal Blucher is in a tough situation. Probably half his men have never seen battle."

"That makes his actions even more stupid and foolish," sputtered Adelman. "All of my men are veterans who have seen the worst battle has to offer. If he had directed us to train his new men they would be battle ready by now!"

"Hmm, hah, yes, well, but many other Germans remember that your king was loyal to Napoleon until the Treaty of Fontainebleu. To be blunt, sir, there is, ah, widespread uncertainty as to the reliability of troops who have recently gone from fighting *for* Napoleon to fighting *against* him."

Adleman spat in disgust. "We fight as our king commands us. All we ask in return for our loyalty is to be treated like any other soldiers. Blucher's officers treated their dogs better than they treated us! My men and I refused to slink home with our tail between our legs. Instead, we determined to exact a revenge against Blucher."

"So, you decided to validate your undeserved disgrace by becoming criminals?"

"We are not criminals! We are modern Robin Hoods. I have men of many skills under my command. We put our heads together to devise a plan that would put those skills to good use."

"And I blundered into your operation at exactly the time you needed someone with my skills to fix your broken smelting furnace."

"Your bad luck became our good fortune. And when you are released, you will be be paid for your services."

"I would never accept any stolen consideration from you," said Barton stiffly. "But I think you are an honorable man who has been turned by anger. I beg you to recall your duty."

"What 'duty' do you speak of? We were dishonorably discharged! Our kingdom has been plundered! It is pointless to argue, but for now I have need of your services. It seems that the smelting furnace has broken down once again."

"I will make you a bargain. If I repair it yet again, promise to let me go."

"I cannot do that, so do not argue. Arguing will only make me determined to keep you here longer."

Adelman's operation was a masterpiece of ingenuity and efficiency. One of his men had worked in the quartermaster corps and had received intelligence that a wagon full of British gold would shortly depart from the port of Antwerp, intended to help pay for the victuals of Blucher's Army. Adelman had fast-marched his men after their discharge at Liege and had intercepted it. Gold could be melted down and recast into an untraceable form; the question was what form would work best. Adleman had decided to recast the coins as small ingots that could be concealed in hollowed out bars of soap. Transporting something so mundane as soap would excite no attention from either thieves or customs officials and would be an easy way to transport the gold the 500 miles back to the city of Dresden in Saxony.

One of the men, Altergott, had been a diamond cutter, and had recognized a diamond merchant an hour after the gold had been intercepted. Altergott had informed Adelman that the merchant was likely bound for Antwerp, the center of the world's diamond industry, and probably had raw stones on his person. So Adelman had ordered his men to detain the merchant and search him. Sure enough, he'd carried a small velvet purse containing twenty stones of various sizes.

"I see great potential here," Altergott had exulted, after examining the stones carefully through a jeweler's lens also liberated from the merchant.

"How much potential?"

"10,000 pounds, if they are carefully cut."

Adelman had debated whether to kill the merchant, but he was not a barbarian and had decided that unconsciousness would do. Once the man recovered, he could whine to the authorities all he liked, but the diamonds would have by then been cut in distinctive ways that would in no way resemble his description.

Now, as Adelman and Barton passed Altergott's work bench, Adelman stopped to inquire about his progress. "How many stones cut so far?"

Altergott pulled the jeweler's magnifying glass from his eye and put down the diamond scalpel he held in his hand. "Ten."

Adelman frowned. "I had hoped for fifteen."

Altergott spoke with the exasperation of the true artist. "Craftsmanship cannot be rushed. One small mistake reduces a diamond's value by half. Diamond cutting is about patience as much as skill. I liken its delicacy to performing a circumcision."

"Very well," said Adelman reluctantly.

The two men next passed three soap makers, industriously boiling lye. Grundel, their chief, answered Adelman's question before it was asked. "It is going very well. I have added some lemon scent to the mix," he said with pride."

"Excellent!" said Adelman approvingly. "The scent is a fine touch."

The next stop was a station with two men fashioning boxes for the soap bars. Adelman nodded approvingly.

The men at the printing press were engaged in making labels for the soap boxes. Adelman picked up one of its products and examined it. The label's design and lettering were impressive yet not too fancy, featuring the words "Gentlemen's Best" ringed by a circle composed of roses, *fleurs-de lis*, and bees. English was chosen for the label because British soaps enjoyed a fine reputation. The flowers and insects referenced The English Hanoverians, the French Bourbons, and Bonaparte's family. The label suggested that the product was of superior quality, yet the printed price was affordable.

Adelman frowned when he and Barton reached the furnace used for melting the gold before recasting it. Steinmetz, the furnace operator, looked distressed.

"Same problem. The feeder value is broken."

"Why won't it stay fixed?" demanded an exasperated Adelman of Barton. "You are not trying to sabotage us, are you?"

"Of course not!" remonstrated Barton indignantly. "As I have told you before, the furnace needs an entirely new valve, but you keep forcing me to repair the old one. This valve has only so many lives. I'm an engineer, not a miracle worker."

"Have you any idea how difficult it is to get parts during wartime? Can't you get one more life out of this one?"

Barton took the valve from the left side of the furnace and examined it. "Maybe. But it will be at least three hours before the furnace will be ready to restart."

Adelman snarled a curse. "Then get on with it, damn it!"

"As your diamond-cutter said, 'Craftsmanship cannot be rushed.'" Barton flashed a sardonic grin.

"Bah!" huffed Adelman, and stalked away.

The last stop on his production tour revived his spirit. Two men were packing soap into finished boxes, then transferring these to packing crates. He counted the boxes: 250, halfway to completion. They were running behind schedule, though not too badly. He could have put larger quantities of gold in each bar, but the smaller the quantity the lower the risk of detection.

At the present rate of production, he figured he needed two more days before he could move his product to Dresden. He estimated that the value of the lot, gold and diamonds together, might be around 30,000 pounds. He and his men would take half for their efforts: 375 pounds per man would pay for a gentleman's home, two servants, and a small carriage for two years. The 15,000 the King would receive would make him grateful, and he might well reward them all with positions and titles. The best way to wipe out disgrace was to better your lot in life.

He had no idea that two sets of interlopers were on their way to spoil his dreams.

Maxwell had stayed uncharacteristically silent during the ride from British Headquarters to the village of Dauphin. Pennywhistle deemed him hungover rather than subdued, and there was a sullen cast to his eye that Pennywhistle distrusted. Nevertheless, he was glad of the silence; Maxwell was the sort of officer whose vain boasting made it difficult to think. He stopped on a small hilltop overlooking the old Royal Engineer Compound and saw to his surprise that though dilapidated it was far from deserted.

He removed his Ramsden spyglass from his saddlebag and surveyed the structures. Two men stood sentry at the river entrance, matched by two men performing the same function on the landward side. They did not wear British uniforms, and so far as Pennywhistle knew the British Crown had never sold the facility. The sentries were in their early twenties and looked fit and alert. They were clad in the nondescript clothing of tradesmen, but their erect bearing was distinctively military, and suggested they had been part of an elite unit. He listened closely and realized two of the guards were conversing in German. Prussian deserters? No, deserters were furtive creatures like cockroaches who stayed in the shadows. These sentries were intended to be seen by one and all.

An 18-foot launch was docked at the quay in front of the river entrance. A wagon with two men on its buckboard emerged from the compound's entrance. The pilot of the launch stepped onto the dock and exchanged some kind of joke with those on the buckboard. After a minute of hearty laughing, all three began unloading the contents of the wagon.

Pennywhistle tilted his head in puzzlement. Whatever was going on here had nothing to do with the British government, and the chaps running the show clearly wanted to keep people out. That implied that there was something worth guarding within, but what?

This, he reminded himself firmly, was no part of his mission. Or... was it? On the verge of sliding shut his Ramsden glass and continuing to town in search of Barton, it occurred to him to wonder if the anomalies of Barton's disappearance and the peculiar activity in the compound might somehow be related.

It was, Pennywhistle decided, time for a show of authority. At best he would gain entrance and discover that what looked suspicious had a peaceful explanation. At worst, he would be able to gauge the strength of resistance and decide whether armed action might be necessary.

Maxwell observed Pennywhistle the whole time, wondering what he was contemplating. He had already realized this assignment was more than the routine retrieval of a missing document. His eyes widened in feral glee as it occurred to him that, as British officers, they had a duty to recover lost Crown property, and so gun and sword play might prove necessary. He was itching to avenge himself on someone for his humiliation at Pennywhistle's hands, and the guards below would be fit fodder for his fury.

Pennywhistle saw the twin black opal lights of vengeance dancing. "Save your energy for when it's needed, Maxwell. Before we make any attempt at repossession, we must find out what and with whom we are dealing. Keep silent, and follow my lead. Stay alert but take no action but upon my order. Is that clear?"

Surly eyes glared back at Pennywhistle and Maxwell replied in churlish tones, "Yes, Colonel." He felt exactly like a dog menaced by the master of hounds' whip.

"I mean it, Ensign. One misstep could imperil our mission and put us in grave danger. A proper reconnaissance is always necessary before acting. How can you prevail in a contest if you do not know the nature of it? Wouldn't you agree?"

"I suppose," muttered Maxwell with ill grace. He all but bared his teeth.

"I suppose... *Colonel.*"

"Yes, Colonel."

"Though I need you to stay quiet, you are more than welcome to appear menacing. Let these sentries know that the British are prepared to back any demands with force. In fact, the more thug-like and destructive you appear, the better."

Maxwell's eyes brightened. "Yes, Colonel!" Instead of wielding the whip, the master of hounds was letting him run after the foxes.

Pennywhistle and Maxwell rode down the hill at a brisk trot, allowing the sentries enough time to note the approach of British officers and communicate that information to their principals.

When Pennywhistle and Maxwell arrived at the river entrance, the two sentries had been joined by a third man who wore the uniform of an officer of the kingdom of Saxony. The uniform had seen better days, as had the officer. When Pennywhistle and Maxwell were twenty feet from the gate, the officer barked a command and the sentries snapped to attention.

Pennywhistle and Maxwell halted their horses as the officer approached. He snapped to attention and executed a crisp salute. Pennywhistle returned the salute, but Maxwell did not, simply glaring at the officer.

Pennywhistle faced a man of medium height and trim build, who looked to be in his middle thirties. His grey eyes bothered Pennywhistle; they were ruthless, predatory, and perceptive.

"I am Lieutenant Colonel Sir Thomas Pennywhistle of the Duke of Wellington's staff," he announced in a firm voice, "and require entrance. By what right do you possess this facility, sir? It is the property of the British Crown."

"Colonel, I am *Premierleutnant* Heinz Adelman, formerly of the Army of King Frederick Augustus. I am sorry you made the journey in vain, Sir Thomas. Evidently you were not informed that we purchased this compound several days ago." The man spoke in the conciliatory tones of a practiced staff officer, but the scars on his hard face suggested he had seen considerable field service. He reached into his pocket and produced an official looking document which appeared to have the Royal Seal. It was almost certainly fake, but it looked convincing. "You will see the signature of Lieutenant Balthazar Barton at the bottom."

Pennywhistle looked closely and it was indeed Barton's signature. Had Barton been here? More to the point, was he still here?

"The gentleman is familiar to me. Is he here presently? Might I speak to him?"

"Alas, no. He departed yesterday evening."

Pennywhistle wondered if Barton was being held hostage. But if so, why?

"Who exactly are you gentlemen, and what is your purpose here?"

"We are a group of Saxon officers and NCOs recently discharged due to wounds that refused to heal. We are greatly saddened that we will not have a chance to fight Bonaparte one last time. We have invested our pensions in this place and plan to turn it into a manufactory that will shortly become famous for producing quality soap such as the gentry are fond of using, but at prices ordinary folk can afford."

Pennywhistle's nose did indeed detect the scents of wood ash and lye, essential elements in the making of soap."

"Your goal sounds admirable, but why the sentries?"

"It is to prevent espionage, Sir Thomas. We have a new recipe and word has gotten out. As soldiers, you and I might find it strange to kill for anything but honor and the glory of our princes, but I assure you, there are men who kill for trade secrets."

Modulating his voice to sound impressed and curious, rather than commandeering, Pennywhistle said, "I should like a tour of your facility, *Herr Premierleutnant*."

Adelman emitted a long sigh. "That would not be convenient right now. We are currently a work in progress. Just as you would not want to parade your men for inspection without adequate warning, so I do not wish to give a tour to such a distinguished representative before our preparations are complete. However, come back in two days' time and I shall be delighted to give you The Grand Tour."

Pennywhistle knew he was being lied to, but it was better to play along and let Adelman believe he had fooled the brave but gullible British officer. He and Maxwell would return clandestinely after dark to discover what was really going on.

"Very well, *Herr Premierleutnant*," responded Pennywhistle pleasantly. "I shall call upon you two days hence and look forward to a tour. In the meantime, I wish you good fortune."

Maxwell shot him a glance that shouted, *Are you insane?!?*

Pennywhistle saluted Adelman, and the Saxon returned the courtesy.

He pivoted his horse and trotted away, followed by a puzzled and angry Maxwell.

When they were out of earshot of the compound Maxwell pulled alongside. "What the hell was that about, Colonel? You're just going to let him take the piss out of you like that? He was lying!"

"Of course Adelman's explanation was misdirection, Ensign, but he clearly had more men inside, likely with muskets trained on us. A precipitous move on our part would have been foolish. I know the value of the element of surprise, and we did not have it. I also know you are eager to resort immediately to force, failing to observe that they have the advantages of numbers, position, and preparation — as did your assailants earlier this evening. There is a better way. *Elepantus non capit murem.*

Maxwell looked sullen and baffled.

"I see you skipped Latin class as well as the seminar on manners. It means, '*The elephant does not catch the mouse.*'"

Maxwell's expression did not change.

Pennywhistle sighed in exasperation. "It means that brute force seldom works in catching a fast, elusive quarry. We must be like cats, cunning and quick. We will return after dark and discover Adelman's real intentions. My instincts tell me that he is holding something valuable that not long ago belonged to somebody else. Furthermore, and more importantly, Barton's signature on that document is authentic. It is my belief that he is being held against his will. We must take care that he comes to no harm. From the smells of the place, there are chemicals within that are highly combustible. Do you take my meaning?"

Maxwell looked puzzled for a second, then a candelabra lit in his head and his eyes blazed. "So we get to blow stuff up?"

"Possibly. Our primary mission is to retrieve the map, and my hope is that Barton has it on his person. I do not know else what they are hiding, but if it might be of value to our enemies and we cannot repossess their secret, we must destroy it. Fast in; a quick, undetected search; and fast out would be ideal; but it is fanciful thinking of the most dangerous sort to believe that all will go according to one's plan. If — no, *when* we run into armed resistance, you will have plenty of opportunity to indulge in violence. You tell me you are good with weapons. This will be your chance to prove your word."

"I am an absolute devil, sir!"

"One more thing, we must watch our backs. Adelman strikes me as smart. I think he might...." Pennywhistle trailed off invitingly.

Maxwell blinked and finished the sentence... "try to kill us first?"

"Very good, Ensign, you are learning. Death by assassins. I have been told there is only one decent inn in town, and Adelman will expect us to stay there. My map indicates there is only one road and it looks to have plenty of twists and turns, well suited to an ambush. Let us proceed alertly, and see what develops."

"Let them try. I will strike them down and they will drown in their own blood." Maxwell gripped the hilt of his sword and literally rattled his saber.

"I am counting on your ferocity."

Adelman thought long and hard after Pennywhistle left. So far no one had died from his efforts. The escort of the gold wagons had been disarmed and left bound and gagged. The diamond merchant had merely been rendered unconscious. But the two who'd just left were a different matter altogether and posed a direct and ongoing threat to his operation. He had slain men in battle, but the prospect of extralegal killing made him queasy. He faced a moral Rubicon, and the price of crossing it would be a piece of his soul. And yet, it made no sense to let moral quibbles queer an enterprise that could guarantee a bright future for good men who had been dealt a bad hand. Being in command sometimes meant that the right thing was not the moral thing.

The two British officers forced him to rethink his transportation timetable. They had been dispatched to reclaim the compound, and he doubted they would long be deterred by the excuse he had offered. It was only a matter of time before the true nature of his operation was discovered, so he had to start moving the soap immediately. Rather than assemble everything into one large shipment, he would instead send out three smaller ones. The first shipment could depart in short order. But first, he needed the two British officers removed from the chessboard; that would buy him a day or two.

He summoned the five men he trusted most, all men handy with a sword and a gun. He explained his predicament and his plan. "I won't order you to do anything; it must be your decision," he told them. "But the first wagons cannot depart unless I am certain those two British officers no longer pose a threat. If the wagons can be made ready, they can follow the annual Procession of the Holy Blood, which will pass through town later today."

"What is the nature of this procession, *Premierleutnant?*"

"It is a Catholic rite," Adelman said, with Protestant contempt in his voice. "It originated during the time of the Great Plague and was intended to attract the Lord's mercy and bring an end to the pestilence. The Procession is undertaken twice yearly. The monks of the Zenne Monastery travel to St Rumbold's Cathedral, bearing a glass vial, which they *claim*" — his voice dripped derision — "contains the blood of Christ. This vial is transported inside a gold reliquary chest, displayed on a black and gold wagon. Other wagons follow, filled with flowers. The monks pause the procession from time to time to toss flower petals into the street, which superstitious peasants gather up in the belief that they will convey a blessing. We will explain to the monks that our wagons are an anonymous donation by a local benefactor. If you are agreeable to my plan, I will dispatch several of our men to buy flowers from the local market."

The men conferred, and all but one nodded agreement. That dissenter was excused without censure. Adelman gave his directions to the remaining four. "Follow those two riders. When you reach Elbert's Alley, kill them."

Adelman's orders were overheard by nine-year Franz Finkel, a wharf rat in the pay of Hans Kinderdokken, the chief of the local underworld. Franz was practiced at being invisible. He made himself useful by penetrating the nooks and crannies of supposedly burglar-proof buildings, then concealing himself until he had assessed the wealth within. He had infiltrated the compound several days before, when Kinderdokken tasked him with investigating a rumor that he had a rival playing for high stakes.

The pale skin of Franz's face was marred by imbedded flecks of grime, a legacy of his years as a chimney sweep. His master had been a bad one: drunk during the day, leaving the hard work to his boy apprentices, and beating them soundly when their work displeased him. One day, after Franz had gotten stuck in a tight chimney flue and been pulled out barely alive, he had had enough and run away. He had been recruited by Kinderdokken, because Hans knew that Franz could describe the interior layouts of the great homes whose chimneys he had cleaned and crawled through.

After one night of spying, Franz had reported back to Kinderdokken that the compound held more gold than Kickerdokken stole in a year. He'd returned a second night to see if he had missed anything, and he had: the diamonds. Now he thanked his lucky stars that he had returned. The new information he had just overheard required immediate action from his master.

Franz wiggled out through a small crack in the southwest wall of the compound and broke into a run. If things went well, he would be rewarded with a tiny chunk of the haul. That would mean this could be his last job on the wrong side of the law. He'd have to travel far to escape the wrath and reach of Kinderdokken, but with coin in his pocket he'd find a way. He arrived at Kinderdokken's warehouse headquarters and was ushered into the presence of the crime lord.

Kinderdokken was as brutal as he was impulsive. A gross man of 300 pounds with three chins, piggy eyes, tiny hands, and bowed legs, he was a man of unbridled appetites and limited imagination. Yet what he lacked in intelligence he made up for with the instincts of the fox. "Excellent news, Franz," he rumbled, "but we shall have to act quickly to relieve these Saxons of their golden soap. I shall emulate Herr Adelman's ruse and use the procession as a mask for our activities."

Kinderdokken considered himself a pious man and attended church regularly, seeing no contradiction between his faith and his nefarious profession. He knew the abbot of the Zenne Monastery well, having frequently donated to the Abbey's building fund. Those donations gave him the public appearance of a solid citizen. The town fathers knew perfectly well what his profession was, but were too afraid for their families to move against him.

A large donation this morning would persuade the Abbot to postpone the start of the Procession for several hours, as well as procure 80 monks' robes for his men, in order, as he would be assure the abbot, for them to make a proper show of penitence for their lapses. He would also need some flowers. Fortunately it was summer; flowers were plentiful. He had wagons, and a carpenter among his men who could cobble together a reliquary chest that would pass muster as long as no one looked too closely. Then he'd stage his own procession.

The simplest plan would be to allow the renegade Saxons to join his false procession and then overpower them, seizing the partial shipment of gold. But doing so would put the remainder of the compound on high alert, and he'd have a hard fight on his hands to secure the rest of the treasure. No, it would be far better to use the elements of deception and surprise to seize the compound and take all the treasure in one sudden assault. Now. Today.

His eye fell on young Finkel, still waiting. "Get yourself something to eat and hold yourself ready. You will be our guide once we breach the compound."

Destination Waterloo

***

Pennywhistle and Maxwell stopped for a late morning meal of herring, pancakes, and coffee at the *Herberg de Pannekoeken*. Four blocks from the guarded compound, the second-floor dining area gave a good view of Dauphin's main street. They were both hungry, but the real point of the brief stop was to await Adelman's riposte to Pennywhistle's visit. Adelman struck him as tough and ruthless; he would likely deduce that the two British officers might return, bringing with them a force of Redcoats to enforce a repossession. Adelman did not seem the kind of man who would tamely submit to being expelled.

Pennywhistle ate in silence, studying a street map of Dauphin as he did so, trying to discover a location to deliver a counterstroke. Since the streets were deserted in preparation for the Procession of the Holy Blood, armed men on horseback would be easy to spot. Sure enough, as Pennywhistle finished the last bite of his pancakes, four horsemen rode into view.

The horsemen, armed with sabers and pistols, trotted slowly down the street and appeared to be arguing among themselves. Their tones were anything but hushed. Pennywhistle did not speak German but the meaning of the verb *killen* was clear. Since it was used repeatedly in conjunction own his surname, Pennywhistle had no doubt what these four men intended.

"Time to go," he said to Maxwell. The two men hurried down the rear stairs, which led to the inner courtyard where their horses were tied to hitching posts. Pennywhistle used his town map to explain his plan to Maxwell. "We can spring our own ambush, but first we need to be seen. I think this spot," he pointed at the map, "will suit our purpose."

Pennywhistle and Maxwell proceeded at brisk trot to the place he had indicated on the map. Then they pulled up, slowed to a walk, and waited for the horsemen to appear. After a short interval, the four horsemen rounded the corner and emerged into clear view. He resisted the insane impulse to turn in his saddle and wave at them.

Maxwell's eyes queried him. *Do we fight them here?*

"There is as alley just ahead with a stable to give us cover. As soon as we round the corner and disappear from our follower's vision, duck into the stable and draw your blade."

"Yes, sir!" Maxwell's eyes glowed with anticipation.

Pennywhistle and Maxwell waited as the horsemen rode by the alley entrance without noticing them. He heard murmurs of confusion from the men, wondering where their quarry had gone.

He was about to say, "Charge!" when Maxwell did so on his own. Even as Pennywhistle applied spurs to the sides of his mount, Maxwell had already split the rear horseman's head in two. The horseman in front turned in surprise, just in time to catch Maxwell's blade across his throat.

Pennywhistle halted his horse and took a sip from his canteen, realizing Maxwell was enjoying himself and needed no help. This was a chance to see if Maxwell was something more than a lout with a loud mouth, a hot temper and a bad attitude.

Maxwell moved fast for a big man. He blocked a thrust from the third horseman aimed at his throat, then ran his blade through the man's chest. He wrenched his blade out so violently that it flung the man clear off his saddle.

Only the fourth horseman put up any kind of fight. His cut at Maxwell's head was blocked. He slashed at Maxwell's ribs, but was parried aside. A thrust at Maxwell's leg was deflected with ease.

Maxwell smiled throughout the fight, but it was the smile of a cat toying with a mouse before eating it. Maxwell could have killed his opponent after any one of the blows but seemed not to want his fun to end too soon. He deflected two more cuts before he tired of the game. He delivered a slashing sweep with the sword that sent the man's head flying.

Pennywhistle pulled alongside Maxwell and saw, not homicidal rage, but murderous glee in the Ensign's eyes. "Maxwell! Stand down! Stand down!"

Maxwell turned in his saddle and raised his blade. His brain was not discriminating between friend and foe. Pennywhistle threw water from his canteen in Maxwell's face. Maxwell blinked hard, then shook his head, as if awakening from a dream. "I got a bit carried away, Colonel."

"You are a master of understatement. And you surprise me. You fought with speed and skill. I may yet make a soldier of you, but we will have to work on the turning off the spigot in your brain that controls the flow of hot blood."

"When the urge to fight takes me, it's difficult to stop." There was regret in Maxwell's voice but an undercurrent of pride, like a child knowing he should not have broken his toys but proud of the strength that enabled him to reduce them to shards and kindling.

"That's why the military has discipline: we want violence to be controlled, not wild." Pennywhistle stroked his chin in thought. "I am surprised Adelman struck so soon. I wonder if it means something is afoot. I was going to wait until nightfall, but I think now we should return and put the place under our watch immediately to get an idea of our opponent's routines and try to figure an easy way in."

"What if there is no easy way in?"

"Then we shall do it the hard way."

Sammie Jo entered the town of Dauphin. Her lack of sleep was catching up with her so she stopped at *L' Auberge Bon Temps*, hoping food would revive her: local inns were also good sources of information about the goings on in the town in which they resided. On her waiter Klaus' recommendation, she ordered a large sandwich of Fricandelle sausages, gouda cheese, and lettuce between Belgian waffles instead of bread. Alongside it on the plate were thin sticks of fried potatoes called *pommes frites*. A glass of Stella Artois provided liquid refreshment.

Her waiter was a talkative young spark, entranced by her beauty. He made a great fuss over her, and when she asked him if anything new had happened in town, he responded with plenty of information that indicated he had a keen eye for observation. She said she was seeking her husband and gave the waiter a description. He told her that he had not seen such a man, but a good place to look might be at the gated compound by the river. "Some strange activity is going on there, and men with military bearing are coming and going at all hours of the day and night." She left him a large tip and mounted Diable for what she hoped was the last leg of her journey.

Kinderdokken's "monks" began their mock Procession of the Holy Blood just before noon, while the abbot conducted an extended mass at the church to delay the real procession and keep the townspeople out of the streets. Kinderdokken's men, who were experienced cutthroats, found it hilarious that they were impersonating holy men. Their weapons, consisting of swords, half pikes, knives, and pistols, were hidden under the flowers in the wagons.

Adelman's four gate guards observed the approaching procession with amused contempt for Catholic superstition. The monks marched in reverent silence at a slow, deliberate pace; several of them stopped just across the street from the compound. Four monks took up baskets filled with flower petals, began walking toward the compound gate, casting petals in every direction as they went. The guards laughed, failing to notice that other monks were drawing weapons from the flower wagons.

At two paces from the two sentry boxes, the monks stopped. "Peace be upon you, my brothers," intoned a tall monk as he tossed red tulip petals toward the sentries. The guards looked at each other in surprise and one replied sarcastically, "I thought you people took a vow of silence."

"On special occasions we may speak." The words were a signal to his three friends, who suddenly produced small pistols from their baskets. The sentries, caught off guard, moved to engage as the pistols fired. Three of them fell dying, but the fourth batted away the knife of the talking monk, then kicked him in the groin. He turned and ran inside the compound, blowing his whistle loudly as he ran.

Bandits disguised as monks charged the gates, waving weapons and howling like demons. Kinderdokken did not lead them. He left that job to his assistant, Karl Mundt, and kept to the rear. Risks were for lesser men. He would take command after the treasures were secured. His eyes blazed with avarice as he thought of how much wealth he would gain today.

The militant Saxons in the compound responded instantly to the alarm dropping whatever they were doing and running for the combination of powder magazine and arms locker. Once armed, they ran into the courtyard, then formed a line in front of the storage building, where two wagons were already loaded with the special soap.

Pennywhistle and Maxwell, hearing gunfire, put spurs to their horses and galloped towards the compound. Pennywhistle in the lead reined in his horse as they came in view of the fort. Three sentries lay dead, and a mob of men in monks' apparel, brandishing edged weapons and pistols, was rushing through the sally port beyond the sentry boxes. Clearly a full scale attack was underway.

"This is our chance, Ensign! We have our diversion. Draw your saber and let's go." The two blazed through the entry port into a courtyard full of running, shouting, fighting men.

While the appearance of two armed, scarlet-clad horsemen would ordinarily have commanded everyone's attention, the two sides were so fixed on the other's destruction that their arrival was barely noticed. The Saxons fired a volley, which cut down ten of the attackers. A number fired back with pistols. Most shots went wild, but one pierced and felled Adelman, causing consternation in the Saxon ranks.

Pennywhistle angled his horse towards an open doorway that he hoped would lead to the interior where, with any luck, he might find a British officer held prisoner in some chamber. Suddenly, Barton emerged from behind two barrels of flour. "Colonel Pennywhistle! You show up in the damnedest places!" he exclaimed.

"So do you, Barton! Do you have the map on you?"

"I do."

"Then get up behind me and let's get out of here."

"Wait, there is something you must know. Stolen British gold is being stored here for smuggling, thousands of pounds worth."

"Well," remarked Pennywhistle, "that certainly explains the unholy interest these men have in seizing the fort, doesn't it?"

Sammie Jo arrived just in time to spot her husband and Maxwell disappearing into the compound. Undeterred by the unmistakable sounds of slaughter, she hesitated not a second. She was no stranger to battle, and her place was beside her man. She put the spurs to Diable and charged.

The Saxon line collapsed with Adelman's death; the battle degenerated into sorties of hand-to-hand combats: bayonets against half pikes and swords. The Saxons were fighting hard and skillfully, but the superior numbers of the brigands were beginning to tell, and the soldiers were slowly falling back.

Barton finished his tale of gold and diamonds. "What should we do, Colonel?"

Pennywhistle had an inspiration. "You speak German, don't you Barton?"

"I do, sir. How does that help us?"

"The Saxons are losing their fight. It's time we turned them into allies. I need you to translate for me." He quickly explained his plan to Barton.

Sammie Jo came through the gate at that moment, spotted her husband, and galloped toward him. She shot two men on the way. She pulled up alongside Pennywhistle, then leaned over and embraced him. "I have never been so glad to see anyone in all my born days," she said warmly.

Pennywhistle blinked in astonishment. "How the blazes did you find us? Never mind; you are here, and I am glad to see you. Come, we need to turn the tide of battle."

Sammie Jo nodded.

The sight of a beautiful woman on a great horse had temporarily frozen both sides in amazement. The men of the compound took advantage of the brief respite to regroup towards the rear.

The four cantered over to join ranks with the retreating Saxons. Barton spoke in a ringing, commanding voice. "Saxon soldiers! It is time to regain your honor and drive these criminals off! My officer promises a full pardon to all who will follow him, and the chance to fight Bonaparte as part of a regular army. What say you?"

The Saxons glanced at each other, then at Pennywhistle and company. That doubt warred with hope was visible on many faces.

Sammie Jo saw their indecision. She drew Thynne's sword, flourished it, then pointed its tip toward the nearest thug, who stepped back in alarm. "Come on!" she shouted "We can take these bastards down!"

Not all the Saxons understood her words, but her intent was clear. It was as if they were being visited by a Valkyrie of ancient legend. Cries of "Yah! Yah!" erupted, followed by a brief cheer.

Pennywhistle turned to Barton. "I'm putting you in charge of our new allies, since you can communicate with them. When I attack, circle behind those brigands. We will catch them between two fires, so to speak."

Barton took up a position behind the Saxons, addressing them in German. Pennywhistle turned to Maxwell. "This is your chance: the two of us are going to stage a cavalry charge. Let your blade do its worst."

"Now you're speaking my language, Colonel."

"Make that the three of us," said Sammie Jo.

"Now," Pennywhistle cautioned, "stay close enough to me so that we are always within supporting dist—"

What happened next annoyed Pennywhistle but should not have surprised him. Maxwell charged, riding forward to crash into a small knot of brigands, slashing wildly yet with skill. He cut one man in the head, one in the shoulder, then pivoted his mount to slash one man in the back of the neck and a fourth between his shoulder blades as he turned to run. He reared his horse in triumph and shouted, "Die, you devils, and know that it was Maxwell who killed you!" His sheer size and swordsmanship likely had more effect than his words. The two groups behind the one he had savaged broke and attempted to flee.

Pennywhistle rolled his eyes and motioned to Sammie Jo. They both charged, and their blades took down two brigands. Pennywhistle deliberately attacked from an angle in order to force the retreating criminals on to the tips of advancing Saxon bayonets.

The felons soon found themselves being bayonetted from the front and sabered from behind. Maxwell decapitated two more men. He was truly in his element; he had become a scarlet tornado on horseback.

The brigands fought fiercely, but when their leader, Karl Mundt, fell to Maxwell's blade, their resolve evaporated. Caught between a rock and a hard place and hoping their lives would be spared, they cast down their weapons and threw up their hands in surrender.

Pennywhistle yelled as loudly as he could, "Stand down, stand down!" Barton repeated the command in German, and the Saxons stopped and waited. The brigands were visibly relieved by this unexpected mercy. But Maxwell saw the gesture as a sign of weakness, and it added fire to his already hot blood. Pennywhistle had anticipated this and shouted at him, "Maxwell! Sheath your blade! Now! These men are our prisoners."

Maxwell stared at him in disbelief, followed by disappointment, and only reluctantly did as he was ordered.

"Dead men tell no tales, Ensign. We need to interrogate them and find out how much stolen British property they have at their hideout."

Pennywhistle rode slowly along the line of brigands, wondering what to do with them and realizing that he simply lacked the time to interrogate all of them. This was a job better handled by the provost marshal, since his men were skilled in such matters. Once the necessary information had been extracted, the provost marshal could turn them over to Belgian authorities, and a detachment of soldiers could retrieve whatever stolen goods they had in their possession. Likely all would hang, but at least they would have received a court hearing, and one or two might have their death sentence commuted.

"Colonel, Look!" shouted Maxwell. "One is getting away!" Maxwell pointed to a grotesquely fat monk running toward the main gate.

"Kinderdokken," murmured the prisoners.

Pennywhistle recognized the name and knew the provost marshal in Brussels would want to have an extended conversation with the man, since he had likely stolen thousands of pounds worth of military supplies. "Get him!" He yelled to Maxwell. "But we need him alive."

Maxwell acknowledged with a quick salute and for once obeyed orders. He galloped off and caught the running man by the back of his collar. His terrific strength enabled him to lift the fat man, administer a quick punch to silence his cries, and manhandle him onto the front of his saddle. The horse's hind quarters sagged under the extra weight.

Maxwell trotted back to Pennywhistle with a smug look of triumph and dumped the dazed crime lord at his officer's feet. Pennywhistle reached down and jerked Kinderdokken upright, staring into his eyes as he tried to get a sense of the man. He had never seen living eyes that looked so dead, and he felt that the soul behind them like a void of cold blackness.

Kinderdokken began to babble. "Don't kill me! Don't kill me! We can make a deal. I can make you a very rich man."

Murmurs of disgust rippled through the crowd of prisoners as they saw how cowardly their leader really was.

"You repulse me, sir, and bribery is abhorrent."

"I have information! Information that will interest you. I know the details of every criminal operation in these parts and can even give you warning of crimes not yet committed. Just spare me!"

Destination Waterloo

Before Pennywhistle could answer, a knife flashed through the air, thrown by one of the prisoners. It buried itself in the back of Kinderdokken's skull. Kinderdokken gasped, shuddered, and slumped heavily to the ground. Clearly, at least one of the prisoners had secrets he did not want revealed in exchange for an amnesty.

"Serves him right!" muttered a prisoner. Pennywhistle recognized the truth of the aphorism: There is no honor among thieves.

Pennywhistle and Barton carried out an inspection of the wagons. Barton showed how the gold was encased in bars of soap, and Pennywhistle marveled at the cleverness of the scheme. "Convenient that this portion of the gold can be moved immediately; Wellington's quartermaster is going to be very pleased. As for the flowers, I think we can find them homes at military hospitals. Flowers can brighten a wounded man's outlook."

Pennywhistle told Maxwell to guard the prisoners, and the young man stalked across the chamber to loom over them, just itching to strike down anyone foolish enough to consider fleeing. Pennywhistle's plan was for the Saxons to march the felons back to Brussels; Maxwell would stay behind to guard the treasure until such time as a small detachment could be detailed to secure it. Pennywhistle asked Barton to call the Saxons to attention and translate his words.

"Soldiers of Saxony, in the past, you have brought distinction to yourselves and your king. I know you were discharged wrongly, but you have shown that you have plenty of fight left in you. I offer you the chance to fight with Hanoverian troops serving under the British Crown. They are green soldiers who would welcome experienced veterans like yourselves. I will extend a general amnesty regarding the stolen gold in return for your service. You will have a chance to reclaim your honor and return home with stories that you will tell your grandchildren about the part you played in humbling Bonaparte once and for all. All those who agree to this bargain, raise your hands."

Every man's hand shot skyward. Some stamped their feet, and a few roared their approval.

Sammie Jo pulled alongside. "They stole British gold?"

"Yes, Hawkeye, quite a lot."

"Looks like you've got your work cut out for you, Sugar Plum. She scowled. "Damn! I was hoping for an intimate reunion directly. Thought we might get a room at the inn I ate at earlier."

Pennywhistle's brows contracted. "That sounds like a splendid idea, but..."

"I know, I know you have your duty," she groaned in exasperation. "You might be married to me, but right now Wellington is 'the other woman'."

"On the way to Brussels you can tell me about your travels." Pennywhistle's face suddenly lit up with one of his rare smiles. "I look forward to holding Nicolas in my arms."

"And I have a surprise for you, Tom. We have a ball to attend."

"A ball? You're joking."

"Not at all. The invitation was issued by the Duchess of Richmond, at the behest of Wellington himself." She smiled mischievously. "He is eager to introduce me to Brussels society."

"I should much prefer to spend the evening in bed with you, Hawkeye."

"I would like nothing better, but this is duty in a social disguise, and as you have often told me, Wellington is He Who Must Be Obeyed."

Maxwell rode up to Pennywhistle and Sammie Jo with a sour look on his face. "What's this about me being left behind as a storage room guard? That's a job for barrack room flunky, not an officer whose blade just savaged the Crown's enemies!"

"Who is this?" Sammie Jo was obviously angered by the rude interruption.

"Someone who does not yet know his place," replied Pennywhistle. "Maximilian Maxwell, allow me to introduce my wife, Lady Pennywhistle."

"Sounds like the name of a racetrack tout," Sammie Jo muttered.

Maxwell glared. "That's no way to talk to someone who just saved your life, Lady Pennywhistle.

Sammie Jo glared back. "From my perspective, I was the one who rescued you."

Pennywhistle turned to Maxwell. "Rather than thinking of this assignment as a cut, regard it as a compliment. You are guarding thousands of pounds of British gold! Do you really think that should be left to an underpaid private soldier who might be disposed to pilfer a small amount? I am not doubting your abilities but reposing confidence in them."

"Oh! I had not thought of it that way, Colonel."

"I will send an English-speaking Saxon to get word to the Antwerp Garrison commander to send a relief party, but until that arrives, you will just have to hold until you are relieved."

Hold until relieved. Hold until relieved. Pennywhistle's words echoed through Maxwell's mind, and he wondered how long he would have to endure this limbo. He hated the condescending way Lady Pennywhistle had spoken to him, yet she was a rare beauty . He studied her from under sullenly lowered eyelashes. She was clearly athletic and would probably be a real terror in bed. He wondered how he might arrange a rendezvous with her. He needed a drink.

Sammie Jo turned to Pennywhistle as they rode out through the gate and into the street. "Maxwell's trouble."

"I know, but Wellington wants me to make something of him."

"I think he will either die in battle or swing at the end of a rope. He wants me: I saw it in his eyes. If he lays a finger on me, I will kill him."

"The trick is to redirect the damage he is capable of doing onto the French."

Pennywhistle's ears perked up as he heard a lone fife in the distance. The melody was "Lilibolero", a popular old tune in the British Army. He unfurled his Ramsden and pointed it toward the source: two slow moving wagons accompanied by ten marching soldiers. He assumed they came from the Antwerp garrison and wondered what they were transporting. He trotted the quarter mile toward them, the wagons stopped at the approach of a British officer. The Sergeant in the driving box saluted.

Pennywhistle returned the salute. "Where are you bound, Sarn't, and what is your cargo?"

"Cartridges sir, for Wellington's Army. My two wagons contain forty barrels, each barrel holds 1,000 musket rounds. A ship unloaded them in Antwerp yesterday and Colonel Smithers thought they should be delivered as soon as possible."

"I am an aide to the Duke of Wellington and am changing your men's assignment. I need your men to perform garrison duty at a Royal Engineer Post that was recently commandeered by unauthorized parties. There is something extremely valuable within that I want protected."

"What is it, sir?"

"Let's just say it was stolen from British forces. It's locked in a warehouse. Your men must make sure that no one enters the warehouse until an authorized officer returns with a detachment to take charge of it. The facility is well stocked with provisions, so your men will have plenty to eat and drink."

"What about the cartridges, Colonel…"

"Pennywhistle. I have some Saxons on their way to Wellington's Army who will take over your escort duties. I shall accompany them, and I assure you that your cartridges will arrive on time and intact. What's your name, Sarn't?"

"Rogers, Colonel. John Rogers."

"A pleasure to have you under my command." Pennywhistle pointed toward the compound. "That is your objective, Sarn't. When you reach it, have the men fall out and form them up for parade. I will explain their new duties, then I will let you determine postings and a duty schedule."

"Very good, Colonel. If you don't mind me asking, do you think a battle with Bonaparte will happen anytime soon?"

"I am certain of it. Probably within a few days, certainly not more than a week."

"I wish I could be there for it. I am a field soldier, sir, not a delivery boy, and I'd like to give that Corsican a damn good thrashing."

"I might be able to help with that, Sarn't. Tell me, is the sarn't commanding the other wagon a capable fellow?"

"Sergeant Fellows is very competent, sir."

"Then I shall place him in charge of the compound garrison. One of the privates can take his place guiding his wagon, and you may continue in your present assignment. If events reach a critical juncture before you start your return journey, then I shall send for you. I would welcome an aide if Bonaparte attacks."

Master's eyes gleamed. "I would be most grateful sir."

It took an hour to brief Fellows and get his men posted, but Pennywhistle was pleased with the arrangement. He wished he could have loaded the soap boxes onto the wagons en rout to Wellington, but the cartridge barrels were packed too tightly for that.

"Thank God for those garrison chaps," growled Maxwell, after he was relieved by the newcomers. "It would have been a damn shame to have been left rotting in that place when a jolly good fight lies ahead."

"No battle is ever 'jolly good', Ensign. No professional soldier talks that way, only rear echelon commentators."

"How do professional soldiers talk, Colonel?" asked Maxwell with barely veiled sarcasm.

Pennywhistle knew he was being baited, but it gave him an idea about how to solve a problem before it began. "Mostly, they don't talk at all, they act. Flapping tongues are generally foolish; worse, they can broadcast information that spies find useful. Are you a betting man?" asked Pennywhistle, certain of the answer.

"Always, Colonel. Have you a wager in mind?"

"I do. I will bet you ten pounds that you cannot refrain from speaking a single word between now and the time we reach Wellington's headquarters."

Maxwell frowned. He loved wagering on curious things, like how many pies a man could consume in an hour, or whether a one-armed, one-legged man could beat a midget in a fight; but what Pennywhistle was wagering required a degree of self-control that he was not sure he possessed. But if he declined the wager he would look weak, and though he hated to admit it, Pennywhistle's respect was something that he would like to have. "Make it 20 pounds and you have a bet."

"Done!" exclaimed Pennywhistle with barely concealed glee. He had dreaded the prospect of having to endure Maxwell's bragging and baiting on the return journey, and twenty pounds was a cheap price to avoid it.

"Have you any last words?" inquired Pennywhistle with intentional irony.

"Only to clarify something. The bet ends the second my foot touches the first step in front of Wellington's headquarters?"

"Agreed. And no talking means no muttering or cursing as well. I consider your question your final words, and so the bet is on as of this moment."

Maxwell narrowed his eyes and nodded.

"Good. Then I shall take my leave of you. I want you to ride alongside Sergeant Rogers and serve as a flank guard for our little convoy. Rogers will inform me if you speak. The one exception to the terms of the bet are if you come under attack, in which case you are, of course, expected to give warning and reply to directions."

Maxwell nodded again, then saluted and trotted to his post.

"You look like the cat that swallowed the canary and a bowl of cream as well," observed an amused Sammie Jo as Pennywhistle trotted alongside.

"I have just bought us a pleasant journey." He explained the wager and Sammie Jo laughed. "From what I have seen that will be pure torture for him!"

"No one ever said an officer's lot was an easy one, and adversity can be good for the soul."

"That's a lot of adversity."

"He needs a lot of fixing."

Franz Finkel had been terrified during the battle. He was a spy and scrounger, not a fighter. He had hated exchanging a bad master for a criminal overlord, but it had been a matter of survival. And now that crime lord would not be able to deliver on his promised payment. Suddenly, Franz realized he didn't need Kinderdokken.

In the chaos, he slipped down to the storage room, pocketed four bars of soap, then wiggled his way through the crack in the wall that had originally granted him entrance. Inside the bars, he had more than enough money to make his way to Antwerp and secure passage across the Atlantic: a chance for a fresh start. He would seek out an American vessel. Perhaps they would even hire him on; that would save him the cost of passage. He decided to look for a ship sailing to Philadelphia, where there were plenty of German speakers.

Chapter 6
Cannons, Lancers, and Command

15 June 1815, 4 p.m., 3 miles west of Charleroi

Fivel's artillery company had halted to regroup after the early morning fight with the Prussians. Officers made sure supplies were replenished, casualties assessed and tended, prisoners interrogated, and enemy bodies searched for anything useful. Fivel's men used the interval to sleep, eat, check their equipment, and gossip.

Jacques Gagne realized that he and his mates had faced only a detachment of Prussians when two squadrons of hussars trotted off to locate the main body. That scouting took four hours, and another two were consumed translating the hussar's information into marching orders for Reille's Corps of 25,000. Jacques' column had then resumed its march, their objective the advanced elements of von Zieten's Corps of 28,000 men, seven miles distant. An hour was consumed narrowing Reille's columns to fit the bridges over the Sambre River, but all the men were across by noon. Three hours of marching followed, with ten-minute halts each hour.

Boom! Boom! Boom!

The transition from country quiet to the terrible roar of battle happened as quickly as the flash of a musket's pan, as advance French gunners opened fire on Prussians amassed to their fore. The din made

Jacques' head feel like a tennis ball being swatted by rackets. He briefly covered his ears, then decided it was pointless; the noise was not going to cease anytime soon. Billowing thunderheads of gun smoke gave off a rotten egg smell so powerful that he gagged. Two of his gun crew had already wretched, one had wet himself, and one was flexing his jaw in a vain effort to equalize ear pressure.

In addition to the noise from Reille's II Corps artillery, d'Erlon's Corps were firing their guns six miles to the east. They were locked in a fight with the Prussians of von Pirch's Corps. The determined knot of resistance in front of II Corps would have to be swept away before any rendezvous between the two French Corps could be achieved.

The fog of war applied in a literal fashion. All Jacques had been told was that 2 regiments of Prussian infantry lay on the other side of the gun smoke, perhaps 300 yards away. An estimated 3,000 Prussians were posted in hedges, a large farmhouse, and the ruins of an old abbey. An abatis blocked the road the French would have to traverse to reach d'Erlon. The interlaced sharpened tree branches with their points directed outward were held together with heavy wire mesh designed to entangle approaching infantry. Coupled with a brook on either side of the road that was swollen by recent rains, a direct French approach to the Prussian position would likely be a costly one.

To make matters worse, the Prussians were supported by eight guns. Four to the right of the old abbey, and four on the slightly higher ground behind the abbey. Half of the guns were howitzers, capable of arcing five-and-one-quarter-inch explosive shells.

While French *voltigeur* snipers worked to kill the gunners, the French artillery worked to kill those Prussian guns. Counter battery fire was generally discouraged as wasteful of ammunition, but here it was the only means they had. One officer climbed a tall oak tree and extended his spyglass, hoping that a small break in the smoke might provide enough information to assist in aiming the guns below.

Sergent Roland Marceau now commanded Jacques' 6-pounder and its six-man crew. Marceau, who projected the image of the crusty veteran, had replaced the much-respected Sergeant Goulet, after Goulet had been incapacitated by a recurrence of malaria. Sergeant Marceau had told his crew that their actions would depend on reports from the infantry *voltigeurs*, who were conducting a local reconnaissance. "Infantry is the queen of battle, and artillery is the king. It's only natural than the queen should tell the king where to put his balls."

Marceau gave every sign of being the perfect non-commissioned officer, but he was hiding a terrible secret. Formerly, he had indeed been as tough and strong as he appeared, but now he was quailing inwardly. Ten years of service as a sergeant and four major battles meant he knew exactly what lay ahead, and the horror became harder to bear each time he had to endure it. He envied the ignorance of his rookies.

Now his nerves sang with tension, and a slight twitching in his right index finger warned him that his survival instinct was preparing an assault on his courage. The stress triggered a boyhood memory of the tall mahogany case clock in the foyer of Chateau Fontaine. As a young servant, he had spent hours cleaning it and had been fascinated by the delicate calibration of its elaborate gears — and how little it would take to upset them. He realized that he had something similar in the foyer of his soul: a case clock of battle. This clock was even more complex than the one at the Chateau and featured a swinging pendulum inexorably ticking off the seconds until it chimed one last time at midnight: the end of a man's combat life, when the bonds of courage, duty, and honor were shattered by the compulsion to break and run. The hands on that clock read ten minutes to midnight, and its pendulum was swinging with frightening rapidity. Despite his inner turmoil, he continued to give the necessary commands.

Jacques' gun and the five others of Fivel's command unlimbered and took positions 10 meters apart, to minimize the risk of a single incoming round damaging more than one gun. They deployed their pieces on level, grassy ground, partially sheltered by a low ridge against which the gunners braced their wheels. The six pounders were sturdy weapons that were simpler, lighter, and more mobile than their Royalist predecessors. They featured a twin tailed wooden carriage 1.5 meters long, wheels as high as a man's shoulder, and a bronze barrel of 1.2 meters length. Each one had an effective range of 640 meters, and their projectiles traveled at 453 meters per second. On dry, even ground the gun's recoil was six feet.

The grey-coated artillery train drivers took charge of the company horses. After unhitching them, leading them to a safe area behind the ammunition wagons, and tethering them to portable posts, they provided each horse with an oat bag from which to feed. The drivers positioned the limbers thirty meters behind the main line, and the ammunition wagons twenty meters behind the limbers. If the company had to shift position quickly, the drivers could get the company underway in approximately four minutes. Jacques thought the six horses who pulled his gun were the swiftest of the lot.

Boom! A shell burst in the clouds over Jacques' head, and lead raindrops spattered at his feet.

"Anyone hurt?" yelled Marceau. A chorus of "No"s was returned. "Then to your posts. For Napoleon and glory!"

What followed next was a military ritual that depended for success on skill, precision, and every action being performed in a set order. One misstep or forgotten action could cause a lethal accidental detonation. Jacques took up his appointed position, as did the rest of the crew. The dog Rifle came over and nosed the back of Jacques' hand. The large poodle remained calm in the midst of gunfire, a comforting presence. The crew had come to consider him something of a good luck talisman.

Boom! Another howitzer shell burst and Jacques heard cries of pain from the gun crew next to theirs.

Marceau, as the battery commander, took up a position behind the gun from where he could operate the barrel elevation screw, help aim the piece, and give the command to fire. The gunners each had a number but were generally called by the name of the function that they performed: every man was also trained to perform the duties of the rest of the crew in case a fallen member needed to be replaced.

Spongeman de Salle stood to the right of the cannon's barrel, while Ventsman Jacques stood two feet behind him. On the opposite side stood Loader Carnot, and two feet behind him stood Firer Le Paul. Gunner Six, Bombardier Guise, stood behind the cannon; he would ensure a steady replenishment of ammunition from the trail box and the wagons to the rear; while Gunner Five, Bombardier Richard, would help Marceau aim the piece with long wooden handspikes embedded in holes in the platform between the cannon's tails.

Marceau nodded approvingly as Gunner Six opened the trail ammunition chest that lay a meter behind the gun. He prepared for the command to select an appropriate round from the eight within. The choices included solid shot, heavy canister, and light canister. Solid shot was good against blocks of men or buildings. It was capable of striking dozens in the heads and chest on the fly, then thighs and kneecaps on the bounce.

Heavy canister was strictly an anti-personnel weapon that turned a cannon into a giant shotgun. It was a tin full of 41 four-ounce balls that was deadliest at the first point blank primitive: the distance when a round rose above a cannon's line of sight, roughly 270 meters. Light canister contained 85 two-ounce balls packed in a similar tin, and was most effective at the second point blank primitive: 365 meters, when projectiles dropped below the cannon's line of sight.

Boom! A third shell burst. Jacques noted it burst far to the rear of the French guns. The previous two shell bursts must have been pure luck. The Prussians were just guessing at the location of their opponents.

"Load!" bellowed Marceau. "Solid shot!" Once the loading ballet began, things happened quickly. Marceau expected the battery to discharge three rounds per minute.

Jacques acted first, covering the venthole with a heavy leather thumbstall to prevent the passage of air. Even though the piece had not been fired, routine had to be maintained. The Spongeman ran his long wooden ramrod with the corkscrew tip into the barrel, twisting it to worm out any smoldering bits of a cartridge bag. He held the ramrod loose and underhanded so that if a chance detonation occurred, it would not blow his arms off. He removed the wormer and took up a second ramrod. He dipped one sheepskin-covered end in a bucket of water and sponged out the barrel to kill any lingering sparks. He removed the ramrod and reversed it, using the other end to soak up any remaining moisture.

The Loader walked to the rear and accepted a sabot from Gunner Six. The sabot contained 2 pounds of powder in a circular flannel bag on a wooden base, a wad above, and a 6-pound ball on top held in place by two iron straps. The Loader returned to the muzzle and carefully inserted it into the barrel. He stepped back and the Spongeman took over.

The Spongeman's ramrod tapped the round three times, then he gave a single hard thrust to seat it home.

Jacques removed his thumbstall from the venthole and took out a long steel pricker from a sack slung over his shoulder. He inserted the pricker into the venthole to pierce the cartridge and expose the gunpowder. He took a thin quiver of fine gunpowder that would detonate the main charge and popped it into the venthole. His job done, he nodded to Marceau.

Marceau turned the elevating screw beneath the barrel upwards by a quarter of a degree. He then took hold of one handspike while Gunner Five took hold of another. Marceau made his best guess about the Prussian battery that had been plaguing them, then he and Gunner Five moved the piece three degrees to the right. He cursed under his breath because for all his knowledge and experience, he was still guessing.

"Make ready!" he bellowed.

Everyone stepped away from the piece. They covered their ears and leaned sideways away from the cannon's muzzle.

The Firer took up his three-foot linstock whose steel tip had anchored it in the ground. Its rope end was a slow burning match impregnated with saltpeter.

"Fire!"

The Firer applied the linstock to the touchhole. There was a bright flash, a hollow boom, and the piece jumped backwards. If the Prussians had been visible, Marceau would have calculated the range by taking the difference in seconds between the flash and boom and multiplying it by 340 meters.

The easy part was done. Now came the hard work.

Jacques and three of the crew raced to the front of the cannon and attached hooked ropes to each wheel hub and to twin hooks on the front of the carriage. Smaller hooks suspended from the fronts of their uniforms. This was known as *en bricole* work. They pulled hard and brought the cannon back to its original position. Doing the drill once was exercise, doing it three times a minute was torture.

Jacques' crew fired rounds in rapid succession. The thunderheads of smoke continued to swell, and the noise grew even more oppressive. Jacques could only see a few yards ahead and to his right and left. Combat became flashes of light blinking on and off in the distance: the smaller ones, musketry, the larger ones, cannon.

Time slowed and minutes became eons: he lost track of how many times his gun flashed, and recoiled, how many times he helped haul it back into position. The men grunted and groaned. Perspiration flowed freely down his forehead into his eyes; he had to wipe them frequently with a handkerchief that had been a parting gift from his mother. His uniform had changed from blue to a gritty grey, and his cheeks and hands resembled a miner's. His leg and shoulder muscles screamed, the incessant *boom booming* hammered at his ears, and his lips grew dry and parched from the saltpeter residue that snatched moisture from the air. His nose became anesthetized to the stink, but his head ached, and it became hard to think. His muscles directed his actions rather than his mind as hours of drill paid off. The crew worked together like clockwork, though as muscles became fatigued that clockwork dropped from three beats per minute to two.

The numerous recoils of his company's guns had churned the soft ground on which they were positioned into a sea of mud. His shoes and trousers were caked with it, and the heavy goo made repositioning his gun that much harder. If the company had to withdraw, the muck would significantly slow their movements.

He felt a mixture of fear, confusion, exhilaration, and pride that he would have been hard pressed to explain to a civilian who had never been in battle. Despite the bewildering sights, sounds, and smells that represented death tugging at his sleeves, his senses had never felt so acutely tuned and alive. His mates were bearing up well, and he judged from their faces that they were feeling the same emotions that he was. His crew had remained untouched so far, but cries and screams from the guns to his right indicated that they had taken casualties.

The heaviest casualties were among the horses, and that tore at his heartstrings. The Prussians were firing high, and their rounds were landing in the rear of the company guns. The horses died horribly, with blighted eyes and ears, missing legs, and unspooling entrails. Some rolled in agony, some staggered slowly, and some sank down on their haunches and waited hopelessly for death to overtake them. Their frantic neighing, piteous groans, and agonized whinnies were high pitched enough to be heard clearly above the bass booms of the guns. The artillery drivers tried hard to calm the uninjured beasts, but their efforts only partially succeeded. At least a quarter of the 179 horses broke their tethers and stampeded. Their loss would significantly impede the company's movement.

And yet, the company had been lucky in a way. Neither Prussian shot nor shell had hit an ammunition wagon. A never-ending line of gunners kept up a brisk flow of ammunition from wagons to weapons.

His crew's luck ran out so fast that he could hardly credit that it happened. One second Spongeman de Salle had a head, the next second he did not. The corpse collapsed and everything stopped as the men stared in confusion. Jacques was surprised that Marceau looked shaken and unmanned. Marceau nonetheless barked at an ammunition passer, "Le Mieux, replace him!" Discipline took over and firing resumed. De Salle had many friends, but mourning would have to wait.

Thunder rumbled in the west, warning of an approaching storm, and a strong wind sprang up. It acted like a giant stagehand, lifting the curtain that had prevented both sides from seeing the damage they had inflicted on each other.

"Cease fire! Cease fire! Cease fire!" was shouted in French and German; officers on both sides wanted to assess the situation, redirect and redeploy. Marceau unfurled his pocket spyglass and put it to his eye. Jacques stared about in awe and muttered, "*Mon Dieu*, what have we done?"

The Prussian abatis had been shattered, and numerous dead soldiers lay behind it. The farmhouse and abbey had been reduced to rubble; the centuries-old hedges were broken and torn. Half of the Prussian guns had been disabled. French *voltigeurs* looked ready to move forward in a skirmish line, and a French infantry column had begun to shift into line, prelude to a bayonet assault.

French hospital wagons moved forward to collect the wounded *voltigeurs*. Designed by the French surgeon general Dominique Larrey, the wagons featured heavy springs to cushion rides, and easy-to-open panels to speed the loading and unloading of casualties.

Jacques blanched as he realized their guns had been positioned too far forward. They were at least 190 meters in front of the supporting infantry, dangerously exposed. The closeness of their guns to the enemy explained the great damage they had done. In the smoke, the French infantry had shifted their position so often that they had lost touch with the artillery they were pledged to support.

Jacques expected that situation would be remedied swiftly, then gasped as an artilleryman's worst nightmare emerged out of a deep gully. Moving upwards was a squadron of Prussian *uhlans* in black shakos, blue coats, and grey overalls. These were big men on big horses, armed with big lances: the Prussian counterpart to French lancers. Three meters long, the lances weighed three kilograms and had swallow tail pennons of black and white just below their razor-sharp tips.

Jacques felt panic rising as he realized that they were only 150 meters away. The muskets of the gunners were behind with the ammunition wagons, but even experienced infantry in line would have been no match for heavy cavalry. The usual tactic for gunners was to temporarily abandon their pieces and seek shelter in the hollow of the nearest infantry square until the danger had passed. Trouble was, the infantry had not yet apprehended the situation and no such square was available.

The *uhlans* stopped briefly, as their commander straightened the 116 troopers into a fifty-meter line, then leveled their lances. Their trumpeter blew a command that made Jacques quake because he knew it probably meant his death. As the distance was short, the squadron dispensed with the trot and canter transitions and spurred their horses directly to the charge. The troopers remained eerily silent, but the thundering hooves of their horses shook the ground.

Tick tock, tick tock, tick tock. Dong! Dong! Dong! Marceau's mind's ear heard his inner clock strike midnight just as clearly as if it had been in a church's bell tower. He broke into the fastest run he that his long legs could manage. The men blinked in stupefaction, left leaderless in the worst of situations.

Jacques estimated that he had a minute left to live. Then remembered a story his uncle had told him, and the moral: *The most audacious action is sometimes the safest one.*

As the Prussian horses thundered forward, Jacques seized command, imitating his uncle's most imperious voice and ferocious posture. "No time to run, my friends. Load immediately! Heavy canister! Zero elevation!" The men were desperate for any leadership, even if it came from a sixteen-year-old. Jacques' ability to inspire trust had never served him better than it did now. The crew complied with a speed that they did not know they had.

Three of the other gun crews ran, but the remaining two saw Jacques' example and began loading their own pieces with preternatural speed. Three guns gave the French a fighting chance, if they were fast enough.

The horsemen were twenty meters away when Jacques' Ventsman inserted the priming quill and his Firer raised the linstock. Jacques could see the scowls on the enemy's mustached faces, and it took every ounce of his courage not to freeze in terror. Instead, he shouted "Fire!"

The six-pounder flashed and boomed, answered by the company's other two guns a second later.

123 four-ounce balls fired at ten meters acted as a devastating meat grinder: the old artillery dictum of "the final round is always the deadliest" showing itself to be true. The three cone-shaped discharges functioned as giant metallic hands, batting the enemy backwards and slapping down 2/3 of the horsemen and their mounts. The rounds flattened on impact; some swelled to the size of small apples, creating terrible exit wounds, crushing bones and entrails if they remained inside a body. A bloody mist filled the air as horses and men partially intact thrashed wildly above ones who lay in ragged pieces. Cries, screams, and shouts created a terrible symphony that neither man nor beast should ever hear. The surviving horses and men stopped and milled around, dazed by what had just happened.

Jacques played a hunch that was counter intuitive but might work against men whose wits had temporarily deserted them. He grabbed a lance from a dead *uhlan*'s hand and thrust it at the nearest horse. Though he had no skill with a lance, his target was a large one, and the mount's rider did not expect an attack. He jammed the point into the base of the horse's neck and pushed with all his might. The horse reared in pain and terror, jerking the lance from his hand, then toppled over, pinning the rider, who screamed in pain.

Jacques picked up another lance and waved it boldly. "Every man grab a lance and follow me!" There were plenty of lances to be had, and his men seized them, realizing that Jacques had shown them a way to go on the attack. What they lacked in skill, they made up for in fury, inspired by Jacques' actions.

Jacques stabbed and thrust with a berserker madness that he did not know he possessed. It sprang less from wanting to save himself than to save the men who had become his brothers in arms. He crippled one horse with a thrust to the fetlock artery. When the unhorsed rider came at him with a lance, Jacques realized the man was unaccustomed to ground fighting. Jacques was stronger and faster on his feet. He sidestepped the *uhlan*'s thrust, then spun and ran the *uhlan* through from the rear.

Aa a second *uhlan* charged, Jacques went down on one knee and thrust the lance outward at a forty-five-degree angle. The horse reared in panic, then fell backwards when Jacques thrust hard at the base of his neck. The horseman survived the fall, but Jacques raced round, grabbed a pistol from his saddle holster, and shot him in the head.

An unhorsed *uhlan* came at him from behind, but Rifle snarled and dove at his leg, clamping his teeth into the man's shin. The *uhlan* howled in pain and dropped his lance. Jacques whirled, picked up the lance, and ran it through his chest.

The *uhlan*s never got a chance to rally from the fury of the French attack. In a way, they were psychologically beaten before the attack began because they simply could not credit that lowly groundlings could dare attack lordly lancers.

The men on the other gun crews saw Jacques' actions and imitated them. Their actions killed another eight horses and broke the *uhlans*' nerve. A trumpeter sounded the retreat, and the survivors spun their mounts round and spurred them back toward the sanctuary of their own lines even faster than they had come. French jeers and cheers followed them.

Jacques could hardly believe what had happened. It all seemed a dream that belonged to someone else. He had always thought of himself as someone who could resume the life of a good Quaker once his duty to France was done. Now he was not so sure. He had seen a side of himself that shocked him and that he could never unsee. Perhaps he had more of his uncle in him than he had thought.

His men surrounded him and clapped him on the back. "You saved us!"

"Well done!"

"It's the quiet ones who turn out to be heroes."

"You're 'Uhlan Killer Gagne' now."

Jacques felt entirely unworthy of the compliments; he had just done what needed to be done.

Capitaine Fivel galloped up on a white horse and halted just in front of Jacques, his face a mixture of relief and satisfaction. He dismounted and extended his hand rather than saluting. Jacques shook it in surprise. "I have had my eye on you since you solved the cannon wheel problem, and I can see my instincts were right. You saved my command, and I shall be forever in your debt. What you did showed the spirit and elan that the Emperor loves. Marceau will never command again, and I need a replacement. This is now your crew, *Caporal* Gagne."

"*Merci beaucoup, mon capitaine.*" It was the proudest moment of Jacques' life. And the most frightening. He felt the weight of command descend hard on his shoulders. He hoped he could do right by his crew then realized that his NCO rank had made them his subordinates rather than his friends. His uncle had taught him that command required a certain distance from the men you commanded. He wondered how he could maintain that.

Fivel handed him a silver flask in celebration, and he took a long pull of some very smooth brandy. In his hot and tired state, the liquor hit him fast and hard. He wanted nothing more than a place to lie down, though stripping off his mud-caked uniform and diving headfirst into a clear, cold stream seemed a splendid idea as well. Looking at the confused tangle of dead men and horses, he wondered where in all this insanity was the camp follower who had propositioned him.

Caporal Le Mans, the giant whom Jacques had embarrassed during the matter of the broken wheel, watched through a dead officer's spyglass and cursed. He became even more determined to exact revenge. He resolved to kill his rival under cover of the next battle.

Rifle bounded up to Jacques, carrying in his mouth a bone from which dangled shreds of flesh. Jacques petted him several times. "You're a good boy."

He wondered if the same could still be said of him.

Jacques Gagne and his company bivouacked on the edge of a small dairy farm, four miles east of Charleroi. Natural clouds and those of lingering gun smoke had brought twilight early. The air was hot, humid, and reeked of the smell of saltpeter. Pickets were posted, foraging parties sent out, and men deposited their packs, blankets, and haversacks around an improvised fire pit. French Army fire pits were laid out in orderly, rectangular streets, a tradition that went back to the ancient Romans. A mess usually consisted of sixteen, but tonight theirs was only 11: his men and those of Gun 5.

The crews cleaned and oiled their cannon ramrods and wormers, then did the same for their muskets, storing them in large bell tents to keep them dry and safe. Tents were not available for the men, so it was every man and his blanket against the elements. Wood was gathered and welcome blazes were lit. The company cook suspended a large pot on a short chain from beneath two forked wooden uprights with a bayonet for a crosspiece; the boiling pot containing the evening meal: a watery soup of potatoes, onions, leeks, peas, and chunks of what had been a dairy cow an hour before. Rations of brandy were issued, and the men sipped slowly as their noses anticipated an evening meal that for once contained fresh meat.

Jacques found that battle had given him a huge appetite. He wished the soup would cook faster. His hands were rock steady; he wondered why the rookie post battle shakes had not appeared. Then he remembered that his uncle had remarked that protecting others often canceled out the tremors.

His men were tired but talkative.

"We really gave those *uhlans* what for, didn't we?" said Carnot.

"That we did," de Paul responded.

"Fritz and his friends will think twice about trying that stunt again," proclaimed Guise.

"This calls for a chorus of '*La Marseilles*'," said LeDoux, and he opened his mouth to sing.

Richard clamped both hands over Le Doux's jaw. "Shut up. *Mon Dieu*, we have heard enough bad noise for one day."

"Too bad about de Salle," remarked Richard, "he had a wife and three children and did not deserve what happened to him."

"No one deserves death" Dupuy said angrily. "I sometimes feel God is playing dice with men's lives."

His comrades nodded.

"I disagree," chided Dacres. "I believe in a God of battles who protects brave men when they stand fast, as we did. I believe He placed his hands upon Gagne's shoulders and directed him to deliver us from evil."

"That makes more sense than saying de Salle died because God is a gamester," de Paul opined.

"I am no philosopher," snarled Dupuy, "but I do know that I would like to meet God in a dark alley and smash a fist into his Heavenly face." He punched his fist skyward.

"De Salle was my best friend, and while I am sad that he is gone," said Dione, "I am glad it was him and not me."

"I hope that bastard Marceau gets what's coming to him," said Carnot angrily. "I can't image how a coward ever became an NCO. That devil left us out to dry! Thank God for Gagne." He raised his tin cup. "May Marceau's next meal be shit stew served in Hell."

"Here, here!" His friends raised their cups and drank.

"I almost feel sorry for Marceau," offered Jacques.

Incredulous cries of "What?!" erupted.

"I think living will be a far worse punishment than death for Marceau. Word of his cowardice will spread far and wide and erase forever any mention of the good deeds he performed in battle. He may return home, but his friends and family will eventually find out and shun him."

"Serve him right," someone muttered.

"I don't think he was a bad man, just a man who broke. Remember, he had fought in many battles. I think the last one was that one too many."

A chorus of catcalls greeted Jacques' assessment.

"I'm not saying that he was a hero gone wrong. But I wonder how we will fare when we, too, bear the weight of a score of battles."

"Bah!" said Jelune, flourishing a deck of cards. "Enough talk! Who will join me in a friendly game?" His mouth widened into a shark's smile. He took out a package from his pocket and unwrapped it for all to see: a slice of apple pie. He took a large bite. "Delicious! Just like my grandmother used to bake. The rest of the pie will be my stake."

The men looked at the slice longingly but eyed him cynically: his reputation as a sharper meant they were unlikely to win the pie.

"You're all damn fools," said Jelune contemptuously, rising to his feet. "I will find some men who don't object to winning big." He stalked off.

De Paul pulled a flute from his haversack and began playing a mocking melody which caused the men to laugh.

"Soup's ready," bellowed the cook.

The men eagerly formed a line with their pannikins held forward.

Conversation ceased as the men ate with relish. The welcome smell of boiled beef and wood smoke blended with the less welcome scents of saltpeter, gun oil, sweaty uniforms, and the effluvia of a nearby cesspit. The men were as ravenous as wolves who had not eaten for a week.

Jacques spotted *Capitaine* Fivel coming toward him, accompanied by a portly man in a bicorne hat wearing a grey wool greatcoat. Jacques blinked twice, gasped, and dropped his spoon as he recognized the silhouette. The man was Emperor Napoleon.

Napoleon liked to see things for himself and had a habit of dropping into units unannounced and without an entourage of aides. He would join men at their campfires, share their food, drink, and gossip, and ask them how they were being treated. The men loved him for having the common touch: he never blamed soldiers for any problems but always laid the fault on the officers who commanded them. On the night before the Battle of Wagram, he had even slept on a blanket alongside the men with whom he had supped.

Such visits were a first-rate way to gauge the morale of his army. as well as encourage the cult of personality that was the bedrock of his rule. While much of what he did reflected the instincts of a master showman, his regard for common soldiers was genuine.

Napoleon had met Fivel only once, on the night before Wagram five years before, but his phenomenal memory came to his aid. He had greeted Fivel like an old friend, then asked what had happened during the past day. Fivel replied by relating how one of his gunner lads had led a victorious charge. At the conclusion, Napoleon had remarked, "I should very much like to meet that young man from Normandy. Men like him represent the future of France."

By the time both men reached the circle around the fire, even the most dimwitted of the mess had recognized the Emperor. They all moved to rise and shout *"Vive l' Empeurer"*, but he motioned them to stay put and remain silent. "My soldiers, please continue eating and do not announce my presence. You have fought hard and well, and I do not wish to disturb your meal. Rather I would like to join you and judge the quality of your provisions for myself. Would that meet with your approval?"

Napoleon's accent intrigued Jacques. His lilting voice was flavored with the long vowels of his native Corsica. He was taller but his oval face was puffier and his body stouter than in the paintings and lithographs that Jacques had seen growing up. His manner was cheerful, but his complexion was waxy.

"My Emperor, it would be an unimaginable honor to have you dine with us," gasped Jacques.

His messmates nodded fervently.

The cook appeared with two plates and spoons and handed one each to Napoleon and Fivel.

"Is this exactly what the men are eating?" demanded Napoleon.

"Th-the same plain faire, Sire," stammered the cook, who could not quite credit to whom he was speaking. He then handed over two tins of brandy.

Napoleon looked over the gathering, then sat next to Jacques Gagne.

Jacques felt a mixture of fear and excitement that was not dissimilar to battle.

Napoleon took a spoonful of soup and slurped it thoughtfully, as if he were a judge at a county cooking contest. He smiled and looked at the cook. "It's good. My compliments to the chef."

The cook stammered, "Uh... thank you, Sire." He had never been called a chef before, let alone by an Emperor.

Napoleon turned to Jacques. "Would you concur, *Caporal* Gagne?"

Jacques managed an astonished, "Yes, Sire." Fivel must have mentioned him to the Emperor.

"Good. I would have shared some harsh words with your commissary officer if the verdict had been otherwise." Napoleon took a few more sips of the soup. "Have any of you men complaints that you wish to bring to my attention?"

The men looked dubious. It was the Emperor they were speaking to, after all.

"Come, come, my soldiers," said Napoleon with a kindness that was unfeigned. "Don't be shy. Surely there is something I can assist you with?"

"I could use some new shoes," stated Carnot matter-of-factly. "Marching 25 miles a day wears them out fast." Rather than being starstruck, he felt like he was talking to a fellow soldier who understood the harsh demands of a campaign. He held up the bottom of his left foot; his toes protruded.

"That is monstrous," remarked Napoleon angrily. "Are the shoes of the rest of you in such bad repair?"

The company showed their soles and heels; not a man had shoes that could be considered in good condition.

"A shipment of new shoes was sent to II Corps but appears to have not been issued. I promise you that II Corps will have a new quartermaster before midnight, and you shall all have new shoes by the time you march tomorrow."

The men smiled. Napoleon was a man of his word when it came to the everyday needs of his men.

"Any other complaints?"

The men shook their heads, then Rifle bounded up and began sniffing the Emperor's hand. The dog made his judgement and wagged his tail energetically. The Emperor petted him with evident pleasure. "Poodles have always been a favorite of mine. What is this noble beast's name?"

"Rifle, Sire," said Jacques.

"A good name for a battle dog. I will bet that he has brought you plenty of luck." Napoleon liked to know if a man or beast was lucky.

The men nodded.

"But he has no collar that bears that name. Allow me to attend to that personally."

The men smiled, pleased that he understood how a mascot boosts a unit's spirits.

Napoleon turned to Jacques.

"*Capitaine* Fivel has told me of your heroism, but I should like to hear the story from your own lips. Would you be kind enough to oblige me?"

"Of course, Sire." His mother's words came back to him: "Always speak plainly, never boast or bluster, and let others judge the merits of your deeds." He began haltingly, while Napoleon's grey eyes bored into his, but gradually his delivery became flowing and confident. The Emperor's intense eyes were all seeing; they radiated a hypnotic magnetism that had a strangely soothing effect. Napoleon gave Jacques his complete attention, making Jacques feel that he was now the most important man in the world. When Jacques finished, he felt strong enough to conquer the world.

Napoleon looked at him with admiration. "A fine tale, *Caporal,* but I suspect you were entirely too modest."

Jacques blushed.

"Such gallant behavior must be rewarded." Napoleon turned to Jacques' messmates. "I must ask you all to come to attention while I present a token of my esteem."

The men complied quickly, wondering what form the Emperor's esteem would take.

"And now, *Caporal* Gagne, prepare to receive The Legion of Honor."

Jacques stood razor straight and puffed out his chest. He felt like he had entered a fairy tale. The Legion was France's highest decoration for gallantry, rarely given to an enlisted man.

Napoleon took from his pocket a white and green Maltese cross with a laurel wreath on top, suspended from a red silk ribbon. It had a *bas relief* of himself in the center.

He placed the ribbon around Jacques' neck, stepped back, and saluted. "Welcome, Legionnaire."

Jacques returned the salute but was so overcome that he could barely speak. His response came out as a whisper. "Thank you, Sire."

Napoleon noted the men around Gagne were staring at him with awe. The Legion was just a bauble to him, but it was by such baubles that men were led.

In the shadows beyond the circle of light cast by the campfire, lurked LeMans. He had left his own mess with the intention of spying on young Gagne, thinking the cover of darkness might provide an opportunity for mischief. Now he spat in disgust that the Empire's highest award was being given to a weakling. When he disposed of the boy, he would make sure to pocket the medal.

Napoleon gave a playful tug of Jacques' earlobe: his odd way of making a direct physical connection with a man who had secured his favor. "I am sure your sweetheart will be pleased, *Caporal.*"

Jacques' face showed confusion.

"Ah," observed Napoleon, "you don't have a sweetheart. Well, you soon will. In fact, you will have your pick of the village girls!"

The assembled soldier's eyes sparkled with a mixture of amusement and longing as they thought of the women in their own villages.

Napoleon handed Jacques a pouch full of coins. "Appointment to the Legion carries with it an honorarium of 250 francs."

Jacques mouth fell open in shock. 250 francs was the equivalent of three-fourth's a year's pay.

"My soldiers, I would love to stay and talk more with you, but Monsieurs Wellington and Blucher require my attention. I promise you glorious victories. Remember: Wellington is a mere sepoy general and Blucher is but an angry old man. It could be that any one of you standing before me will join *Caporal* Gagne as a member of the Legion in the days ahead. When I leave, every man here shall be issued a second ration of brandy."

Napoleon's words triggered joyful shouts of *"Vive l'Empereur! Vive l' Empereur! Vive l' Empereur!"*

Jacques' eyes filled with tears as the glory of this remarkable moment hit him fully. He could never go back to being what he had been, and he would be the Emperor's man for the rest of his days.

LeMans scowled and slunk off. Young Gagne was too much the center of attention for him to have a chance tonight; besides, he was still hungry, and there were soldiers who carelessly left their food bowls lying about.

At an adjacent campfire, Jelune looked up from his card game and in the direction of the loud cheering. *It couldn't be. It was not possible!* But the silhouette was unmistakable. He cursed that his greed had caused him to miss the chance of a lifetime.

As the Emperor disappeared into the distance, Jacques' eye picked out the camp follower whom he had been seeking. She waved at him from behind a tree, and he realized that she had probably seen Napoleon's presentation. She beckoned to him and smiled, her expression letting him know her services were available free to such a gallant soldier. His joy changed to lust, and he smiled back. He heard his mother's voice in his head whispering Quaker platitudes about not consorting with trollops, but right now he was not thinking with his brain. The banishment of his battle virginity had left him proud; the banishment of his physical virginity would leave him triumphant.

Napoleon observed the scene as he mounted his horse, and it pleased him. If virtue was not rewarded, it withered on the vine. Medals and money were well and good, but a carnal reward gave a young man a special kind of confidence that nothing else could replicate.

Jacques walked over to the woman. He had never really gotten a close look at her. She was about 5-foot-4 inches, with brown hair, green eyes, a long nose, and a pointed chin. It was an imperious face rather than a beautiful one, yet its character was alluring. She looked like she had seen tough times but had refused to be broken by them. She had looked forty at a distance, but up close, if one ignored the furrows of worry, she seemed not more than 23 or 24.

She wore her hair gathered up with a red scarf under a wide-brimmed straw hat and sported large bangle earrings. A close-fitting blue hussar jacket topped a long dress, and she was shod in brogans that were also army issue. A large haversack hung from her left shoulder, and a pipeclayed white belt encircled her waist, featuring the belly box cartridge pouch popular with *voltigeurs*. The musket leaning against a nearby tree probably belonged to her; Gagne noticed that it had been fired recently.

The musket was incongruous for a trollop but not for a *vivandiere*. He revised his estimate of her. Not a prostitute; likely she had been an army wife at some point, and some of her equipment had come from a deceased husband. His lust subsided. He wanted to know her story. He decided upon the direct approach. "I am Jacques Gagne, and it is a pleasure to meet you at last."

She smiled at him without coyness. "I already know your name. This meeting is not a coincidence: I have been following you for some time. Been your guardian angel in fact. Saved your life during the *uhlan* attack." She pointed to the musket.

Gagne searched his memory. A *uhlan* about to impale him had suddenly acquired a musket hole in his forehead from an unknown source. "I am much obliged. Have you a name?"

"Pauline Fourès."

"A Sergeant Fourès completed my training. He was a man I much admired."

"That was my husband. I miss him very much. He died from dysentery, but one of his company spread a rumor that I had poisoned him. It caused the regiment to shun me. That is why I have kept to the shadows. I have no one to trust and nowhere to go. I grew up in the army and it is the only life I know. I spotted you during training and, well... had a feeling about you. My instincts have never failed me, and they told me 'Here a good man with a kind heart.'"

"Why did you proposition me instead of introducing yourself?"

"I wanted you to come to me, rather than me appealing to you as a creature who would only excite your pity. You would have viewed me as a vagrant beggar, not seen me as a woman."

"So, you are not a prostitute but a widow in distress?"

"I have not yet been reduced to selling myself, but if things do not improve, I may have to resort to that. I have survived by hunting small game, but I am out of powder and shot. My last rounds were expended in your defense. I have buried two husbands, both fighting men. I would never want anything but a soldier for my next one."

"You are seeking a third husband?" He blinked in shock. "Are you considering me for that post?"

She laughed. "Don't look so frightened! I just want to get to know you for the time being. I offer myself to you as an introduction, but I do not do so casually."

Gagne wanted her badly, but his mother always told him that good things were worth waiting for. This was a woman of pride and dignity, worth more than a quick coupling behind a tree.

He said nothing for a full minute as he pondered his options: whether to be a paladin or pirate, Quaker or cad.

Pauline eyed him with worry, hoping her frankness had not offended him. Her two husbands had been good men, but not deep thinkers. It looked like Gagne was a man who took life very seriously and was determined to do the right thing rather than the easy thing.

When Gagne spoke, it was with a smile in his voice. "I like you. I want you. I might even come to need you. But not here, not now."

Pauline looked crestfallen.

"You misunderstand. I am not rejecting you, it's just that I am unwilling to settle for silver when I could have gold. I want to help, so I can see you at your best." He pulled out the pouch Napoleon had given him and extracted five gold coins worth a hundred francs. He squeezed her hand gently, then opened her palm and deposited the coins. "This should tide you over. Get some food, drink, and a new dress. Rent a room at an inn and get a decent night's sleep. When you are feeling better, come and talk with me. With your skill at tracking, I am sure you will know where to find me."

Tears sprang to Pauline's eyes. "I never imagined I would meet a Galahad. That is the kindest thing anyone has ever done for me. I see I was right about you. Give me two days and you will see a new woman."

"I like the old one quite a lot."

She kissed him hard, but it was with warmth rather than lust. "For luck!" she said, then kissed him again, more gently.

He had closed his eyes to absorb the huge weight of emotions that pummeled his heart and mind. He felt her lips retreat. When he opened his eyes, she was gone. She had left behind the red scarf that she had worn in her hair. He picked it up and realized she had left it to keep his memory of her fresh. It was her way of saying Au *revoir*, until we meet again, rather than A*dieu*, goodbye. Right now, he prized this scarf far more than his medal or the gold coins remaining in his purse.

"Damn fool," said Carnot, who had witnessed the scene.

"No, damn lucky," said Le Paul. "If only we all could meet women like that."

Chapter 7
The Ball that Bonaparte Spoiled

15 June 1815, 6p.m., Brussels

It took Pennywhistle and his entourage longer to reach Brussels than it had to traverse the roads that morning. Soldiers were moving about and townsfolk were fleeing. Barton immediately conveyed the map to Wellington, but the processing of the criminals was time consuming, and Pennywhistle felt he had to remain long enough to see that it went smoothly. One brigand broke almost immediately, begging the provost marshal not to turn him over to the Belgian authorities. The provost marshal agreed only if the man could provide a complete list of the British goods stolen by his master. As Barton translated, the brigand revealed an encyclopedic knowledge of Kinderdokken's operations. His accounting of barrels of flour, salt pork, and gunpowder stolen by his master indicated a haul worth close to 10,000 pounds.

Pennywhistle trusted only himself to see that his pledge to the Saxons was carried out correctly. He personally escorted them to the headquarters of Major von Hammerstein, Commander of the Saltzgitter Landwehr Battalion consisting of 22 officers and 622 men. Von Hammerstein welcomed the veterans with delight and swore them in immediately. He spoke to the assembled group with kindness and understanding, promising to treat them with the honor and dignity denied them by Blucher. The Saxons saluted von Hammerstein with three loud "Huzzahs!" though Pennywhistle had the impression they were intended just as much for him.

A joyful reunion with Sammie Jo's party followed at Lady Densham's. Hugs and stories of the past few months were exchanged, but baby Nicholas was the chief object of attention. Pennywhistle teared up as he held the frail infant in his arms. Sammie Jo had not told him their son's health was precarious, nor that, during the first week, she had feared that he might depart life at any moment. Pennywhistle knew that she had done so to spare him worry, but the smallness of the infant he held in his arms shocked him. She reassured him that the worst was past; the child's appetite was good and he was gaining weight, although his breathing problems persisted. The child's cooing delighted Pennywhistle and soothed his worry.

Sammie Jo knew another way to banish it, at least for the time being.

They retired to their room and made love twice in quick succession. The first round was hard, fast, and short, speaking of loneliness, physical need, and raw passion. The second was leisurely, the joining of two kindred souls. They lay quietly in each other's arms after the second release, two bodies silently conversing.

"You have no idea how much I have missed you," murmured Sammie Jo.

"I felt as though I was missing my right arm these past few months. I don't want to be parted from you for so long ever again. When this campaign is over, so is my military career."

"Are you sure? I believe you could end up as Commandant of the Corps.'

"When I first joined, becoming Commandant seemed the most glorious dream imaginable. Now... I just don't care. I am tired of war;

its trophies and emoluments mean nothing to me. I have lost too many friends and seen too many innocents suffer to think that war is anything but a terrible evil. I feel that I am encased in a world where everyone is striving for something not worth having. I will finish this campaign and then be done with this madness. I am concerned about Nicholas, and I want to be by his side as he grows up. I want more children, too. I want to wake up in bed every morning with you lying next to me, not a sword and a pistol because I fear an attack from enemy soldiers. I've spent much of my life killing people and destroying; I'd like to help people and build for a change. Perhaps we both need a fresh start. Now that peace has been made with America, we might consider your homeland. My half-brother left me a considerable amount of property in North Carolina. That might be an option worth exploring."

"I agree, but right now we must make it through the next few days. Do you think a fight with Bonaparte is imminent?"

"I am certain of it."

"I wish we could skip this damn ball. Margaret and the Earl are not going. Vienna gave them enough balls and soirees to last a lifetime, and they are enjoying playing the doting godparents."

"And you were the one who was so keen on me going earlier! But you were right then. Most of the Duke's senior officers will be present, and it is a good opportunity for me to gauge their mood and outlook. I assure you I would far prefer to stay here the rest of the night. I don't relish putting on my dress uniform and behaving like a good little soldier instead of staying put and being a husband and a father."

"Since we must go, I am glad my trunks arrived in time. Lady Densham is three inches shorter than I and none of her dresses will do. Do you think the dress I wore at the Razoumovsky Ball will serve?"

"It's probably too fancy. Remember, in Vienna you were in the presence of the crème de la crème of Europe: kings, czars, and emperors. Tonight, you will be facing... let's just say lesser lights. Appearing too well turned out might put some ladies noses out of joint. I would suggest something subdued in muted colors. Go easy on the jewelry, too. That blue silk frock with the high neck and puffy sleeves might be just the thing. It's in the best of taste. Your beauty is so great that you could be dressed like a washerwoman and you would still be the belle of the ball."

"You do know how to turn a girl's head." Sammie Jo smiled. The clock struck ten and she started. "I was so focused on you that I never heard the earlier chimes."

"Neither did I. We will just have to arrive fashionably late."

During their short journey to the ball, Pennywhistle's borrowed carriage passed groups of ten to twenty soldiers hurrying toward various regimental assembly points. The largest one would be in The Grand Place, the large central square that constituted the heart of Brussels, a place of magnificently extravagant gothic guild halls, a royal palace, and lots of hot chocolate shops whose scents permeated the square. He witnessed knots of three or four soldiers pouring onto the cobblestones from the taverns, inns, and homes where they had been quartered.

Two departing soldiers received hugs from an innkeeper's wife and a bottle of gin, a round of cheese, and a loaf of bread from the innkeeper himself; a testimony to the good behavior of British troops whose presence was welcomed.

Pennywhistle heard drums beating, bugles blowing, and bagpipes skirling as well as the creaking and clanking of artillery pieces and supply wagons moving forward. Uniformed messengers on horseback dashed by, and small gatherings of civilians normally abed conversed urgently on street quarters. This was a city in a state of animated expectancy.

Two of those urgently conversing civilians observed the approach of Pennywhistle's coach.

"There is a war on, and people are still going to parties! Who would believe it. Better lock up your daughter," said Hugo van Dreelin, a stocky man clad in the round hat, blue tailcoat, and grey trousers of a prosperous haberdasher. "Bonaparte's men will be hungry for women and not too particular about whether they are willing partners."

"I have already sent my wife and daughter to the country," replied Jan van der Beek, a spare man and a fellow member of one of the most powerful guilds in the city. "I dispatched all my bolts of fine wool and silk to the country yesterday as well, and closed my shop. The French will steal anything that is not hidden or locked down."

"Are you going to follow your family or remain in the city? Your opposition to the French the last time they were here was well known and might be a problem if Bonaparte wins the day."

"I'm staying," stated van der Beek. The British troops have impressed me, and I have confidence in Wellington."

"You think he can win?"

"I do. I know you think dancing has no place here, but the fact that Wellington told the Duchess to proceed with her ball tells me he is the confident, unflappable gentleman of whom I have heard so much. Unlike most of Bonaparte's opponents, I do not believe that the Duke fears him."

"I am staying as well, though for a more personal reason. My son Lucas is an ensign in Byleveldt's Battery of artillery. I believe he is stationed somewhere in the general vicinity of Quatre Bras."

"I had no idea." Van der Beek's voice rippled with concern. "I thought he was going to take over the family business."

"He is, God willing, but he has been drilling with the city militia for the past year. When Bonaparte returned, he answered our new King's call to arms. Since he knew his way around a drill book and liked matters technical, he was appointed an ensign of artillery. He takes his responsibility very seriously and drills his men hard," proclaimed van der Beek with pride.

"And yet, ... artillery."

"I am concerned, but he is doing a man's work, and if your wife and daughter are to have a home to return to, men like my son must do the needful thing. It is difficult. Some of his men wonder if they are fighting on the wrong side. He worries that in battle they may either run or defect."

"I have heard that Wellington has doubts about the loyalty of some of his Dutch and Belgian units," observed van Dreelin.

"I think I may have figured out a way to keep tabs on Lucas, improve morale, and assist the men of his company, all at the same time."

"How is that?"

"My son told me battle is a very thirsty business. I am in the process of organizing a small convoy of four wagons filled with water, beer, wine, and spirits. I have three wagons filled and could use your assistance preparing the final one. Some spare guilders from you would persuade a few reluctant wine merchants to surrender the last of their stocks. You would be an angel of mercy."

"Does that mean you would be staying to dispense your supplies?"

"It does."

"Am I right in thinking that it will be done under fire?"

"You are."

"So, you could die?"

"Quite possibly."

"Have you any official authorization?"

"None, but I have spoken with the captain in charge of supply convoy departing at 2 a.m. He winked at me and smiled. We would be unofficial but welcomed."

"This is madness," remonstrated van der Beek.

"Insane," agreed van Dreelin. "A middle-aged merchant playing a young man's game makes no sense, unless you factor in patriotism and paternal concern."

"My patriotism has always been based on coin, making Brussels strong by increasing the prosperity of the best of her guilds," confessed van der Beek. He stroked his chin in thought, then his eyes flashed as he reached a decision. "I am coming with you. I am about more than money!"

They clasped hands and a bargain was sealed. Both men were practical, prosperous businessmen, but this night they had just become something much more.

"If Lucas dies, God forbid," vowed van der Beek, "I shall be there to comfort you."

"I would ask more than that. I might be too distraught to manage his burial, so I would ask you to arrange it."

At ten minutes past 11, Sammie Jo and Pennywhistle alighted from their carriage a quarter block from the gatehouse of the Duke of Richmond's mansion at #23 *Rue Blanchisserie.* This was an area of the lower town dotted with residences; the administrative, royal, and guild buildings occupied nearly all of the upper town. The carriages of partygoers jammed the narrow streets surrounding the mansion, so a short walk was necessary. The Pennywhistles traversed an avenue of manicured trees and shrubs until they reached the ante room in front of the entrance.

"This don't look like no ballroom," scoffed Sammie Jo.

"This building was only recently converted to its present role," responded Pennywhistle. "It has been a workshop, carriage storage facility, and a children's playroom. When the Richmond's first arrived last year, many of their fourteen children played shuttlecock and battledore within. I understand Richmond leased it from a Swiss chap named Jean-Michel Simons, a carriage builder fallen on hard times."

"Not exactly the Razoumovsky Palace," observed Sammie Jo. "In fact, this 'mansion' is about the size of Razoumovsky's gatehouse." The Razoumovsky Ball had been attended by 4,000 guests, who were treated to a 36-course dinner and a concert composed and conducted by Beethoven.

Pennywhistle presented their formal invitation to a major who was acting as the major domo. They would have been greeted by the Duke and Duchess themselves had they arrived on time. The major whispered to a sergeant, who guided them from the ante room down the short corridor to the ballroom's entrance. He announced their arrival in stentorian tones that belonged in a barracks. All eyes regarded them, but only for an instant. The room vibrated with tension, and since the newcomers were not bearing any messages or dispatches, everyone went back to doing what they had been doing: dancing, gossiping, or gathering in small groups to speculate about Bonaparte's intentions and whereabouts.

Sammie Jo surveyed the ballroom and whispered to her husband. "I see what you mean about this place once being a carriage house; those beams above us look like they belong in a barn. But the wallpaper looks brand new. I can see plaster marks." The wallpaper was of a trellis and rose pattern, and was overlain with silver and gold swagging. Garlands adorned the swagging; copper, rather than crystal, chandeliers provided plenty of light. Red ribbons hung from the ceiling and rose petals covered the floor.

"It's certainly truncated," observed Pennywhistle. "This whole affair is the product of quick improvisation. Rather fitting, since the Duke's campaign will have to be quickly improvised as well."

"Life reflecting art, isn't that how you would put it?"

"Exactly. Although, speaking of art, I predict that when painters render tonight's events on canvas, fifty or sixty years hence, the result will appear far grander and more glamorous than the real event."

Sammie Jo stifled a laugh.

Pennywhistle did his own slow survey of the room. "The Earl informed me that 103 officers were invited. Adding their ladies and miscellaneous civilians, the attendance looks to be about 250 present. I see a fair number of nobles, and the royalty of the army is well represented. Look: two corps commanders, three divisional commanders, three brigade commanders, and at least 20 regimental commanders. The junior officers here are all well connected and influential beyond their actual ranks. "

"Shouldn't the officers be with their men, if a battle is just around the corner?"

"Judging by the number of soldiers we saw thronging the streets, I surmise Wellington's orders to the regiments, brigades, and divisions of his army were issued after the officers present had already departed for the evening's entertainment. I should not be surprised if in the next few hours messengers arrive informing the officers of developments and calling them away. But having most of the influential officers in one location is actually advantageous to Wellington. Should any actionable intelligence be received this evening, all his important officers will be in one place. That's far more convenient than having to send a slew of messengers speeding round to a variety of encampments."

"I'm still surprised the ball wasn't cancelled," said Sammie Jo.

"The Duchess asked Wellington if she should do just that. He told her to proceed. They are great friends, and he did not want to spoil the social event of the season. But I think he had another motive. The city is tense, and he wants to send a message that he has matters well in hand. It's a bit like Drake's response on being told the Spanish Armada loomed on the horizon: 'There is time for me to finish my game of bowls and beat the Spanish too.' I would also point out that the show of confidence is intended just as much for the friends of Bonaparte present tonight as for those who support the Allies."

Sammie Jo looked at him in puzzlement.

"There are prominent citizens here whom the Duchess would not want to slight, yet knows for a fact that they are not supporters of Britain and her allies. Probably a third of the city is generally sympathetic to Bonaparte."

"Like that old saying, 'Keep your friends close and your enemies closer.''

"And allow the spies among them to communicate to their master exactly the message you wish sent." If Bonaparte thinks the British are too distracted by a silly social event to ready themselves for his next strike, so much the better."

The orchestra of fifty stopped playing and the musicians took a short break. The dancers mingled with the rest of the crowd. The conversation became general, but both Pennywhistle and Sammie Jo knew that conversational tones were different from what you would hear at an ordinary ball. Instead of being relaxed and expansive, the conversations seemed hushed, hurried, and carried the taint of worry and desperation. The usual cheerful flirting and banter between the sexes was minimal, the laughter sounded brittle and hollow. The small knots of people reminded Pennywhistle of furtive conspirators discussing plots, possibilities, and timetables, wondering which of their members would still be alive several days hence.

The most telling oddity was the sobriety of the officers. Ordinarily most would have been sporting a happy glow, while a few would have been reeling drunk. The large punchbowl serving the gathering was down by only half, not empty and demanding a refill as would have been usual in happier times. The officers present instinctively understood that with a battle imminent, an extended conversation with John Barleycorn would make them vulnerable to the traps laid by his good friend, the Grim Reaper.

"We've got about twenty minutes until the next dance," said Pennywhistle to Sammie Jo. "Why don't we split up and mingle. We can reunite when the waltz is played and compare notes."

"Good plan. You handle the military gossip, and I will take care of the civilian side. I see our hostess. The Duke believed she would like to meet me and I think it's time to oblige her." Sammie Jo's eyes alighted on a passing officer dressed brilliantly but cursed with one of the ugliest faces she had ever seen. He appeared to be making friendly eye contact with a young lady of fashion, who returned his glance with scowling eyes then flounced away.

Pennywhistle noticed her observing the two and answered her unasked question. "That is Henry Hotham, one of the richest officers in the army — and one of the most miserly. She is Lady Georgiana Lennox, one of the Duke of Richmond's seven daughters. Her father and mother sought to arrange a match between the two, but she was having none of it. They were exceedingly disappointed, but it appears Hotham has not yet abandoned hope."

"Good for her! I can't imagine waking up every morning next to someone who would give Medusa a fright. Nice to see someone with an independent streak. I get why marriages are arranged, but the idea still runs counter to my nature. Compatibility matters!"

"I agree, but the peculiar circumstances that brought us together would be very difficult to duplicate. As for the Duchess, she certainly has her finger directly on the pulse of this gathering. Ah! I see two prominent naval officers I should like to speak to. I have heard the army's assessment of our present situation; now I would like to get the Navy's." He kissed Sammie Jo quickly. "Remember that most of the women here have not set foot in Europe for a long time and will be eager for news of the latest fashions. It's a certainty that none of them have ever danced with a czar."

Sammie Jo chuckled. "Ain't that a hoot. A little ol' country girl from America knowing more about what's fashionable than women with family lineages as long as your arm."

Pennywhistle and Sammie Jo separated and embarked on their separate missions. Pennywhistle walked over to the two naval officers, who were in an animated conversation that looked on the verge of transitioning to a heated argument. He had met Rear-Admiral Sir Pulteney Malcolm after Trafalgar and liked him. A straightforward Scot with a distinguished battle record, Malcolm currently commanded a squadron in the North Sea that protected the Scheldt Estuary and the key port of Antwerp. He thus corresponded regularly with Pennywhistle. Like Pennywhistle, he favored Nelson's approach to discipline, looking for the best in a man and cultivating it, rather than assuming the worst and using the lash to suppress it.

Pennywhistle recognized the other man, Vice Admiral Sir Sydney Smith, from Vienna, where he had been an unaccredited, informal member of the British diplomatic community. His salon had attracted a well-connected following, and Smith had sometimes provided Pennywhistle with tidbits of gossip that had helped in negotiations. Pennywhistle considered him a brilliant, ingenious, and resourceful man, though his argumentative nature sometimes left Pennywhistle feeling drained after an extended conversation. He was as eccentric and theatrical as Lord Cochrane. He was also one of the few men living who could say he had beaten Bonaparte: that had been at the siege of Acre in 1799. Napoleon had remarked of Sir Sidney, "He cheated me of my destiny."

Smith's chief problem was his arrogance: he always had to be the brightest light in a room. He thought he knew better than anyone else — and mostly he did, but he never failed to let others know that he was cleverer than they could ever be. He treated orders as mere suggestions. When under Nelson's command, the two had butted heads frequently. Loved by those who served under him, he was resented by his peers. Currently he was heavily in debt, on his way back to England to secure reimbursement for his services in Vienna.

"Good evening, gentlemen," murmured Pennywhistle in his most soothing tones. "I hope you do not mind my intruding on your conversation. I should welcome your take on the events now unfolding."

The two men smiled at him briefly, seemingly relieved that their contentious exchange had acquired a referee.

"Good to see you again, Sir Thomas." Malcolm said heartily.

"A pleasure, Sir Thomas," said Smith politely.

"The honor is mine," replied Pennywhistle.

Brief bows were exchanged.

"You have faced Bonaparte before, Sir Sydney, while most of us here have not. What do you think are his present intentions?"

Smith loved playing the expert. "Bonaparte is aggressive and will come at us from the East. I suspect he has advanced much farther than the Duke guesses. If I were he, I would not do the expected and advance directly on Brussels. I would execute a flanking movement toward the village of Ligny, smash Blucher, then proceed to Quatre Bras and beat Wellington before he can assemble his scattered forces. I should not be surprised if he launches an attack on Blucher by midday tomorrow."

"That soon?"

"Yes, Sir Thomas. Speed and surprise are the only ways he can win. And I fear that he may have stolen 24 hours' march on Wellington."

"I think you are wrong, Sir Sydney," retorted Malcolm. "Bonaparte is a master strategist and will come at us from the West; he knows the best way to destroy an army is to cut its supply line. He will circle round Wellington's right flank near Hal, then sever his supply line to Ostend."

"Most interesting, gentlemen. You both offer cogent arguments, yet the fog of war is a very real phenomenon. The information that Wellington has received so far is spotty and confusing. General von Dornberg's outpost cavalry skirmished with Bonaparte's men this morning near Mons, and he sent a message to that effect that arrived around five. Bonaparte has crossed the frontier, but his men are spread out; von Dornberg was unable to discover if his main thrust would be to the east, north, or west. Von Zieten's 1st Corps of Prussians fought a short but spirited engagement with the French at Thuin, 20 kilometers southeast of Mons and 10 kilometers southwest of Charleroi. The message von Zieten had sent was similarly inconclusive. Thus, much as Wellington wishes to deploy his forces, he must wait until he discerns which of Bonaparte's efforts are feints and which are main thrusts. He has given orders for the several divisions of his army to assemble at their headquarters and be ready to march at a moment's notice. There is a rumor that the Prince of Orange has sent a Nassau brigade to the hamlet of Quatre Bras, so that may provide a clue as to the directions of Wellington's next movements. But rumors abound tonight, and it is difficult to discriminate between fact and speculation."

Sammie Jo introduced herself to the Duchess of Richmond. Custom dictated a lady should wait to be introduced by someone of higher rank, but Sammie Jo knew the Duchess wanted to meet her and decided not to stand on ceremony. Soon the two women were conversing like old friends. The Duchess liked eccentrics and Sammie Jo certainly fit that bill. Her American background intrigued her hostess, since the only American she had ever met was Colonel DeLancy, Wellington's chief of staff. Other ladies joined them until there was a large circle around Sammie Jo. She gratified everyone's curiosity about Vienna fashions. She answered scores of questions about who wore what, who ate what, and who was involved with whom. It amused her that she was being elevated to the position of influential social arbiter. Everyone laughed at her story about how she had rejected Czar Alexander's advances, and they gasped to hear that Chancellor Metternich and Czar Alexander had nearly fought a duel over the favor of the Duchess Sagan. The women were eager, even desperate, to pretend to the nonexistence of the elephant in the room, that many of their beaux would die in the hours ahead.

Sammie Jo excused herself when the orchestra musicians resumed their seats and the conductor rang a bell, signaling that a dance would commence in two minutes. As she approached her husband, Lady Mary Alvanley pulled her aside. Tall, spare, sixty years old, and with a judgmental gleam in her death-grey eyes, she exuded an intimidating dignity. Her expression indicated that she had not enjoyed Sammie

Jo's informality and was determined to censure her. "I heard your annoying little stories," she began in an imperious voice, "and I shudder to think of the pall you cast over the British diplomatic community in Vienna. You are an ill-bred upstart who does not deserve the title of lady. You neither know your place nor how to speak to your betters. I can't see how you gulled a scion of a respectable family into marrying you."

Sammie Jo knew these sentiments were shared by many people in her husband's social set. Usually she disregarded the glares and snubs, but tonight her dander was up. "Maybe Ah am an upstart," she drawled, deliberately emphasizing her backwoods dialect, "but Ah count Mistah Playun Truth among my friends, and Ah ain't shoah you've ever met that particulah gentleman, preferring the company as you do of his no account cousin, Mistah Privilege. Mah husband choose me because Ah *wasn't* a scheming fawtune-huntah, despahrate foah a husband with a title, but a woman who could howald huh own, and who knew a good mayun when she found him. If the Duchess accepts me foah who and what Ah am, why should Ah be afraid of a li'l old pissant like yoahself?"

Alvanley froze in shock. She had never been spoken to so impudently.

Sammie Jo's eyes sparkled like ice crystals. Her voice become honey-coated thorns, snd now she spoke in her clearest accents. "I am worth my weight in wildcats. I've lived a life of adventure, while you followed the rules. And I'll bet it's been damn boring. As for my husband, he ain't blinded by prestige, and he married me out of love. The magic we have is rare, and I can see why an old prune would envy something that she will never know."

Alvanley put her hands on her hips and glared. "Well, I never—"

"You got that right. I wouldn't trade my life for yours for all the wealth in King Solomon's mines. I've met kings, emperors, and czars. How many do you know?" Sammie Jo gave a mocking curtsey, then turned on her heel and sashayed away.

The music started up with an introductory passage. As she and Pennywhistle prepared for the waltz, they shared what they had found.

"Well, Sugar Plum, As I see it, most of these women are plain scared. They remind me of pregnant women expecting to go into labor at any moment who've been told their babies might not survive. Believe me, I know how that feels."

"Their fears are understandable. Without question, some of these officers will not live to see their homes again. As for my reconnaissance, my two naval acquaintances offered compelling arguments about Bonaparte's intentions that were mutually exclusive. We shall have to bide our time and await developments. Perhaps we shall know more when Wellington arrives. It's nearly midnight, and I find it telling that he has made no appearance yet. Let us dance until the Duke arrives or until supper is served. According to our invitation, it is scheduled for 1 a.m. We can at least pretend to forget the dangers hovering offstage and focus on the pleasures of the present moment."

Pennywhistle took Sammie Jo in his arms as the waltz proper began. Both counted to three before cueing themselves to the beat of the music and surrendering to the commands of ¾ time. The duo were skilled dancers, and their gracefully executed swirls, twirls, and exquisite footsteps were performed more neatly and precisely than those of the other couples on the floor. Several doughty senior officers paired with younger partners paid close attention. These gentlemen had been taking dance lessons, just not enough of them. Two subalterns and their partners sought to copy their movements as well, but they'd had numerous glasses of punch and their efforts resulted in crushed toes and graceless movements. Five other dances followed, featuring varied tempos and steps: a minuet, a reel, a quadrillion, a polonaise, and a sarabande.

The oddest thing was the presence of three children scampering about. Sammie Jo had no idea how they had gotten there or to whom they belonged, but they seemed to be having a fine time playing hide and seek among the dancers and dignitaries. One boy who looked about ten raced toward the sitting Duke of Brunswick and plopped himself on the duke's knee.

"That young fellow is the Prince Eugen Lamoral de Ligne," murmured Pennywhistle, "son of the Countess Oultremont. I believe the other two children are his siblings. Brunswick is an amiable fellow and behaves like a godfather towards them."

Sammie Jo's perceptive eyes assessed the fashions that both sexes were eager to show off. While the men's scarlet uniforms were colorful, dashing, and well cut, the women's dresses looked fashionable only if one pretended it was 1803, the last year British women in any numbers had been able to visit the Continent. The gowns were made of satin, silk, damask, or taffeta and came in royal blue, ghost white, ice grey, evening teal, morning peach, or bottle green. Most featured décolletage that was considered daring in Britain but reckoned hopelessly déclassé by Continental mavens of fashion. At least the hair styles were in keeping with European tastes: lots of buns, Psyche knots, braids, and ringlets, copied from those found on Roman statuary.

Expending nervous energy through dance eased the tension but did not come close to eliminating it. The orchestra stopped briefly to allow the dancers to catch their breath, then four kilted sergeants stepped onto the main floor. Lieutenant Colonel Claude Alexander of the 92nd saluted his Colonel, Sir John Cameron of Fassiefern, with a sword.

Pipe Major Alexander Cameron stepped forward with his bagpipe. The sergeants crossed four claybegs on the floor: double edged, basket-hilted swords erroneously called claymores by non-Scots. Pipe Major Cameron announced that the tune he was about to play was called "Ghillie Callum" which had first been played after the defeat of one of Macbeth's chieftains at Dunsinane in 1054.

"The Duchess' father was the colonel of a regiment, and she loves Highland dancing," whispered Pennywhistle. "I think this is meant to entertain the Belgians; they have been captivated by the kilts and exotic ways of the Scots soldiers stationed in the city."

Sammie Jo smiled. "Men in dresses playing footsie with swords. That is exotic."

"That's uncharitable, Hawkeye. They are splendid warriors. The French once called these men 'the ladies from hell'."

Cameron brought the mouthpiece to his lips and commenced blowing. A pipe major had to have exceptional skill with the bagpipe as well as exceptional lung capacity. The distinctive sound of bagpipes was beloved in Scotland but sometimes received mixed reviews in other countries: its friends averred that bagpipes 'skirled', its detractors insisted they squealed. Sammie Jo was of the latter persuasion; to her the sound was a combination of dying pigs, scalded cats, and cawing crows.

The dancers first danced outside the weapons, and then danced across them. They used a fast, exact step to avoid touching the blades, which tradition held would bring bad luck. As the dance continued, the pace speeded up; kilts twirled and hands held high slashed motions through the air that mimicked a broadsword in action. The tempo increased to a frenzy and the men's feet moved with blinding speed. The music reached a resounding crescendo then ceased abruptly. The crowd broke into thunderous applause in which Sammie Jo did not join. She found the performance more curious than compelling. Her husband, who was half Scots, clearly enjoyed it.

The Pipe Major then played a quick tune that brought smiles to the Duchess of Richmond. "Lady Charlotte Gordon's Reel" had been composed in her honor, reflecting the title that she had held before her marriage.

Pennywhistle noticed the arrival of three messengers during its performance. They spoke in hushed tones to three senior officers, who discreetly departed. Wellington must have issued orders.

The orchestra struck up a stately polonaise. The room had grown humid from all the dancing. Two officers remedied the situation by opening the large French doors to admit a cooling breeze.

Just after midnight Wellington entered the room. All eyes fixed on him. He was wearing his brilliant scarlet coat replete with his many orders and decorations, which he wore only on ceremonial occasions. For battle he always wore civilian attire: a blue frock coat, white kidskin breeches, and the distinctive boots that would eventually be given his name. It was a simple outfit that made him easily identifiable on the battlefield. Ironically, this and was of a piece with Bonaparte's approach to military dress. Bonaparte generally wore the basic uniform of a colonel of *chasseurs à cheval*, which distinguished him from his marshals who wore the gaudiest and most elaborate uniforms possible.

Wellington was accompanied by Baron Friedrich von Muffling, a Prussian colonel and liaison officer. A messenger dashed up to Wellington with a dispatch that he read quickly. The messenger was Charles Lennox, Earl of March, son of the Duchess and brother of Lady Georgiana Lennox. Sammie Jo recognized him, and instantly realized he was not here to claim a dance. Lennox's 17-year-old sister, who was a particular favorite of Wellington, broke off her dance and walked briskly up to the Duke. Pennywhistle and Sammie Jo moved closer.

"Are the rumors true that Bonaparte has entered Belgium?"

"Yes, they are true; we are off tomorrow." Pennywhistle noted that Wellington spoke loudly, clearly wanting his response to be heard. He briefly conferred with the Prince of Orange, then began chatting with the ladies who had gathered round him. Pennywhistle knew that he was charming the ladies to allay their fears. A ripple of excitement spread through the crowd. Several officers took leave of their ladies and quietly exited the room.

"What do you plan to do, Tom?" asked Sammie Jo.

"My job is to secure the supply line from Ostend to Antwerp and thence to Brussels, but I have already done that. The route is well guarded and supply wagons are arriving as scheduled. Right now, I am something of a fifth wheel, but Wellington is desperately short of aides, and I expect I can make myself useful in that respect. He knows that I share his regard for proper logistics. I shall just have to do as he has done with respect to Bonaparte: wait and see."

Wellington continued to chat with the ladies, staging his own version of a Kabuki drama of pretended serenity. It was moderately effective, but small groups of officers continued to slip away.

The orchestra played various dances, though fewer and fewer couples took to the dance floor.

An aide to the Prince of Orange arrived; Pennywhistle recognized him as Lieutenant Henry Webster of the 9th Light Dragoons. Webster strode over to the Prince and handed him a dispatch. The Prince glanced over it and looked puzzled; he was personally brave but an inept commander and not quite sure what to make of the dispatch. He passed it to Wellington, who read it quickly, frowned, conferred briefly with the prince, then signaled to the orchestra conductor that he wanted him to resume playing.

The conductor began a lively waltz. Worried looks were exchanged between women and their beaux, and desperate contingency plans were hatched. Sammie Jo sympathized; she knew her time with her husband was growing short.

Pennywhistle checked his watch: 12:15. "Wellington is trying to spread calm, but I infer from the number of departures that Bonaparte has humbugged us and now we must make haste to catch up. It's time for me to report in. Get back to Lady Densham's and keep yourself and Nicholas safe. Guard Diable carefully. If the day goes against us and civilians in the city panic, everyone will want to flee, and good horses will be as rare as hen's teeth."

"No, Tom, the Earl has another horse I can use. You will need Diable's speed to get clear of any tight spots. And I know you will be in plenty of them."

"He is a spirited animal, and I am not a good horseman."

"I've gentled him down enough that you'll be able to manage. I will fetch him here."

"Very well, Hawkeye. I know Wellington: he will try to maintain the appearance of the status quo and so will stay here at least until he finishes supper. That will probably be my last meal for quite a while. That gives you about ninety minutes to run a few errands." He reached into his pocket and extracted a short list which he handed to Sammie Jo. "These items would be helpful, though I can survive without them."

She glanced over the list and nodded. "I will pack a picnic hamper as well: Smithfield ham, a round of cheese, bread, those waffles you told me you like, and some hard candy for quick energy. I will send several bottles of root beer. — oops! I keep forgetting the English call it spruce beer — and ask Lady Densham to select her best bottle of wine from her cellar."

"Excellent. Get a message to Rogers that I will grant his wish, and bring him with you. And pay a call on Maxwell at his quarters at #2 *Rue Basse*. He is probably ensconced in some den of iniquity or gambling, but you might apprehend him, and he is assigned to me. I shall meet you where we parked our carriage. And bring Nicolas with you. In case the worst happens, I want to kiss him goodbye. For now, I must depart." He kissed her hard and was gone.

Damn it, thought Sammie Jo. *I thought I would have him for a few more days. I hate war!*

Wellington behaved as Pennywhistle expected. He alternated conversing with women and officers, his expression growing grimmer and grimmer despite his attempts to convey the impression of an even keel in heavy seas. Pennywhistle waited for an opportunity to speak to Wellington privately for a few moments, but none came.

The trickle of officers leaving the ball progressed to a steady stream. The Duchess positioned herself at the entrance to the ballroom and implored exiting officers, "Please, please don't leave. You will ruin my ball." Most made polite excuses and left anyway.

Wellington rallied to her defense by making an elaborate show of going upstairs for supper. A gaggle of officers followed him. Pennywhistle joined the retinue, still hoping for a short private audience. The orchestra moved upstairs as well and serenaded the dwindling crowd as they supped on chicken broth, cold cuts, and sweetmeats. The majority of diners were women.

Wellington rose at 1:45, announcing he needed to grab a few hours sleep. As he headed toward an exit, Pennywhistle seized his moment and finally got his private audience.

"Your Grace, how may I be of service? I have not yet received any orders and wish to help."

"Ah, yes, Pennywhistle. I do have an assignment for you. There has been skirmishing at Quatre Bras, where I shall be headed in a few hours. I think a sharp contest likely there on the morrow. Though most of the men are being issued 60 rounds as we speak, we may burn through that quickly. A convoy of ammunition wagons should be arriving from Antwerp in the next hour or so."

"I am aware of that, Your Grace."

"I want you to see to it that the convoy arrives in Quatre Bras at the earliest possible moment. Those two wagons you rescued yesterday will be part of it. I can spare ten hussars from the King's German Legion for escorts, and you may select any personal assistants you deem necessary. The roads will be crowded, so you will have to be as much of a traffic manager as a soldier. I caution you to be alert for stray French cavalry patrols bent on mischief. I know it's not an assignment you would wish for, but I cannot spare anyone else, and that ammunition may prove critical to our success."

"I quite understand, Your Grace. I will do my duty."

"I never had any doubt. Now if you will excuse me, I need to seize a few hours sleep. I shall depart the city by eight."

"I shall be on the road as quickly as possible, sir." Pennywhistle saluted, which the Duke returned, then left the room.

As Pennywhistle exited the ballroom he overheard Lord Uxbridge, Wellington's second in command, speaking to young officers who had just arrived. "So, the French have engaged us at Frasnes? That is unexpected. The French are less than 30 miles from Brussels. That's two days average march or one day's hard march." He turned to the few officers still dancing in the ballroom and spoke loudly, "You gentlemen who have engaged partners had best finish your dance and get to your quarters as fast as you can."

The orchestra played "Auld Lang Syne" as the last officers departed.

Pennywhistle calculated it would take two hours to organize the convoy and get it moving. At best, it would be 4 am before the wagons were ready to roll. Assuming things went well — always an unwise assumption in war — the wagons might make 4 miles an hour. Quatre Bras was 27 miles away. Allowing for stops to rest, feed, and water the horses, he might arrive there as soon as 2 pm; but of course, a stray French cavalry patrol could slow that timetable. His job would not be the kind that found its way into any history books, but it was vital, and he had long ago lost any thirst for glory. As Wellington had often remarked, "The amateur soldier worries about tactics, the professional about logistics."

Chapter 8
Old Debts and a Second Chance

15 June 1815, 8 p.m. Brussels

Ensign Maxwell returned to his quarters and did what he usually did at day's end: he poured himself a strong drink, dropped into an old leather chair, and began planning a night of gambling and debauchery. The company he attracted on those outings were acquaintances of convenience rather than friends, even more debased and rudderless than he. He did not have to report back to Pennywhistle for 12 hours, so he had plenty of time for revelry. Pennywhistle had warned him to stay alert because events were approaching a crisis, but he dismissed this; the colonel was being an alarmist.

He picked up the engraved invitation to the Duchess of Richmond's Ball from the table next to the chair, stared at it, and laughed. Normally the Duchess would never have sent an invitation to a lowly ensign; the invitation was clearly his grandmother's doing: yet another example of how privilege worked. His grandmother loved him after a fashion, but her primary concern was advancing family members to positions of influence so that the family would gain greater glory.

Maxwell's had never worked for anything in his life, until today. He had been deemed incorrigible growing up, but his father had covered up his misdeeds until, at age 18, he had caused a scandal. His father had packed him off to the army. His army superiors, not daring to offend his influential family, gave him easy assignments and made excuses to the effect that "the lad is just sowing a few wild oats."

The twenty pounds he'd won from Pennywhistle's bet represented a kind of effort he had never made before: studied inaction. Strangely, keeping his mouth shut had opened his eyes and ears. He'd seen and listened to the sights and sounds of the convoy as it moved, watching good soldiers go about their business without any fuss or fanfare. The soldiers displayed a sense of purpose — something that had been absent in his life. The Saxons in particular demonstrated a degree of commitment he could not help but admire. He had never committed to anything, save the headlong pursuit of his own pleasure.

"Grow up! I am not your damn babysitter" — Pennywhistle's words echoed in his mind. The remark was insulting, but it carried the sting of truth. He had never really grown up. Shirking responsibility, living each day carelessly... on some level he knew he was wasting his life, but rather than confront that reality he plunged himself into reckless adventures. He was neither observant nor introspective, but he was not the complete fool that many, especially his father, believed him to be.

He took a long, greedy pull of his drink and reflected on the men he had killed in his first taste of combat. He would never know their names or backgrounds, yet he could recall every detail on their faces as they died. Their groans as life left them rang in his head as he stared at his drink. He wondered why anonymous dead men were spoiling the pleasure of his expensive Glen Livet.

He had once killed a man with his fists in a bar brawl, but the fights today felt different; the deaths he had inflicted had served a purpose. No charges had been filed after the bar brawl because his father had spread around large sums of money to the right people, including *wergild* to the man's family. He could not recall who had started the fight or what it had been about, not even the man's name. What he did recall vividly was an overwhelming feeling of rage. Once that fight started, his sole *raison d'etre* became beating his opponent to a bloody pulp, and the satisfaction of winning had burnished the image he had formed of himself: a man with whom strangers trifled at their peril and to whom women were drawn because of his strength.

No one had ever beaten him in a fight until this morning. Suddenly, the same rage he had experienced during the bar brawl swept over him like a hurricane, and he pounded his fist on the table as he saw Thomas Pennywhistle's face in his mind's eye. He wanted him dead! Not an easy death but an excruciatingly painful one. His fertile imagination began to conjure ways to bring that about.

The muscles in his neck seized up and for a moment he could hardly breathe. His right eyelid commenced twitching, he shuddered violently, and he compulsively clasped and unclasped his left hand. The rage was so great that he feared he was going mad. Madness ran in the family; his grandfather had died a raving lunatic. Maxwell's own dread of madness had at times been so great he had come perilously close to a drastic solution. On one occasion, he had placed a loaded pistol under his tongue. Now he topped off his drink, took a quick gulp, and did what he always did in these situations. He began to write.

His quill committed his darkest and most perverse thoughts about Pennywhistle to paper. As the terrible sentences unfurled, the madness began to abate. Each word reclaimed a piece of his soul from the monster that possessed it, because writing functioned like a lightning rod: attracting dangerous energies then sending them to earth. He wrote for an hour, and at its end he placed the letter atop a pile of others that he intended to burn. He burned his letters once a month.

The height of the stack worried him, and he wondered if it was time to reconsider his bully boy personality. Pennywhistle had been generous in victory; showing no animus and promising him a clean slate. "Bombproofed" seemed to think his belligerent personality could be put to good military use.

The life of a staff officer had bored him, but he liked to fight, and since he was in the military he'd decided to learn about military weapons. Out of his own funds he had hired a series of tutors in marksmanship, fencing, and riding. He had enjoyed his lessons, and his instructors had remarked that he showed a natural affinity with weapons, as well as being blessed with sound instincts and exceptional hand and eye coordination.

He took a few more sips of his drink. Perhaps he was doing this soul searching because he knew he had reached the limit of the protection that privilege could offer him. Wellington had little tolerance for bad officers, and he would have cashiered any other ensign long ago. That he had turned him over to Pennywhistle's untender mercies meant he had reached the limit of his patience. He guessed that Wellington had told the colonel something on the order of "Either fix Maxwell or throw him in the dust bin." He'd initially viewed Pennywhistle as a tormentor, but wondered now if he'd gotten it backwards: the man might show him how to turn the military into a career rather using it as a way station on a journey to oblivion.

A memory came to mind: Lady Pennywhistle on horseback, hugging her husband and regarding him with naked hunger. The image was arousing. He pictured her writhing and moaning in his bed. That she was remarkably self-possessed, fierce-willed, and saw him in adversarial terms added to her appeal. Then he reproached himself. Poaching a man's wife had never presented problems, but it now seemed... ugly. The bonds between her and Pennywhistle were much stronger than what he was used to seeing in marriages of convenience or necessity, and he realized he envied something that he had never had, something he might not even be capable of.

He finished his drink and poured himself another. Alcohol usually liberated a burst of voluptuary optimism and a surge of confidence, but tonight it was provoking a long, thorough look into the mirror of his own soul, and he did not like what he was seeing. The face staring back at him was a grotesque parody of his own handsome one: the eyes bleak and hollow, the cheeks lined and sunken, and the mouth frozen halfway between a frown and a snarl. It was the face of a self-destructive man who knew he was doomed but was powerless to stop himself.

He took a gulp of the Scotch, then set the glass down on the table. Part of him wanted to continue drinking to cast that horrid inner face into the pit of forgetfulness, but another part of him screamed that the face was that of what he would become, not what he was at this present moment. There was still a small candle of hope in his soul, but it was flickering, and its pale light was threatening to go out forever. Pennywhistle had averred that battle could change things quickly, and a big one that men might speak of for centuries could be mere days away. It was a once in a lifetime opportunity to chart a new course. He might perish, but even death would have more meaning than if he died from the ravages of a life of debauchery. He remembered what Macbeth had stated about The Thane of Cawdor: "Nothing became him in this life like the leaving of it."

He stared at his drink in anger, then picked it up and threw it across the room. A moment later he did the same thing with the bottle of Glen Livet. He checked his watch: Midnight. Late, but there was still time to attend the ball; it was only three blocks from his residence. Pennywhistle and his wife would be there. He would show himself capable of behaving like a gentleman rather than a barbarian. Wellington himself would be in attendance and might take note of his good behavior, which would reflect well on Sir Thomas. He rose to his feet, having had enough whiskey to numb his qualms but not impair his senses or his reflexes.

He changed quickly, strapped on his sword, then dashed down the stairs and walked briskly into the night. He was only a quarter block from his destination, approaching a line of waiting carriages, when his wayward past caught up with him. Three men stepped out from behind a blue and red carriage, blocking his path. "Hold it right there, Maxwell," rumbled a familiar and unwelcome voice. "I have been patient, but it's time to honor the promissory note you gave me. I figured you'd find your way to the Duchess' Ball and all I had to do was wait."

The voice belonged to Captain Hartwell Harcourt of the 3rd Regiment. He sounded drunk and aggressive. The two officers who stood behind him looked deep into their cups as well. "You owe me 200 pounds and it's time to pay up."

"My dear Captain Harcourt," snapped Maxwell with sarcasm, "I have written to Coutt's Bank in London for the funds but have not yet received them. There *is* a war on, you know. Or maybe you don't. You've been in the service ten years, and I do not believe you have ever seen any action save at the gaming tables. Whereas I killed a dozen men with my sword today, in the service of The Crown."

"Stuff and nonsense! A dozen fleas on the head of your latest tart, perhaps! Stop baiting me and start paying me! You used the same excuse last week and I am weary of waiting! But..." his eyes narrowed and he advanced two steps, "I am prepared to accept something as a downpayment. Your oh-so-fancy sword will do nicely. My own wants replacement and your saber is an Osborn of Birmingham, crafted by the King's own sword maker. Just the sort of weapon for a man such as I."

Maxwell bristled. No officer of character would surrender his sword without a fight, certainly not a sword that had just drawn its first blood. Harcourt wanted the sword not for its value but to humiliate Maxwell in front of his friends. "Satan and all the imps of hell shall not take it from me! But I have 20 pounds on my person and I offer it to you."

Harcourt exchanged looks with his friends. Maxwell realized to his chagrin that Harcourt and his companions were rakes on a tear — not so very different from himself. Their dissolute and jaded faces were cousins to the one that had glared back at him from the mirror of his soul.

"How about this, Maxwell. I will take your sword *and* your money, and grant you a week's grace."

Harcourt's friends snickered.

"No!" Maxwell riposted. "Consider the offer rescinded. You will get your money in full when it arrives. I give you my word as a gentleman."

"Your word, your *word*?" Harcourt laughed derisively. "That's worth no more than a whore's Sunday promise that she will sin no more. I would run you through here and now, but dead men do not pay their bills!" Harcourt and his friends laughed evilly.

Maxwell wanted to arrive at the ball with dignity, with his uniform in a presentable state. On the other hand, his temper was surging on the rising tide of alcohol in his blood. He'd give one more warning. If it were ignored…. "I will say this only once. Stand aside and let me pass."

"Not likely," sneered Harcourt. "My friends and I—"

Maxwell's fist smashed into Harcourt's chin, lifting him off his feet and sending him sprawling. He turned his attention to the officer on Harcourt's left and floored him with a right cross. The third man in the trio threw a left hook at Maxwell, which he blocked easily. He was about to finish the man with an uppercut when a bright light flashed, cobblestones rushed up to meet him, and darkness engulfed him.

He had been hit from behind by a woman with a heavy cosh. She simpered at Harcourt. "Well ain't you boys in a pickle barrel. You should have known better than to take on that one. Everyone knows what a fighter he is. But I figured I'd help you out, since you three are my best customers."

Harcourt and his friends rose unsteadily to their feet. "Thanks, Marie," wheezed Harcourt. "He caught us off guard."

Marie laughed. "Your secret is safe with me. Now take what you want off that toff and come back to my place a. My two friends and I know how to soothe the pain of bruises."

Harcourt bent down and took Maxwell's sword and wallet. He also took his expensive Swiss watch. "And now, Marie, we are yours for the night. Lead on, fair lady."

The foursome strolled off for a night of bumps, tickles, laughs, and lust, but not before Harcourt's two companions administered several admonitory, muddy kicks to the unconscious Maxwell.

Maxwell felt himself being shaken awake. He had no idea who had hit him or how long he had been splayed on the cobbles. As his vision cleared, he found himself staring into the face of none other than Lady Pennywhistle.

"Looks like you ain't so tough as you advertise. I was on my way to the carriage parked over yonder when I spied you sprawled here. The French are on the move, and my husband thinks your worthless hide might have some value to him. What happened?"

"Ran into three acquaintances and we... had words. Someone must have hit me from behind." He rubbed the back of his head. "I was on my way to the ball."

"You were, were you? Hmph. My husband predicted I'd find you at a betting house or a bordello."

"No! It was my intention to see if I could be of service to Colonel Pennywhistle."

"You turning over a new leaf? That's as likely as a tiger losing his stripes."

"I don't blame you for being skeptical, but I want to chart a new course."

"Well, heavy seas lie ahead! My husband is more trusting than I will ever be, but I suppose you could be telling the truth. If you are, pull yourself together and assemble your kit. Then we must call upon Sergeant Rogers before rejoining my husband."

"The chap from the convoy?"

"The same. He wants a chance to fight, and now that the French are active my husband intends to give him that chance."

"I share his desire."

"We will see about that." Sammie Jo helped Maxwell do his feet. "You do realize that your sword is missing."

Maxwell stared in horror at the frog in his sword belt that was now empty of a sword and scabbard. He searched his pockets. "Damn it! The blackguards robbed me! I will get that sword back if it's the last thing I ever do! Those scoundrels—"

"There isn't time for that," Sammie Jo cut him off. "You can use my husband's spare sword. The troops will be marching soon and there's no time to waste.

"I will do my best." he swallowed his pride. "My lady."

"If you're going to be with my Tom, you're best better be damn good!"

Chapter 9
The War Wagons

16 June 1815, 2 a.m., Brussels

The haberdashers van Dreelin and van der Beek kept their convoy of four wagons moving steadily toward the city gate known locally as *Le Porte Napoleon*. They rode together in the driving box of one wagon; the three other vehicles were each manned by two volunteers from the Haberdashers' Guild, which had endorsed their errand of mercy. The extra manpower would be necessary to distribute their liquid supplies when they arrived at their destination. Though most of their cargo was water, they also had beer, wine, and spirits, which would have to be carefully policed, since soldiers liked to overindulge if given a chance.

Though it was 2 a.m., the city's street lights and the many additional lanterns that had been hung gave good illumination to avenues that were nearly as alive as at midday, with soldiers rushing about, civilians boarding carriages in preparation for flight, wagons of various kinds rumbling to unknown destinations, and couriers trotting briskly to deliver messages that in some cases meant life and death. The two haberdashers witnessed plenty of tearful farewells, and it seemed that every vagrant, urchin, and refugee in the city had taken to the streets to beg. Some women tossed loaves of bread to passing soldiers from second story windows, while others threw flowers.

Patrictic maidens stood on doorsteps, waving and shouting, *"Vive le Roi!"* or *"Vive Wellington!"* when soldiers marched past. A few cranky veterans defiantly bellowed *"Vive l'Empeurer"* from their windows, but rather than angering the Redcoats, it amused them.

Some of the smaller, fearful merchants had boarded up their shop windows; the more optimistic ones had set up small tables in front of their businesses to sell items that soldiers might find useful: sewing and mess kits, cups, mirrors, brushes, pins, pipes, playing cards pocketknives, razors, and dozens of other items. Informal food stands sprang up selling everything from apples to strawberries to hard sausage and rounds of cheese. Many of the soldiers had been paid recently and knew coins would do them no good on a battlefield; far better to exchange them for something of immediate benefit.

Fiddlers stood on street corners playing popular tunes and airs, some patriotic and pulse-pounding, some sentimental and sad, some silly and sidesplitting. "Johnny Cope", "Over the Hills and Far Away", and "Garryowen" were especially popular. The turned-up hats at the street musicians' feet gradually filled with coins.

Van Dreelin had started the wagons rolling early because he knew movement would be reduced to a crawl in a few hours as more and more soldiers reported to their assembly points.

"I wonder what my son is thinking at this moment," said van Dreelin.

"Probably wondering what you are doing," replied van der Beek. "Then seeing to the needs of his men."

"I pray that he is well."

"Lucas is a brave lad. He will weather the hours ahead, but I worry that we may face scavengers and robbers once we leave the city."

"I have considered that possibility. Perhaps the best way to gain protection is to find a military convoy to which we can attach ourselves. We could offer their men refreshment in return for protection."

"A fine idea, van Dreelin. Where do we find a convoy?"

There will be several on the road soon enough. We will let them find us, then strike a bargain."

"I hope to God this will be the end of war for a good long time. We have had 22 years of war, and I think how much wealthier the Haberdasher's Guild would be if the Revolution had never happened."

"At least the Revolution freed us from Austrian control. They were bad administrators who did not understand the role guilds play in Flanders' economics. It's a pity the Republic we established did not last."

"You can thank Napoleon for the end of the Republic. That's why Napoleon needs to go once and for all."

"What do you think of our new king, Willem I?"

"Too soon to tell. It's only a few months since the Congress of Vienna proclaimed him king. From what I have heard he looks favorably upon the Guilds and wants to expand industry and trade. I understand he wants to establish new universities which will be friendly to modern industries. On the other hand, I am a free thinker and I have heard he wants to reimpose the Dutch reformed faith on Belgium. I have also heard that he wants to discourage the speaking of the Walloon tongue, which would be bad for business."

"My opinion is that Belgium must eventually split off from the Netherlands and chart its own course as an independent nation."

The political discussion stopped abruptly as two rough looking men on scruffy horses pulled alongside van Dreelin and van der Beek's wagon. The one with a long scar down the left side of his face spoke. "Do you gentlemen and your cargo need any protection? My friend and

I will be glad to provide it. Can't be too careful. Some strange types prowling the streets."

Van Dreelin looked him up and down and didn't like what he saw. He glanced at van der Beek, who nodded. Van der Beek pushed aside the blanket covering his knees and raised his double-barreled shot gun, aiming it at the scar-faced man. "This is our answer. Now be gone before I use this."

The two toughs blanched in fear, clearly not expecting resistance from two mild looking middle-aged gentlemen. They quickly turned their horses away and departed.

"I am glad you insisted on the shotgun," said van der Beek."

"Even angels of mercy need protection. Those two may be only the first of the dangerous characters that we will encounter today. We must find some lasting protection quickly."

"Assuredly. We need real soldiers."

Pennywhistle trusted Sammie Jo completely, and tonight she kept her word and more. When Pennywhistle showed up at the rendezvous site he found Sammie Jo standing in front of her carriage, cradling Nicholas in one arm and holding the reins of Diable in her other hand. Maxwell, on horseback, was stationed a few feet to her left, and twenty feet behind him Sergeant Rogers sat atop the driving box of an ammunition wagon. Another sergeant sat in the driving box of a second wagon. It puzzled him that Rogers and his fellow NCO had known they would be under Pennywhistle's command even before he did, until he recalled Wellington mentioning that he had already issued orders.

Most surprising was the sight of Andrew Dale, clad in his old scarlet jacket and round hat, mounted on a black mare. His Baker rifle resided in a leather sheath attached to the saddle, and a brace of pistols were visible in holsters just astern of the saddle's pommel.

"What are you doing here, Dale? You're on the retired list, with a pension and a family. I don't want your son growing up without a father. Your place is at Lady Densham's, guarding your family."

"Begging your pardon, Colonel, but I think the battle to come will be the end of Bonaparte, and I want to be there when it happens. I thought I could stand down, but when Captain Thynne left to report back to his regiment, the old instincts woke up and I knew I had to get back in harness. My wife was not pleased, but she accepts that I could no more sit this one out than a guard dog could stand by and watch a fox raid a henhouse."

Pennywhistle knew it was pointless to argue, and having Dale at his back always made him breathe a little easier. With the solid build, ruddy cheeks, and dependable manner common to the English yeomanry from which he sprang, Dale was the quintessence of reliability. "I don't seem to have much say in the matter, do I? If you weren't retired I could order you to return, but as I am not your commanding officer I can only accept your decision."

"That's right, Colonel."

Pennywhistle turned toward Maxwell. "Glad to see you could make it to the party, Ensign." His voice had a stern edge. "Your dress uniform looks rather the worse for wear, but I shall refrain from asking how it got that way. All I need to know, Maxwell, is whether you ready to do your duty."

"Yes, Colonel." His eyes gleamed. "I am champing at the bit to slash any Johnny Crapaud who gets in my way!"

Pennywhistle smiled sardonically. "Then you may be disappointed. Our job is to provide an escort for an ammunition convoy to Quatre Bras. We will pick up the other four wagons at the supply depot on the

Rue de Lorraine as well as a contingent of ten hussars. It is my hope we will reach our destination unscathed."

"That's disappointing," remarked Maxwell sullenly. "I want some real action."

"The fortunes of war, Ensign, are not always to our liking. But our assignment may teach you a valuable lesson. Victory often goes, not to the army that fights hardest, but the army that is best supplied. No matter how brave men are, without bullets their courage is useless. Armies gobble ammunition the way a drunken spendthrift burns through money, and ammunition bankruptcy means death on the battlefield. Our task may lack glamour, but it is nonetheless vital."

"I see," Maxwell answered in a surly voice that suggested he did not.

Pennywhistle turned away from Maxwell to make his important farewells. He kissed Sammie Jo hard, then took Nicholas in his arms. He held the baby close, and tears started to his eyes. He kissed the child tenderly, then spoke in a quavering voice. "He looks so tiny, so helpless. Take care of him, keep him safe. I could not bear to lose him, anymore than I could bear to lose you." His arms enfolded his wife and child with all the love in his heart, and he mouthed a silent prayer for their welfare. The rational part of him believed God was a detached watchmaker who stood aside from his creations, but the sentimental part hoped that God might sometimes be induced to protect the valiant and the innocent.

Sammie Jo's pregnancy had come at a time when she had scrambled and struggled to survive, and she wondered if her strenuous activities had affected the delicate internal chemistry necessary to give birth to a robust child. Margaret had warned her to be more careful in future pregnancies, for what happened to the mother was transmitted to the child in the womb. The nagging guilt Sammie Jo felt led her to think that the quiet life that she and Tom contemplated would be of benefit, not just to them but to generations yet to come.

Maxwell was touched by the scene. Not by Pennywhistle's affection for his wife, but for his son. Maxwell possessed a secret: he had fathered a child he had never seen. The mother had been a servant girl in the employ his arranged fiancée. The pregnancy had queered what would have been a marriage between two great families. He had been packed off to the army; the girl and her child had been sent God knows where. To prevent any attempt to reach her, his furious father had refused to tell him what arrangements had been made. The child would be two years old now, though Maxwell did not even know if it was a boy or girl, alive or dead. He might be hell on wheels with adults, but he had always had a soft spot for children and enjoyed their company, seeing in them an innocence that he had been stolen from him by a father who always pushed too hard and too fast, who favored corporal punishment and humiliation over kind words.

He wondered if there might be some way to track down his lost child once the campaign was done. Of course, that was predicated on his surviving the campaign. He had a rare moment of pause as he realized that the men he had slain had been amateurs, and he would now be facing the finest fighting professionals in Europe.

Rogers was touched by the scene as well. He had a wife and two children back in Winchester. He had served thirteen years and only had one year to go until he could claim his pension. He and his wife had been frugal during their fifteen-year marriage, and had their eye on a small yeoman's farm run by an aging widower with no children. There was a quiet understanding that when Rogers collected his pension, the yeoman would sell them his farm. All Rogers had to do was survive the present campaign and a few months of uneventful garrison duty, then the life he had always wanted would be his.

Destination Waterloo

Sammie Jo pulled back from the long embrace, barely holding back her tears. She handed Pennywhistle a clothing sheath. "Inside is your undress uniform: I knew you'd want your working gear." He accepted this, then entered the carriage and changed quickly, finally feeling like a real soldier instead of the facsimile he had portrayed at the Ball. When he emerged, Sammie Jo brought Diable up to him.

"I have packed everything on your list in Diable's saddlebags, Tom. One contains food, one contains drink, one contains tools, and one contains cartridges. I put your Nock pistols in the saddle holsters, your cutlass in a saddle sheath, and your Ferguson Rifle in a saddle bucket. The only thing I could not pack was luck and my love."

Maxwell was impressed by her competence and attention to detail. He had never considered the possibility that a woman might provide the kind of assistance that made a man something more than he would ever be on his own, a woman who was a partner, not a pet or plaything.

Sammie Jo kissed Pennywhistle deeply, then her manner became brusque and gruff, the only way she could keep from breaking down. "Now you'd best be off. Don't take any damn fool chances, and don't try to be a hero. I swear to God if you get yourself killed, I will curse your memory for the rest of my days." Her voice softened. "Send word when you can. I have never loved anyone the way I have loved you."

Pennywhistle blinked hard as he mounted Diable. Then the sentimental husband disappeared, replaced by the military man. He turned to his small command. "Gentlemen, our destination is the depot on the *Rue de Lorraine*. Follow me, and let us make the best time we can."

What Pennywhistle did not know was that his convoy had a stowaway. Eleven-year-old Johnny had hidden himself behind the trunks on the luggage board at the rear of the carriage. He had slipped away when no one was looking, raised the tarp covering the powder barrels in the rear wagon, and hidden his small form there. He knew Pennywhistle would never have permitted him to come. Johnny had seen battle before; he had no illusions about what it portended, but he wanted to get a glimpse of Bonaparte: the great, bad man who had changed the face of Europe. It never occurred to him that if he got close enough to glimpse Bonaparte, that might be the last thing he ever saw.

A little way off, Van Dreelin and van der Beek saw Pennywhistle depart and decided to make a detour, hoping the distinguished looking British officer and his group were exactly the escort they needed.

Chapter 10
The Boy Who Cried "Hussar!"

16 June 1815, 7 a.m., near the hamlet of Quatre Bras

It was just after 7 am near the hamlet of Frasces, 4 kilometers south of Quatre Bras. There had been some skirmishing half a kilometer to the west yesterday, nothing of any great moment, but now the French *voltigeur* advance scouts had come under attack, and Colonel Tousseau had directed 1st company of the 1st Battalion forward to provide support.

"Battery halt and unlimber! Deploy in open order!" Fivel shouted. Jacques Gagne's men, posted on a low ridge, obeyed efficiently. The ground in front of their six-pounder was a field of green clover. The ridge overlooked a paved road called the *Chausse de Charleroi*. Their targets were green-coated skirmishers from Herzogtom-Nassau, a small German-speaking duchy on the Rhine, now affiliated with the Anglo-Allied efforts. Their musket rate of fire was half-hearted, what you would expect of inexperienced troops. However, the Nassauers had also brought up six guns, posted to cover a crossroads three hundred meters in front of Jacques' position. Fivel recognized their uniforms as belonging to Byleveldt's Battery, composed largely of recruits from Brussels and the southern Netherlands. Their fire was spotty and inaccurate.

Fivel's battery of six cannons was in position ninety seconds after unlimbering, and Jacques' six-pounder fired its first round shot thirty seconds after that. The thunderous discharges flushed clouds of birds from trees and pheasants from the meadows and hedges nearby; the vibrations from the guns' recoils startled waves of scampering field mice. Fivel, standing next to Jacques, unshipped his spyglass and examined the result of his battery's discharge.

"Excellent shooting, Jacques. Your round just dismounted one of their howitzers. One piece down, five to go."

"Thank you, Captain," Jacques replied. It was his first round fired as a gun commander. The result was more luck than calculation, since he had a lot to learn about aiming, but it boded well for the future.

A return shot from the Belgian battery whizzed over Jacques' head and buried itself in a small sandpit. His men laughed briefly, then commenced loading their piece. Jacques gave the command to fire.

The gun flamed, boomed, and shot backwards six feet. The crew manhandled it back into position and fired a second shot forty seconds later. This rate distressed Jacques; he wanted his crew capable of three rounds a minute. The pace improved as the crew hit his stride.

The five other guns of the battery kept up a steady fire. "One gun gone, one damaged, two caissons destroyed and ten men down!" shouted Fivel. "They will crack soon."

And then it happened. Carelessness, not the enemy, struck. A spongeman on gun five had not swabbed the cannon bore properly, and a ventsman had failed to cover the touch hole completely. Ramming caused compression that ignited a smoldering flannel fragment from the previous round. The premature explosion hurled the spongeman thirty feet in the air, still clutching his ramrod. The sight riveted the entire battery, which temporarily stopped firing. The spongeman cartwheeled twice, then plunged to earth, ricocheting off a rock into a patch of nettles. His crew rushed over to retrieve what they expected to find a corpse. To everyone's surprise, the man rose and began talking. Though he had powder burns on his face and hands, he appeared lucid and evidently had no broken bones. The ventsman was not so lucky. His thumb had been severely burned and he would likely lose it.

The cautionary tale warned Jacques to slow his guns rate of fire, and the other gun commanders did the same. That rate was still faster than the enemy guns, and the slower rate of discharge allowed for greater accuracy. The huge clouds of smoke generated by the guns made aiming increasingly difficult, but a brisk breeze created gaps long enough for the French to see their opponents for a few seconds. Jacques got a fast glimpse of the previously damaged enemy cannon. He cranked the elevating screw of his piece up a quarter degree, then gave the command to fire.

His round landed squarely on the enemy six-pounder's barrel, ripping it from the carriage and hurling it through the air. The ventsman, loader, gun captain, and three men near the limber were killed in midair by jagged, searingly hot bronze shards, chunks of their bodies flying in every direction. The remainder of the gun crew turned and fled, abandoning their caisson and a nearby ammunition wagon. The other gun crews panicked motions signaled that they had had enough. Their commander began shouting commands for his remaining crews to limber up and depart for a less exposed position.

A sudden gust cleared away the smoke and Jacques' men cheered at the ignominious departure of their foes. Small groups of French *voltigeurs* began to advance in short rushes, and the entire Nassau infantry began a hurried withdrawal.

Fivel strolled up to Jacques and clapped him on the shoulder. "Good shooting."

"Thank you, sir. Should we begin pushing the guns forward manually and switch to canister? Shower it on the retreating infantry from point blank range and turn a retreat into a rout?"

"No, we stay put and await orders."

"Shouldn't we 'march to the sound of the guns' as the Emperor says?"

"I would, but Reille has been instructed to advance no further than that farmhouse which the *voltigeurs* are approaching. Marshal Ney will be in charge today, and I do not expect him to show up until at least nine' clock."

"But, sir, it looks like more Belgians, Dutch, and Germans are arriving as we speak."

"We will push them out of the way soon enough."

"So, we do nothing?"

"No, Gagne, we eat, drink, and grab what rest we can. We should rejoice that the enemy's fire wounded but two of our men, and only slightly. The balls never touched them, only wood splinters generated by the ball's impacts. We will engage the enemy again soon enough. I don't think anyone got more than four hours sleep last night; the rest will do them good. And part of war is just waiting." He gestured to a group of 10 approaching foragers, each carrying two throttled chickens. "A feast awaits us, Gagne. A far better reward for our efforts than any medals, wouldn't you agree? Now why don't you have your crew build a campfire so they can enjoy their share."

"Very good, sir," he replied without enthusiasm. He ground his teeth in frustration as he turned away.

The chicken proved tasty, but Jacques did not enjoy it. His instinct was to push the cannons, Napoleon's "beautiful daughters", forward aggressively, as the Emperor had done on many occasions, and he would have been more than willing to stay hungry to do so. Sitting still and letting the enemy regroup made no sense; it was not what his uncle would have done. Every ounce of ground they did not gain, and every enemy they did not slay, spat on the memories of his friends who had died. He started briefly as he realized just how much he had changed in the last few days. The forgiving farm boy who was a friend to all was becoming a memory, yet he felt curiously untroubled.

He liked and respected Fivel but thought he was making a mistake. It was not his place to judge the actions of his superiors, yet the novelty of independent thinking felt right. Or was it a distrust of unquestionable authority that had only awaited the right circumstances to manifest?

He had defied his mother to join the service. She had wept and accused him of being "just like your uncle!" Both his parents considered his uncle a dyed-in-the-wool contrarian, a man who questioned everything, perpetually one step away from becoming an outlaw. Jacques wondered how much of his uncle's persona he could adopt without losing who he himself really was. That was the real question: who is Jacques Gagne? Two days ago, the answer would have been simple, but now he was seeing sides to himself that he never knew existed. He had always tried to please others, but now he was trying to please himself.

He glanced over to the campfire of the crew next to his and saw the recently airborne spongeman chomping on a chicken leg without a care in the world. That he was still alive was a miracle, but the spongeman acted as though it was a matter of luck. A miracle suggested predestination, while luck suggested random chance. The two seemed diametrically opposed, yet Napoleon believed in both destiny and luck. Gagne had no idea how that could be, but perhaps that was why he was a *caporal* and Napoleon was an emperor.

***

Sergent Jean-Paul Gagne was experienced enough to sometimes treat orders as recommendations rather than rules. While his nephew Jacques was enjoying a well-deserved repast, he and the twenty men of his platoon slithered forward on their bellies. Their objective was a burned-out stone farmhouse in which forty green-jacketed Nassau infantrymen had taken refuge. Gagne had seen the Nassauers' sole officer killed earlier, and since he judged that today was their first fight, a clever and determined assault could probably put them to flight. The frightened faces, appearing now and then at the house's smashed windows, confirmed that they were leaderless and confused. The infantrymen inside were *jaegers,* German for hunters, and had been designated as such because they were expert marksmen.

The infantrymen were less important than the building, which stood on a small knoll and would, if seized, provide an excellent view of the Anglo-Allied positions. The farmhouse would also also serve as an assembly point for the advance of more *voltigeurs*. A conventional NCO assessed a situation; a wise one thought several moves ahead.

Sous Lieutenant Gerard Le Clair, nominally in charge, had been commissioned only a month before. He had dutifully issued the recall orders given him by his captain, and was surprised when Gagne argued against them. Gagne's insolence was as much a part of him as cunning was of a fox, and he knew that part of every new new officer's training was the lesson to heed to the recommendations of his senior sergeant. And so Gagne had argued that it was safer to advance than remain in an exposed position, that success would attend a surprise assault, and that victory would bring the sort of renown that could result in an promotion for the lieutenant who gave the orders.

Le Clair had accepted Sergeant Gagne's plan and taken charge of half the men. The lieutenant's men would advance in a feint, while Gagne's men would comprise the main assault.

Gagne's men had learned a lot from their first fight a few days earlier. The difference in a soldier between his first battle and his second was the difference between a bee and a wasp. A bee could sting but once and the venom was mild; a wasp could sting repeatedly and the venom was harsh. He would lead the assault, followed by the four men he judged the most stalwart: Collette, Rochefort, Le Duc, and Tremblay. The remaining six would do well enough but were better at mopping up.

Gagne's men snaked their way forward, the only sounds the swooshing of the reeds. *Sergent* Gagne issued his commands by hand gestures. Their uniforms acquired a coating of mud as they advanced, and daubs of the stuff thrown up by their movements speckled the powder grime on their faces. Gagne's keen ears were attuned to sounds: French muskets sounded slightly different from German muskets. The French had fired twenty times, the Nassauer's half that.

Gagne stopped advancing when they were ten feet from the farmhouse door, which was open. The men inside were not prepared to defend this position to the death; they wanted to be able to flee quickly. He motioned to his men, who fixed bayonets while still lying prone. Gagne took from his pocket a small wooden whistle that he had carved himself. He popped to his feet and blew it as loudly as he could. The whistle's high notes were a good imitation of a courting whippoorwill and carried above the reports of musket fire. This was the signal for Le Clair's men to fire a diversion volley and for his own men to form up.

Behind him, his men sprang to their feet. Gagne brought his weapon to the charge musket position, and his men did the same. His expression changed to one of controlled ferocity. Gagne inclined his head toward the door; his men nodded in understanding. Gagne barreled through the entrance, followed by his men.

The gun smoke-filled room stank of saltpeter, sweat, and fear. The closely packed Nassauers were facing away from Gagne, distracted by Le Clair's gunfire aimed at the windows. Gagne speared one through the back, then another, and another. Three men had hit the floor before the rest had even turned round.

In that short interval, the remainder of Gagne's men charged into the room. The Nassauers froze in shock; not one thought to using his musket as a club. Men often ran or surrendered abjectly when faced by a line of bayonets; the mere threat often forestalled real bloodshed. Here terror and no place to run stimulated the darkest predatory instincts in attackers. No quarter would be given and the Nassauers were too frightened to even think of asking for mercy. What followed was not battle but butchery.

Collette stabbed one man through the heart, and one with an upward jab to the sternum. Rochefort accounted for three, all with thrusts to the stomach. LeDuc polished off four, favoring slashes across the throat. The dubious record for slaughter went to Tremblay, who killed six. The small former housebreaker, who moved with the swiftness of a cat and the instincts of a tiger, employed all six of the thrusts recommended by the training manual. The madness of the quartet was infectious, and the rest of the men became less soldiers than demons.

Halfway through the killing, Le Clair burst through the door. Seeing, and worse, smelling the carnage, he retched, the normal reaction of any sane man. He was about to order a stop to the madness when Gagne put a hand on his shoulder and murmured, "They won't listen. Just stand back and let it play out."

Le Clair knew Gagne was right, but doing nothing ran counter to everything he had learned in training.

The killing frenzy continued for five minutes, at the end of which no enemy soldier remained alive. Gagne's men stood over the corpses with grins of satisfaction, the blaze of feral triumph hot in their deranged eyes. Many clapped each other on the shoulders as if they had just won a sporting contest. Two men spat on the corpses, and one dropped the front flap of his trousers and methodically went from body to body, urinating into mouths frozen in terror, confusion, and regret. The worst was the usually mousey Private Barbeau. He ripped the trousers off one corpse, severed the testicles, then stuffed them in the corpse's mouth. He laughed loudly for a full minute.

Private Le Mat, who aspired to be an artist at the end of his service, removed a small sketchpad from his haversack and began to record the scene.

Sergeant Gagne recognized the symptoms. The madness did not immediately vanish with the end of killing; it would slowly fade away over the next hour. Extreme fatigue and hunger would follow, and it would not be until nightfall that regret, shame, remorse, and tears would make appearances.

Le Clair's men stared at the carnage in horror but spoke no words, not understanding, yet refusing to condemn. Their eyes were those of men who had seen an evil genie unleashed and wondered if it could ever be put back in the bottle.

"This is not war," brooded Le Clair with deep melancholy. "This is Satan's dreams come to life. I would never in my worst nightmares have believed men capable of such monstrous deeds. I see none of the honor, glory, or patriotism that caused me to follow the colors. I wish I had some magical power to wipe away any memory of this day."

"I was once like you, Lieutenant," said Gagne with sympathy. "You will never forget this day, but perhaps in time you will learn how to deal with it properly."

"How do I do that?"

"I cannot say, Lieutenant. Every conscience must find its own path to sanity. The needs of my conscience may be entirely different from the requirements of yours. The aftermath of war is a lonely business, a man's struggle with his inner demons and angels cannot be fought by anyone else."

Le Clair let out a long, sad sigh. "Marshal de Saxe stated it well: 'Real battle is terrible so that we do not grow too fond of it.'

"Soldiers know that, Lieutenant, but politicians never learn."

***

16 June, 1815, 2 p.m., on the road to Quatre Bras

From the city of Brussels, the cobblestone road of *Le Chausse de Charleroi* bore the tramping, clopping, and creaking of thousands of marching British soldiers, their horses, and their wagons. The cool air was turning humid as the sun rose higher in the sky and promised a sultry day. The wool uniforms of the soldiers chafed and itched under the straps holding their packs and accoutrements. Their tongues grew dry as their mouths became parched. The horses which towed the heavy wagons suffered even more, roiled lather around their mouths signaling incipient dehydration. Pennywhistle's mission was urgent; his wagons carried 60,000 musket rounds, but common sense and humanity both demanded that he order an early rest stop. His caravan of ten wagons and fifty men stopped for a thirty-minute break at 10 am, rather than at 11, four hours after it had departed from Brussels. Though he'd departed an hour late, he was averaging four miles per hour and was 13 miles from his destination.

Destination Waterloo

Four wagons had joined his convoy led by two prominent members of the Haberdashers' Guild. Pennywhistle liked them both for their patriotism and their generosity, and perfectly understood the worry one had for his son who was a serving officer. Van Dreelin, their leader, stated that every man in his convoy would receive all the water he wanted, but only one bottle of beer and no wine or spirits. Pennywhistle's sergeants could be trusted, and his hussar escorts had been selected for their reliability, but Maxwell liked to drink rather too well.

So far, Maxwell had been uncharacteristically silent, as if he had something on his mind. Pennywhistle was grateful for the quiet, having feared a steady stream of brag and bounce on the journey. He wondered if Maxwell was pondering the fact that they would soon be facing the best soldiers in Europe led by perhaps the greatest Great Captain of all time. Pennywhistle knew what lay ahead, but having worked closely with Wellington, he had absorbed something of the man's calm confidence, granting Bonaparte a healthy respect but no fear.

Pennywhistle passed various groups of soldiers in improvised bivouacs cooking rations, eating, filling canteens, and massaging tired feet. Most of the clearings by the road were occupied, and he needed a considerable space for his horses and wagons. He unfurled his Ramsden and surveyed the road ahead. Two hundred yards away, he spotted an abandoned farmstead that had plenty of space and a well.

"Convoy, halt!" bellowed Pennywhistle five minutes later. "Deploy and replenish. We resume in thirty minutes." No further commands were necessary, because Pennywhistle had taken the trouble to brief everyone in the convoy on his expectations and their duties, exactly as Nelson did at sea. His detailed instructions had delayed their departure, but thorough preparation was the best way to cope with any emergency. He had outlined contingency plans, chiefly how to respond if attacked by infantry, cavalry, and artillery. Even if he himself were killed, his men would know what to do.

The convoy pulled off the road and the drivers arranged the wagons in a small circle. The horses stood placidly in the center. Drivers strapped feedbags filled with oats to their mouths, then proceeded to the well to fill buckets with water. The man accompanying each driver not only acted as a guard but had been selected for his experience as a farrier. They checked the horses for sores, examined their hooves and the integrity of their iron shoes, brushed the sweat off their coats, adjusted the harnesses and checked for chafing.

Pennywhistle conferred with Lieutenant Karl Sommers, commander of the hussars, finding him a bright, imaginative chap after his own heart. Two of his men would act as mounted sentinels, while two would perform the same duty on foot. The remainder would feed the detachment's horses from a supply of hay each horseman carried in a net suspended on either side of his saddle.

Van Dreelin and his drivers set up small stands and tubs of water behind their wagons. Once their other duties were complete, the men of the convoy lined up to receive a large mug filled with water, as well as a bottle of Lindeman's Beer, considered the finest brew in a city famous for its beers. To Pennywhistle's surprise, the merchants had also laid in a stock of baguettes and small rounds of Gouda cheese, which provided a welcome accompaniment to the sharp tang of the beer.

Though rest stops were often used to boil salt pork rations, no cooking would be done today, since fires and ammunition could form a lethal friendship.

Pennywhistle rode slowly round the improvised camp and satisfied himself that everything was ship shape and Bristol fashion. He had nothing to do for the next twenty minutes and decided he could permit himself a short break. He knew little about beer, since he seldom drank the stuff, but decided he would give Lindeman's a try out of curiosity. He dismounted, accepted a beer from Van Dreelin, then found for himself a shady spot. He had just opened the bottle when Maxwell sat down next to him, clutching his own bottle of Lindeman's.

"This is a fine brew, Colonel. I could go for a whole case right now, but I do understand your order. We need to have our wits about us. I am eager to have a go at Monsieur Crapaud."

"Be careful what you wish for, Ensign. Every minute that goes by without us engaging the French is a godsend that gives Wellington more time to assemble his troops. The cavalry screen he has deployed appears effective. I have received no reports of French scouts in the area, though we must remain vigilant. It only takes one man with a practiced eye to make a detailed accounting of our units and our numbers."

Two German hussars laughed loudly over some private joke, giving the lie to the English belief that Germans had no sense of humor. "Enjoy that sound, Maxwell, because it is a precious one that you will likely not hear again in the next several days."

Pennywhistle opened his bottle and took a sip. "Rather good," he remarked to Maxwell, "though on a hot day like today, I wish it had been chilled. They chill their beer in America, Ensign; that is something we English ought to try."

"But that would diminish the flavor," Maxwell countered.

From where he had concealed himself, Johnny pushed back the tarp above him just enough so he could see over wagon's side. Everyone seemed occupied and no one was looking in his direction. He was hungry, thirsty, and needed to empty his bladder. He wondered if he could tend to any of these things without being seen. The Belgians had finished dispersing their provender and the water buckets, beer, and food stood unattended. It was now or never.

He slid over the wagon's side, then crouched beneath it, making one final survey and plotting a course to his objective. As an orphaned pickpocket in London, he had developed a sixth sense that enabled him spot lurking constables, watchmen, or wardens whose actions could have resulted in him eventually dancing at the end of a hangman's rope.

He saw movement in a grove of trees, fifty yards behind the improvised camp. It might have just woodland animals about their business, but his intuition suggested the movements were human. It might just be frightened peasants, but it could also be something more serious. His time with Pennywhistle had taught him to take no chances and plan for the worst. He put his hunger and thirst in a mental lockbox and focused his attention on the trees. He had not planned on being a self-appointed sentry, but since no else had seen the movements, he would just have to accept the job.

The men making the movements were six wounded French hussars, the remnants of an earlier patrol involved in a deadly skirmish. They had been left behind as a rear defense at their own request so their mates could escape, then their opponents had been recalled before they themselves could be captured or dispatched. They had found refuge in the grove of trees that they presently occupied.

One hussar sentry lay dead at Etienne Le Coq's feet. The German had not seen them while making his rounds, and it had cost him his life. He would soon be missed, so the hussars knew they had to act quickly.

The six men held a whispered council of war. "We're all dead men anyway," brooded *Caporal* Le Coq, their leader. "We might as well go out in glory by torching those ammunition wagons. Our deaths would accomplish something and help the Emperor.”

“No! We must not give up. We can take horses and make a run for it,” objected Private Barbier.

“We’re in bad shape, and those troopers look pretty damn fit. They would put up a hell of a fight. We wouldn’t stand a chance,” worried Private Allard.

“Maybe we should do both,” suggested Private Alaire.

“What do you mean?” queried Private Abelard.

“We torch the wagons and steal horses during the confusion. If we were ready to pounce the second after the explosion, we stand a fair chance of pulling it off. But there is one problem.”

“What is that?” asked Private Cassel.

“One of us would have to die. For the man carrying the torch it would be a suicide mission. He would have to throw it at very close range for it to be effective and would go up with the blast.”

“Why couldn’t he just light it and throw it from a distance?” inquired Abelard.

“First,” responded Le Coq, “it would be hard to throw a torch from any distance great enough to afford protection from the blast. The torch might also miss its target, and there would be no opportunity for a second try. A man running with a lit torch would be spotted far sooner than one who lit his torch only when he was right next to his target. No, the only way to be sure is for the torch bearer to actually place the lighted torch inside a wagon.”

Grim nods were exchanged.

“But it could be worse than that,” continued Le Coq. “I have no idea what the blast radius would be from the explosion: perhaps none of us would survive. I will volunteer because I am the senior man and have the gravest wound.”

"No, Jean," protested Abelard. "We have always shared the risks of battle, and today shall be no exception. We shall draw sticks. The one who gets the short one carries the torch. Does everyone agree?"

Every head nodded.

"Very well," agreed Le Coq reluctantly. "I shall gather the sticks. You will hold them, Abelard. I will hand them to you with your back turned away from the others and your eyes closed, so you do not know which stick is the short one. I do not want you to cheat and draw the short one for yourself."

"I would never…" Abelard stopped himself and gave a grim smile. "No, you're right. When it comes to the lives of my best friends, I," he stopped and looked at the assembled anxious faces, "no, none of us can be trusted."

Le Coq found six small fallen sticks and handed them to Abelard.

The sticks were drawn quickly. Those who got the long ones bore expressions of both relief and regret.

Cassel drew the short one. He gave a gallic shrug and huffed ruefully. "Well, my pension would not have amounted to much and I would not have made a very good husband."

"*Omnes pro uno, unus pro omnibus*" observed LeCoq.

He saw puzzlement among his men.

"It's Virgil. 'All for one and one for all.'"

The eyes of the six glistened briefly.

Johnny spied a figure move to the edge of the trees. The man angled his head round a tree trunk and surveyed the ground in front of him. He had a baby face, but his expression was hard: a mixture of determination and pain. Johnny recognized the elaborate lime green dolman, pelisse, and breeches as belonging to a member of 7th

Hussars. Then he saw that blood seeped from a wound on the soldier's left side.

Johnny tensed, wondering if he should shout an alarm, then decided he should wait until the man had committed himself. Besides, it would be well to find out if he had brought any friends. Johnny guessed he was a scout, assessing the numbers and makeup of the convoy. No, his eyes seemed fixed on the ammunition wagon just in front of Johnny, ten yards away. He looked to be calculating the distance to it; fifty yards by Johnny's reckoning. He had no carbine, no pistol, and no sword. Hussars were aggressive by nature and training, and it made little sense that one in a dangerous situation would be unarmed. The only reason one would shed his weapons would be for swift movement on foot; odd, since hussars were mounted troops known for their fast horses. Perhaps, Johnny reflected, the same encounter that had caused the man's wound had also killed his horse.

The man picked a long wooden stake that looked to have a lumpy head. He then removed a small metal box from a haversack. He stared at it briefly then his lips began moving silently, in what Johnny guessed was a prayer.

Johnny made the connection in an instant of insight. The stick was a torch soaked in pitch, and the box contained a flint and striker to ignite it. The man intended to throw it at a wagon and blow the supplies sky high. He must be praying one last time because he would be meeting his God very soon.

Suddenly, the wounded man broke into a fast run. Johnny burst from his hide, jumping up and down and waving his arms as he shouted "Help! Help! Fire! Fire!"

It took critical seconds for the small capering figure to be noticed, seconds the convoy did not have. The hussar would reach the wagon before any of the guards could stop him. Johnny was the only one with a chance.

He darted forward. The hussar was so focused on his objective that he did not see the small figure racing to intercept him. Johnny was far too small to wrestle the man to the ground, but he could bring him down if he used his body as a flying wedge and aimed below the hussar's center of gravity. He remembered something Pennywhistle had told him about close quarter combat, "If a man cannot see well, he cannot fight well."

Pennywhistle was alerted by the shouts. He spotted Johnny, then saw the hussar a fraction of a second later and drew the same conclusion as Johnny. "Get up!' he shouted to Maxwell.

Johnny flung himself sideways and hit the man just above his shins, a scant ten yards from the wagon. Cassel went down, but did not relinquish control of the torch. He flung Johnny aside and rolled left, reaching for the flint and striker. Johnny jumped on him and clawed his eyes. Cassel howled in pain and anger. Johnny drew his small pocketknife and plunged it into Cassel's hand, causing him to drop the flint and striker.

Le Coq and his mates saw the whole thing from the tree line. "He's not going to make it. One for all and all for one, right? I would rather destroy this convoy than return to France as a cripple. Do you agree with me?"

Everyone nodded.

"May God have mercy on our souls. Light a torch and follow me!"

Cassel grabbed the flint and striker with his other hand as Johnny fought to wrench it free. During the struggle, the striker hit the flint and a large spark alighted on a large patch of nettles under the wagon, and the dry nettles began to burn. Johnny rolled away from Cassel and kicked out blindly. His shoe connected with Cassel's chin, stunning him.

The nettles burned rapidly, and it would be only a matter of seconds before the fire spread to the wagon wheels. Johnny jumped to his feet and threw himself upon the burning nettles, the patch just about the size of his body. He rolled frantically, singing himself but finally extinguishing the blaze.

Out of the corner of his eye, Johnny saw Maxwell thrust his blade through the arsonist's throat.

"Colonel!" shouted Maxwell frantically. "Look!"

Pennywhistle saw five hussars running toward the wagons, all bearing lighted torches. It was not so much a run as a fast shamble. All of the men were wounded, and this looked to be a final effort.

Pennywhistle admired their bravery, yet they had to be stopped. The trouble was they had spread themselves out, each going for a separate wagon. He and Maxwell could account for two, perhaps three, but two might get through. He just had to hope someone else was alert enough to assist. He charged toward one hussar and cut him down with a thrust to his chest. Maxwell killed another with a diagonal slash to the neck. Pennywhistle accounted for a third with a thrust to the stomach.

The other two made it to within five feet of the wagons when two shots rang out. The hussars staggered, then collapsed like sacks of grain emptied of their contents.

Van Dreelin and van der Beek held smoking pistols.

"Good shot, van der Beek" said Van Dreelin. "I had no idea you'd brought a pistol, or that you'd been practicing."

"I fought in the uprising against the Austrians in '90. I kept my pistol and never forgot my training."

"And I served with the Bruges Militia and brought my old pistol. But I thought you were a peacemaker, devoted to the arts of conciliation and compromise."

Van Dreelin sighed. "A smart peacemaker always has a plan if those on the other side want to cancel the negotiations violently."

Pennywhistle next did something that baffled Maxwell. He ordered a dozen men of the convoy to collect the bodies of the hussars and place them in a dry gully. They filled the gully with sand from its banks, making an improvised grave.

"Colonel, I do not understand. Why on Earth would you not just leave those hussars as food for crows? They tried to murder us all!"

"You see them as foes, and so they were. But they were also fighting men who died gallantly. Did you see the shape they were in? Nearly walking corpses! They would have been much harder nuts to crack had they been unwounded. Instead of trying to extend what little time remained to them, they gave their final moments over to a heroic gesture. Yes, it was heroic, even though we were on the receiving end. If I had been their commanding officer and they had survived, I would have seen to it that each man received the Legion of Honor. I admire courage, wherever it may be found, and their earthly remains deserve consideration. Their internment required no great effort and represented to me a small point of honor: such courtesies separate us from barbarians."

Maxwell rolled his eyes.

"There is also a lesson here for you, Ensign. Take note of the devotion Bonaparte inspires in his men. You may despise the Emperor, but you cannot deny that he ignites a loyalty that is as remarkable as it is dangerous. Wellington's Army is in for the fight of its life."

"I still would have left them to rot."

"You are not alone, Maxwell, but as long as men remember to extend kindness to their enemies, wars can come to an end."

Johnny walked hesitantly up to the two, his face a mixture of triumph and trepidation. He might have saved the convoy, but he had still disobeyed Pennywhistle's direct and emphatic order to remain at Lady Densham's.

Pennywhistle glared at Johnny in exasperation. "What am I to do with you? We are too far advanced toward our destination to send you home, yet I dislike rewarding people who give their word to me then break it when my back is turned."

"Mr. Dale is going to adopt me. I wanted to stay close to him."

Dale came dashing up at that moment, a scowl on his face. "Sorry I missed the fracas, Colonel, but I was talking to Lieutenant Sommers and those elm trees prevented me from seeing what was happening. I came as soon as I heard the gunshots. Blast you, Johnny! You promised you'd stay home. What have you to say for yourself?"

Johnny kept silent. Pennywhistle quickly related the lad's part in saving the convoy.

"Well, at least that's something. What use shall we make of him, Colonel?"

"Not sure, but we are always in need of messengers, and he rides a horse reasonably well."

"Gentlemen," interjected Maxwell, "might I make a suggestion?"

Pennywhistle had not expected initiative from Maxwell; he was curious to see if the fellow was thinking of somebody other than himself. "Go ahead."

"If the lad here is going to be a messenger, he should have some means to defend himself. He should have a sword, but I am willing to wager that he has never had any instruction in the blade. I would like to provide that: short lessons whenever we stop for a rest, and when we reach our destination. Nothing fancy or complicated, just basic life-saving movements."

Pennywhistle blinked in surprise, then laughed quietly. "You want to be his teacher? You want to mentor him in the blade?"

"I know how to shoot, and I would love to learn to use a sword," Johnny said eagerly.

"I realize that I have a history of unreliability, Colonel, but wouldn't you agree that the road to redemption starts with a single step? You took a chance on me, and I'd like to take a chance on this young lad."

Pennywhistle looked dubious and turned to Dale. "What say you?"

"I have my doubts, but Maxwell has had some fine teachers and knows his way around a blade."

"And I will allow," offered Pennywhistle, "that though his judgement is sometimes questionable, his nerves are steady in battle."

"I would want to keep a weather eye on both of them," replied Dale.

"As would I. Perhaps we should ask Johnny before proceeding further."

Dale nodded.

"Johnny, would you agree to follow Ensign Maxwell's instructions to the letter? Be honest now, I need something better than the piecrust promise you gave your stepfather and me."

Johnny's face turned solemn, a mixture of reflection and regret. "I am sorry for not keeping my word, but I can't say I'm sorry I came. I will do exactly as Mr. Maxwell says. I don't intend to be a bystander; I wish to slay Frenchmen!"

"Well spoken!" Maxwell's eyes gleamed. "A man after my own heart."

Johnny smiled. He liked being referred to as a man, not a boy.

"Very well, Mr. Maxwell, you have a pupil." Pennywhistle fixed Maxwell's eyes with a hard stare. "Take care that he acquires only those habits you wish to teach and none of those habits that you wish to shed."

"Could I get something to eat?" pleaded Johnny. "I'm so hungry, I could eat a horse."

"Just make sure it belonged to a Frenchman," said Maxwell.

Chapter 11
Dangerous Medicine

16 June 1815, 10 a.m., Brussels

Anger reigned in a room that was supposed to promote peace and rest. The improvised nursery rang with Sammie Jo's shouts. "What the hell did you do to Nicholas, Mrs. George? He was fine when I left two hours ago, but now he can barely breathe! He's tossing and turning as if a devil was playing with him! I ain't seen this since we left Vienna!"

"It will pass, milady," Mrs. George said soothingly. "I just gave him his medication. It requires an hour to take full effect, and at first it makes a baby restless. Nothing to worry about, milady."

Sammie Jo's ire tossed her newly learned manners out the window. "What the hell! Nothing to worry about? Nothing to worry about? You never told me about any medication!"

Mrs. George replied with a studied calm, as if explaining to a child having a tantrum. "I did not want burden you, milady, with extra worry, since you already fear for your husband's safety. The medication was recommended to me by one of the midwives in Vienna. She told me the Hapsburgs themselves use it regularly on any of their infants in distress. The medication facilitates sleep. I ran out of it after we left Vienna, but this morning I purchased a new supply from a local apothecary."

"Show me the goddamned stuff!"

Mrs. George reached under the baby's changing table and extracted a large glass bottle. The label proclaimed in fancy gold lettering "Barker's Royal Infants Preservative", and a representation of the arms of George III stood above the lettering, implying the king himself used the medication for his family, though that endorsement was probably fictional.

Sammie Jo snarled as she seized the bottle from Mrs. George. "Why, it's nothing but a god-damned patent medicine! We have traveling salesmen back home who peddle quack concoctions, and I ain't never see a one of them scoundrels who knew a jot about making people well. Mostly their stuff was just liquor with some fancy flavorings and a few spices. I get laughed at for my back country ways, but it seems to me that the lot of you can be tricked right easy, providing someone puts the word "Royal" somewhere on a label."

Sammie Jo unscrewed the top, muttering, "Let's find out what this stuff really is." She rubbed her finger round the rim and touched it to the tip of her tongue. Her face hardened into a grimace, and she spat. "Damn it, woman, didn't you ever taste the stuff? It's laudanum. This is potent stuff that would be dangerous for a grown man. Who the devil would prescribe this for an infant?"

Mrs. George face went white. Her shocked expression suggested that she would never in a million years want to harm a child. "You must believe me, milady, I only want the best for Nicholas."

Sammie Jo glared at Mrs. George. "Part of me wants to beat the living tar out of you, give you a dose of the suffering that you have caused Nicholas." She paused, sighed, and the fire in her eyes went out. "But you ain't bad, just stupid. Nicholas likes you. It ain't in my nature to give folks a second chance, but my husband did so with me, and it seems right that I should pass that on. What kind of dosage did you give Nicholas?"

"A tiny one, milady, half the recommended dose. A quarter teaspoon midafternoon and a similar one just before bed."

Laudanum explained Nicholas' chronic breathing problems and restlessness. Sammie Jo had seen officers stumbling from opium dens in London displaying those symptoms. And she knew how addictive the stuff was: her husband had suffered agonies, weaning himself from the laudanum prescribed for the pain of a severe wound. This also answered the question of why Nicholas' health had improved on the journey from Vienna. His natural defenses had begun working to restore his health.

Sammie Jo considered; was there anything she could do to help her son recover from this setback?

Years ago, she had gone down with a bad case of pneumonia and nearly died — not from the pneumonia, but from the local doctor's treatment, which had consisted of repeated bloodletting, a tartar emetic, and the administration of Rush's Bilious Pills. What had saved her life was the intervention of a neighboring woman, who'd brought over a Piscataway medicine man who went by the name Walks-in-Water. He'd compounded a tea of various herbs and roots which had proved to be an efficacious tonic. When she'd recovered and could walk again, she'd begged him to teach her, and for much of the following spring and summer she had followed him around to learn the medicine plants. When she'd left America, she'd brought some dried herbs with her.

Now she decided to make a tonic similar to the one that had saved her life, since it had eased difficult breathing as well as promoting rest and healing. She hoped that if she drank the tea, some of its benefits might pass into her breastmilk.

Sammie Jo repaired to the kitchens beneath Lady Densham's residence and set some water to simmer, then added cardinal flowers, horsemint, pleurisy root, black cherry bark, and sassafras. When these had steeped, she strained the liquid, poured herself a cupful, and set the rest aside for later. Drinking the aromatic tisane brought back memories of the woods and meadows where she'd walked and hunted. She felt herself relax deeply.

When she went upstairs, Nicholas was still fussy and weepy, but he was hungry too, and put his lips to her nipple and suckled eagerly. His was still restless, but after 20 minutes he became sleepy. Sammie Jo laid him in his cradle and rocked it gently. She quietly sang a few lullabies.

She decided to wait by Nicholas' side for an hour or so, to see if there were any changes. Gradually, his fitful tossing and turning calmed. After an hour, his occasional wheezing had cleared. After ninety minutes, his breathing was regular and deep.

Mrs. George came over and gazed down at Nicolas. Even she could hear the difference in the infant's breathing; this was the restorative sleep of health, not the deathlike slumber of the drugged.

"Why, milady! Whatever did you do?"

As she listened to Sammie Jo's explanation, she was first disapproving, then astonished.

"Goodness!" exclaimed Mrs. George. "I thought Indians scalped children!"

"Damnation, Mrs. George, scalping weren't something the Indians thunk up! The French and British took to scalpin' when they was fightin' each other. Both sides paid bounties for killing each others' colonists, and it's lots easier to transport scalps as proof of your kills than bodies."

"That is barbaric," gasped an astonished Mrs. George. "And here I thought the British spoke only with the voice of civilization."

"The truth ain't always pretty, and more often than not, it's different from what you got told. Well, at least we can get Nicholas back to health. And, Mrs. George, the next time you have a bright idea about medication, talk to me first."

"I certainly will, Lady Pennywhistle."

Healing was the also topic of discussion in the morning room, two floors below. Five women were talking animatedly and making careful lists.

"Where is Sammie Jo?" asked Deborah Dale. "It's not like her to miss a meeting that she was so keen on having."

"Some problem has arisen with Nicholas, and she is attending to it. I do worry so about that child," lamented Margaret.

"What is the matter with him?" inquired Lady Densham.

"He was born weak and frail," stated Margaret." His health had improved markedly during the journey, but this morning he suffered a relapse. I have no idea what caused it."

"I pray that he gets well," offered Lady Densham with deep sympathy. "But now let us turn our attentions to the health of our gallant soldiers. I find it disgraceful that so many of the British community here are fleeing in terror, afraid of what will happen if Bonaparte prevails."

"I think they expect Bonaparte to reenact The Terror of '93 and '94, when the guillotines ran 24 hours a day," responded Margaret. "Our government likes to promote Bonaparte as a bloodthirsty tyrant, and they have been very successful, perhaps too successful. I know two French *emigrées* who returned to France after he issued a general amnesty in 1803, promising no harm would come to them as long as they refrained from overt political activity."

"Did he keep his word that time?" inquired Deborah, her keen reporter's instincts seeking more detail.

"Yes, he did," replied Margaret. "A number of exiles returned, and they have remained unmolested. And when he installed his brother Louis as the ruler of this area, his administration was much more benign than the Batavian Republic which proceeded it. My belief is that the Belgians know if they cause no trouble, they will survive a change in government with a minimum of disruption."

"So you are saying that Bonaparte is *not* ruthless?" demanded a surprised Sarah.

"Oh, he can be ruthless! When he put down a revolt by the Paris Mob in 1795, he gave them more than just a whiff of grapeshot, he gave them a cannonade that last more than an hour! I would say he is a pragmatic tyrant but not a bloodthirsty one."

"I for one believe he will be soundly thrashed," snapped Densham. "But either way, there will be many wounded, and it is terrible they will be left to the care of Belgians. Not that the Belgians won't give them good care, but it reflects badly on us."

"I have heard that many monasteries and nunneries are already freeing up space to treat the wounded," offered Deborah. "There has been so much fighting in the area since the 90s that they have had plenty of experience with injured soldiers. I understand the guilds want to pitch in too."

"Be that as it may," said Densham, "space for the wounded will be in short supply. I have cleared the rooms on the next floor up. We should be able to accommodate perhaps 200 soldiers. Now what we need are the means to care for them. Please check your lists to make sure we have not forgotten anything. We don't have much time, and the situation on the streets below is becoming increasingly disorderly."

The lists were based on the recommendations of Densham's personal physician, Dr. Hiram Hathaway: silk and linen for bandages, fine thread for sutures, ice to reduce swelling, laudanum to relieve pain, leather to help seal amputations, hay to cover the floors, and mattresses for the wounded to lie on.

"I have taken up a collection from courageous British ladies in the city," continued Densham, "so we have plenty of coin for our purchases. Don't hesitate to pay high prices if it is the only way to get what you need. I have purchased three wagons to fill, two of you to each wagon."

"Perhaps the wagons could be kept in readiness to transport wounded, once they are emptied," offered Lady Magdalene de Lancey, the wife of Wellington's chief of staff, Sir William de Lancey. "The Army is always short of conveyances to move the injured and sick."

"Surely you are not suggesting we drive them?" huffed Lady Densham.

"Only for a short distance. We could give lifts to the walking wounded who have made it to Brussels but are too weary to continue to a place of treatment."

"Shouldn't we have an escort?" asked Sarah Thynne. "It might be dangerous for us with all the chaos of battle."

"There are sufficient British soldiers traversing the streets that no one will dare to offer you harm," replied Lady Densham. "It's three o clock now. Let's all meet back here by nine. I know some of the shops have closed, but many are staying open, trying to liquidate their stocks before French looters help themselves."

"I wish I knew more about nursing," sighed Sarah.

"We all do," said Lady Densham kindly. "But our hearts our good, and if we trust them we cannot go very wrong."

A door opened and Sammie Jo walked in. "Sorry I am late. What did I miss?"

***

16 June 1815, 2 p.m. on the road to Quatre Bras

After parting ways with Sarah and the Earl's party, Thynne had rejoined his regiment in Brussels barely in time for its departure. Presently, his Squadron of the 1st Lifeguards cavalry regiment was sixteen miles from Quatre Bras. The sounds of distant cannon and musket fire reached his practiced ear, the intermittent sounds were those of a battle just starting, not the steady ones of a battle well underway. At the present rate of advance, 4 kilometers per hour, and allowing for the heavy congestion on the road, his squadron of 135 horsemen should arrive in the general area of Quatre Bras in the early hours of June 17.

Lieutenant Colonel Ferrior, the regimental commander, had decreed that the horses should advance at the slow walk to conserve their energy. Thynne thought it was time to increase the pace to a brisk walk, 6 kilometers per hour. A forced rate of 10 kilometers per hour was possible, but that would fatigue the horses and lessen their ability to carry out the kind of shock action for which heavy cavalry was designed.

Thynne pulled alongside Ferrior and made his recommendation to increase the pace.

"I shall wait for Somerset's orders," countered Ferrior. Lord Edward Somerset was the commander of the prestigious Household Brigade, to which Ferrior's Regiment belonged. The brigade of 70 officers and 1,100 sabers was the elite of British Cavalry, since their original function had been to protect the Royal Household. Ferrior stroked his chin in thought. "On the other hand, Somerset respects initiative and is something of a fire eater. We can set an example to the rest of the brigade. Very well, Thynne, have the trumpeter blow the appropriate commands."

Thynne saluted. "Very good, sir."

The two squadrons proceeded at the new pace in columns of four, with the 253 sabers of the enlisted men and the 12 of officers taking up 48 meters of roadside ground. Like Thynne's horse, Mandrake, the regiment's horses were large and black, with their manes combed to the left, to differentiate them from the other regiments in the brigade who combed to the right.

Each trooper wore a brick red jacket and light grey trousers with a long red stripe down each leg. Each sported a helmet that resembled something a Roman gladiator might have worn: red and black jappaned leather, with a brass crest and short bill. The leather was hard enough to deflect all but the strongest sword cuts, and the long black horsehair plume suspended from its top was designed to foul an enemy horseman's blade.

Each trooper's primary weapon was the Pattern 1796 Heavy Cavalry Saber, whose broad, 35-inch straight blade was much feared by French cavalry. It was, however, several inches shorter than its French counterpart, sometimes putting the British at a disadvantage. Secondary weapons included two Heavy Dragoon pistols of .75 caliber and a Paget Carbine, 32 inches long with a .65 bore. Gunpowder weapons were seldom of much use in a charge and were chiefly useful when squadrons were employed for outpost duty.

Coronet Septimus Lacy pulled his horse alongside Thynne. Coronet was the lowest commissioned rank in the cavalry, and Lacy, who had just turned 18, had only held it for six weeks. "I say, Captain, it sounds like we shall see action presently."

"You are not mistaken, but I would warn you not to expect a grand charge today. I hazard to guess that we shall be held in reserve to cover Wellington's retreat this evening."

"Retreat?" gasped Lacy. "You expect Wellington to be beaten?"

"Calm down, Lacy. Not beaten, just making a fighting withdrawal. Now that Bonaparte has committed himself, Wellington needs time to reassemble the scattered portions of his army. He also needs Prussian help to finish the job, but the disposition and morale of Marshal Blucher's men is an unknown, a question mark. The Duke is fighting a delaying action at Quatre Bras, not trying to defeat Boney but to slow his advance. I expect Wellington will make a stand somewhere in the next seventy-two hours and fight the kind of defensive battle for which he became famous in Spain."

"You served under him in the Peninsula, did you not? Have you any notions as to where that stand will be?" Lacy looked around, as if expecting to see a sign with an arrow saying, "Wellington's Last Stand."

"That little hamlet we passed through a while ago, Mt. St. Jean, a mile from the town of Waterloo, would serve nicely. It has a low ridge that would enable Wellington to use reverse slope tactics: shelter the men from cannon and musket fire until just before they are needed. Napoleon loves his artillery, but if his gunners cannot see the men they are shooting at, the effectiveness of their fire is substantially diminished."

"You've fought against the French cuirassiers and dragoons. What is your assessment of them?"

"First rate warriors. Exceptional riders and exceptional swordsmen. Despite what you may have been told, they are fully our equals. Now, Coronet, I see that Trooper Bennett has fallen asleep in his saddle. Would you be so good as to rouse him?"

"Of course, sir!" Lacy saluted and rode off.

Thynne was glad to be where he was, yet regretted his placement as well. He was more than willing to do his duty, but three months of marriage had changed him. He found to his surprise that the arranged marriage that he had avoided for so long was turning into a love match. Sarah's surprise appearance in Vienna had persuaded him to take the plunge on impulse, and her sheer enthusiasm for the match was infectious. He had once been the army equivalent of the sailor with a girl in every port, but found that he missed his rakish ways not at all. Domestic bliss was real, not the silly goose myth he had always deemed it to be. He realized now that Sarah, while plain looking, was the kind of woman with whom he could build a family. Marriage to Sarah was making him a better man; a solemnity of character and conduct that he did not know he possessed was emerging. He was beginning to see that his former attitudes towards life had been a prolonged adolescence, devoid of any responsibility, save to his military obligations. Responsibility now felt right as well as good, and he wanted to see where this new path would lead him.

He withdrew a locket from his coat pocket and opened it. It contained a miniature of Sarah as well as a coil of her hair that smelled of sandalwood. He gazed at it longingly, realizing he was engaging in the rankest sentimentality. It was the sort of thing you would expect from a callow coronet like Lacy, and he would have laughed at officers performing such a silly ritual a few years ago. Now contemplation of his beloved filled his heart with joy and hope. He kissed the locket, and he made a solemn vow to return to her. Widowhood was something she should never know.

Destination Waterloo

16 June 1815, 2 p.m., Brussels

Thynne's wife, Sarah, was thinking about him at the same moment. She had been paired with Sammie Jo on a buying expedition to procure sundries for the soon-to-be hospital at Lady Densham's. The pair had bought up the entire stock of silks and linens from three dress shops and were on their way to a fourth. Silk was a superb material for bandages because it was much less prone to carry infections than linen.

Tears welled up in Sarah's eyes as they approached the next shop.

"What's wrong?" Asked Sammie Jo.

"I was just thinking about the many terrible wounds our bandages will have to cover. Then I think of my Steven lying hurt and lonely and I can't bear the thought. I do not know what I will do if I lose him."

Sammie Jo stopped the wagon and put her arm around Sarah. "I'm worried about Tom, too, but don't give in to fears. I've seen Steven in action Sarah, and he knows how to take care of himself. Don't be like a dog chasing a porcupine. Steven would be proud of what you are doing. He cares for his men, and he would want any wounded ones to have the gentleness of a woman's touch. I've been through a heap of fighting and I won't sugarcoat it; what happens is awful. You will see some mighty bad stuff in our improvised hospital. Now listen to me. Weeping, wailing, and hand wringing may help you, but it's useless to the wounded men in your care. You may want to run away and puke, but remember, to many of the men you are a literal angel. Your face may be the last sight some of them will ever see; your hand might be the last one they will ever hold. Sometimes it just takes a kind word, a smile, or a comforting touch to give a glimmer of hope to a wounded man. Every so often, that glimmer is like a floating spar to a shipwrecked sailor: something to save him from going under."

"That is a grave responsibility." Sarah fanned herself rapidly with a silk fan that she pulled from her skirt pocket.

"You are stronger than you know, Sarah," rejoined Sammie Jo. She knew Sarah was self-conscious about her plump figure, and this sometimes caused her to doubt herself. "Put the fan away. I am a good judge of people and I ain't wrong about you. You came all the way to Vienna to wed Steven without informing either your family or his, and that tells me a lot about your spirit. You got a lot of grit at your core. You trusted it in Vienna; if you trust it again, you will find you are stronger than you ever thought. When things look darkest, focus on your love for Steven."

"There is one other thing, Sammie Jo." Sarah's face paled, and her expression became at once apprehensive and awed. "My menses stopped some time ago, and yesterday I felt several flutters that I think is the start of quickening."

"Oh!" exclaimed Sammie Jo, eyebrows raised in understanding. "Well, I'm right glad you spoke up. That puts a different light on things, don't it? God forbid that Steven should fall, but if he does, he will live on in the child you hold in your arms. But it also means we need to take good care of you, Sarah, you and your child. I won't let you exhaust yourself caring for others. If I'd been more careful while I was pregnant, I'm certain sure Nicholas would be healthier, so let's not let you make the same mistake I did."

Privately, Sammie Jo was also thinking that Sarah's pregnancy was a potential solution to a thorny Thynne family problem. Steven was the second son of the Marquis of Bath; his elder brother was in poor health and his wife has had never given birth to an heir. Even if Steven himself were to die in battle, a son of Sarah's might eventually become the next Marquis.

Margaret was giving her version of Sammie Jo's talk to Magdalene de Lancey, who, like Sarah, was a newlywed and shared similar fears for her husband.

"So, focusing on the immediate goal, rather than worrying about what is over the horizon, is the best medicine?" asked Magdalene.

]"Just so," replied Margaret. "We have already accomplished a great deal. Our wagon is nearly full of hay and straw mattresses. One more stop and our journey will be complete."

"I wonder where William is just now," said Magdalene wistfully.

"Do I understand correctly that you two have not spent much time together since the wedding?"

"We shared a few months together before duty called William to the Low Countries. He has been phenomenally busy, coordinating myriad details as Wellington's Chief of Staff. I just arrived on the 13th, and we were barely able to spend the night together before he had to dash off again. I pray that William and I will have children and happily grow old together."

Lady Margaret sighed. "That is my one regret, Magdalene, that I was never able to have children. Tom Pennywhistle is my godson, the closest thing I will ever have to a child. I pray for his safety in the battles ahead." She smiled. "I think Tom is a lucky man and will come through this war, as he did the previous ones."

"A lucky man?"

Margaret laughed softly. "Tom would look askance at my belief in luck, but it is one thing I have in common with the dreaded Bonaparte. Some men are born survivors, with the hand of Providence set upon them. Tom is one of those men."

"I pray that William is as well."

Two blocks away, Lady Densham and Deborah were arguing. "That is a perfectly horrid idea, so put it right out of your mind, Deborah. Your duty is here helping the wounded."

"But, Lady Densham, think of it! I would be witnessing a major battle as it happens, not piecing it together after the fact from second and third hand accounts. I could witness events unfolding and interview the principals on the spot." Deborah's usual thoughtful expression was replaced by one of barely suppressed excitement, which suddenly darkened. "Besides, my husband is there, and my stepson Johnny has gone missing. My guess is that if I find my husband, I will find Johnny as well."

"Don't be ridiculous! You have never been anywhere near battle, and you have no notion of how chaotic and dangerous a battlefield is. Rather than finding your menfolk, you are likely to lose yourself, and quite possibly your life. Furthermore, I strongly doubt that all those busy men will stop what they are doing to answer your foolish questions! Stay here and help me collect supplies of laudanum and ice."

"Very well, milady." Deborah's voice was polite, but her dangerous expression suggested that, far from obeying Lady Densham's orders, she was prepared to defy them at the first opportunity.

"Sixty pounds for that old nag is outrageous!" huffed the Earl Grosvenor, pointing to an old grey mare. "Those three standing behind her look to be in even worse shape. I should think you'd be offering me a discount, because we British are defending your city from Bonaparte. That horse isn't worth ten pounds on her best day, and those were a while back."

Emil de Jochmins shrugged. He was a Belgian horse trader with a long jaw, a sharp nose, eyes set close together, and a sly expression.

"On the contrary, my lord, I am offering a good price because you are British I have but to wait a few hours," he gestured to the heavy traffic in the streets," and I can get triple what I am offering you. Many British citizens are fleeing, fearing the worst, and it has created a demand for horses that exceeds the supply. We Belgians have seen regimes come and go, and while we do not wish to see Bonaparte return, we will adapt as we always have done. If that happens, I shall miss the British because they pay me in gold, as I expect you are prepared to do now."

The Earl scowled. "I would not be in this predicament, except that two of my best mounts turned up with severe cases of colic this morning. My farrier says it was probably the result of bad oats. The horses will need a week to recover. The people in my party need horses, so I am compelled to look at second rate animals out of necessity."

The Earl turned to Grimsby, an ex-Royal Marine Sergeant, who had been invalided from the service when he lost his right leg. He had become a butler, but he had never lost his love for horses, and his knowledge of them was exceptional. "Grimsby, would you be willing to give this horse an examination? I should like to be sure his purchase will not be a complete waste of money."

"Yes, my lord, but don't expect me to return a verdict that says your money is well spent."

"Ah!" exclaimed the Belgian in smarmy triumph. "Then you do wish to buy! I am glad you see reason."

The distant *boom boom* of cannon increased the urgency of the Earl's mission and his determination to plan for contingencies. "I will buy all four at thirty pounds per head, providing Grimsby tells me they are not at death's door."

The Belgian's jaw clenched, and his eyes flamed with indignation. "Such a price is highway robbery."

"Remember, monsieur, that the military authorities are industriously commandeering horses as we speak. If you do not take my offer, there is a good chance the nags will be taken, and you will not receive a penny in compensation."

"Sadly, there is truth in what you say," sighed Jochmins in exasperation, "so I will reluctantly accept your proposal."

"Good! Let Grimsby make his inspections and we shall conclude our business."

Grimsby took an hour to inspect the horses. Eyes, teeth, nostrils, forelocks, fetlocks, and hooves received detailed examinations. When he spoke, there was concern in his voice. "Under any other circumstances, I would advise against buying them. Their health is indifferent, and I would not answer for their usefulness beyond a year."

"I just need them good for a month. Are they up to that?"

"They are, as long as they are not pushed too hard or too fast."

"Mr. Grimsby, you are unfair to these wonderful animals," reproached Jochmins. "Your inspection did not account for character, and these beasts have character in abundance! In times of adversity, these animals will surprise you."

The Earl and Grimsby rolled their eyes at this shameless puffery. The Earl's expression turned hard. "I shall expect saddles and tack to come with the beasts."

"Of course! Though my best saddle and tack was sold some hours ago."

"Let us shake hands to seal the deal." The Earl extended his hand — a privilege that flattered the horse trader. An Earl generally only shook hands with another aristocrat or gentleman. The trader returned a firm handshake. "Patience, Hope, Charity, and Faith will serve you well," gesturing at the horses as he named them.

At least their names are appropriate to what we need, thought Grosvenor.

As they led their newly acquired equine property through the twisting streets, Grosvenor noticed the abundance of hastily improvised, fruit, vegetable, and pawning stands. The people in the area were selling off any crops, and any items that contained silver or gold that could be looted by the French. The vendors all looked to be solid citizens who had suffered armies of occupation before. Everything went for a fraction of its true value, but coins could be transported easily, or just as easily buried.

"Perhaps, my lord, we should send some servants out to buy up all the fresh fruit they can," remarked Grimsby, "to benefit the wounded men you wife and her friends intend to nurse."

"She and Lady Densham dispatched a legion of servants on that very errand just after dawn. I do so hope the butcher's bill will be low for the contest ahead, but given Bonaparte's aggressive style I think that my wife and her friends will be extraordinarily busy."

"I agree, my lord. No matter how much fresh fruit they buy, it will not be enough."

***

16 June 1815, 5 p.m., Brussels

After returning to the house with Sarah, Sammie Jo retired to her room to nurse Nicholas and rest. She decided to dress for dinner, only to discover that one of her favorite earrings was missing. Frowning, she recollected they had been part of her ensemble for the Duchess of Richmond's ball the night before. The earring was important to her because it was part of a set that Tom had bought her in Bermuda, just after their wedding. Their marriage had prospered despite the many dangers they had faced, and she had come to regard the earrings as good luck talismans. Mentally retracing her movements, she concluded that she must have lost the earring sometime between rousing Maxwell out of the gutter and helping him to hurriedly gather up equipment for his rapid departure.

Sammie Jo saddled up one of the newly purchased nags and retraced her steps.

Maxwell's flat was messy and disordered. Clothes had been tossed over chairs or in heaps on the floor; plates of half-eaten food crowded a small dining table; a bookcase was carelessly stuffed with old newspapers, scuffed shoes, and three bottles of scotch; the floor was littered with discarded rum and scotch bottles. A half empty wash basin contained stale water, and a smelly chamber pot indicated that it had not been emptied of its contents. The sheets of the unmade bed were twisted into knots, as if the owner seldom enjoyed an untroubled night.

In the far corner of the room stood five empty scotch bottles that had been neatly placed on a low shelf, then used for pistol practice. .Their tops had been shot off, as broke glass and pock marks in the wall behind attested. Sammie Jo was momentarily impressed. Higher up the wall was a large "G" shape of additional bullet holes. She guessed it stood for King George, though she had no idea if the letter was intended to honor or ridicule him.

The smell of the room made her feel like she had stepped into a stomach gurgling with bile. She wondered why a servant had not cleaned the place, since Maxwell could well afford one, then decided that a drunken man with a nasty temper and a gun probably discouraged the retention of servants.

She kicked aside bottles and clothes and searched the floor. She had almost given up in disgust when she saw the silver gleam of the earbob. Relieved and delighted, she scooped up her earring and pocketed it carefully. Her job was done, it was time to leave.

Something incongruous on Maxwell's desk caught her eye: a small oval miniature of a young woman. She was pretty and dressed in simple country garb. A single rose lay at the base of the stand which held the miniature, like a votive offering at a shrine. She wondered what manner of woman provoked that sort of gesture from a man whom she sensed was used to chasing women as determinedly as a hound dog pursued foxes.

As if to complement her analogy, she noted a small bronze statue of a leaping Newfoundland dog, placed near the miniature and equally well cared for. It looked to be expensive sculpting, possibly specially commissioned. Did it represent a pet from boyhood? Sammie Jo's background had taught her to pay attention to the way in which a stranger treated an animal. A man who showed a beast kindness was worthy to do business with. If he treated an animal badly, he was not to be trusted.

Also on the desk was a stack of papers, closely written, face up.

Sammie Jo had no intention of reading someone else's correspondences, but a very personal name caught her eye. This lout had been writing to her husband, or about him.

Sammie Jo's curiosity wrestled with her conscience. Whatever was on that paper might tell her Maxwell's cast of mind and give clues to his future actions. She weighed good manners against good sense, and the later won. She took off her green bonnet and satin gloves and sat down on the Sheraton chair in front of the writing table, picked up the top paper, and began to read.

She blanched. This was no letter to a superior officer, this was a paean to hate, filled with vitriolic rage against an officer that Maxwell felt had wronged him. It enumerated perceived offenses in the manner of an accountant enumerating debts. Some people collected objects; Maxwell apparently collected grievances. He was not a man with a chip on his shoulder, but an entire forest.

The most alarming parts of the letter came after the accounting of offenses. There was an extended description of bloodthirsty actions to be taken, which included shooting in the back, beheading, dismemberment, and wiping a man's entire family from the surface of the earth. *Nicholas*! Her hand clenched, crushing the paper. She smoothed it out and continued reading. She noticed the handwriting changed as the words became more extreme. The earlier writing was in precise penmanship, which changed to the wandering, unsteady hand of a man ingesting high proof alcohol. Drink made some men funny, some amorous, some sad, and some combative. Maxwell fell into the last category, though perhaps hateful was a better label than combative.

Sammie Jo skimmed the other pages in the stack. Most of them were about fellow officers, but several were about women whom Maxwell evidently believed had betrayed him. There was an odd undercurrent in the letters; that of an angry child who was bewildered by what was happening to him and dimly sensed that the real cause of his misery was some failing of character.

She picked up the one about her husband again. The final sentence riveted her attention. "If he crosses me again, I shall kill him." She knew that Tom knew how to handle all manner of external threats, but would it occur to him that the deadliest one might be riding alongside him?

Destination Waterloo

Was her husband taming a beast or harboring a madman primed to unleash his demons? There might be a third possibility. She thought back to a visit she had her husband and made to the menagerie at the Tower of London. She had enjoyed the sight of domesticated lions who did tricks for tourists under the watchful eyes of their handlers. The trouble with such beasts was that they sometimes reverted to their true natures at the most unexpected moments and savaged their handlers.

Sammie Jo ordinarily was as decisive as her husband, but now she felt lost and uncertain. Her job as a mother was to see to the safety of her child, and that meant staying in Brussels. Her duty as a wife was to see to the welfare of her husband, and that would involve radical and dangerous actions.

The most optimistic interpretation of the letters was that they were a way for a deeply troubled soul to lance the festering boils of his emotions, but Sammie Jo had survived a hard life by being wary of optimism that seemed too good to be true. A pretended attempt to reform would be the easiest way to win someone's confidence and cause him to drop his guard.

She could die if she tried to warn her husband, but he might die if she did nothing. If the worst happened, their baby would be left an orphan

It was a horrible choice to have to make, but war had a cruel agenda with many nasty permutations. Every minute she hesitated increased the danger to Tom. Doing nothing was not in her nature, and neither was avoiding risk. She asked herself if what she contemplated was a damn fool risk or a calculated one. After a minute of the deepest soul searching, she concluded it was the latter.

She knew where Tom and the convoy were headed and had a good idea of the route they would take. She would have to forego nursing wounded men, but perhaps her new mission could be used to aid the soldiers, if she drove a wagon full of medical supplies. Once those were distributed, the wagon could then be used to transport the wounded. The Earl might be willing to help if he approved of her plan, although he and Margaret would undoubtedly try to argue her out of the action she was about to take. But... Deborah! Deborah wanted to report the battle from the field, and though everyone told her that was a bad idea, she was just as headstrong as Sammie Jo and might prove a useful ally.

Boom! Boom! The distant cannon fire was gradually increasing in volume and intensity. She grabbed her bonnet and gloves and headed for the door, kicking aside bottles as she did so. There was not a moment to lose.

Chapter 12

Four Arms and Three Battles

16 June, 1815, 3 p.m.

Quatre Bras was a prosperous farming village of two dozen buildings and three hundred souls that in peacetime was notable for its un-remarkability. The name, Quatre Bras, meant "Four Arms" and referred to two broad cobblestone thoroughfares which intersected in front of a large stone and brick walled farm compound known as the *Ferme de Quatre Bras*.

The *Chausse de Charleroi* road ran south to north, the chief inland artery from France to the Low Countries, becoming the *Chausse de Bruxelles* once it exited Quatre Bras. The *Chausse de Nivelles* ran east to west and became the *Chausse de Namur* east of the village, part of a major route from The Channel to the German states along the Rhine. Both roads had four-foot ditches and wide verges on either side, convenient for sheltering troops. Dredging to level the roadbeds had created substantial berms, now bursting with foliage, creating north-south covered ways that concealed the passage of columns.

Three wide ridges with level tops running east to west crossed the landscape, branching off at 45-degree angles from the *Chausse de Namur*: well suited for the placement of artillery. The gently undulating dips between ridges meant soldiers might not easily be seen during an advance. Fields of wheat and rye nearly six feet tall could provide additional concealment and the hedgerows which bordered the fields were thick enough to be formidable defensive features. Two major streams furnished clean, clear drinking water for farm laborers. On both sides of the *Chausse de Charleroi* were large patches of dense woods that were honeycombed with well-trod paths. Farm buildings dotted the landscape, the most important being the walled compound known as *Ferme de Gemiancourt*. Gemiancourt, two thirds of a mile south of the crossroads, was particularly well suited for defense: four substantial structures arrayed around an open space, surrounded by vast fields, gardens, and orchards. To its north was mostly open ground, good for cavalry or forming infantry squares.

Wellington had a fine eye for defensive ground and so had selected the area to fight a delaying action. If he could hold the crossroads, it would buy him time to assemble the scattered units of his command and fight his major action against Bonaparte on terrain of his own choosing. Whereas if the French should take it, they could sever communications between Wellington main army and Blucher to the East, making it easier for Napoleon to beat both armies in detail.

Jacques Gagne, soaked in sweat, covered in grime, and stinking of saltpeter, took advantage of a brief lull in their advance to finish the last bite of his remaining loaf of bread and drained the last ounce of water from his canteen. The heat generated by his guns was amplified by the hot, humid weather. He had stripped off his coat, stock, and shako after the first hour of marching, and dispensed with his waistcoat after the second. He now stood bare chested, covered in flecks of rye that the wind had blown against his sweaty form.

His section and the rest of Fivel's guns were posted ten meters to the left of Gemiancourt's western wall. He had just received an order to advance the two guns of his section a further quarter kilometer. He was not pleased, yet he respected Fivel's aggressive attitude and knew it was the right thing to do. He issued the appropriate orders, which were received with a mixture of resignation and resentment.

He had never spent a more exhausting hour. It was not just serving the guns but manhandling them meter by meter up the Charleroi Road. They had foregone the horses because each advance was so short. His guns had occupied four different positions since the engagement began, remaining in each spot only long enough to roust enemy infantry from hedges, woods, and fields of wheat and rye. The exhilaration of battle was a potent drug, but its effects were eventually outweighed by the debilitation of exhaustion.

He looked in exasperation mixed with understanding at eight of his men struggling to move a 1,200-pound cannon over ground that was grassy on top, but thick mud just beneath. They were giving their all, but it was not enough.

"Bend your knees more, Dubois, and put your shoulder into it," shouted Jacques at the man pushing the six-pounder cannon's five-foot-high left wheel. "The same goes for you, Bonfils, you've done far too much shirking today." Bonfils glowered but obeyed. He was behind the gun's right wheel.

"Barbier and Boucher, more force on the handspikes. The higher the tail, the less the drag." They grimaced, adjusted the two handspikes embedded in the cannon's twin tail, and raised it an additional foot.

"You're a slave driver, Gagne," retorted Barbier, whose shirt was plastered to his chest. "This is the fifth time we've moved this damn gun."

"And if we have to move it five times more, we will do so. Can't you see our infantry needs our help? Think of them, not yourself," retorted Jacques. "And you four," he jabbed his finger at the men in front of the guns. Each pulled on a rope attached to either the hub of the wheels or twin hooks attached to the cannon's undercarriage. "Pull harder!" This quartet particularly resented his commands; they were not artillerymen, but infantry hurriedly drafted to provide brute force.

Round shot whizzed and shrieked through the air, coming from the combined ten guns of Dutch batteries commanded by Byleveldt and Stevenaar, with whom they had been dueling since morning. The Dutch gunners were firing too high to hit their intended targets of French cannons and crews, but cries and screams to the rear indicated that some of their rounds had bitten the men with the wagons. Those hits could be critical, because just as actors could not perform without the support of a stage crew, gunners' efforts were worthless if denied a steady supply of ammunition to fuel the guns and water to cool them.

The gun lurched forward another ten feet, then stuck fast in a patch of marshy ground. Cries of anger and frustration rose, spurring Jacques to put his own shoulder to a wheel and lead by example. This had the desired effect: another man put his shoulder to the opposite wheel and a pair positioned themselves in the space on the axle between wheel and carriage. "On my mark, one, two, three...heave! Heave!"

The piece lurched out of its hole. Its wheels found firmer ground, and the pushing of a dozen men propelled it forward efficiently, if not easily. "Stop here!" shouted Jacques, when the piece came parallel with the other gun of his section. "Well done! Now let's get Claudette ready to fire! Babbette has already completed her preparations." French artillerymen often named their weapons after women and whispered entreaties to them in battle that were reminiscent of a lover's talk.

The men of gun 2, Babbette, were covered in sweat and grime as well, but they'd had a much easier time moving their piece, since it had been on the cobblestones of the *Chausse de Charleroi*. There was a friendly rivalry between the two crews, and the men of gun 2 smiled that they had won the race to the new position, even though they knew they had enjoyed an unfair advantage.

The other four guns of Fivel's battery were not yet in position. Jacques congratulated himself that his section had moved fastest. As his men loaded, he surveyed the ground in front of him seeking targets for Claudette and Babbette's next kisses.

Jacques' small world had little to do with the battle as a whole; it centered on the *Chausse de Charleroi* three hundred meters ahead of him and the *Bois de Boisseau* that lay 500 meters to the left of the road. Three hundred green coated Nasseurs had taken refuge in the heavy woods, employing logs, trees, and bushes for cover. Four hundred black coated Brunswickers were pouring into the north end of the wood to lend additional support. The forest was dense; he hoped that the artillery could land enough rounds to knock over trees or create a hurricane of splinters that would dislodge the Nassauers and discourage more Brunswickers from entering. Once that was accomplished, the French *tirailleurs* would go after the survivors with bayonets, and the cuirassiers on their heavy horses could run them down.

Jacques had been in action without respite since the engagement became general at 2 pm. He estimated his section had fired 5 rounds of solid shot and 5 rounds of canister in that interval, shifting the guns between salvos. For men who were new to battle, they had acquitted themselves well. But the fighting had taken its toll. Men's movements were slow and clumsy. Tempers frayed, and the air was hard to breathe. Low hanging clouds of gun smoke wafted across the battlefield whenever a stray breeze sprang up; causing those briefly enveloped to cough and retch. The men's parched lips remained unwetted because most had already emptied their canteens. Though his cannons were beyond the effective musket range of the men in the *Boisseau*, two men had been hit by spent rounds which caused painful bruising though they did not incapacitate.

Jacques saw Fivel looking down the line of his guns, assessing their readiness. Satisfied that their positions, thirty feet apart, barrel elevations, and range to targets were correct, he slowly raised his sword. Every gun captain and second chief watched him, anticipating what came next. Fivel's sword flashed down, and six portfires flashed as they touched the priming quills. Six guns roared and shot backwards. Clouds of smoke filled the air.

Crews began to reload, even before Fivel could assess the effects of the salvo though his spyglass. Brun, the loader in Claudette's crew, suddenly collapsed, with a death grey face and clammy skin. He writhed on the ground, vomiting between spasms. Jacques examined him and realized he had a severe case of heat exhaustion. Jacques himself and several of his men were showing signs of the same affliction. They needed water quickly.

Jacques looked to the twin water buckets attached to each gun as a supply source. He blanched in shock as he saw that they were nearly empty. Evaporation, the heavy use of the guns, and the sloshing of water as the pieces were violently heaved forward accounted for why the 17 liters that each bucket contained were no longer in evidence.

The water for the buckets came from barrels called rundlets. It took three rundlets to fill the 12 buckets of the battery. Jacques looked to the rear, hoping to see a wagon bearing fresh barrels, but the stream of wagons that brought ammunition and water had stopped. He took out a spyglass that a retreating officer Dutch officer had left behind and surveyed the ground to the rear. Many wagons lay in shambles, and wagons that should have been present were gone; driven to safety by panicked teamsters.

Jacques cursed himself for not realizing it earlier, but fatigue had dimmed his powers of observation. He had been wrong about the enemy batteries; the commanding officers were not inept, they were brilliant. They had purposely been shooting at the rear echelon in the manner of someone who wants to bring down a man on a stool, targeting the legs of the stool rather than the occupant of it.

The situation was even worse that Jacques realized, for the reserve train of ammunition and water had taken a wrong turn in the woods to the rear, the *Bois d H'ulte*, and was hopelessly lost, with horses suffering the effects of heat. Lost supply trains had plagued the campaign from the start, due to bad maps, a lack of guides, and difficult local terrain.

Jacques felt a fierce grip on his shoulder. Looking round, he met the earnest gaze of Private Vachon, his eyes wide with alarm. Vachon had once worked at a cannon foundry and would have still been employed there had he not trifled with the wife of the foundry's supervisor. A new soldier he might be, but he was the artillery equivalent of a ship's sailing master and possessed a wide knowledge and wisdom about ordinance.

"Do not reload again, *Caporal*, I beg you."

"What's wrong?"

"The heat of the battle is causing the barrels to warp. It is not something that happens to iron guns, but it does to bronze, especially if the guns are old. Our pieces are very old, relics from forgotten wars, they belong in museums. The Emperor needed to equip an army quickly, and as one of the last batteries formed, our unit received leftovers that no one else wanted. The barrels need to be cooled to arrest the problem, or else the warping will change the shape of the barrel, rendering the cannon inoperable. Or worse, the barrel will explode when a round is fired! It might not happen the next round, but I dare not answer for the health of these guns after three more salvos. If they can be cooled thoroughly, they might yet be salvaged. Something must be done!"

Jacques suddenly felt like a very old man. The weight of command was a real thing and weighed on his shoulders like the heavy stones once used to press a witch to death. It seemed utterly fantastic that the fate of his guns came down to a simple thing like water, but it did. The rest of Fivel's guns probably suffered from the same problem, since they were part of the same lot. He had to warn him.

This was a bad time for the battery to go out of action. Absent any artillery fire, more Brunswickers would enter the *Bois de Boisseau* and put heart into the Nassauer's within. Columns of red-coated soldiers could be seen emerging from the shelter of the berms and advancing south toward Gemiancourt, while green-jacketed ones were weaving their way through the bushes and brackens to the north of the Gemiancourt stream. The stream gave him an idea: the problem was one of water, and Nature might have the solution he needed.

He ordered his section to cease firing, to their astonishment. He had Vachon explain the situation, then turned command over to him.

"Couldn't we just piss on the guns to cool them, like the infantry who clean fouling by peeing down the barrels?" inquired St. Martin, not known for his intelligence.

"Of course not!" retorted Jacques in exasperation as he rolled his eyes. "It would take a regiment of men to generate that volume of piss." He told his crews to take no action until he returned, then ran as fast as he could toward Fivel. Rounds from Byleveldt's and Stevenaar's Batteries continued to slash the air, adding urgency to his errand.

Fivel received him with surprise but trusted him sufficiently to listen to what he had to say. Fivel frowned, then ordered the guns to cease fire. He quickly inspected each gun personally. "You are right, Gagne. I curse myself for ever accepting these guns in the first place. Our buckets have enough water left to service the guns, but not cool them enough to prevent damage. I got so caught up in the fight to our front, I failed to notice what was going on in the rear."

"I have a plan,"stated Jacques with a confidence that was only half real.

"Bold talk from a youngster! But I will hear your plans because I am in an impossible situation," conceded Fivel. "I can't withdraw, and things are going to get a lot hotter in the next half hour. Even if no more wagons arrive, I have ten rounds in reserve and I damn well intend to use them. Show me how I can do that."

Jacques explained as fast as he could, aware that the drumbeats that accompanied marching soldiers had gotten louder in the short interval in which he spoke. Fivel paced back and forth with his head down as Jacques talked, something he often did when he was deep in thought.

"That's a ridiculous plan, Gagne! But I cannot come up with one that's any better. Hmm, aggression is a better defense than passivity. So we increase the aggression in your plan because often the bigger lie is more readily believed than the smaller one."

Fivel had his bugler sound the assembly. His men gathered round, wondering why they had been called away from smashing the enemy. Fivel's explanation was succinct; soon every crewman knew the plan and as his specific part in it. Their faces reflected mixtures of determination and uncertainty, fortitude as well as fear. Fivel knew they had realistically appraised their chances but would face the long odds with a courage borne of a regard for their mates, himself, and the Emperor. He thought he had never seen such a fine body of men.

"To your posts!"

The men gathered the tools they would need for their jobs and scurried to their appointed positions.

Fivel noted with alarm that a Hanoverian Battery and a British one had begun unlimbering on the *Chasse de Namur*. His position was at the outside range of their weapons, but they could still pose problems. The rhythmic rat-tat-tatting of drums became more insistent and the muffled thudding of footsteps on downed stalks of grain signaled the measured advance of disciplined, deadly men. Both batteries were coming from the rye fields north of the Gemiancourt Stream. The distant six-foot stalks swayed, and not from the wind. He unfurled his glass and caught flashes of red among the rye. A British force of unknown strength was advancing, possibly intent on retaking the Gemiancourt farmstead.

The swaying stalks reminded him of the hand motions of a beautiful woman who had once jilted him: taunting and beckoning at the same time. His hardest task would be to remember that his job was to command and direct, not rush headlong with his men into danger to show himself the bravest among them. That was the problem with their commander today, Marshal Ney. He was justly called "the bravest of the brave", and he led charges personally, but too often Ney's emotions ran away with him. Fivel correctly understood his job was to save lives, which could best be done by remaining physically and mentally detached; the finest instrument of war was a good brain thinking clearly.

He surveyed the main objective of his men with his glass. The Gemiancourt stream had turned blood red and was partly coated with a thin layer of slime from the effluvia of wounds. Thirty or so wounded men of assorted nationalities lay on both sides of it, trying to fill their canteens, drink with cupped hands, or cleanse their weeping wounds. An informal truce had been declared on the water's shore: the men were objects of pity, no threat to anybody.

A flash of green in the brackens to the east of the stream caused him to direct his spyglass in that direction. A steady stream of men were advancing from the *Bois de Chesnes,* two thirds of a kilometer to the northeast. He swore loudly because he recognized the uniforms: the green jackets of the 95th Rifles. They were the finest shots in the British Army, armed with the Baker Rifle which had more than double the range of an infantry musket. Even a few could do his men enormous harm.

The situation was dire, so Fivel resorted to a theatrical gesture. "Men of France! Our enemies bear down upon us! If we do not complete our mission rapidly, we will not live to lament our slowness." He raised his loaded pistol and fired it. "Go!"

The men dashed to their guns and began pushing them twenty paces forward. It was even more back-breaking work than usual since it was done at the fastest possible pace, but it sent an unmistakable message of strength and aggression. Once the guns were in position, two of the gun crews opened fire with canister on the rye fields; manning the pieces that looked to be in the best repair. Two quick rounds generated sufficiently large clouds of smoke to give the rest of the crews cover.

Half of the remaining crews grabbed muskets and formed a loose skirmish line that passed through the guns. Once on the other side, they began descending the shallow hill, firing as they advanced. They were putting on a show designed to divert enemy attention and force them to keep their heads down. The remaining crewmen grabbed a bucket in each hand and made for the stream.

Jacques reached the stream first. He had run the fastest because this had been his idea and he wanted to inspire his men. Two dying men at the water's edge pleaded for help, but he elbowed them aside, feeling terrible as he did so. He dipped his buckets sideways in the water, then brought them up. *Zip zip.* Two rifle bullets sang past his head. He ignored them and rose to a low crouch. He felt something pluck at his left thigh. He looked down to see a fragment of trousers was missing, yet the skin beneath was neither cut nor blemished. The cries of the wounded along the stream bed swelled to a chorus that was painful to hear because it had to be deliberately ignored.

A good friend on Jacques' left clutched his chest in a vain effort to stop a spreading red stain. He was a kindhearted soul who always had a good word for everyone. It took every ounce of Jacques' self-control not to drop the buckets and lift him over his shoulder to carry him away.

Jacques started back toward his guns at a brisk walk, being careful to spill as little water as possible. Bullets continued to whizz past, but his luck held.

The rest of the crews arrived at the stream bed in groups of three or four, composed of men who shared a personal bond beyond the general fellowship of the battery. They dropped to their knees the second they reached the stream and frantically began filling their buckets. They were quickly spotted by the green jackets hidden in the bushes north of the stream, who opened a steady and accurate fire. The diversion provided by the artillery skirmishers had worked on the Redcoats, but the "grasshoppers" of the 95th were Peninsular veterans and were not fooled at all.

Two Frenchmen fell forward into the stream and lay unmoving. A third man caught a glancing blow to the shoulder but did not drop his buckets. A fourth absorbed a spent round to his leg that left it badly bruised, but he managed to rise and start moving toward his gun. Panic spread like wildfire, but the artillerists knew safety lay in the completion of their task, not in giving into their survival instinct. Several men wet themselves, but they persevered, and before long a stream of men was headed toward the guns like a line of bucket passers at a city well answering the sound of a fire bell in the night.

Satisfied that the Redcoats were temporarily quiescent, the *voltigeurs* changed direction and advanced toward the stream. They fired into the brackens and thickets, directing their weapons at the area that seemed to be generating the greatest volume of fire. The amount of enemy fire diminished. Lips grew parched from biting cartridges and faces that were already begrimed with powder turned black as midnight. The air smelled like a sulfurous outpouring from the lowest circles of hell, and their eyes stung from the smoke. Several had eyebrows singed off from being too close to the flash from the pan of the man next to him. Once the last artillerist had filled his buckets and exited the stream, the men about faced, shouldered their weapons, then raced back to the guns.

Jacques waited by his section until the bucket men appeared. The buckets would all have to be thrown together to gain the desired effect. He instructed his men to get ready, then pointed to the place on each barrel where each man should direct his water. "One, two, three, heave!"

The barrels hissed and clouds of steam rose as the water hit. Jacques gingerly touched the barrels of his two guns, and both were merely warm to the touch, not searingly hot. The incipient deformity had been halted, at least for the time being.

Fivel panned his glass toward the field of rye as his crews reloaded. The stalks in the near distance were swaying heavily and the splotches of red were becoming more frequent. The drumbeats swelled in volume. He saw the top of a regimental color and then a king's color. He redirected his glass toward the green-jacketed men coming down from the Namur Road. Riflemen specialized in sniping at artillerists, but they had paused to reform and reload. Judging them the lesser threat for the time being, he again directed his glass toward the rye field.

He caught glimpses of kilts and bonnets and guessed he was facing Scotsmen of the 92nd. Gordon Highlanders under the command of Colonel Cameron. As if to confirm his hunch, bag pipers commenced playing a lively air that told him that their commander no longer felt he needed the element of surprise.

Fivel's crew chiefs signaled they were ready. He furled his glass and drew his sword, signaling to his men that the command to fire was imminent.

The first man to emerge from the rye field was a Highland officer on horseback, possibly Cameron himself. He must have been walking the horse through the field and mounted it at the last moment. The Gordon Highlanders exiting from the field formed themselves into a two-rank line with fixed bayonets. The regimental colors drooped on their poles in the heavy air. Fivel withheld the order to fire because he remembered the Emperor's wise observation to "never interrupt your enemy when he is making a mistake."

Even as the Redcoats straightened their ranks, a line of British riflemen rose like dragon's teeth from the undulating ground east of the stream. These were the dreaded 95th Rifles, who wore green uniforms with black shakos and carried Baker rifles. They advanced in short rushes, working in groups of four, with plenty of space between the men. Their method of advancing, combined with the color of their jackets, had won them the nickname "the grasshoppers". Fivel knew he was in a terrible race against time. If he could fire the guns before the greenbacks brought their rifles to bear, the smoke would throw off their aim. If he miscalculated, his men would die, having failed. But Fivel's cannons were double-shotted with canister, and their targets were an artillerist's dream: closely packed, downhill, and without a speck of cover.

The Highland drummers had just begun to beat the advance when the guns of Fivel's battery exploded. The rounds ripped huge gaps in the two lines of red, as if they had been punched by six giant fists. Corpses and a carpet of writhing, moaning men marked the places where proud soldiers had just stood. The remaining men staggered backwards. The officer with outsize epaulettes lay badly wounded alongside his dead horse. Several men dragged him back to the safety of the rye field. A second officer on horseback appeared and took command. He frantically redirected his Redcoats toward the shelter of the rye. The Redcoats were sufficiently dazed that their movements were slow.

Jacques' short-handed crews were cheered by the sight and miraculously squeezed off a second salvo. It was less deadly than the first in terms of casualties, but more deadly in terms of morale. The Scots left standing ran helter skelter.

Fivel's men reloaded quickly and directed their next salvo at the green-jacketed riflemen. Since riflemen advanced individually or in small groups rather than in lines or columns, the rounds did less damage, but they had the desired effect. The riflemen faded back into the brackens and scrubby dips from which they had emerged.

Fivel had no time to congratulate himself on the outcome because a messenger arrived and relayed an order that astounded him. He was being directed to give up the position he had fought so hard to retain. "This cannot be," he remonstrated to the messenger. "It makes no sense. I believe there is a potential assault brewing on Gemiancourt and we can break it up before it begins if we simply continue firing."

The messenger sighed in exasperation. He was tired of dealing with commanders who disputed orders, and he had dealt with many this day. "The orders come directly from Marshal Ney. He has been informed that Lord Wellington has arrived on the field and is in direct command at the crossroads. He believes your fire would be better employed at a new location to the east. Another messenger will arrive momentarily to give you the exact placement."

Fivel glared at the messenger, then sighed in resignation as he realized it was as pointless to argue with a messenger as it was to teach tricks to a cat. "Consider the order acknowledged and understood."

The lieutenant saluted crisply, pivoted his horse, and galloped away.

Officious little prick, thought Fivel. *Those staff officers are all cut from the same cloth.*

A chorus of moans and groans met Fivel's order to withdraw.

Jacques was shocked and dismayed. Claudette and Babbette had proven superb kissers, and his men had planted their kisses in exactly the right spots. *This order is a punishment, not a reward,* he thought indignantly. He wondered what Marshal Ney was thinking. Perhaps Ney knew something he did not, but he was learning to trust his instincts and they demanded that the fight should be pressed from their present position. His Quaker upbringing had taught him to disdain waste in any form, and that's what today had been, sheer waste.

His men saw his depression and they whispered among themselves. One man had an idea that produced giggles. A single bucket of water remained full, and they had the perfect use for its contents. "Gagne!" one shouted.

He turned to face them and was met with the full contents of the bucket. The water felt good and refreshing on his face and bare chest, and it arrested his disordered thinking. Some might have seen the act as one of insubordination, but he knew his men intended only the best. They laughed merrily, glad to have something to distract them from the blood and gore they had endured and inflicted. He joined in the laughter; the spirit of good fellowship making him realize his ridiculous appearance reflected the ridiculousness of the situation.

They had just begun to limber up the guns when he heard a familiar and unexpected voice. "Jacques, I knew I would find you where the action was hottest. I took your advice. A good night's sleep in a decent bed, good food, and a new wardrobe can do wonders for a girl."

It was Pauline. She was clad in a brand-new high-waisted, bottle-green frock of fine wool, a cashmere shawl the color of amber, and a white silk bonnet that featured a pattern of roses and tulips. She looked healthier and happier. She also bore the scent of a perfume based on roses and peaches — a refreshing change from the smells of saltpeter and sweat. Her post battle appearance was as incongruous as a rose gracing a dung heap.

Rifle bounded up to her, flashing teeth in a poodle's grin, seeking a pet or two. She obliged attentively. Rifle usually exhibited hostility to newcomers, so his approval was a good sign.

"How is it you always appear after one of my battles? How do you manage it without supernatural intervention? I am pleased to see you, but you should not be here."

"When a woman cares about someone she finds a way to be near him. I have been through battles before; I know how to thread my way through while avoiding harm to myself. I hired a local guide who needed money and was charmed to assist the cause of love. You have a very handsome chest, by the way."

The talk of love and his chest unsettled Jacques. He was attracted to her, but he had been raised to regard private relations between a man and a woman as something that belonged to marriage. Nevertheless, he was loath to send her away. He needed feminine tenderness and understanding badly.

He decided his course in an instant of insight. He was a marked man, targeted by this woman's attention and intent, and could not for the life of him decide whether that was a good thing or a bad thing. *One step at a time*, he told himself. His decision felt right because his depression retreated and his energy level surged. "Very well, Pauline. You may stay... for the time being."

***

16 June 1815, 4 p.m., the fields and farmlands of Quatre Bras
Boom! Boom! Boom! Boom!
Sergent Jean Paul Gagne's *voltigeurs* covered their ears each time *Capitaine* Tacon's Battery of six guns fired on their right and *Capitaine* Barbeaux's Battery fired on their left. The target of this converging fire was a gathering of 1,800 men who had taken shelter in the *Bois de Boisseau*; the 1st and 3rd Battalions of the 2nd Nassau Regiment, and a volunteer Jaeger Company. Their woodland hide was well suited for defense: plenty of tall trees, dense thickets, fallen logs, and shallow ravines that offered refuge for troops who had undergone a harrowing baptism of fire earlier that morning. Their dispositions and formations were nearly impossible to see, concealed by the drifting clouds of gun smoke from artillery and muskets.

The guns of Tacon's Battery alternated firing canister with solid shot. The round shot was directed at the trees behind which the men sheltered. There were loud cracks as trees fell, splinters flew, and logs were upturned. But the only way to be sure of a victory was by direct infantry assault, followed by charges of cuirassiers and lancers once the concealed men had been flushed into the open. The five six-pounders of Stevenaar's Battery, arrayed in open ground to the east of the forest, had ceased firing at the French guns. Likely they were reserving their fire for when the French infantry assault began.

Jean Paul Gagne's men would form part of the spearhead of that assault, although his platoon was down to 15 men of the original 24. Some had been victims of battle, others of disease. He gave his soldiers a quick, brutally honest summary of what to expect. He emphasized seeing to the safety of their partner, the man who provided cover while one reloaded. But he warned the men never to bunch up, for a group was an easier target. Lastly, he gave an instruction that surprised everyone, yet it made sense.

Six French battalions totaling 3,000 men formed up for the attack in three lines, with three feet between each man, occupying the half mile of open ground between the *Bois de Pierrepont* and the *Bois de Boisseau*. Gagne's men were at the extreme right of the first rank. The lines moved uphill at 76 paces per minute with bayonets advanced and drummers beating the *pas de charge*. The officers pranced, danced, and twirled their shakos atop their upraised swords. They cheered their men on, while the men chorused *Vive l'Empereur!* almost as if it were a holy incantation. Complete silence issued from the woods.

Gagne expected the first enemy volley to come at 130 meters, but it did not materialize. A further thirty-meter advance provoked no response. The enemy commander was displaying sound judgment by delaying his fire. The closer the range, the greater the chances that shots would find homes.

At eighty meters, Gagne felt a tingling in his temples as goose bumps formed on his arms, old scars on his leg pulsed, and the hairs on his arms, legs, and back stood on end. He liked to believe his intuition had a supernatural quality to it, as if powers far greater than he were interested in his protection; but deep down he knew it was the product of good instincts mated to plenty of battle experience.

"Platoon One, oblique right at the double quick and... down!" he shouted at the top of his lungs. His men veered right ten paces and threw themselves flat into the field of clover. Their faces had barely touched the ground when a rippling volley exploded from the edge of the wood. It ripped large holes in the front rank and left a carpet of dead and dying who chorused a hellish outpouring of shrieks and moans. Smoke filled the air as did the acrid smell of saltpeter.

Some of Gagne's men moved to rise but he hissed, "No! Only on my command." Another volley followed in short order, not as destructive as the first but enough to kill and wound dozens of Frenchmen. Gagne had guessed correctly that after the first rank fired those men would retire a few paces, to be replaced by a second rank that was already loaded. Once they had discharged their weapons, both ranks would have to reload. "Now, now's our time!" he shouted to his platoon. "Up, up, and have at em!" His men obeyed with alacrity and thrust their bayonets forward. "Charge!"

The same command was shouted by dozens of other officers and NCOs. French dead and dying were stepped over as the entire line raced toward the edge of the forest, howling like devils and screaming a variety of curses.

Tremblay and Le Duc were the first of Gagne's men to pierce the woods, and each caught a Nasseaur in the act of biting open a cartridge. Tremblay took his man in the neck, while Le Duc accounted for his with a thrust to the chest. Rochfort and Collette fired their weapons from the hip at point blank range, killing two more, then dispatched the men at their sides with bayonet jabs. Martin and Du Bois each fought an opponent who knew how to use a bayonet and went through a quick cycle of thrust, low block, thrust, parry, high block, slash, medium block, and jab. Both clashes resulted in fatal denouements for the Nassauers. Fontenoy as usual refused to fight, but he performed his function of reloading for the others, also holding himself ready to drag any wounded clear of the fight.

Sous Lieutenant Le Clair engaged in a sword duel with a green-coated lieutenant. He looked to be about the same age as Le Clair, just as frightened and just as lacking in skill. Le Clair won simply because he was faster.

Gagne surveyed the line ahead for the most experienced-looking NCO, and shot him.

The French forced their way slowly through the forest, their skirmish lines becoming many short ones rather than several long ones because of the broken nature of the ground. Men stumbled, fell, picked themselves up, and staggered on. Some were shot as they rose; others were too frightened to rise and hugged the ground.

The Nassauers gave ground grudgingly, but the superior training and experience of the French gave them the edge. Most business was done with the bayonet, but significant numbers of ragged volleys were fired by both sides. The trees and heavy foliage trapped the gun smoke and made breathing difficult; Gagne heard wheezing, coughing, and retching. The tall trees, rutted trails, heavy foliage, and undulating terrain meant that rather than being one large fight, the battle changed into innumerable smaller ones, often one knot of three or four men fighting an equal number of foes, completely isolated from the rest of the conflict. Each man's world became a few square meters of turf.

After four close quarter encounters, Gagne stopped counting the number of individual fights his platoon had engaged in. Rochefort was slightly wounded but continued to fight. Gagne had not yet lost a man, and his platoon had accounted for at least two dozen of the enemy.

The first line of gradually retreating German Nassauers did most of the fighting and took most of the casualties, but they bought time for the second line to take up locations behind a line of logs, fallen trees, boulders, and declivities. They opened a destructive fire on the increasingly chaotic French advance. The woods were dark, and with the choking clouds of gunfire it became difficult to distinguish friend from foe. Some of the French wore green and blue uniforms much like the Nasseaurs in color and cut, which added to the confusion. Shouts and curses in French or German were better indicators of who was where than visual identification.

Officers on both sides who sought to bring order to the chaos were the first ones to die. Their shouts and exhortations generated lots of noise, and so turned them into aiming points for men for men firing blind. The contest turned into an infantryman's fight where every man exercised a considerable degree of personal generalship. The real leaders became experienced NCOs like Gagne. The targeting of ill-defined shapes moving in and out of the twilight haze resulted in a considerable number of deaths from friendly fire. Gagne had told his men to look at the silhouette of the shako first, because Nassau shakos were lower and more rounded than those of the French.

The smoke facilitated many chance collisions. A typical one involved Private Jacques Roux of the 4th Legere, who ran headfirst into Private Hans Huizinga of the 2nd Nassau, as both emerged from the smoke, bushes, and brambles at the same moment. Both blinked in shock and surprise, as if each could not quite credit that he was literally face to face with the enemy. Neither thought the other looked like the demon that he had been told he faced. They looked equally ordinary to each other and were of the same age build and age. Despite their training, neither wanted to kill the other. Both lowered their muskets and stared uncertainly into each other's eyes. The matter was settled by Roux's colleague, Private Morel, who bayoneted Huizinga without giving it a moment's thought.

For an increasing number of survivors, looting took precedent over fighting. The French were short on nearly all supplies, so Anglo-Allied haversacks were prime targets for the rations they contained. Boots were also much sought after. In the crucible of prolonged warfare, food and footwear were more valuable than gold. Few prisoners were taken, because sending them to the rear under guard was not possible. No quarter was asked, and none was given. The cries of the wounded for water were ignored.

A few scattered fires broke out, caused by sparks from the flashes of musket pans. Most were quickly stamped out, but a few progressed sufficiently to detonate the contents of cartridge boxes of wounded men; granting them a quick death rather than a lingering one. The smoke these fires generated added further to the stinking murk.

As the atmosphere grew heavy, men dropped from heat exhaustion. Most recovered after a few minutes of stupefied rest, but some suffered fatal results. A few died silently from carbon dioxide poisoning as that deadly gas, given off by firearms and gasping men, accumulated.

Gagne's men threaded their way through the roiling chaos, dispatching opponents as they encountered them. The platoon's movements reflected Gagne's mastery of small unit actions. Each action sharpened the bonds of fellowship, loyalty, and skill; concerns for personal welfare faded as the identity of the group strengthened.

At the north edge of the wood, the platoon's forward progress was blocked by a two-story cottage that stood directly astride the path ahead. The square structure of thick, whitewashed stone, thatched roof, and grey half timbers looked like it belonged to Snow White.

The structure was surrounded by a large, gated garden with three-foot-high brick walls. Four German Nassauers had barricaded themselves in the cottage at its center; two musket barrels protruded from windows on the second floor and two from those on the first. Two men lay flat on their bellies in the garden, and two crouched on either side of the gate.

Gagne motioned for his men to take cover while he assessed the situation. He took his time, but two other platoons rushed past, emboldened by the impetuosity of combat. Gagne watched two assaults fail because of the hubris of their commanders.

In the first assault, five Frenchmen charged the gate which the defenders had left open. The Nassauers slammed the gate shut and turned the enclosure into a kill zone. The French had counted on using bayonets and had not even loaded their muskets. They were cut down by accurate musketry fired from three directions.

In the second attempt, six Frenchmen opened a lively musket fire on the enclosure from a single position, not deigning to employ enfilade fire. They were led by an officer who goaded his men on with the flat of his blade. The Nassau commander correctly judged that the Frenchmen hated their officer and obeyed only out of fear. The Nassauers ignored the rest of the men and focused their fire exclusively on the officer. When he fell, his men seemed almost grateful and departed quickly.

Gagne's plan came down to horse sense. Tremblay had discovered three beasts tethered to a tree at the edge of the woods, 400 meters away. Officers had probably left them before the start of the battle, since riding into combat in heavy forest was impractical. *Sous Lieutenant* Le Clair loved horses and would have liked to have appropriated the trio for his personal mounts, but Gagne saw them coldly: not as lovely animals but as assets that could be used to spare the lives of their men. Whether they died mattered less than whether they prevented his men from doing so. He needed horses that were fast and skilled at jumping. The other requirement, that they not be frightened by gunfire, was a given.

Gagne divided his platoon into three sections. One put the cottage under fire from the left, one from the right. Le Clair, the only horseman amongst them, rode straight at the enclosure, sword extended and yelling madly. His horse leaped the gate, followed by the other two. The sudden appearance of three war stallions shocked the defenders, and they froze momentarily. Le Clair cut down two as they rose from the garden. The other men managed to shoot two wildly kicking horses, but doing so caused them to reveal their positions and they were systematically picked off by musket fire. Gagne's third section rushed the gate and finished off the last few defenders.

Then the men looted the corpses. Tremblay was pleased to find their officer had worn a money belt under his sash that contained gold coins worth more than he would be paid in ten years. That he had an expensive watch was a mere bonus.

The cottage was stocked with beer, sausages, and cheese. Gagne knew more fighting lay ahead, but his men were hungry and thirsty and deserved a reward. The Emperor could spare them for a quarter hour. The men pitched into the victuals with the same determination they had shown in battle.

Sous Lieutenant Le Clair was content to let his NCO issue orders. Tears came to his eyes as he contemplated the dead horses. They had been thoroughbreds. Such a waste!

The main body of the French infantry gradually pushed the Nasseaurs to the northeast edge of the woods. The Nasseaurs were down to their last few rounds. Colonel Prince Sassen-Weimar, their commander, made the decision to withdraw towards the crossroads, making for the tall fields of wheat and rye which would shield their progress. He managed to extricate two thirds of the survivors and had them quick marching north in columns when disaster materialized.

The 485 green-and-azure-coated men of Pire's cavalry had skirted the woods. The 1st *Chasseurs* were cuirassiers, so named because of the steel cuirasses which encased their chests and back: large men on huge horses with 45-inch swords. The Nassauers were weighed down by muskets, accoutrements, and fatigue. By the time they saw the cuirassiers charging them it was too late to form a square, the preferred method of dealing with cavalry. Indeed, the cuirassier's assault was so rapid they could not even form a line.

A saturnalia of slashing, cutting, and trampling commenced that shattered the Allied columns into a mass of fleeing fugitives. They raced for the imagined safety of the rye fields a hundred meters ahead, but horses were faster than even the fleetest of feet.

Chasseur Bardet decapitated two fleeing infantrymen and laughed as he did so. Chasseur Pomeau's horse trampled three men to death, then his blade accounted for another three. *Chasseur* Souchon killed so many men with his sword that he grew bored and decided to test his marksmanship for amusement. His heavy Year XIII pistols of .67 caliber were accurate only at close range, but his eye was good. He shot one man in the base of the skull at twenty meters and another in the lower back at thirty.

Scarcely half the Nassauers made it to the rye fields. At that point, the cuirassiers pulled up their mounts and halted, preparatory to turning the show over to the lancers. A nine-foot lance was better suited than a sword for skewering fugitives cowering among stalks. A man might avoid a sword by throwing himself flat, but he could not escape a lance.

The 412 Frenchmen of the 5th Lancers charged into the fields. The ensuing screams of pain, fear, and confusion indicated they were doing their jobs. Nassauers died by the dozens, most impaled from the rear rather than the front. One lancer rode ahead to the edge of the field and planted his lance as a marker were it could be seen above the tall rye: a signal the 381 men of the fast-approaching 6th Lancers.

Lancer Luvais, in a fit of foolish bravado designed to showcase both his tremendous strength and his contempt for his enemies, hurled his heavy lance as if it was a javelin. Its impact did not so much impale the man it hit as crush him. He trotted over to his victim and jerked the lance free as effortlessly as if it had been a pin in a pincushion.

One lone gun of Stevenaar's Dutch battery attempted to keep pace with the battle, even after the other guns had been destroyed or recalled. Acting on his own authority, Sergeant de Groot, the commander, now ordered the six-pounder unlimbered and loaded with a charge of canister. He was inexperienced, and that affected his ability to estimate the proper range and elevation. His aim was badly off when the piece fired. Instead of the 85 musket balls hitting the lancers or cuirassiers, most of them reached the tree line. But they were not ineffective, for the French infantry had sheltered there. Some of the canister landed among Gagne's men.

Duquesne and Frontenac, the two privates who usually preferred to fire lying on their bellies, died. One-minute there were men, the next flying body parts. Gagne had the presence of mind to hurry the remainder of his platoon to cover. The men whispered to each other in disbelief and anger.

"It's monstrously unfair!" exclaimed LeDuc. "To make it through a battle where men are deliberately trying to kill you, only to die from a stray shot that isn't even aimed at you."

"Who ever said battle was fair?" rejoined Rochfort.

"Their luck ran out. Mine is still in," said Tremblay. "I look forward to spending my newfound fortune."

"I am just glad to be alive," muttered Collette.

"That is all any soldier can wish for," remarked Gagne. "The battle is finally going our way. If Marshal Ney will follow up our success here, the Emperor will have himself a victory." He looked at the sky and the sun's position. By his soldierly estimate , it was not yet 5 p.m.

***

16 June 1815, 5 p.m., near Quatre Bras

Pennywhistle, near the front of the convoy, spotted an approaching horseman riding hell for leather, and nudged Diable into a canter to intercept the messenger ahead of the scouts. His alertness transformed into sudden alarm as he recognized first the horse, then the rider. The chestnut-colored stallion was Copenhagen, Wellington's campaign companion since 1813. Copenhagen was famous for his strength, endurance, and battlefield intelligence. For Wellington to push him thus meant the Duke was about urgent business.

"What took you so long?" demanded Wellington. "We are hard pressed, and the outcome at the crossroads is far from certain. Many soldiers are out of ammunition."

This emergency explained why the Duke had ridden a quarter mile from the crossroads to meet him.

"I did the best I could, Your Grace. The roads were crowded and traffic stoppages frequent. Two of the wagons suffered broken wheels, three of the horses went lame, and two collapsed from heat exhaustion.

We will deliver the cargo, I just need to know which units are in the severest need."

Wellington rattled off a quick appraisal of the situation at the crossroads, as well as detailed account of the ammunition supply of each regiment, yet another example of his mastery of logistics. He drew a map from his pocket and pointed out the positions of his various units.

Tragically, the Duke of Brunswick had been killed at the *Bois de Boisseau*. Brunswick had been one of the brightest lights of the Anglo-Allied High Command, a skillful commander who had many times led his soldiers to victory during the Peninsular Campaigns. Ousted from his Duchy by Bonaparte in 1809, he had fled to Britain, taking with him several thousand well-trained soldiers. They were promptly put on the British payroll, with the duke commissioned as a lieutenant general. He'd chosen black uniforms for his men, topped by shakos bearing a skull and crossbones front plate, to signify mourning for their occupied country. Brunswick had hated Bonaparte the way a man with perfect pitch hates an off-key singer. His remaining men thirsted for revenge, and had taken up positions as flank guards for the British 33rd Regiment.

On the side of the *Chausse de Charleroi,* soldiers of the 69th, 44th, 42nd, and 32nd Regiments were holding off determined assaults of French infantry, their eventual objective being the Gemiancourt Farm. George Cooke's division was just arriving on the field and was moving to reinforce both efforts, as well as the 95th which held the army's left flank.

Wellington's army had 18 guns in play, three batteries of six guns, situated along the ridge known as the Batti St. Barnard. From right to left, commanders Rogers, Van Cleeve and Lloyd directed the batteries to cover the *Chausse de Namur*, keeping the French guns on the opposite ridge of Gemiancourt in check.

The one area where Wellington was deficient was cavalry. He simply did not have enough, and those of his Dutch and Belgian allies were unseasoned and ineffective. Pire's cavalry was causing havoc, and Pennywhistle would have to get the convoy past them.

Most British regiments had formed squares against Pire's cavalry: a four-rank-deep formation where the two front ranks kneeled with fixed bayonets while the two standing behind them poured volleys into any cavalry that came too close. Officers directed events from the hollow center, which also formed a place of refuge for the wounded. Since a horse will not jump over a fixed bayonet, squares were nearly impenetrable to cavalry so long as their integrity was maintained. The squares were holding the cavalry in check, while reducing their numbers with well-directed fire.

"Of course," Wellington remarked, "that was twenty minutes ago. By the time you arrive they will have rearranged themselves in accordance with the stresses of battle."

"Your Grace," Pennywhistle said, "I had a bit of luck on my way here. One of the Belgians in my convoy grew up in the area and knows it well. He has furnished me with detailed information about the roads and key features of the terrain. With what he told me and the information you have provided, I just need to make a quick personnel reconnaissance to determine how best to distribute the ammunition.

"How much reconnaissance time?"

"Fifteen minutes."

"That is a lot to ask. While you are mincing about, men will be dying for want of bullets. What good is delivering ammunition to dead men?"

"It comes down to this, Your Grace. If I proceed immediately, some of the ammunition will certainly get through in a haphazard manner. If I act with circumspection, nearly all of it will be delivered where it is most needed. May I have your permission to borrow various personnel? I would like to say I act with your full authority."

"Hmm. Very well."

"Then I will borrow men of Major Whinyate's rocket troop and some of their equipment."

The Duke looked startled. "Whatever for? They are a useless set of fellows who would be better employed as regular artillery."

"Congreve Rockets can be employed for a variety of unconventional uses."

"Very well, Pennywhistle, take what men you will. Now be off with you." Wellington turned his horse and galloped down the road.

A short ride brought Pennywhistle to Whinyate's sidelined rocket troop. The men looked disconsolate at being granted no role in the day's fighting. Even Pire's cavalry were ignoring them as inconsequential.

Major Edward Charles Whinyate was a bright, enthusiastic young man who believed as wholeheartedly in his rockets as Wellington disdained them. He was quick to appreciate the potential of Pennywhistle's plan, and made practical suggestions. "I can lend you Lieutenant Gascoigne and five men who are skilled fuse cutters. They are tired of being ridiculed and will welcome a change to show what they can do." Gascoigne, Pennywhistle was please to discover, had seen considerable service in Spain. He projected an air of quiet confidence.

With the six rocketeers and eight Congreves, Pennywhistle rejoined his caravan.

Maxwell was angry that he was assigned to the ten hussars who would bring up the rear and constitute a mobile defense force. He was somewhat mollified when told that he was placed where he was because Pennywhistle had been impressed with his swordsmanship on horseback. Lancers were a danger, but his size and agility might make Maxwell the one man who could handle them. A swordsman was always at a disadvantage with a lancer, since the nine feet of a lance outranged any sword. The only way to defeat a lancer was to move faster than he and turn inside the arc of the lance so he could not wield it effectively.

Pennywhistle moved his caravan briskly but carefully. Men and horses darted back and forth across the road at frequent intervals, limiting its speed and causing several halts. He altered his course just before he reached the crossroads and executed a circular half turn to the north. He halted at a clearing two hundred meters east of the *Quatre Bras* farmstead and a similar distance north of the *Chausse de Namur*. The wagons were partially shielded from enemy view by the several berms, and it would be a central location from which to distribute ammunition. He instructed van Dreelin and van der Beek to set up their waterworks and instructed the men to start unloading the wagons.

He rode Diable a hundred yards to higher ground and unfurled his Ramsden.

He panned his spyglass over the chaotic scene in front of him. Swirling clouds of smoke, thunderous noise, and fast-moving men and horses made him realize his distribution plan was flawed. He had conceived of an orderly dispersal based on an orderly environment. Most of the men were formed in squares and had to stay where they were.

He slapped himself on the forehead as a flash of insight made him realize that he had entirely misread the situation. If the squares could not come to him, he would come to them. It would be a tight fit, but with the horses untethered a wagon could fit inside a square, making ammunition distribution easy and direct.

Five squares stood firm, but there seemed to be hesitation in the 69th Regiment. Seven of its ten companies remained in line, two just milled about, and one had begun to form the front of a sixth square. A harassed looking colonel argued violently with a major expostulating madly with his hands: a look of confusion suffused the face of a sergeant standing to their right. Pennywhistle could not for the life of him guess the problem, then he saw an entourage of 14 aides following a foppishly dressed man and understood everything.

Dear God! It was "Slender Billy," the Prince of Orange. Personally brave and reasonably intelligent, he was as devoid of tactical intuition as a desert was of water. The 22-year-old was heir to the Dutch throne and had seen action in Spain. He had been educated in England and had until recently been engaged to one of George III's daughters. His nickname supposedly sprang from his ridiculously slim neck, but others suggested it had more to do with his thin acquaintance with common sense. The bloody fool Prince must have told his men to stay in line formation.

The pounding of hooves from the rye fields increased in volume and suggested the imminent arrival of a fresh wave of cavalry, possibly lancers. Experienced British officers knew the prince's commands were an affront to good tactics and were struggling to reconcile the execution of a lawful order with their aversion to the certain death of great numbers of their men. Pennywhistle was skilled at reading battlefields and knew an entirely preventable disaster lay just ahead. He could not stop it, but he could mitigate its severity. He saw with dreadful clarity what must shortly come to pass, and his revulsion spurred an intense calculation of competing variables.

When he got back to his men, his plan was fully formed. His men were no fools and had noticed the peculiar configuration of the 69th. "We are going to bring the ammunition to the squares. Half of the contents of the wagons will remain here for later dispersal. The captain of each wagon must choose a regiment, then make for it with all possible speed, using the king's colors as a focal point. Keep the straightest possible course and halt for nothing. You may well be under fire, but the faster you move the sooner you will be under the protection of your square's musketry. It's the wagons that matter, the horses are expendable. Cut them loose as soon as you are close enough to the squares and let the men to grab hold of the wagons.

"I will command the sixth wagon. Empty it of the regular barrels and load it with the ones made into bomb barrels." He pointed to Gascoigne. "Lieutenant, you and your men will light the fuses and lay the bombs at my command. I also want you to have your two Congreve's ready to fire at a moment's notice."

Gascoigne smiled. "The rockets have a very unsettling effect on horses."

Pennywhistle continued. "The hussars will follow behind and try to keep enemy cavalry off our tails." He turned to Maxwell and Sommers. "Don't engage until the bombs have been detonated. I want any horsemen you face disoriented. Remember, your job is to provide a distraction for the infantry, not seek glory for yourselves."

Sommers nodded, but Maxwell frowned.

The wagonners looked at each other in surprise. It was a strange plan, but given the odd circumstances, appropriate.

"Now, get moving."

Pennywhistle's sense of urgency was infectious, and the men completed their preparations in short order. The wagon captains positioned their wagons in line abreast order and awaited his command. The humid air reeked of the twin scents of rye pounded into rubble and equine sweat. Pennywhistle drew his sword. He pointed to the squares ahead, then slashed downward. "Go, go, go!" he shouted. The captains cracked their whips and the wagons clattered forward.

Wagon one steered towards the 30th Regiment and wagon two towards the 33rd. They were quickly taken into each of the squares just as the French cavalry burst from the rye. The bandsmen distributed enough cartridges to ensure the French cuirassiers were met but plenty of lead greetings.

The resulting volleys staggered the French squadrons, tumbling horses and men to the ground. A few horsemen got to their feet and desperately sought wayward mounts. Those still in their saddles flashed by in a blur, their horses unwilling to get close to the line of steel. French officers gallantly reformed the survivors and led another assault on the north and east faces of the squares. It met with the same result and added to the carpet of writhing, moaning human and equine flesh. A line of unwounded men jogged toward the safety of the rye fields whence they had come.

Wagons three, four, and five reached the squares of the Guards, 44th, and 73rd Regiments without incident and were met by choruses of cheers and huzzahs. Cartridges were distributed and a brisk fire maintained on horsemen who, seeing the fate of their brethren, maneuvered with more caution than elan.

Deflected by the galling fire of the five resupplied squares, the remaining horsemen directed their wrath against the 69th. It had almost formed itself into a square when one officer made a fatal mistake. The line of men he commanded could have closed the square, but he instead told it to about face and delivery a volley into the faces of cavalry hot on their heels. The volley was devastating, but the French cavalry was so close that their momentum was unstoppable. They shattered the line as if it had been glass and sent the fugitives scurrying for cover that did not exist.

A quarter of the cavalry pursued the fleeing men with vigor while the rest charged the partially formed square. A volley emptied a few saddles, but the force of the charge caused the incipient square to implode. The French smashed British morale utterly as they cut, slashed, and drove their swords into men who had no effective way to resist. The men who were not felled by swords were trampled by thundering hooves. The remainder gave the cavalry its dream: defenseless running men with their backsides exposed. Many horsemen shouted *"Vive l'Empereur!"* in triumph as they dug their spurs hard into their mounts.

The fierce impetuosity of the French charge meant the horsemen were uninterested in taking prisoners. The few men who held their hands up in supplication were ruthlessly butchered. Some threw themselves on the ground and played dead, hoping to rise as soon as the horsemen had ridden past. They had not anticipated the lancers just emerging from the distant rye.

A fierce struggle commenced for possession of the 69th's regimental colors, a large green flag containing the regiment's number in Roman numerals in the center. The numerals resided on a shield surrounded by roses, thistles, and laurel leaves. A small Union Jack occupied the upper left quadrant. The large standard furnished a way to pinpoint the regiment's position in battle as well as serving as a rallying point. Its loss would be a great blow to the regiment's honor. A young ensign, an older sergeant, and a gentleman volunteer were fending off the attackers. Three cuirassiers died before two of the British succumbed.

The mortally wounded ensign tore the silk flag from its pole, wrapped it around his body, and dropped to the ground.

The horsemen left the dying ensign rather than having to dismount and unwind the flag from his middle. Another struggle had erupted over the regiment's king's colors a few meters to the east. This was a large Union Jack with the regiment's number in Roman numerals on a shield in the center. They joined in the assault on this second group with determination. The four defenders of this standard went down hard, one gentleman volunteer suffering a panoply of wounds, yet refusing to die. Triumphant, the French galloped off, holding the captured standard high and shouting *"Quelle Glorieux!"*

Pennywhistle calculated trajectories. Bombs exploding where the two were intermixed could kill friend and foe alike. He spotted a group of horsemen who were as yet unengaged— an ideal target. He gave the command for the wagon to move, but at a deliberate pace. He wanted it to be seen, to act as a lure. As Gascoigne readied the Congreves, Pennywhistle trotted ahead of the wagon. British infantry men scurried past, but he ignored them, realizing the best way to help them was to cut down the strength of their pursuers.

A shout from a French officer indicated his wagon had been seen. The officer formed his men up for a charge.

"Now, Mr. Gasgoine! Aim for that fierce looking fellow who appears to be in command." He pointed to the approaching squadron. "Once the first rocket has stirred things up, unleash the second."

"Right sir," replied Gascoigne cheerfully

Gascoigne's first rocket hissed evilly, trailed sparks, and zigzagged crazily once it departed its launcher. Its malevolent sound reminded Pennywhistle of a dragon reacting badly to be woken from a sound sleep. The rocket soared high in an unpredictable pattern then plunged to earth, landing in front of the charging squadron. The shards of its cone gutted five horses, but that was not the chief damage. The shocking noise it had made panicked the horses nearly as much as it panicked their riders. The horses neighed and reared, and their riders struggled to keep them under control.

Gascoigne fired his second shot, but this time it did not land anywhere close to its target. Its noise and appearance, however, had more effect than all the shards it contained. The horses turned and stampeded in the opposite direction. Pennywhistle knew it would be some time before their riders would be able to bring them under control, so they were effectively out of the fight.

Pennywhistle's efforts had attracted the attentions of another squadron of lancers, so he gave the command to the wagon captain to move in a direction parallel to the approaching horsemen. As he did so, Gascoigne opened the rear flap of the wagon and readied his flint and striker to light the fuses of the bomb barrels. When Pennywhistle judged the moment right, the wagon master changed direction, back toward the *Chausse de Namur*. Gascoigne's men lit the fuses and dumped the barrels at two second intervals.

The first four barrels exploded too soon and did no damage, alerting the pursuing French to the danger, causing them to slacken their pace. Their caution proved exactly the wrong move; a faster pace would have taken them past the barrels before they exploded. When the barrels detonated it was like the effects of one giant volley. It was an unaimed volley, the bullets flying in every direction, but enough flew in the right direction to take down two lines of charging cuirassiers and cause the rest to pull up hard. The wagon master had angled in such a way that the Frenchmen could not see whether the wagon contained more deadly surprises.

Small groups of fugitives streamed past the wagon. A few waved and shouted at Pennywhistle, thankful for the respite he had given them. Pennywhistle wished he could do more, but it was time to go. He had just given the command to head for the rear when his peripheral vision detected his worst nightmare: a line of cavalry wearing the distinctive *czapskas* — red and gold square topped hats — and *kurkas* —tight fitting blue jackets with yellow front panels called plastrons — that were worn only by lancers. Their lances were leveled and headed his way.

There were at least a hundred, and they would reach him before he could reach his own lines. He drew his sword and prepared to make his best defense, wishing yet again that he were a better rider.

Sommers knew it was time to act, even if his chances of survival were slim at best. He and his ten men charged headlong at the lancers. Hussars, which were considered light cavalry, did not generally oppose lancers. Light cavalry generally struck quick glancing blows then dashed off, while heavy cavalry remained in place to engage in extended struggles.

Two of Sommer's men were impaled and unhorsed by the leading troopers of the lancer squadron, but the rest made it past, slashing sideways with their blades as they rode, severely wounding four of their enemy. Hussar's horses were smaller and faster than those of the lancers and could turn tighter corners. Sommers used this to his advantage, as his men pivoted and attacked the rear troopers of the squadron from behind. Slashing downwards, Sommer's men killed five lancers before the rest could react. But react they did, eventually boxing in Sommer's and his remaining eight men into an ever-tightening circle. Sommer's men had no chance, but they sold their lives dearly, taking five more lancers with them as they bought time for Pennywhistle and his wagon to escape.

Pennywhistle watched Sommer's sacrifice with sadness. He did not spur Diable to the gallop, choosing to keep pace with the wagon.

Maxwell had remained behind as part of a plan he had agreed upon with Sommers. He had made it his job to act as Pennywhistle's personal guardian angel. He was not doing it out of selflessness but to prove to Pennywhistle that his limited trust in him had not been misplaced. More than anything he wanted that harpy of a wife to know how wrong she had been about him.

He saw five troopers break free of the melee with Sommers to pursue Pennywhistle. Maxwell charged straight at them.

He swept aside the lance of his first opponent, stabbing the rider's horse in the flank to disable it. The second lancer aimed straight at his chest, but he used his blade to deflect the lance upward, then shot the man with one of the two pistols he carried on either side of his saddle. He shot a second man with his remaining pistol. Continuing past the other two, he pivoted and ran one lancer through from the rear. The fifth brought his horse round and stopped. He stared fiercely into Maxwell's eyes and Maxwell returned his gaze with an equal ferocity.

Suddenly it was not 1815, but 1415. Maxwell had the feeling he was about to fight a knightly duel of the sort that would have been at home at Agincourt. Each man nodded briefly in acknowledgment, then charged straight at the other. The Frenchman's lance struck Maxwell in the shoulder and knocked him from his horse. The wound was painful but far from fatal, spurring Maxwell's rage and determination. Maxwell rolled hard to the right, then slashed at the rear legs of his opponent's mount. The horse reared in pain, then fell sideways. His rider leaped clear, landing on his feet like an enormous cat.

Maxwell rose quickly. Everything had changed in his favor. He was a man with a sword fighting a man with a lance without a horse. The Frenchman readied his nine-foot lance but had only brought it to his waist when Maxwell severed his arm with a mighty blow. Blood jetted from the stub as the man sank to one knee, a stunned expression on his face. Maxwell's imagination had likened this to a medieval contest, but chivalry was not in his character, and he dispatched the Frenchmen with a slash to the throat. He then remounted his horse and galloped back toward Pennywhistle, engaged in combat with two lancers. He was holding his own, but only barely.

Just before Maxwell was within range, Pennywhistle skewered one lancer, but his companion swung his lance as a club as Pennywhistle rode past. The three-inch diameter oak shaft dealt Pennywhistle a heavy blow to the temple, and he toppled unconscious from Diable. The lancer circled back, gloating as he prepared the *coup de grace.*

Johnny had been sheltering in the wagon. Now he leaped down and tried to pick up the dead trooper's lance. It was far too heavy for him, but Dale saw what he intended and joined him. Together they raised the lance and stabbed upward, driving the lance through the back of Pennywhistle's assailant. He gave a loud cry, dropped his lance, and slumped forward over the neck of his steed, who cantered away.

Dale and Johnny helped the unconscious Pennywhistle to his feet. He came to, sort of. "Get the wagon moving," he whispered.

Maxwell came galloping up, two Frenchmen hard on his heels. Dale wondered if Maxwell was aware of the threat astern and guessed that he was not. Then the troopers suddenly disappeared from their saddles. Dale heard the hollow rattle of musket fire. A group of fifteen or so soldiers from the 69th had rallied, seen the predicament of Pennywhistle and his men, and had just given their solution. Dale waved in acknowledgment. Some of the men waved back.

Maxwell's horse ground to a halt in front of Dale and Johnny. "Leave this to me," he shouted. He dismounted, and despite his wound, threw Pennywhistle over his shoulder and then onto the back of his saddle. "It's the fastest way."

He galloped off as Dale clambered back onto the wagon. The small group of the 69th had induced caution in the remaining lancers, giving Dale time to escape. Johnny mounted Diable and raced after Maxwell, his seat surprisingly confident given how much larger the horse was than his small frame.

The next thing Pennywhistle remembered was clear water lapping at his lips from one of van Dreelin's cups pressed to his mouth by Johnny. He sat with his back propped against a tree. Fifty or so tired, begrimed men of various regiments and ranks sat next to him, some sipping water and some gulping it. He felt exhausted and his head hurt but other than that he was fine. He looked up to see Dale, Johnny and Maxwell staring at him with concern. "What happened?"

"Well, Colonel, it's a bit of a story," replied Dale.

"Did the..."

"Yes, Colonel, the rest of the ammunition has been distributed."

"What time is it?" Pennywhistle guessed it was late evening from the fading light in the western sky.

"Getting close on 10 p.m."

He had been out three and a half hours.

"Went the day well?"

"We have suffered heavy casualties, but we have retaken the ground we lost and more, inflicting severe losses on Marshal Ney. A day's work well done, I should say. My guess is we will move toward Mount Saint Jean at dawn."

Pennywhistle noticed the recently bandaged wound on Maxwell's shoulder. "How bad is it?"

"Tis but a scratch, Colonel." It hurt like hell, but Maxwell was damned if he would let Pennywhistle know that. He had fought like a berserker, and berserkers never admitted pain.

Chapter 13

Sabers in the Rain

17 June 1815, 4 a.m., the crossroads of Quatre Bras

Pennywhistle slept fitfully. He had wrapped himself in his boat cloak and used a knapsack for a pillow, choosing a location under one of van Dreelin's water wagons just north of the Quatre Bras farmstead. Dale, Maxwell, and Johnny slept next to him each wrapped in a horse blanket that had belonged to a fallen French mount. Those mounts had furnished dinner as well. Dead horses might be a tragedy, but they made good steaks. Dale had assumed the roles of both butcher and cook; finding that a French cuirassier's sword made a superb meat cleaver and his steel breastplate, when inverted, made an excellent frying pan.

Pennywhistle was awakened periodically by the sounds of French and English pickets exchanging gunfire. His ears told him it was the routine conversation of men trying to determine their enemy's exact location, but the periodic pop popping kept his sixth sense of danger from fully surrendering to the demands of sleep. The low moaning of the wounded concealed in the fields of rye, bothered him as well. Men were out searching for their fallen comrades, but it was a difficult task in the dark. He heard occasional cries of recognition and relief as seeker and fallen friend found each other but he heard frustrated swearing too, indicating that either a comrade had not been found or if he had he was no longer among the living. The cries and swearing were in French as well, those on errands of kindness informally agreeing that mercy swore allegiance to no flag.

He knew some French were searching haversacks for food; their policy of living off the land had caught up with them. Wellington's policy of always paying for goods and punishing looting severely had guaranteed the British a more reliable food supply.

He also heard the unwelcome sounds of numberless scurrying creatures, likely field mice for whom corpses provided an easy meal. Owls hooted at the prospect of a carrion harvest.

The smells of stale sweat, old gun smoke, and ground up rye did not vanish with the onset of night.

Men called runners arrived periodically. These were usually NCOs acting on their own volition: both delivering and seeking information, darting from encampment to encampment. They were much esteemed because their information was always accurate and up to date. They generally had a better and more accurate understanding of the post battle situation than Wellington's own intelligence officers.

Pennywhistle gave up on sleep at 4 am., when he heard a particularly talkative runner announce that Blucher had received a sound thrashing from Napoleon at Ligny, ten miles to the east. Pennywhistle sought out the runner to ask for details.

"Well, sir, I got this information from a Prussian hussar two hours ago, and I am pretty certain that its good. Blucher's Army is withdrawing to the North and West, not the North and East."

Pennywhistle found that development worrisome, but took heart from the fact that Blucher's Prussians had not withdrawn in a direction suggesting they were heading home. The direction they had taken put them in a position to link up with Wellington, though it would happen later than planned.

Destination Waterloo

Knowing that Wellington was an early riser, Pennywhistle decided to pay him a visit. At this point, he was a man without a job, but he still wanted to play a part. The runner had told him that Wellington was currently conversing with officers of the 92nd at their bivouac, half a mile to the East.

Pennywhistle mounted Diable and headed toward Wellington's expected position. The road was crowded with wounded soldiers who had been slung over the backs of cavalry horses for evacuation, since the wagons were wholly inadequate to the enormous task.

Those whose wounds were judged to be less severe rode upright, two to a horse. Upright was a relative term because many swayed back and forth and side to side, as consciousness threatened to desert them. More severely wounded men were piled on four to a horse, like sacks of old grain.

Pennywhistle had never understood horses, but he could have sworn these beasts were displaying an almost human compassion for their damaged riders; moving with great care and gentleness as if to ease the pain caused by their forward movements.

He arrived to find Wellington sleeping with a newspaper over his face. He knew Wellington liked quick cat naps and suspected this was one of them. Taking his cues from the Highlanders surrounding Wellington, he kept quiet and waited.

Wellington abruptly sat up and threw the newspaper into the fire. Fully awake, he summoned his military secretaries to his side and began dictating orders, which they dutifully recorded. The orders were careful and detailed. Pennywhistle realized Wellington had not been sleeping but meditating. The scribes could barely keep up with the pace of Wellington's words, even though they used the most advanced form of shorthand. There was not a second of hesitation in his dictation: his design was fully formed and devoid of doubt.

Pennywhistle was impressed. He saw in his mind's eye what Wellington intended. The Mt. St. Jean Ridge was a region of low ridges, deep cut lanes, small forests, and hidden avenues of approach, a mile and a half in front of a village of 1,500 souls called Waterloo. He was recreating the topography in his mind when his name was called.

"Pennywhistle! Damn my soul, just the man I want to see! It is all very well to issue orders but seeing them carried out with intelligence and initiative is quite another matter. I need you and your people to report to the assistant adjutant general to carry out my orders regarding the Hougemont Farmstead."

Pennywhistle searched his memory for the recollection of the area, and realized Wellington was talking of a walled farmstead. Typical of the area, Hougemont was much like the farm fortress at Quatre Bras that he had just defended.

Pennywhistle saluted in obedience. "What would be my purpose there, Your Grace?"

"My orders direct regiments to a general area, but the initial positions of each company are left to the determination of the adjutant general. He sends out men with stakes to mark those positions. I would like you and your people to perform that function for Hougemont."

"It would be my honor, Your Grace. Do I have your permission to make small adjustments in those dispositions subject to the conditions on the ground and the weather?"

"You do, but very, very minor ones. I anticipate our men will begin moving around 10 am, so you had better depart immediately to have things ready for them when they arrive."

"Very good, Your Grace." Pennywhistle saluted, turned on his heel and walked away, deep in thought.

Pennywhistle's new assignment was not met with favor by his friends.

"After all we did yesterday, this is a fine thanks," huffed Maxwell. "You don't treat heroes like flunkeys."

"With all due respect," said Dale, "couldn't Wellington have found you a position in the line? Many officers were killed yesterday, and I am sure many regiments would welcome an officer with your considerable combat experience."

Even Johnny frowned.

Pennywhistle shook his head. "You have all misread the situation. This job is extremely important. I will have the chance to influence the outcome of this battle to a far greater degree than if I commanded troops or acted in some other capacity. The small changes I may make in Wellington's name could have enormous consequences for thousands of men. Though the decisions will be mine, any insights you give me on where the stakes should be driven will be listened to with respect. So, you see, by assisting me you may have a chance to save many, many lives and contribute far more to the battle than you could in an ordinary capacity."

His companions looked at each other in surprise. Dale spoke for all three. "Sorry we doubted you, Colonel. It's just that we are eager to see Bonaparte thrashed and we did not want to end up as rear echelon errand boys."

"I appreciate your eagerness, but you will more likely be in the forward echelon." Pennywhistle spoke gravely. "I believe a battle that will change history will be fought on the morrow. It will be a meat grinder of epic proportions. Tomorrow many will echo Westmoreland thoughts in Henry V, 'Would that we had one ten thousandth of those men in England that do no work today.' I hope that all of us will be alive 48 hours hence, but if I were a betting man, I wouldn't lay a wager on that happening. If you do survive, you will be able to tell your grandchildren, 'I fought at Mount Saint Jean.'"

Maxwell pursed his lips. "I like the idea, but not the name, sounds too damn French. We need a name that comes more readily to the English tongue."

"Wellington is making his headquarters in a town a mile and a half south of Mt. St. Jean. It's called Waterloo. How does that sound to you?"

"Waterloo, Waterloo," Maxwell muttered thoughtfully. "I like that."

The first few hours of the journey to Hougemont passed without incident. Various bodies of cavalry trotted by, on their way to cover Wellington's retreat. He was surprised when one officer of the 1st Lifeguards cheerfully hailed him. "I say, Pennywhistle! Hold up a bit."

Thynne trotted briskly to his side. "I did not expect to see you here."

"Nor I you."

"I presume you are coming from the fight just ended. I have heard only rumors about it. How did we fare?"

"We held our ground, then pushed the French back, but frankly it was no more than a bloody nose to Bonaparte. In a way, we were a warmup, a novelty act like those you see in a Covent Garden theatre: an act designed to whet an audience's appetite for the play yet to begin."

Thynne snorted a laugh. "Novelty act, ha! Very appropriate. You think the play will happen on the morrow?"

"I am certain of it."

"I presume you and your people are heading for the theatre where the play will take place."

"That we are. Special orders from Wellington."

"Then before I go, allow me to make a request. If we both survive this ordeal we shall meet for a splendid dinner at Boodles and treat the entire club to a round of drinks to celebrate our good fortune."

"I shall look forward to it."

"Excellent. One other promise I should like to exact from you. If I should fall, will you and Sammie Jo look after Sarah?"

"Do not give it a moment's thought."

"Thank you, that lightens my heart greatly. Now I must be off. Good luck to you!"

"And to you."

At 2 p.m., the uneventful ride changed to a miserable journey. The hot humid air and low hanging clouds finally gave way to a thunderstorm that quickly turned in a deluge of biblical proportions. The pouring rain soaked everyone to the skin in its first fusillade and the ones that followed made the quartet look like bedraggled animals covered in dirt.

Though Pennywhistle felt glum, the infantry hours behind him would be suffering far more. The verge on either side of the road changed to pure mud which would make marching difficult. The driving rain would also make campfires difficult to light. The sensible thing to do was seek shelter but that was an option open neither to Pennywhistle nor the soldiers marching from Quatre Bras.

The storm increased in fury as the hours passed and the miles ground miserably by. Pennywhistle guessed that the storm would persist through the night which would change certain aspects of the battle ahead. Wet ground would severely limit the effects of ricochet artillery fire and he would have to factor that as he made the dispositions for Hougemont. The troops would probably go into battle wet, tired, and hungry: exactly the opposite of those heroic stalwarts pictured in battle paintings by artists who had never seen the thing they painted.

The rain became so intense at times that the quartet could barely see three feet ahead. Because of that they nearly rode into a wagon and two old horses when they came around a bend. Pennywhistle could not see faces but the wagon driver and riders all wore bonnets. He halted his men and slowly rode up to the wagon.

He got the shock of his life when it's driver spoke. "Tom, is that you?"

The voice belonged to Sammie Jo.

***

17 June 1815, 3 p.m., Genappe Bridge

The driving rain retarded the progress of Thynne and his men. The horses proceeded at the slowest of walks instead of the brisk trot that was expected. His squadron was two miles north of the Dyle River crossing at Genappe, eight miles south of Mt. St. Jean, when the inability to see anything nearly had fatal consequences for the commander of British Cavalry.

He had warned Lord Uxbridge that the cavalry should stay close together because of stray French patrols, but Uxbridge and his entourage had ridden ahead, well in advance of the main body.

Uxbridge was doing as Thynne feared he would: forgetting his job was to be a manager and director of his men, to lead from the rear rather than the front.

"You worry too much, Thynne," Uxbridge had admonished him. "I am quite sure any cavalry we meet will be Prussian, not French. I should be glad of their assistance."

"Forgive me, my lord, but the Prussians did not do well yesterday. It seems to me that any spare cavalry would be covering their retreat instead of plodding through the rain on roads they do not know to link up with Allies they barely understand on a mission that is vague at best."

"They would be scouts, Thynne, designated to provide information on the lay of the land so the Prussians may proceed with confidence in the hours ahead. We have nothing to fear."

Those last words haunted Thynne. All too often they were uttered by unreasonably optimistic men who actually had reason to fear, or at least for caution.

He heard rather than saw the tumult that developed. Uxbridge's alarmed voice rose above the peals of thunder. "Make haste! Make haste. For God's sake gallop, or you will all be taken!" Shapes in red came racing toward him out of the pouring rain, pursued by some enemy that Thynne could not yet see. The horsemen scattered before they reached him, frantically jumping walls, hedges, and fences, seeking shelter in the gardens and enclosures fronting the *chausse*.

Uxbridge was personally brave, but he had lost control of the situation. Thynne could now see the outlines of the men who had caused the headlong flight: the cut of their uniforms made it clear they were French, and they were on a tear.

Thynne pivoted his horse and galloped back a few yards to Captain Cavile Mercer, heading a detachment of horse artillery. "Mercer, unlimber two guns and give those fellows coming up the road a whiff of canister." The rain was coming down so hard that Thynne feared it had extinguished their slow matches.

Mercer complied and his two nine pounders fired two rounds in rapid succession. They aimed at the sound of clattering hooves on the cobblestones because it gave them a better target than fast moving misty shapes. Thynne did not know if they hit anything, but the sound of hooves suddenly stopped. When the sounds resumed, they started to fade. After a minute they ceased entirely.

The French had been driven off, but the situation highlighted the chief weaknesses of British cavalry: too much dash and too little common sense. Too much emphasis on personal bravery and derring-do and too little focus on the regiment's general impact on an engagement.

The lightning stopped, but the rain continued unabated. Uxbridge returned chastened and proceeded with more circumspection. Upon reaching the north edge of Genappe, he posted his own regiment, the 7th Hussars in a position blocking the main road. The 23rd Light Dragoons were posted two hundred yards behind them, and the Lifeguards stationed an additional 200 yards beyond them.

Because the rain had turned everything not paved into a sea of mud, any French advance would have to come up the road in that Thynne now surveyed with his spyglass. The rain slackened briefly and gave him a chance to view the town's single street. It was choked with troopers of the French 2nd Lancers. The advance guard had halted and leveled their lances, but troopers continued to flow forward creating a muddle that the French were struggling to sort out.

The leveled lances made it plain that a charge was imminent. Because the ditches on either side of the road were filled with water, any French advance up the road would have to come on a very narrow front. He had a vision of a gloved hand stopping a punch: the first representing the British and the second the French. The sensible thing to do was stand on the defensive and let the fight come to them. Lancers were particularly dangerous, but the narrow, constricted road and rain would limit their ability to build up the speed necessary for effective use of the lance.

Destination Waterloo

He redirected his glass toward Uxbridge and saw what he feared. Uxbridge was forming up the 7th Hussars for a charge. Light cavalry against lancers was not a good match. Here again, British eagerness to get at the enemy was overwhelming good tactical sense. He could predict the outcome, but he could do nothing to stop it. The only question was when his troop and the Lifeguards would be called upon to bail out their comrades.

He quietly moved among his men and told them to do a last-minute equipment check, telling them to pay particular attention to the flints on their pistols. The driving rain would greatly decrease the effectiveness of pistols as moisture was the enemy of gun powder but in a close quarter fight against lancers, pistols came in very handy.

The 7th charged headlong at the 2nd lancers, with plenty of dash and vigor though not with the accompanying skill. The long lances impaled many before they got within striking distance of their swords. The combat quickly degenerated into a series of individual combats in the driving rain with no generalship evident. British slashes and cuts were met by French thrusts and jabs. The British used no pistols. The battle seesawed back and forth but gradually the skill and experience of the French began to tell. The retreat was sounded, and the British began to pull back in small groups. The British had reduced French numbers slightly but had not dampened their spirits at all.

Uxbridge next launched the 23rd at the French and the result was much the same. Ten minutes of close quarter combat resulted in heavy losses to the British but this time they had inflicted significant losses on the French. As the British withdrew, Thynne surveyed his men, knowing his turn was next. They looked confident, un dispirited by the two British reverses. He trusted they would remember his instructions: close quickly on your opponent and fire your pistols at the moment when you are just outside of thrusting range of the lance.

Thynne felt the familiar emotions as the regiment's trumpeters sounded the charge: fear, exhilaration, uncertainty. He thought of Sarah and wondered if she was well. His men moved forward at a brisk trot since road and weather argued against the gallop.

His men did as he had instructed and fired their pistols first. Since the French did not expect it, it unnerved and unmanned them. Thynne noted they looked weary. Lances were heavy affairs and the two previous encounters had greatly reduced the energy with which they wielded them.

He engaged in six personal combats. He shot two men with his pistols then drew his sword to engage the third. His breath came hard and fast as his jaw burned then clamped shut. He swept aside two jabs with his sword; one aimed at his leg and one at his chest. His flailing heart struggled to escape its cage as he cut the Frenchman on the leg. His nose drank in the scent of terror as cuirassier reared back in pain. His cheeks flamed and a burst of heat rippled across his chest as he slashed his opponent across the mouth. He drooped sideways then slipped from his saddle.

The fourth man lunged expertly but Thynne used the quickness of his horse to outmaneuver him. His mouth and throat felt like cotton in a desert, though his tongue turned slick and slippery and was suffused with a metallic taste. Sweat glazed his forehead and a latticework of goosebumps materialized on his arms and legs. His skin grew clammy, and blood drained from his face as his body shunted toward it towards his arms, chest, and legs. His body understood it was in the fight of his life even though his mind retained the calmness necessary for survival. He blinked sweat from his eyes as he cut at his opponent's lower back from the rear, the pain causing his target to lose his balance and tumble from the saddle.

Destination Waterloo

The fifth man fought well. Since Thynne had closed the distance quickly, his opponent had used his lance as a club. He hit Thynne once in the thigh and once in the temple. The glancing second blow caused him to see stars. His breath caught in his throat, his stomach lurched, and fear plunged the dagger of uncertainty into his heart. Desperate, he did the unthinkable for a man who loved horses. He thrust his blade into the eye of the Frenchman's horse, causing it to rear in pain before it collapsed. Its rider lay pinned beneath its bulk, dazed but alive. He was out of the fight.

His last opponent grazed his sword arm with the tip of his lance. The superficial wound was nonetheless painful; causing him to wince, groan, gnash his teeth, and drop his sword though it remained attached to his wrist by its silk sword knot. He maneuvered his horse with his thighs and reached for his Paget Carbine with his good hand. The stubby weapon only weighed five and a half pounds and the .62 ball could do serious harm at close range. The lancer had opened his mouth to curse him and Thynne used that as his target. The pain maddened him, and he shoved the Paget's muzzle under the man's tongue with anger and pulled the trigger with satisfaction. The back of the man's head disappeared, and he flew off the saddle as if he had been riding a Congreve rocket.

A seventh lancer came at him, but at that moment, a trumpet sounded the recall, and he veered off at the last second. The lancers retreated slowly, defeated but still disciplined. Several troopers looked eager to pursue but he had his trumpeter sound their recall. Fatigue swept over him like an ocean wave putting out a fire of beach gorse: his body paying the price now that the immediate danger was past. He was not Uxbridge: his job had been to stop the lancers and he had done that. It was a limited victory because he never forgot the cavalry's ultimate object was to secure Wellington's retreat.

The rain continued its depredations and made him long for the comfort of a good fire, a decent meal, a mellow brandy, and the arms of his wife. The breezy, nonchalance for which he was famous struggled to reassert itself but the pain in his arm sent it packing. He would need to have the wound dressed by a surgeon but there should be no lasting damage.

Cornet Lacy rode up to him, holding his bloody sword aloft and wearing a half smile of triumph. Thynne's recognized the symptoms of very young man who had survived his first fight and whose mind had probably exaggerated his role in it. He could easily learn the wrong lesson from the battle just fought, and it was up to Thynne to make sure he learned the right one.

"I say, that was rather bracing, Captain. We really gave those French devils what for."

"We accomplished our mission, but at high cost. This encounter could have been better handled."

"How so, sir?" Lacy sounded both shocked and dubious.

"Uxbridge gave up the advantage by charging."

"Well, we drove them off and that is what counts. As soon as I am able, I shall pen a letter to my father telling him of our glorious conduct."

"The objective counts, but the butcher's bill matters, and ours is far too high. As for the letter, I doubt you will have time to write. We shall be very busy for the next day or two. For now, see to your men. They did well. A word of praise here and there would not be amiss."

"Might I ask question, Captain?" For once, the young man sounded less than sure of himself.

"Of course."

"All through the fight I keep seeing my fiancée's face in my mind's eye. Does that mark me as odd?"

"Not at all, Lacy. Confronting death, it is natural to think of those who make life worth living."

Sarah's face shone into his own mind, and he wondered how she was fairing. He had no idea that she was but eight miles distant.

Pennywhistle moved his sopping horse close to Sammie Jo sitting in her wagon's drive box. Her face, when he could see it clearly during the brief flashes of lightning, was a mixture of relief and anxiety. She stretched her arms out uncertainly, seeking an embrace but not sure if she would receive one.

"Are you mad? Why on earth are you here?" The perplexity in his voice carried a strong undercurrent of anger. "You have a lot of explaining to do, risking yourself and the future of our child." Fear lay at the root of his response, as he envisioned the cold void his life would be without her.

Sammie Jo retracted her arms in a protective self-embrace, unused to her husband's anger. Deborah, sitting on the box next to Sammie Jo, quietly put her arm around her friend. Sarah, seated in the back of the wagon, peered around, her eyes wide with concern.

Sammie Jo took a deep breath and pointed at Maxwell a few yards behind Pennywhistle. "I came because of him. I found letters he wrote in which he made the gravest threats. It sounded like he meant to do you mortal harm. I had to act."

Pennywhistle started. He had no doubt she was sincere, and her fierce response tracked with her love of him rather than a flirtation with insanity. He wondered what letters she was talking about. "And yet, you see I am unharmed."

"He may just be biding his time."

Pennywhistle wanted to settle this ridiculous business quickly. He gestured to Maxwell. "Ensign, get over here." He stowed his anger and moved Diable closer to place his hand on Sammie Jo's shoulder. He spoke reassuringly. "He saved my life yesterday. Without him, we would not be having this conversation."

Sammie Jo looked thunderstruck. "But... but... the language of the letters was so violent, so horrid! I had to assume his threats were real. And they weren't just about you! He wrote about doing terrible things to other people — even women!"

Maxwell pulled his horse alongside Pennywhistle. He glared at Sammie Jo. Pennywhistle addressed him.

"My wife says you wrote threatening letters about me, which I find puzzling, given your actions yesterday. Explain yourself, and be quick about it."

Maxwell did so with ill grace: a man reluctant to reveal thoughts he himself did not want to hear. "I do not deny I wrote the letters," he allowed grudgingly. "I should not have written them, but they were not meant for any eyes other than my own. I can understand how your wife saw them as a matter for concern but... and I know this is no excuse, but they reflect the urgings of John Barleycorn, with whom I have kept too much company. He stirs up resentments, unleashing an inner beast goaded by hatred and anger. When the beast is upon me, I commit my thoughts to paper. Then in a calmer state I burn them. I am sorry my indulgences have caused distress."

"I know our first meeting was contentious, but I thought we had evolved a rough understanding. Why all the paper threats?"

Maxwell hesitated for a moment; he was a man rallying his resolve to scale the walls of some inner prison of torment. Then he spoke with a candor that Pennywhistle had never heard. "I know the senior officers despise me, but I also knew they feared me. Everyone feared me, if not for my size, then for the influence my family could bring to bear." A brief expression of brag and bounce flitted across Maxwell's face, then faded. "That changed when you appeared. I realized that you were far more dangerous than I, not because of rage and hatred but because of discipline and skill. I resented that."

"So, I represented the end of your play time and the beginning of hard work?"

Maxwell nodded and his face became wistful for a moment, as he recalled a happier time. "My mother was disciplined, like you, and kept our household in good order. She died when I was six." He scowled as he continued, his voice bitter. "Father was — is — a hard man. Mother had a dog named Jigsy, a giant Newfoundland. I admired my mother, but I loved that dog. My father shot him in the head, after Jigsy bit him when he was about to strike my mother."

"Did your Pa often beat on your Ma?" demanded Sammie Jo.

"Frequently. He despised her Quaker values. They were too peaceable for a man of his temperament." His face turned dark. "I was told my mother died from a fall down the stairs. I think my father pushed her."

"That's terrible!" Sammie Jo exclaimed.

Maxwell paled, remembering certain past behaviors, then muttered, "I fear I would be no better as a husband, or a father."

Pennywhistle found revelations in a driving rain a peculiar turn of events, but he was glad for the enlightenment. "So, you saw me as a surrogate parent attempting to introduce unwelcome order and purpose into your life."

"I did, and 1 poured out my resentments on paper. I had discovered that if one creates chaos, one gains a sense of control, because only the chaos maker knows what comes next."

"So, most of your resentments of me were directed at your father? A man you feared you might become?"

"At first, I saw the two of you as indistinguishable. The words I wrote about you were directed at him as well."

"But you have concluded that I am not him?"

"I have. You are... everything he is not. He wrote me off; you were willing to take a chance on me, even after I had turned everyone against me. Might I ask why you took that chance?"

"You mentioned a beast within; I saw something of that during our first encounter. But as I observed you, I came to see you less as a man-eating lion and more as an unbroken stallion, rendered violent by mistreatment. The first is mere dangerous, but the second can be useful, if properly tempered. In a way, you are like Diable."

"Like Diable?" Sammie Jo exclaimed.

Pennywhistle turned to her. "Yes. He was a beautiful animal who had bucked off so many riders that he became an outcast. You bought him for a fraction of his true value. Instead of breaking his will you cultivated his spirit, gentled him, and he became the magnificent beast I ride today."

"And that's how you see me?" inquired Maxwell.

"It is. You fought with a fury I have seldom beheld, but I sensed something other than anger and hate in you. I have seen you fight valiantly, and of your own will you have chosen to fight your king's enemies rather than your fellow countrymen. You have earned a measure of my respect, and I am willing to extend more if you will give me, and my wife, your solemn word that you will never again pen such foul letters, and that we will have your true faith and allegiance."

Sammie Jo's voice turned hard. "Think before you speak, Maxwell. I understand you better now, and you are probably telling the truth, but my gut warns me to have a caution. Where I come from, a man's word is everything. If you mean what you say, I am willing to declare peace. But so help me God, if you lie, if you ever hurt my husband, I will hunt you down and grind you into food for crows."

Maxwell's face bore the expression of a man struggling with strong emotions, like a man sounding the devil's tritone in his soul. "I have never been more wrong about any man than I have been about you, Colonel Pennywhistle. Lady Pennywhistle, I do not blame you for suspecting me. It is foolish to do as I have done, going through life collecting grievances as if they are trophies." He cleared his throat. "I solemnly pledge on my life and honor that I shall do everything in my power to advance the lives, fortunes, and safety of the both of you. May God strike me down if I falter for even a moment in that endeavor."

"That must have hurt," drawled Sammie Jo," but I accept your word."

"I do as well," said Pennywhistle. "I should welcome the chance to extend the hand of comradeship."

Deborah looked on in pleasure and surprise at the impromptu reconciliation. Her face fell a moment later, when she beheld her husband glowering at her.

"Lady Pennywhistle's explanation makes sense to me," growled Dale, "but I can think of only reason why you are here. It's to get 'the story', isn't it? I thought you had agreed that family should come first. Have you any idea what you have gotten yourself into?"

"It s not that simple," Deborah replied, steadily meeting her husband's angry look. "Allow me explain. I helped Lady Densham nurse a dying officer, and the words he wrote in letter to his wife haunted me so much that I committed them to memory. I want to see for myself the environment that such extraordinary and loving men must endure."

"What were those words?" Dale asked, curious despite himself.

Deborah's expression changed to one of loving solemnity, and she recited with gravitas mixed with kindness:

"My Mary, let the recollection console you that the happiest days of my life have been from your love and affection, and that I die loving only you, and with a fervent hope that our souls may be reunited hereafter and part no more.

"What dear children, My Mary, I leave you. My Mariana, gentlest girl, may God bless you. My Anne, my John, may heaven protect you. My children, may you all be happy and may the reflection that your father never in his life swerved from the truth and always acted from the dictates of his conscience, preserve you, virtuous and happy, for without virtue there can be no happiness.

"My Mary, I must tell you how tranquilly I shall die since it seems my fate to fall. We cannot, my own love, die together —one or other must witness the loss of what we love most. Let my children console you, my love, my Mary."

Tears rose to more than one pair of eyes. One of the horses purchased by the Earl chuffed in instinctive sympathy. Sarah sniffed and scrubbed her eyes.

Maxwell said nothing, but thought of the child he had fathered and wondered how he could find it.

Dale's expression softened. "I still wish you had not come."

"That is exactly how I feel about you, Hawkeye," said Pennywhistle, clearing his throat.

Sammie Jo looked at Pennywhistle with concern. "Have you written such a note?"

"I have, but not with such expressiveness of heart. I entrusted mine to the Earl, but it does not say anything that you do not already know." Pennywhistle turned to Sarah. "Speaking of loved ones, I encountered your husband on the road a few hours back."

"My goodness!" gasped a startled and pleased Sarah. "He promised that he would send word of his whereabouts, but I have heard nothing and had begun to worry. Was he well? Is he hale and hearty? No wounds or..."

"He is fine, I assure you, and his thoughts are chiefly of you."

"I must see him! I have news that he will want to hear. I... I am with child."

Pennywhistle smiled. "That is the best news. I am not sure how to get that message to him, but I will try to find a way. In the meanwhile, since you ladies are here, we shall have to make provision. I wish I could send you back, but the road from Brussels is likely clogged with the baggage and supplies of the army moving forward. And I confess I am curious what lies under the tarp of your wagon."

"Medical supplies," stated Sarah. "We know the army is short of them. We thought we could assist in their distribution, and then help load wounded into the empty wagon. We brought three horses to convey us back to Lady Densham's once our mission here is accomplished." She gestured towards the back of the wagon, barely distinguishable in the downpour. The three horses were champing their bits side by side, their lead ropes tied to the rear of the wagon.

"Naïve, but praiseworthy," remarked Pennywhistle. He briefly explained his own assignment. "You ladies can help. You are already soaked, and a little mud won't hurt you. Once we finish, you can take your wagon to the ammunition park in the Forest of Soignes and we can see to its disposition. Now let's head for Hougemont."

John Danielski

***

17 June 1815, 6 p.m., the walled farmstead of Hougemont

The little caravan arrived at Hougemont, sodden and shivering, as the deluge turned roads to mud and streams to swollen watercourses.

The farm estate was situated on an escarpment three hundred yards in front of where Wellington's main line would be positioned, and would function as a breakwater for any attacks on his right flank. 12 buildings were grouped around a central courtyard, surrounded by walls that varied in height from six meters to just over two. It had three gates, the chief of which was the North Gate, which stood at the end of a long-covered way that featured a sunken road and thick hedges. South of the covered way was the Small Apple Orchard, and to its east, the Great Apple Orchard, an area of roughly 200 square meters. Two fields of tall wheat and rye lay southeast of the Great Orchard.

There was a kitchen garden on the west side of the compound with a tall, surrounding hedge. A much larger formal garden, with well-manicured paths that wound between rose beds and ornate topiaries, lay behind the Great Orchard, surrounded by a seven-foot-high wall that was thick enough to be impervious to musketry. To the south of this garden lay a wooded area 300 meters wide and 250 meters deep. It was well tended and free of underbrush, and would allow semi-clear lines of sight as well as cover, but the sluicing rain was dissolving the ground into thick muck.

Pennywhistle and his entourage entered through the North Gate and halted, dripping wet and hungry, in the courtyard; he directed everyone to take shelter in the chateau. He rode alone and north, seeking the assistant adjutant general, Sir William de Lancey, Wellington's chief of staff, and found him half a mile away, sheltering beneath a lone elm tree at a crossroads, looking as bedraggled and

340

forlorn from the rain as Pennywhistle felt. They spent the next half hour discussing troop dispositions, and de Lancey promised a supply wagon would shortly deliver the stakes.

The stakes had already been prepared by the Quartermaster Department. They were four feet high, and each had been inscribed with India ink, which would not run or fade. The information on them was terse, such as "2 Grds Lgt. Cy.", signifying the position was to be occupied by the Light Company of the 2nd Guards Regiment, the famous Coldstream Guards. There would be companies from several regiments, about 1300 men, stationed in and around the chateau and the stakes associated with each regiment were topped with small pennants: the varied hues of the pennants matching the facing colors of the uniforms of particular regiments.

When Pennywhistle left de Lancey, he spent ninety minutes slowly riding Hougemont's perimeter, wanting to use his time effectively while waiting for his supplies. He dismounted at key points to get the lay of the land, as best he could through the grey veil of rain. Like many gentlemen who owned land and wanted to be sure of its exact dimensions and configurations, he had received youthful training as a surveyor. He had borrowed the basic tools of the trade from an officer of the Royal Engineers, a surveyor's scope, chain, compass, theodolite, and plumb line. He paced off distances as carefully as he could; his boots became so caked with mud he had to pause every twenty steps to knock and scrape them mud off.

At the end of each short survey, he knelt and used Diable as a shelter against the rain. He recorded the positions on his map, then stowed it, rose, remounted, and moved on to the next position. The defensive possibility of the grounds impressed him. Properly positioned, a small number of troops could deny entrance to a much greater number.

The only official resident was the gardener and his five-year-old daughter, whom he greeted pleasantly when he encountered them, then advised them to evacuate. The gardener understood but was reluctant to leave, worried for the elaborate topiary work whose maintenance constituted his chief responsibility. Pennywhistle finally persuaded them to go by handing a gold napoleon to the gardener and a small box of hard candy — his emergency ration of battlefield energy — to the girl.

By the time he returned to the chateau, supernumeraries from the baggage train had filtered into the courtyard, and he pressed them into service. Counting his men, Johnny, and the women, he had twenty-eight operatives. He assembled everyone in the foyer of the chateau for a briefing, during which his map was passed around. He had divided Hougemont into seven sections, since there would be detachments from seven companies, each section to be staked out by 4 men or women. Everyone was issued a mallet and a collection of color-coded stakes, with instructions to pound hard enough that wind and rain would not knock over their markers.

What followed was three hours of backbreaking labor in muddy, water saturated ground that threatened to suck the boots from everyone's feet. The rain fell in sheets, making it hard to see and hear. The were exclamations of pain and frustration when rain made the tools slippery and mallets struck fingers instead of stakes. When the job was done, Sammie Jo plopped down on the chateau's front steps, next to her husband. "I feel like a field hand on the worst plantation in the South."

"At least we do not have the South's heat."

"This rain ain't much of an improvement."

"At least it is only rain, not a storm; there is no wind to chill us, no lightning to strike us."

Sammie Jo laughed through her weariness. "I see you are determined to see the best in our circumstances. I say it's time we get a fire going and cook up some vittles."

"We will have to move inside to make room for the soldiers soon to arrive. At least we have the areas marked out for them. That will reduce the chaos or setting up camps, if not the discomfort."

"Now all you have to do is win the battle," said Sammie Jo wryly. "And make damn sure that that letter you gave to the Earl never gets sent." She cleared her throat. "Now I have some good news for you. I wanted to tell you earlier, but with all the hullabaloo about Maxwell, I could not find the right moment. It's about Nicholas. He is going to be fine." Her smile was a mixture of joy and relief.

"That is wonderful news! But how do you know this?"

"Turns out he was being poisoned."

Pennywhistle's brow darkened. "I will tear that man limb from limb."

"It's not a man, it's a woman, Mrs. George."

"His nanny?" expostulated Tom violently. "Why in God's name would she do that?"

"That's just it. The poison came from a patent medicine she had been giving him. She thought she was helping. Turns out our son had become addicted to laudanum. When Mrs. George ran out of her medication on our trip here, his body weaned itself. His health improves daily."

"I feel like a great burden has been lifted, my dear. The prospect of a great battle reminds one of what is important in life, and nothing is more important than family."

"Speaking of family, Tom, maybe we should work on a second child. I know we both look like a couple of wet hens, but I think we could manage some privacy in the chateau before all the troops arrive." She grinned slyly.

"Are you suggesting..."

"Why not? A lot of people are about to die, so why not do something that creates life? If anything should happen to you, it's a memory I should like to carry with me."

Pennywhistle laughed. "You're right! A quick bout of disport and dalliance is a splendid idea."

Sammie Jo rose and took him by the hand. "I had in mind something long and vigorous. The house is empty and bare but there is a bedroom on the second floor that still has a bed and sheets."

"Then lay on, MacDuff,'" proclaimed Pennywhistle lustily, "and damned be him, or her, who first cries, 'Hold, enough!'"

Chapter 14
On the Eve of Battle

17 June 1815, on the road to Napoleon's Headquarters

Pauline marched with the men of the 2nd Regiment of Artillery throughout the day of June 17, having packed up her finery and donned the more sensible garb of a camp follower: a sergeant's great coat, a sapper's moleskin trousers and the boots of a hussar, the whole topped off by a wide brimmed straw hat. The men accepted her because she understood them; she had twice been married to NCOs, and indeed, the coat she wore had belonged to her second husband. She bantered with the men in rough soldier's language that yet avoided vulgarity, cracking jokes designed to ease the burden of a hard march in filthy weather. She was an experienced forager and twice vanished for an hour. Both times she returned with pouches containing loaves of fresh bread and cheese obtained from God knows where, and freshly gathered berries and greens which the hungry and grateful foot soldiers ate on the march. Thus fortified, a few began to sing the *"Chanson de l'Oignon"* and *"Le Pas Redoublé de la Garde Impériale"*.

She kept a close eye on Jacques that was affectionate but not cloying. She understood that he was ambivalent about her presence, and she wanted to persuade him, not push him into accepting her into his life. She knew he desired her, yet she also understood and respected the power of his strong Quaker beliefs. It was refreshing to meet a man whose principles regulated his penis, and not the other way round.

The night of June 17 would have been the most miserable of Jacques' life had it not been for Pauline. Fivel's men camped at the edge of a small woodland. Rain ricocheted off the leaves and everyone was shivering with cold and covered in mud. Their camp equipage had not caught up with them, so the gun crews created "Portuguese tents" out of five stacked muskets covered in two thin blankets. Gagne and his two crews cut clover from a nearby field that made a sweet-scented carpet that blocked out the worst of the mud. Men usually liked to sleep in a circle with their feet toward the fire, but the broken, uneven ground precluded this, and three attempts to start fires failed. The men finally gave up, wrapped themselves in their blankets, and hoped for the best.

Pauline slept next to Jacques, her presence nurturing rather than sexual. He felt like a discarded sack of laundry, but she stroked his hands and head, and her kind words finally caused sleep to overtake him. He awoke frequently, plagued by bad dreams about the fight ahead, but each time she soothed him back to sleep. When he awoke and stood, he felt weary and dull. He took several deep breaths of the morning air, fingered the Legion of Honor in his pocket, and stamped his feet.

The cooks were finally able to build fires to heat their breakfasts — possibly the last meal they would have before going into action. The wood was so damp that the fires hissed and hesitated, generating large clouds of smoke which stung the eyes.

A forager managed to locate a stray sheep, which was summarily butchered. The company added some leeks, onions, and potatoes to create a stew. The meal was much anticipated, but the cook found he lacked salt. He substituted saltpeter, which destroyed the flavor. One man punched him, and he was cursed roundly by the entire company.

What saved the day were the loaves of bread and rounds of cheese supplied by Pauline. The men looked upon her with great affection. Never was the aphorism "The way to a man's heart is through his stomach" more apt.

No wine was available, but several of the men had filled their canteens with beer plundered from the cellar of a local farmhouse. One of the scouts had found the farmhouse, but it was Pauline who had suggested the search of its cellars; she knew many farmers were also part time brewers. Jacques was unused to the taste of beer and did not particularly like it, but his mates assured him that the brew was to beer what champagne was to wine.

Before beginning the day's march, men checked and cleaned their equipment. In their wet and muddy uniforms they resembled down-on-their luck day laborers, but they were betting their lives on the functioning of their equipment; so when they were done, their guns and accoutrements looked like they belonged to bandbox soldiers.

***

18 June, 1815, 5 a.m. on the road to Le Caillou

Jacques Gagne and his artillery company began their progress toward Le Caillou, the farmhouse estate where Napoleon had established his headquarters and whose grounds would serve as the assembly area for the various units of his Army: half a mile from Hougemont and three quarters of a mile from Wellington's main position on the Mt. St. Jean Ridge.

Because of the weather, Napoleon's Army had fallen considerably behind schedule. The rain had reduced the roads to a sea of mud, which slowed marching and made it difficult to shift the great guns.

Napoleon enjoyed a considerable superiority in guns, but the absence of hard turf to facilitate ricochet fire would severely limit that advantage. Jaques knew that Napoleon favored early morning attacks, but now he would have to wait.

Rumors rippled through the marching men, but as usual they were vague and sometimes contradictory. All that Gagne knew for certain was that Wellington's Army had halted some miles ahead and seemed about to make a stand. Many of his comrades were of the confident opinion that Wellington would flee before the Emperor could attack.

Several horses towing the guns had developed problems that were beyond the ability of the company farriers to treat en route, though there was hope for the beasts if they could make it to a garrison town. The horses of artillery were generally overworked and underfed; pulling heavy burdens at anything from a walk to a brisk trot aged a horse quickly. An advance column outran its supply of hay and oats, and cavalry horses generally received priority in feed over those of the artillery. It was not uncommon for artillery horses to be put on half rations mere days after a campaign began.

Though many of his crews viewed horses as mere beasts of burden, Jacques saw them as intelligent creatures with distinct personalities. One had become something of a friend. "Pierre" was old but friendly, and Jacques delighted in feeding him and stroking his warm neck.

After the column had slogged on a few miles, Pierre stumbled, went down on one knee, and would not rise. This forced the other horse in harness to stop, and the limber they had been towing blocked the road, causing the entire column to grind to a halt. Jacques walked over to the horse and saw confusion in his eyes. A farrier trudged up and gave Pierre a cursory examination.

"He's done for. We need to cut him loose and shoot him. We'll bring a horse from one of the wagons."

"Is there really nothing to be done? Perhaps rest, or water, or…"

"Waste of time." The farrier recognized the symptoms. The corporal cared for the beast. "The faster the deed is done the better for all concerned. We can't delay the army because of one horse." The farrier cut Pierre out of his harness, the beast wearing a pleading expression.

Tears came to Jacques' eyes, knowing the farrier was right.

"He is your friend," the farrier said, "you should do the deed. Remember, it's not an execution, it's a mercy killing." He handed over the pistol.

Gagne took it with shaking hands. He steadied himself and put the gun to Pierre's head. His uncertain eyes locked with the trusting ones of Pierre. "Good-bye, old friend." He wept as he pulled the trigger.

Jacques staggered back as the beast collapsed. The pistol hung in his listless hand, then dropped to the ground. He doubled over and retched.

Doing the right thing had never felt more wrong. He got himself back into line and spoke no more words until the column had reached its destination, around 9 a.m. Pauline tried to cheer him up, but for once she failed. Jacques did a lot of thinking in those hours and reluctantly concluded that what he had had to do with Pierre was less tragedy than training. Today would be an equine massacre. Pierre was only the first horse would have to be put down.

Pauline saw his distress and knew it was dangerous. Depressed men became careless men and careless men often became dead men. She needed to give him hope, confidence, and a belief in his own strength. She knew the best way to do so, but with the army readying itself for battle, privacy would be difficult find. She cast around for a place where the two of them could stretch out, and spotted a flying hospital wagon that awaited use. It was fully enclosed and capable of transporting four stretcher cases.

She came up to him, smiled, and seized his hand. "There is something I must show you. It's important."

Puzzled, he accepted, wondering what could possibly outweigh his duty to his men. When they arrived at the hospital wagon, she opened its doors and smiled at him.

Gage grasped her meaning but protested. "Pauline, this is not the right moment. Our first time together should be slow and beautiful, and I am willing to wait until—"

She cut him off abruptly. "No! Right here, right now. Please trust me, Jacques, this is vital for your survival. Men who have no will to live... don't." She clutched both his hands in hers, gazing into his face earnestly.

Jacques saw his mother's disapproving face in his mind's eye, but that image faded as he focused intently on the face of the woman before him.

"Very well, Pauline, I am yours to command. But...but...well, I have never done this before and am afraid that..."

The smile in her voice arrested his doubts. "I will be your guide, and you will follow my lead." She stepped nimbly up, into the back of the ambulance. "Now, Jacques, I have just what the doctor ordered. Step into my parlor, and know that you are safe and loved."

Jacques did as she asked, and when she closed the doors, he entered a completely different world, one in which they were the only two inhabitants. She was assured but gentle, and guided his vigorous, youthful ardor with a deft touch. Things happened quickly, as she expected. When his climax came it was suffused with joy.

"That was incredible," gasped Jacques.

Destination Waterloo

Pauline stroked his head gently. "Now let me teach you how to pleasure a woman, so that you will both enjoy love-making."

For a little while longer, time ceased to matter.

***

18 June, 1815, 5 a.m, Hougemont

Pennywhistle and his entourage had spent most of the night before guiding the newly arriving troops to their positions. When pioneers of the King's German Legion arrived, he had helped supervise the construction of firing steps and firing platforms on the high walls of the main enclosure, and then the furrowing of loopholes through the bricks of the garden walls so muskets could be fired through them.

He had slept four hours. It was less rest than he needed, but reasonably restorative. Sammie Jo had brought a spare undress uniform on the chance she would encounter him, so when he departed the chateau in the morning, he appeared in stark contrast to bedraggled fellow officers, who "looked like they had been sent for but couldn't come," as Sammie Jo would say.

The men outside Hougemont's walls had spent a night in pouring rain, most without shelter. They had gotten little sleep after a long march; their uniforms were sopping wet and smelled of mildew. Very few had had a hot meal in the last 24 hours, and some had had no food at all. Pennywhistle took in the general air of misery compounded with resolve, an atmosphere familiar to him from many campaigns. All at once, he was struck by a realization. When paintings were made of this battle, years after the fact, artists would depict the Redcoats in uniforms as fresh and trim as if ready for a parade ground inspection, without any of the mud or grime that presently was ubiquitous. His own skills with the brush were mediocre, but if he ever called upon them to reproduce what he now witnessed, he would show the truth of these soldiers' conditions.

Pennywhistle had a difficult decision to make. Hougemont seemed to him a sturdy, defensible location; should he order his entourage to remain here, behind the protection of its walls? Certainly their support, both military and medical, would be welcomed by the defenders. Or should they accompany him to his next assignment, the supply dump from which would radiate out the supply lines for the coming battle?

He had seem too many "secure" places overrun and seized in the course of battle to believe the walls of Hougemont would keep everyone safe, and he knew all too bitterly what could happen to prisoners taken in the madness of war, even women and children. Would they actually be safer with the supplies, among the Anglo-Allied camp followers? They would al least be among other women and children who were also performing supportive tasks. As for young Maxwell, he would be sure to get his fill of fighting whether he remained here among the defenders or accompanied his colonel on supply runs.

This was not a decision that could be made rationally; the dangers and responsibilities were too even in the balance. He had a premonition that, either way, he would have cause for pride in his people, and for regret. And perhaps, the decision was still theirs as much as his. He turned on his booted heel and reentered the chateau to consult with Dale and Sammie Jo.

***

18 June, 1815, 10 a.m., before Le Caillou
After his tryst with Pauline, Jacques felt renewed, invigorated, and confident. He returned to his artillery company, arriving just in time to

see something that had never been done before: Napoleon's entire *L'armée du Nord* forming up for battle in clear view of the enemy. The spectacle made a virtue of necessity: the ground had only just become dry enough to support a major attack, and Napoleon's delayed timetable demanded the assembly be done in the open so that a major assault could be launched once the forming up had been accomplished. The grand pageant was awe-inspiring, and Jacques was certain it was intimidating to Wellington's troops.

The clouds dissipated as a breeze sprang up. The sun began warming the landscape, finally drying out soggy uniforms. Jacques took the medal of the Legion of Honor from his pocket and affixed it to his uniform.

With bands playing, drums beating, flags flying, and bayonets sparkling, four massive columns approached their deployment areas on the left and right of the low ridge in front of Le Caillou. They were followed by seven smaller columns several hundred yards behind. An army of 77,500 men was deployed: 53, 400 infantry, 15,600 cavalry, 6,500 artillery, 246 great guns, and 2,000 staff officers. Napoleon had 7,000 more men than the army he faced, and the advantage of 89 more great guns. Most importantly, the majority of his men were veterans, whereas as many as a third of Wellington's men had never seen combat.

After an hour, Napoleon's Army was assembled. In front were two lines of infantry with hussars guarding the flanks. The third and fourth lines were cuirassiers, the sunlight sparkling off their steel breastplates. The fifth and sixth lines were the Imperial Guard and its cavalry.

Napoleon rode out in full view of his troops, clad in his familiar black and gold bicorn hat and grey overcoat. The effect as he passed was electric: thousands of shakos, helmets, and fur caps were put on the tips of bayonets or swords and waved about in wild enthusiasm. Loud shouts of *"Vive l' Empereur!"* filled the air. Jacques straightened his shoulders with pride. This was a glorious moment that he would never forget.

The cheering for the Emperor stopped, the bands ceased playing, and the banners, guidons, and pennants that had flapped gloriously in the rising wind drooped, then sagged, as the wind died. The staged drama was complete; the real one was about to begin. Napoleon's Army occupied the space between the *Chausse Nivelles* and the *Chausse de Charleroi*, facing Wellington's army three quarters of a mile away. While much of Wellington's army was sheltered behind a low plateau, hidden from direct French view, many of Wellington's guns were visible, positioned on the forward edge of that plateau to afford clear fields of fire.

Those guns concerned *Sergent* Jean Paul Gagne. He and his ten men would have to traverse 1,000 yards of ground, and would likely be under fire every step of the way. They would be deployed as skirmishers, along with a battalion of the 2nd *Legere* from Baudin's brigade: roughly 500 men in all, under the command of *Chef-de-brigade* Dupont. They would be followed by 3,700 men of the 1st and 2nd Legere, led by Baudin. Their target was a walled farm complex called Hougemont, which was concealed behind woods, orchards, and crops of wheat and rye. Gagne could only guess at how many men lay within Hougemont and its grounds. He had been told the defenders were a mixed lot, as was Wellington's entire army: British, Hanoverian, and Nassau troops.

Three batteries of horse artillery and two of foot artillery would support the French assault. But the woods and orchards formed an effective shield against artillery, so the degree of aid they could provide would be minimal. His nephew's battery was deployed to the east of Hougemont; he panned his glass over their formation. He was pleased to see Jacques confidently giving commands to the gunners of his section.

Gagne's company commander had planned their move to coincide with the commencement of an French artillery bombardment aimed at the woods and fields around Hougemont.

Boom! Boom! Boom! Thirty-four cannons crashed out in quick succession. Gagne and his men broke in a brisk jog. Their objective was their jumping off position, the undulating folds of ground 300 meters south of the Hougemont Wood. They moved in groups of twos and threes.

The nearest British batteries opened fire. At first, Gagne's men were barely within the range limit for solid shot. Most of the balls landed nowhere near them, and of the ones that did the balls simply stopped a few feet after striking the ground, the ricochet effect almost nil.

Suddenly, two of his men screamed. Fontenoy clutched his left shoulder, while Martin clutched his head. Both twitched for a seconds, then collapsed. Gagne swore in frustration. Their deaths came not from the side, but from above, caused by a weapon that he had never encountered because it was unique to the British, whom he had never faced before. Its official name was "spherical case shot", but it was commonly called by the name of its inventor: Lieutenant General Henry Shrapnel.

Shrapnel featured a hollow shell filled with gunpowder and up to 40 musket balls, lit by a fuse that was activated by the explosion that fired the round. When shot from a howitzer, it arced at a high angle and acted like a lethal rain. The trick was to cut the correct length of fuse so that the shell would not detonate too soon but would explode over the heads of its intended targets. Mastering fuse cutting had taken several years, but the British gunners were now very good at their jobs.

Gagne and the rest of his men reached the fold of ground where their fellow *voltigeurs* sheltered, from which they had a clear view of the Hougemont Wood. His men took cover, hoping the three-foot declivity would give them some protection. Gagne and the other platoon commanders did roll calls and found they had lost a quarter of their men to shrapnel.

Gagne was resigned but not disheartened. British artillery fire had stopped because the French were now close to the wood and further salvos might damage friend as well as foe. Gagne unfurled his spyglass and focused it on the forest ahead. He could only see flashes of uniform, but he did notice that the men were not carrying muskets but jaeger rifles. That meant his skirmish line would come under aimed rather than volley fire, probably at 250 yards rather than 100.

His men's fingers pawed the clay soil nervously as they bent low, waiting for the main assault force to fully assemble. He moved quietly among them in a crouch, telling them they faced three hundred yards of killing ground and the best way to survive its depredations would be to gain the shelter of the woods as quickly as possible. "Load your weapon but trust your bayonet," he instructed. "Remember, the enemy riflemen will not have bayonets, so the sooner we close, the sooner we have the advantage. Fire only when you are inside the wood and face an opponent. Stop for nothing. If a mate falls, keep going. Remember, rifles might be more precise than muskets, but they are slower to load."

General Baudin, conspicuous on horseback, signaled with his sword to Dupont, leader of the skirmishers, that the six lines of the main assault were ready. Dupont acknowledged with a flourish of his own sword. A bugle sounded. The skirmishers rose, bayonets fixed, and spread themselves out quickly, three feet between each man.

To their rear, drummers began beating the *pas de charge*.

The *voltigeurs* moved forward in a brisk trot rather than a flat out run. It was important that they pierce the wood as a group, not individuals.

The sharp crack of rifles commenced mere seconds after the *voltigeurs* had departed their assembly points. The men in the wood were good shots and killed or wounded at least thirty men before the French had traversed the first hundred yards. Gagne saw the line slow and stagger, yet it did not stop.

The *voltigeurs* had advanced a further hundred yards when they were struck by another round of shrapnel fire from the ridge. That lethal cloud killed or wounded another hundred men. The line bowed and sagged, but the survivors never lost sight of their objective and moved forward: walking, limping, or crawling.

The final push of sixty yards cost the French skirmishers only ten men. The remainder ran the last twenty yards, each man silently choosing a target based on muzzle flashes.

Once Gagne's men and 340 of their mates burst through the tree line, they began stabbing madly at anything in a green uniform. The expressions on their opponents' faces did not reflect the fear the French expected; many had hoped the mere sight of French steel at close quarters would cause their enemies to flee in terror. What the French saw instead was anger and loathing. These men had had their homeland despoiled by the French and were hungry for revenge. The riflemen fought furiously, resisting the French stoutly with swords, rifle butts, and improvised weapons; but none of these were a match for a bayonet. They sold their lives dearly, accounting for more of the French than one had a right to expect of rookie troops.

A Nassau private hurled a log at Le Duc, a considerable feat of strength that came to naught when Le Duc deflected the log up and away with his musket. He then made a quick side slash with his bayonet, which slit the man's throat. The man clutched his bloody throat in agony, gurgled, dropped to his knees in the mud, then pitched forward.

A Nassau corporal brandishing a hunting knife leaped from a tree and landed atop Du Bois' back. He had pushed Bois' face into the dirt and raised his knife to strike when Tremplay skewered him from behind. The force of the thrust lifted the corporal off Du Bois and propelled him toward the ground. Rochfort defended Tremplay from a side attack, killing his man with a bayonet thrust to the heart; demonstrating, once again, the merits of teamwork.

Collette killed an officer who had fired a pistol at him. It was amazing that the man missed from a range of five feet, but the strain of battle often impaired hand-eye coordination. The officer's servant drew a hunting knife, but seeing the fire in Collette's eyes, turned on his heels and ran.

Gagne concentrated on leading rather than fighting, but an aggressive, green-coated NCO forced him to demonstrate his own considerable expertise with a bayonet. One low block pushed his opponent's sword sideways, then he used the butt of his Charleville to ram the man in the teeth. The man staggered back, and when he reached a distance that allowed Gagne to use its full reach, he ran his bayonet through the German's stomach.

The unequal contest at the edge of the wood ended. The Jaegers withdrew all at once, as if each man had received a magical "retreat" signal at the same time. They fled headlong to the north, hoping to find someplace to regroup.

Gagne commanded his men to halt and reorder themselves. Their immediate job was done: they had acted as hammers, smashing open a locked door. His men would be needed again shortly; once the wood was secure, the large orchard would be the next area to attack. He told his men they could rest, smoke their pipes, or eat. Most had already emptied their haversacks, and so they discussed the next attack with eagerness. Not because they were eager for a fight, but because conquest of the orchard promised plenty of apples.

But Gagne's men got no rest. The shrapnel that had stopped once they reached the tree line now recommenced. Rather than dampening the effects of shrapnel, the trees increased it. Splinters and shards of wood flew every which way; some as great as three feet in length. There was no place to hide, so the best the men could do was to hug the earth and hope for the best.

It angered Gagne that French cannon were doing nothing; he wondered why they were not engaging in counter battery fire to stop the shrapnel at its source. In fact, his nephew's battery had just been redirected to do just that, but lying flat on his face without a shred of dignity, Gagne had no way of knowing.

***

18 June 1815, 11:30 a.m., Allied field ammunition dump, forward of the Forest of Soignes

The echoes of gunfire resounded through the ammunition park in the Forest of Soignes, a mile behind the village of Waterloo. The grounds bustled with purposeful activity of, but the camp was a mess, and messes annoyed Pennywhistle's orderly mind. He frowned at the sight of acres of supply wagons that had been abandoned by their civilian drivers the day before. The civilians had been panicked, not by actual French attacks, but by rumors of them. Royal Wagon Train drivers were reliable, but there were too few of them for the demands of such a large army as Wellington's.

These wagons contained ammunition that the troops would need later in the day, as ammunition consumption would be prodigious.

Even though most men of the infantry had been issued sixty rounds, if the battle lasted an entire day, many soldiers would run out. As for artillery, the Dutch were already begging rounds from the British.

Everyone was so preoccupied with the exigencies of battle that no one appeared to have a master plan to get that ammunition to the men at the front. With Wellington's assent, Pennywhistle began rounding up spare soldiers and civilians and pressing abandoned wagons back into service. His impromptu command would form an emergency delivery service, dispatching wagons at a moment's notice to whatever section of the front needed supplies.

The ammunition park, he realized, would also have to be moved forward to a position just out of range of the heaviest of Bonaparte's guns.

The 300 medical personnel of Wellington's Army occupied an area adjacent to the ammunition park. Upon their arrival, Pennywhistle had offered to escort the three women and introduce them to the officer in charge. To his surprise, all three expressed a preference for helping him organize a reserve ammunition shuttle service.

"I'd rather help men avoid being wounded than minister to them after they have been," Sammie Jo said, matter-of-factly.

"It would give me a chance to witness battle firsthand, rather than merely hear about it from wounded men." Deborah's devotion to finding and telling the truth reminded Pennywhistle of a nun's devotion to God.

"I don't know where Steven is, but being with the wagons might give me a chance to find him," Sarah said, hopefully.

"Absolutely not!" bellowed Pennywhistle with exasperation. "I will not hear of it. You all belong where you are safe, and the errands the wagons will perform will be the opposite of that."

Dale added his angry voice. "You've no business risking your life, Deborah."

Maxwell pronounced firmly, "War is man's business. You will just get in the way."

It was Johnny who came up with the compromise. "Why don't the women work as dispatchers?"

Everyone looked at him in surprise.

Johnny knew he was speaking of matters far beyond his years, but he knew Pennywhistle welcomed initiative, wherever it came from. "They could take the orders, organize wagons, and supervise their loading, freeing up men to drive them. Since you are shorthanded, it makes good sense."

Pennywhistle pondered Johnny's words, noting that the women did not object. "That's an interesting proposal, a classic compromise: each side getting some of what they want but not all, and it would work. Ladies," he queried, "what say you?"

"I'd rather be conning a wagon, "replied Sammie Jo stubbornly, "but I understand this would help you. I assume you'd want to make the military decisions, assessing priorities; deciding which needs are critical and which can wait. And I know commanding from the rear is not be easy for you, since you are always hot to be where the action is thickest. So it's a compromise all around. That's fair."

Pennywhistle knitted his eyebrows, bowed his head, and began to pace. Sammie Jo was right, but he also knew that a critical delivery might require his presence to ensure the job was done right. He didn't want to be an Uxbridge; he would delegate the duties of a field officer to other drivers — with one caveat. That was Hougemont. What was supposed to be a sideshow for both armies was sucking in men fast, and the British were burning ammunition to defend the walls and grounds like there was no tomorrow. The other deliveries could be made from behind Allied lines, but getting through to Hougemont might require punching through French lines.

Sammie Jo recognized the warning signs of deep thought and kept silent, though she was bursting with suggestions.

He came to a decision that would have shocked a conventional officer. He would trust a woman to do a man's job and allow a civilian to play a military role. Sammie Jo was uniquely fitted for the role of his understudy: smart, adaptable, and brave. She had shown in Vienna that she was immune to intimidation even by heads of state. Authority and command were rooted in her character.

"I know my place is here in the park, Sammie Jo, but I might have to desert my post for a short period, and you would be left in charge."

"Me?" exclaimed a stunned Sammie Jo. "I ain't no officer."

"No, but you have seen me work, you know my methods, and you have been through enough battles to know how an army works, better than many junior officers. Most importantly, you instinctively know when a man is talking rot and when he is being straightforward. Wellington likes and admires you and might even support my decision, if I had the opportunity to tell him. I will furnish you with a good map and detailed instructions, should the exigencies of battle command me away. There are three categories of supply demands: critical, important, and impossible. Your judgment plus your physical presence, title, and sheer energy will cause men to listen to you."

"I declare, Tom Pennywhistle," exclaimed Sammie Jo with amusement mixed with admiration, "you're talking like a revolutionary and making Mary Wollstonecraft's ideas on women's rights seem downright practical. I may make an American of you yet!"

"Battle often causes custom to be cast out the window in the interest of common sense."

"So, Sammie Jo would be in charge if you were gone, and we would be her assistants?" inquired Deborah.

"Yes, she would," replied Pennywhistle. "The shorthand that you use for reporting will come in handy taking orders. In addition, you would get a chance to quickly query men arriving from critical sectors. Rather than you going to the stories, the stories will come to you. You could also ask returning deliverymen for their impressions of the battle."

"Ah," said Deborah, "the best of both worlds."

"Sarah," inquired Pennywhistle, "your opinion?"

"I could give the driver's a description of Steven and ask them to tell me if they had seen him," she murmured, thinking out loud. "Yes. Yes! I shall be happy to lend my best efforts."

"Good," said Pennywhistle. "While nursing requires a compassionate heart, which you all have, this task requires quick thinking and good judgement, qualities much harder to find in any human beings."

Deborah realized she might gain the material not just for a series of articles, but an entire memoir. She pictured the title in her mind: *Recollections of War by a Woman of Character and Compassion*. No, that sounded too much like a military Jane Austen. She could work out the title later.

Pennywhistle and company rounded up ten wagons and sets of horses, arranging them in a compass rose. Half the wagons contained infantry cartridges, and half artillery rounds. The Dutchmen van Dreelin and van der Beek set up their water wagons nearby, ready to provide relief to thirsty messengers and drivers. Van Dreelin was particularly joyful; he had found his son, who had been sent by his regiment to request more ammunition.

Twenty Englishmen and ten Dutchmen were drafted into service, and a cat named Marvel insisted upon accompanying his owner. Half of the new men were civilians, half military. All were what Pennywhistle called "drifters": men who for one reason or another had lost their units. None of them could be accused of zeal, but with close supervision there was hope that some useful service could be coaxed out of them.

Three women who were not camp followers attracted attention, as Pennywhistle meant them to. Inquisitive officers approached, and so found out Pennywhistle's purpose.

He felt like the captain of a volunteer fire brigade standing by for his first alarm. He did not have long to wait. Messengers began arriving at the gallop, requesting ammunitions for their units. At first, all the work was focused sending out supply wagons, but as the sun arced across the sky past midday, the wagons began returning with wounded men. Soon the medical staff were overwhelmed, even with the help of camp followers. Deborah and Sarah found more than ample opportunity to put the bandaging skills they had practiced to good use.

Sarah was amazed to discover that camp followers included wives and even children. Among the women assisting the ambulance staff was a mother with a five-year-old daughter. The young child quietly played by the side of the tent.

It was after 2 p.m. when a runner dashed into the camp with the message that ammunition was urgently needed for the defence of Hougemont. Pennywhistle had been holding the sturdiest supply wagon in reserve for just this eventuality. Leaving Sammie Jo in charge of deploying the wagons, he assembled his team, mounted Diable, and set out.

***

Destination Waterloo

18 June 1815, 1 p.m., the fields east of Hougemont

The pounding of Fivel's cannons mirrored the pounding in Jacques Gagne's head. An hour of firing his two guns had given him a headache the like of which he had never had. Napoleon had sent 12 more cannons forward: there were now 42 cannons blasting away in the relatively small space around Hougemont. The clouds generated by so many guns rose 500 meters above the cannons, exactly the thunderheads you would expect from a storm, though this was of lead not water. The multiple discharges impregnated the air with saltpeter, making it hard to breathe and causing him to cough frequently. The grit in the heavy air smelled and tasted like rotten eggs with the consistency of oatmeal mixed with gravel: a thin layer of it covered clothes as well as equipment. Saltpeter sucked moisture from everything; making his lips and throat as parched as if he were in the Sahara.

The discharges had heated the air almost 20 degrees and the heavy moisture in the atmosphere acted like a wet blanket, keeping the smoke from rising too far. A heat dome formed, making him feel as if he were fighting in a hothouse. Only in war could you feel parched and soaked at the same time.

Casualties had been light in Fivel's battery. None killed, one badly wounded, and three moderately so: all victims of shrapnel. The cannons were all intact because the enemy had been firing solid shot slightly too high; most of the rounds smashing wagons and limbers well to the rear. His men were showing their fatigue, but morale remained high.

Boom! Boom! Boom! Boom! His battery fired two more rounds in quick succession at the guns on the ridge behind Hougemont. He watched the balls for the split second before they vanished into the smoke, satisfied that his aim was true if the enemy batteries had not moved. Hougemont was entirely concealed in smoke, and he located the infantry fight chiefly by shouts, screams, and slogans. A big fight was on, though it was impossible to tell who was winning.

The enemy batteries were visible only at intervals through the heavy smoke. Their fire had actually increased rather than decreased in the last hour. Jacques' cannons had probably disabled some of the British guns with their kisses, but Wellington was feeding more batteries into the fight. The attack against Hougemont was not Napoleon's main thrust but a distraction to cause Wellington to dissipate his already slim resources. So far, it seemed to be working.

"Cease fire, cease fire!" echoed down the line of cannons. Fivel knew they were down to their last rounds and had called a halt so more ammunition could be brought forward. *Caporal* Gagne told his men to stand down and rest; Pauline distributed spare canteens she had filled with water from the barrels 20 meters to the rear. She had been an angel of mercy throughout the fight, capturing the gratitude of every man in the battery; filling men's cups with water, oblivious to shot and shell. She had transferred water from barrels to four large botas she wore round her neck. The weight of the water was heavy, and she was not a large woman, but she nonetheless moved backward and forward along the line of guns with determination and dispatch. When she was not doing that, she bandaged up the wounded and dragged them to safety.

Jacques plopped down next to the right wheel of gun number one and gulped the last of his canteen's contents. Pauline sat down next to him and handed him a biscuit and a round of sausage. "Battle always makes men hungry, so I kept this for you."

He accepted both gratefully. "Always thinking of me. You seem to know just what I need even before I do."

"I've had a lot of experience looking out for men, and I think you need a lot of looking after."

"You do it very well." He cleared his throat and rallied his conflicting thoughts.

He both admired her and lusted for her, but he was unsure of his other feelings. The confidence love making had given him was undeniable and had made possible his exceptionally strong performance today; he would always be grateful and would never forget the magic of the act of love. He also felt great affection and friendship for Pauline. In his upbringing, if a boy slept with a girl, it meant a wedding must follow soon after. He was not ready for marriage, yet his background made him feel compelled to consider proposing it. Pauline had been married twice before; perhaps she could instruct him on the mysteries. She was a good woman and he wanted to do right by her though she was not the kind of woman his mother would have chosen for him. He heard his mother's voice in his head: *Marry within the Quaker faith; chose a bride of high morals and sound industry who comes from a background similar to your own.*

"Pauline, there is something we need to discuss. I..."

"Stop right there, Jacques. I recognize the expression and know what you are about to ask." Her voice became brisk and businesslike. "I do not think you are ready for what you're contemplating. Perhaps in two or three years, but not now. I am happy that we have met, but in peace our paths would never have crossed. You fight well, but your nature is not that of a soldier. You are a gentle soul in an ungentle place and time; a maker, not a destroyer. I see you returning home and growing old with many grandchildren, a happy and prosperous apple grower. You deserve a wife who loves that life and prospers in it."

"Is it wrong to desire that vision?"

"Not at all, but I am a restless spirit, unused to staying long in one place. It unwise to forecast the future; I prefer to live in the present moment. For now, I am content to continue our association and explore it as it unfolds."

Gagne was stunned. For a woman so passionate in lovemaking, her appraisal sounded like a land speculator appraising the value of an undeveloped plot of land, seeing herself as a crop that would not grow well in the soil he would prepare. Perhaps she was right; their two worlds might not be compatible, and he should just focus on the one they were in right now.

She saw the confusion in his face. "Don't try to force yourself to feel something that is not there. Don't try to will love into existence. I am content to know you regard me with tenderness and affection."

"I do, Pauline." He sighed and scowled. "It's all so...complicated. I always thought my feelings for a woman would be simple, clear, and direct. Now I feel like a blind man who has never seen a human face trying to puzzle out its expression by touch."

Fivel's shouted orders ended the conversation. The ammunition had been delivered and the battery was ready to recommence firing. Jacques rose, helping Pauline to her feet.

"For now, Jacques, banish any worry and just focus on doing your job and surviving."

He nodded and took up his appointed position. Pauline returned to the water barrels and began refilling her botas.

The battery had fired two rounds when disaster struck. Cannon number 2's barrel exploded, not as the result of enemy action but metal fatigue. The blast killed three of the crew and threw Jacques to the ground. He was unconscious for a few seconds, and when he awoke, everything seemed clouded by a fine mist. His vision eventually cleared, and he realized that, other than a ringing in his ears and a few bruises, he was unhurt. Bits of bodies lay scattered around him, and he felt his stomach churn, but it was not until he rose and looked left that he got the shock of his life. Tears started t his eyes he muttered, "Oh, no! No!"

Pauline lay on her back, a shard of metal imbedded in her forehead. Her expression was one of surprise. He walked slowly toward the body with a trance-like expression on his face, his brain unwilling to accept the verdict of his eyes. He bent down and stroked her hair gently, then shut her eyes. He picked the body up reverently and carried it to an ammunition wagon that had been emptied of its contents. He plucked a clover and placed it atop her body. He offered a silent prayer for her soul, then covered her body with a tarpaulin.

He felt a comforting hand on his shoulder and turned to see Fivel's sympathetic face. "I am so sorry, Gagne. She was a rare spirit and will be missed."

"I will never forget her," Jacques whispered, as if making a knightly vow. "Never. Ever." He turned on his heel and walked back toward his remaining gun. Sadness gave way to anger at the sheer waste of a good and decent life. He needed to lash out at somebody, and the British would do just fine.

***

18 June 1815, 1:30 p.m., Napoleon's camp

At his headquarters in Le Caillou, Napoleon sat slumped in a canvas camp chair. He had slept poorly the night before, in great pain. His health, which had suffered during the Russian campaign and the German campaigns of 1813, had declined during his exile at Elba. He was no longer buoyed by the indomitable fire and drive for which he had become famous; at times he lapsed into inexplicable torpor.

One of Bonaparte's messengers, *Capitaine* Rene Coignet, galloped up, dismounted quickly, and saluted his Emperor crisply. The salute went unacknowledged.

Coignet was an old man by army standards, having seen fifty summers. He had been promoted from the ranks and had known the Emperor since the Corsican had first been appointed to command the Army of Italy, at the age of 26. The person Coignet saw before him was nothing like the rail thin, sharp-eyed, phenomenally energetic general he had known in those days: a commander who seemed to be everywhere at once, inspiring men with his bold ideas, bolder risk-taking, and genuine willingness to share the privations of his men, no matter how physically demanding. Now Coignet beheld an individual with a stout belly, thinning hair, and waxy skin, who seemed barely awake. His grey eyes lacked their former fire, and as he assessed Coignet, he shifted in a way that suggested he was suffering from a bad case of piles. Yet despite not having seen Coignet since Marengo in 1800, Napoleon addressed him by name. His memory, at least, was as sharp as ever. "Well, what is it, Coignet?"

"Message from Prince Jerome, Sire. His men are poised to strike at the North Gate of Hougemont. He is certain he can gain entrance if his soldiers are reinforced by at least two brigades."

"What does Reille say?" Reille commanded the corps to which Prince Jerome's division was attached.

"Comte Reille says that since Prince Jerome is closest to Hougemont, he will defer to his judgement."

Coignet knew that though Reille was in nominal command, the fact that Prince Jerome was the Emperor's brother guaranteed that Jerome's "suggestions" would be *de facto* orders. Jerome was a likable fellow but had no head for commanding a division; however, Napoleon had a huge blind spot when it came to the capabilities of his brothers.

"Speak to Marshall Ney about the matter, Coignet," replied Napoleon listlessly. "Tell him to give my brother whatever resources he requires." With that, Napoleon drifted off into a light sleep.

Coignet shuddered inwardly. The actual command of the battle was apparently being delegated to Marshal Ney! Ney was loyal, brave, gallant, and... stupid.

Coignet realized it was Ney who had allowed Hougemont to become a vortex that sucked in every available local resource. It should have been walled off with a minimum of troops, not be allowed to become a battle within a battle.

This Napoleon was pale copy of the man who had invaded Russia in 1812, and Coignet wondered what it would take to get Bonaparte to resume actual command. Reluctantly, he concluded it would take a miracle.

Chapter 15
The Crisis

18 June 1815, 1:45 p.m., the Ohain Road

Captain Steven Thynne's horse, Mandrake, was skittish: pawing the muddy ground, chuffing frequently, and turning his head rapidly from side to side as he gripped his bit hard. The huge black stallion, eighteen hands high, was exceptionally intelligent and intuitive, and he knew something important was about to happen. His mood mirrored the anxious expectancy of his rider.

Mandrake had cost Thynne more than a year's salary, and never had his money been better spent. The stallion seemed to understand his intentions almost before he did and had saved his life on numerous occasions. The bond between the two was so strong as to be almost supernatural; if there was ever a horse guaranteed to bring his master back alive no matter how hard the fighting, it was Mandrake.

Thynne and his squadron of 135 Life Guards had endured forty minutes of intense shelling from the 80 guns of Napoleon's Grand Battery, six- and twelve-pounders firing solid shot. Wellington's center had taken more than 4,000 rounds during that time, a hundred per minute. And this bombardment was merely the prelude to Napoleon's major effort.

Destination Waterloo

Wellington's use of terrain had so far protected the British from the worst of the bombardment. The majority of Wellington's army were posted on the reverse slope of the Mount Saint Jean ridge, out of sight of the gun crews. And the muddy ground was reducing the effectiveness of the French barrage. Cannon balls were often more deadly on the bounce than on the fly, and on hard ground could usually be counted on for three devastating bounces. Each bounce was called a graze, and today most balls had only managed a single graze.

The 1,100 troopers of King George III's Household Brigade, of which the Life Guards were one regiment, was posted in an undulating fold of ground well to the rear of the British and Allied infantries. Thynne's curiosity got the better of him, and he trotted Mandrake forward several hundred yards to the crest of the ridge. He unfurled his spyglass and surveyed the downward slope in front of the Ohain Road, which was ten feet below the ground on either side, with a thick hedge on the higher ground; it marked the forward edge of Wellington's lines. What Thynne saw took his breath away. It was a sight never to be forgotten, as magnificent as it was frightening.

Four French divisions were approaching the Ohain Road, marching steadily up hill: 17,000 soldiers spread over 2/3 of a mile. Each division marched in a column with a front of 125 yards and a depth of 24 ranks. The unusual formation had the unstoppable momentum of a column but a great enough width that it could immediately deploy sufficient firepower from its front two ranks to reap the benefits of a line. The divisions marched majestically through tall fields of rye, only the tops of their shakos visible; the densely planted stalks and rain-soaked ground slowing their movements.

800 French cuirassiers protected the flanks of the columns of the French infantry assault, followed by several batteries of horse artillery.

The 28 guns of Wellington's batteries, which were posted well in advance of his main lines, opened fire. Their fire proved deadly but not decisive. Whole files of the French columns were mowed down, but their loss did not stop the advance.

Thynne had seen enough. He pivoted Mandrake, returned to his post, and waited. And waited. And waited. Each second seemed an eternity though the hands of his pocket watch told him only thirty minutes had elapsed since his visit to the crest. It was hard to see much through the smoke, but a furious infantry fight was underway several hundred yards ahead. The French had reached the crest and had pushed back the divisions of Picton and Von Alten. Thynne sensed the battle hung in the balance.

Uxbridge came riding up and spoke urgently to Lord Edward Somerset, the Household Brigade's Commander. It did not take a genius to guess a cavalry charge had been ordered. A cavalry charge usually gathered momentum gradually, from walk to trot to canter to gallop but here the brigade would be moving uphill over broken ground; they would have to proceed at the pace known as "a march walk."

Cornet Lacy pulled alongside, his face brimming with vigor and enthusiasm. "This charge will be long remembered."

"I hope it is remembered for the right reasons," replied Thynne.

"What do you mean?" inquired Lacy.

Thynne reproached himself. His job was to inspire, not sow doubt. "Nothing at all, Cornet. I am sure we shall succeed... ah... gloriously."

"I am sure the Peer will see we all get medals," Lacy chirped.

The trumpeters blew the appropriate commands, and the brigade's seven squadrons formed into line. Thynne's command was posted on the far right. The British horses advanced up hill slope. The muddy terrain reduced everyone's movements to slow motion.

Destination Waterloo

The goal of the Life Guards was to reclaim the hill from the cavalry of French cuirassiers who were currently riding back and forth, slashing at the disorganized and dying soldiers of the British infantry. Thynne's men encountered a line of French cuirassiers, and a furious contest ensued. The French had longer swords and superior reach, but the British horses were larger, giving their riders the advantage of height. On this occasion, the decisive factor proved to be the mounts.

French horses suffered from generations of indifferent breeding; Napoleon's campaigns had consumed horses at a prodigious rate, so quantity, not quality, had become the driving principle. French horses were trained for slow moving maneuvers, stressing formality, discipline, and obedience. In marked contrast, British horses were trained for the hunt and the race course. They were bred for speed, endurance, responsiveness, and initiative. As a consequence, they were much sought after as prizes of war. The eyes of French cuirassiers lit up with desire: if they could kill these riders, the best prizes would be not their haversacks and weapons, but their horses.

Mandrake embodied the epitome of British equine stock, and Thynne's strategy relied upon the stallion's agility: cut, run, cut, and run again, damage his opponents before they could react, then move out of range. He moved past one cuirassier who had raised his blade to strike raking the man's ribs with his saber. This cuirassier had attracted Thynne's attention because he had shouted in broken English, "I'll stop your damned crowing!" The Frenchman dropped his sword and drooped sideways in his saddle, not dead but out of the fight. Thynne ducked a sword slash aimed at his head from a Frenchman on the right, then darted past him and sabered the man in the back of the neck. The man tumbled from his saddle.

A third opponent proved craftier. He kept the fight at close quarters, using his smaller mount to move inside Mandrake's wider movements. He wielded his sword fast and expertly, slashing successively at Thynne's head, arm, and leg. Thynne blocked them, barely. His own cuts to the man's chest and thigh were parried away. As they continued to slash, block, and thrust, it dawned on Thynne that Mandrake was his best weapon. He maneuvered to gain some distance, then sent Mandrake leaping forward. Mandrake's bulk shoved the other horse violently to the left, and causing the rider to lose his balance. As he tried to recover, he dropped his guard for a few critical seconds. That was all Thynne needed to thrust the tip of his blade through the man's throat.

The cuirassiers' discipline broke all at once and they began to abandon the field, leaving the French infantry exposed and off balance. Thynne and his men tore into them, slashing and cutting madly with swift and deadly blows. The carnage was terrible, and what had been disciplined infantry soon became a rabble streaming down the hill whence they had come. The Household Brigade on the right and Union Brigade on the left had broken the back of Napoleon's infantry assault. Both cavalry brigades pursued the fugitives closely, turning a retreat into a rout.

Uxbridge, as usual, forgot himself and led from the front, behaving like a hot-blooded cornet rather than a responsible director of a large body of horsemen. An extended debauch of riding and killing commenced, each man a law unto himself, seeking nothing but individual glory. The French infantry was slaughtered in droves, and once they had been reduced to impotency, the cavalry rode hard for the guns of the French Grand Battery. They overran its position and drove off the gunners, but the riders had no way to either spike the guns or tow them away.

A shiver of fear lanced up Thynne's back and his mouth went dry. The charge had kept no squadrons in reserve. There were no troopers to defend against the inevitable counterattack. He swore in frustration, knowing what was coming, but also knowing he could do nothing to prevent a general slaughter. There was one action he could take, and he prepared to do so.

The exuberant troopers had ridden their magnificent mounts to the brink of exhaustion when all at once they were confronted by seasoned cavalry whose commanders knew their business. General Jacquinot had plenty of reserves, and he knew exactly when to release them.

Thynne, unlike most squadron commanders, retained some control over his men. He had sounded their recall when the rest of the brigade was halfway to the Grand Battery, and his squadron began a trot back toward the ridge, their horses tired but not blown.

Jacquinot's counterattack of lancers shattered the two brigades of horsemen who had ridden to the guns. A British triumph transitioned to a British disaster, then a rout. The British horses were not only exhausted and slowed by the heavy mud; riders attempting to flee died with lances through their backs.

Thynne halted his men, trying to form a bulwark upon which retreating riders might rally, but the momentum of the French was too great, and the British riders were too dazed and shaken to notice what he offered. Soon the French lancers were among his own men, proving once again that tired men with swords on winded horses were no match for fresh men with lances on fresh mounts. His men died in a farrago of bloodletting. "Help me! Help me!" shouted Coronet Lacy just before a lance pierced his heart.

Thynne killed two lancers before one succeeded at thrusting a lance through his leg. The pain was so terrible he twisted in his saddle, causing a lance aimed at his chest to miss and merely graze his shoulder. He felt himself losing consciousness, but before he did, his glance alighted on the locket that his left hand had unconsciously grasped. The thought of his beloved gave him the presence of mind to whisper six words: "Take me home. Take me home."

Mandrake's acute sense of smell took in the scent of sandalwood with which the locket was suffused, associating it with Thynne's wife, who had always given him particularly delicious apples. Even as Thynne slumped forward in the saddle, Mandrake took off like a rocket; breaking past the four horses circling Thynne and astonishing their riders. He headed straight back for the British lines with a speed that would have been remarkable for a champion racehorse, let alone a horse had just endured heavy action on a crowded battlefield.

The lancers galloped in pursuit, less concerned with killing his rider than capturing a steed the like of which they had never seen. Mandrake threaded his way around knots of fighting men, making their pursuit difficult. The four lancers finally gave up and turned to find softer targets.

Mandrake made himself a legend, commanding the awe of both sides as he thundered past. Once inside British lines, he did not stop but proceeded toward a surgeon's station well to the rear of where his journey had started. He halted abruptly near the entrance.

A startled surgeon emerged from the operating tent, stunned that a lone horse had provided the most efficient ambulance service he had ever seen. He and two of his mates gently removed Thynne from the saddle. He examined Thynne quickly. "If we take off that leg, we can save him, but we must be quick. Come, let's get him inside, he goes to the front of the line."

Mandrake snorted in approval as Thynne was carried into the tent. The wounded soldiers who lay outside the tent looked up in amazement, wishing they had such a friend. They felt no resentment at Thynne being placed ahead of them; his arrival was miraculous, and no one wanted to interfere with a miracle.

Several surgeon's helpers, what the Navy called loblolly boys, scurried to round up hay and water for Mandrake. One brushed

Mandrake down while he chewed his hay contentedly as if what he had just done was all in a day's work.

***

18 June, 3 p.m., the fields east of Hougemont

Jean-Paul Gagne faced a garden of death. In time of peace, it was a large, vine-covered field where mixed vegetables were cultivated, but today it represented a thirty-yard-wide killing ground devoid of cover. The muskets of hundreds of Redcoats and Hanoverians poked through the seven-foot-high brick walls that surrounded Hougemont's formal garden to the north. The enemy stood on fire steps and would be able to blaze downwards on their opponents at point blank range; even a blind man couldn't miss. The gnarled, twisting vines were perfect for ensnaring feet, making a fast run through them a high casualty proposition. The unexpectedly heavy volume of fire indicated that those who were not on the fire steps were reloading muskets for those who were.

Covering the garden were dozens of bodies, some moaning and twitching, but most silent and still. Every so often, a wounded man tried to crawl to safety, but he was quickly noticed and dispatched. The British were inclined to show mercy to such men, but the Hanoverians never: they had not forgotten how the conquering French had treated their land.

The men of the 1st *Legere* and 2nd *Legere* who had gained the orchard had paid a heavy price; it would fare no better for his men unless Gagne could devise a clever ruse. He scowled; none was forthcoming.

Gagne's men would have to traverse that deadly garden diagonally to reach their objective of the apple orchard which lay to the East of the Formal Garden. Before they reached the shelter of the trees, they would come under musket fire from the west wall of the garden, also lined with British and Hanoverian Troops.

The orchard was swarming with French regulars, but they were being pushed back, tree by tree, by a counterattack led by two companies of Lord Saltoun's 1st Foot Guards. The fighting was hot and fierce, and the French needed something to even the odds.

The equalizer had arrived five minutes ago, in the hands his nephew Jacques, and Gagne's job was to shepherd it through the gauntlet of fire. His nephew seemed in the grip of a deep melancholy, at odds with his normal optimism. Jean-Paul felt this when he embraced the lad, but they neither had time nor inclination to discuss anything other than professional concerns. Lives were at stake, and each minute that passed left more men at risk.

Jacques had arrived with a 5.5 inch howitzer. If it could be gotten into the orchard it would be deadly at close quarters. He had brought with it a real prize: shrapnel ammunition. A British supply wagon containing ten rounds of spherical case shot had been captured by Pire's lancers and turned over to commander *Capitaine* Fivel. Fivel only had a general idea how the thing worked; remembering the incident with the wagon wheel and Jacques handiness with machinery of all kinds, Fivel had entrusted the weapon to his young *caporal* to work out its particulars.

Gagne theorized that the trick lay in cutting the fuse to the correct length. Since he had neither knowledge nor experience, he would be engaging in rank guesswork. His job would be to ensure that the shell burst mere seconds after impact, far more difficult than having it burst hundreds of meters beyond its dispatch point. Many men's lives rested on his judgment, and he shivered for a moment at the grave responsibility.

His uncle noticed. "Are you all right, Jacques?"

A vision of Pauline's face shimmered in his mind's eye and his doubt vanished. He felt her presence and her inspiration. The image had the effect of reducing the discordant voices in his mind to a single clear narrative that had all the variables figured out and was confident of success.

"Yes, Uncle," he replied with a force that surprised him. "More than fine. I believe I know how to employ my special ammunition. And I have a good idea of where. All that is necessary is to get me in position. I leave that to you." Jacques looked at the ground ahead of him and wondered how he could get a heavy piece of ordnance past fast-firing soldiers who would stop at nothing to kill men towing an instrument that could alter the outcome in favor of their enemies.

Jean Paul knew there was a solution, but he hated it. It involved giving up what you claimed to love in the interest of something you had vowed to love even more. His men were human beings, not drones to be mindlessly sacrificed. He finally decided his duty should command his instinct. To send men on a suicide mission was wrong, but necessary. At least he could call for volunteers and give each man the choice between playing the lion or the sacrificial lamb. The lions would lay down diversionary fire, while the lambs would engage in a mad charge against the garden wall. His nephew and his men could use that cover to drag the howitzer across the garden and into the orchard.

Jean-Paul explained his plan to Jacques. Jacques thought it could work, but like his uncle, regretted that men would have to be deliberately sacrificed as a diversion.

The two had just finished working out details of the feint when God intervened. Well, perhaps not God, but benighted souls certainly under God's direct protection. A group of twenty or so women came wandering toward the garden, clad in long white smocks with a red cross on the front of each gown. They had vacant looks on their faces that indicated they had no idea they were in a war zone. They babbled in low tones, each seeming to be talking to herself rather than the others. Private Collette recognized them.

"They are the Little Sisters of the Faint Light," stated Collette. "It's an asylum run by Benedictine Nuns, near Genappe. Looks like these women escaped its confines. The nuns must be too busy with their own difficulties to be looking for them."

The French soldiers in the way of the escapees instinctively moved away, the quality of pity not dead, despite the ravages of battle. They let the women pass, and that gave Jean Paul an idea. The lunatics would be the diversion. The British, despite being the enemy, were familiar with the laws of mercy, and would cease firing to allow passage of these sad folk.

Jean Paul issued his orders quickly, while his nephew's men loaded the howitzer. Collette volunteered to guide the women. He transformed the waistcoat of a dead comrade into an improvised flag of truce. Waving this flag vigorously, he stepped into the killing ground.

As hoped, the British held their fire, respecting the flag of truce. When they saw the reason for it, and an officer atop the wall shouted, "They may pass." Unspoken was the understanding that the temporary cease fire would last only until the lunatics were out of range of musketry.

Collette gently took the hand of the lead lunatic and began escorting her. The women followed Collette single file, like ducklings behind their mother. They were docile and obedient, moving islands of calm in a sea of war. British eyes followed their passage, the odd spectacle like the attraction of a freak show at a county fair. They relaxed their vigilance, and this gave the French an interval of safety that Jean Paul and Jacques put to immediate use.

While the British looked left, Jacques men dashed right, each of the four men carrying a tow rope attached to hooks under the front of the gun. When they had reached the limit of the ropes, they threw themselves to the ground and waited for the command to commence pulling.

The women continued their passage as Jacques cut the fuse for a round of case shot. He had no idea of the burn rate of British detonation cord, but settled on one and a half centimeters. If it detonated too late, it would still kill soldiers, just not the ones he needed disabled. His men loaded the howitzer, and he elevated its stubby barrel to fire in as steep an arc as possible. He sighted on a British officer's shako thirty yards away, the man incautiously exposing himself to gape at the lunatics. Jean Paul's men lay on their bellies, ready to provide covering fire.

Once Collette judged the distance safe, he pointed the women in the right direction and offered a short prayer for their welfare. They still had plenty of dangerous terrain to navigate, but he hoped they would meet with the same responses of pity and mercy in others that they had with his men and the British; they were harmless doves seeking refuge.

Collette was a man of honor and needed to signify the truce was at an end. He shouted at the British, waved his flag twice, then ripped it from the stick to which it was attached. He tore it in half, threw it to the ground, and gave a deep, gallant bow. He raced for the cover of the woods and was not followed by any British bullets.

The second Collette gained the wood, Jacques fired, and his uncle's musketeers delivered a volley. Jacques' instincts proved sound; the round detonated thirty feet above and ten feet behind the British defenders. Shouts of pain, confusion, and anger issued from the garden walls.

Jacques knew the chaos would be short-lived. His men rose and pulled hard on the howitzer ropes, and the gun began to move over the muddy ground, faster than he'd expected. Its wheels stuck once, but some vigorous pulling wrenched them free. Jean Paul's men followed the gunners in twos and threes, stopping twice to kneel and send a few diversionary shots toward the British. By the time the British opened fire, the French had reached the orchard, all but one man.

Collette had the farthest to run, and he made the mistake of stopping for one lunatic who had fallen asleep and been missed. She had jolted awake, startled by the gunfire. In her panic, she ran into the killing ground, then stopped abruptly, in complete disorientation. Bullets whizzed and whined on every side of her, but by some miracle she remained untouched.

Collette ran toward her. He swept her off her feet, cradling her in his arms, and made for the safety of the woods. He had just reached the edge when a bullet caught him in the back. He sagged, but had enough energy left to thrust the girl into the shelter of the trees. Collette's last sight was of a sobbing girl who had temporarily regained her senses and mourned the man who had saved her.

The howitzer proved decisive in the continuing fight in the orchard. By the time Gagne had fired the rest of his spherical case shot, The Guardsmen under Saltoun were in retreat. It was an orderly retreat, not a panicked one, and the Guardsmen were still dangerous. French infantry proceeded cautiously. Volleys were exchanged frequently, and the British yielded ground grudgingly.

Jacques felt a tug on his arm and saw that a bullet had grazed it. Since it had come from behind, it was likely friendly fire. He turned in the direction whence the round had come and saw it was distinctly unfriendly fire, intended for him personally. *Caporal* Le Mans, whom he had publicly embarrassed days before, glared at him, lowering the musket he had just fired.

It was hard to believe that anyone would try to kill him based on the pettiest of slights, but Jacques had learned that war amplified everything to a peculiar degree, particularly human emotions. War afforded an aggrieved man the opportunity to get away with murder, and Le Mans had just taken it. But war also gave Fate an opportunity to play tricks, and Fate now intervened. Le Man's angry glare changed to one of confusion as a purple blotch blossomed in the center of his forehead. He shivered for an instant, then collapsed.

The French reached the sunken road at the north edge of the orchard. The road led to the North Gate of Hougemont, which had remained open to allow for the passage of ammunition wagons. This gave the French a priceless opportunity for penetrating the heart of the enemy defenses.

It was at that moment Pennywhistle's supply wagon and escort pulled up, two hundred yards to the rear of the low hill above Hougemont. He unfurled his Ramsden and pointed it toward the orchard and then the gate, frowning deeply at the sight of French troops advancing. He was baffled. Why was Napoleon so focused on taking Hougemont? It was not strategically important.

A lieutenant of the Coldstream Guards galloped up to Pennywhistle and jerked his horse to a halt alongside Diable. "You've come just in time, Colonel..."

"Pennywhistle, Royal Marines."

"Lachlan MacGibbon at your service, Colonel. Colonel McDonnell's men's inside Hougemont are down to their last few rounds. He sent me to beg, borrow, or steal any ammunition I could lay my hands on, and it appears Providence has placed you directly in my path to answer his pleas."

"Getting through will be a dicey proposition," observed Pennywhistle, "but it can be managed if we can coordinate covering fire and any distraction you can contrive."

"Four companies of the 2nd Battalion under Colonel Woodford are readying an attack, sir," MacGibbon pointed to 400 Redcoats forming into lines in the near distance, "presaged by a five-minute barrage of canister and shrapnel from the several batteries on the slope. They should be able to clear a path for the supply wagon."

Pennywhistle again surveyed the area near the gate, his mind calculating and variables with the speed born of necessity: terrain, rate of infantry movements, volume of fire from the parapets on either side of the gate, and a dozen other elements that alone were trifling, but together constituted significant obstacles.

He furled his Ramsden and addressed MacGibbon with quiet confidence. "Tell Colonel Woodford I shall be ready to move as soon as his men stop to fire their first volley. You may tell him that, come hell or high water, I shall deliver my ammunition to Colonel McDonnell."

"I am relieved to hear it. And now, sir, I must depart." He turned his horse and galloped off to Woodford.

Pennywhistle readied his men and issued the necessary orders. There was no point in riding Diable into the fray, since mounted officers were conspicuous targets, and his job was to be an inconspicuous delivery boy. He handed Diable off to a trustworthy looking sergeant and told him there was a guinea in it for him if he kept the animal safe and sound. Against the advice of Dale and Maxwell, he decided to drive the wagon himself.

The British cannons stopped their thundering and the infantry drums of the Coldstream Guard commenced beating. Two lines began moving down the hill at the quickstep of 120 paces per minute. Their muskets were loaded, their bayonets leveled, their faces hard. Remnants of Saltoun's men who had been driven from the orchard rallied to them and formed a third line to their rear.

The French maintained a steady fire as the British advanced. Men dropped from time to time, but their comrades stepped over them, closed ranks, and continued the advance. At forty yards, the Redcoats halted, dressed ranks, then fired a devastating volley deliberately aimed low.

Pennywhistle's wagon began to move, but he refrained from cracking the whip. It was not yet time for a burst of speed. The Redcoats were using a well-tested formula developed in the Peninsula, and he wanted to let it play out. Dale sat next to him in the drive box with a Baker Rifle, while Maxwell rode alongside, ready to dispatch any miscreants with his saber who were not felled by fire from the three Englishmen and two Dutchmen, kneeling with muskets at the rear of the wagons. Pennywhistle did not expect much from the Anglo-Dutch drifters, but they were the only spare men he'd been able to find.

The Redcoats reloaded and fired a second volley. Pennywhistle sped up his wagon. The British reloaded and fired a third volley. This time they shouted "Hip, hip, huzzah!" three times.

"Charge!" bellowed Woodford. The British began to run down the slope, bayonets leveled.

Pennywhistle cracked the whip and the wagon leaped forward. He focused his attention on the open gate 200 yards ahead. He could see men on the parapets cheering him. A group of ten riflemen advanced beyond the gate to lend to led closer fire support. The wagon gathered speed. The five drifters in the wagon fired wildly, acting like quills on a porcupine that warned enemies not to get too close. Maxwell sabered three Frenchmen who had slipped past Woodford's men, and Dale shot another with his Baker.

They were twenty yards from the gate when Fate played a wild card. Dale dropped his Baker as a bullet entered his chest just above his left pectoral. He gasped and slumped backwards, grimacing in pain. Pennywhistle knew it was a severe wound, possibly fatal, but he could not stop to treat it. The wagon barreled along, crossing the last five yards to the gate. More and more enemy fire focused on them. Two of the drifters were killed, and the sideboards of the wagon resembled a sieve. They rattled over the threshold and continued toward the centre of the enclosure.

Colonel McDonnell bellowed, "Shut the gates! Shut the gates!" He and two others hefted a stout timber that would bar the gate. But the men closing the gates were pushed back by a group of thirty Frenchmen who charged through, accompanied by a drummer boy. Their leader was an exceptionally tall, bearded man in the uniform of a *sous lieutenant*. He wielded a heavy axe that he had used to smash through part of the gate. His companions cheered, calling him by his nickname, *"L'Enforcer"* — appropriate, given his size and savagery.

What followed was a clash of bayonets. The French were gradually driven toward the center of the courtyard. McDonnell and company finally managed to bar the gate, cutting the French off from retreat or support.

Pennywhistle set the surviving drifters to opening the barrels and distributing the ammunition. Groups of soldiers rushed forward haphazardly, madly filling their cartridge boxes, haversacks, pockets, and anything else that could hold a cartridge.

Maxwell had taken a dislike to the bearded man with the axe leading the assault, and leaped from the wagon to engage him in personal combat.

Destination Waterloo

The Frenchman was the same size as Maxwell, but moved more slowly. Maxwell dodged two swipes from the axe, ducked under a third, and landed a strike that sliced the man's thigh. The cut slowed the lieutenant but enraged him and increased his ferocity. Maxwell's sword blocked one blow, but shattered under the second. He threw what was left of the sword in the Frenchman's face.

The shattered blade glanced off the Frenchman's forehead and he staggered back, momentarily stunned. Maxwell put his head down and charged, giving no thought to strategy. He struck the Frenchman hard in the stomach, and both went down. They rolled over and over, each man fixing his hands on the others throat and squeezing for all he was worth.

The battle came down to a contest of raw will and endurance. Their wills were equal, but the Frenchman was bleeding from the cut to his thigh, and his strength began to ebb. Maxwell continued to squeeze like a choleric Titan. The Frenchman's tongue turned purple as his eyes threatened to burst from their sockets. His own grip loosened, he wheezed desperately, but Maxwell continued to squeeze, then he lay still. Maxwell rose slowly, his chest heaving. "Stupid bastard," he snarled under his breath.

The death of their leader burned the heart out of the few Frenchmen who remained alive. They were dispatched until only one left, the 12-year-old drummer. He clutched his drum and cowered in fear. McDonnell approached slowly and spoke gently. "Have no fear, lad. We do not kill children."

Pennywhistle, meanwhile, had laid Dale out on the back of the emptied wagon. He ripped open the shirt and examined the wound. Dale's breathing was raspy and bubbled; he hovered on the edge of consciousness, and his pulse under Pennywhistle's fingers bounded frantically, then began to fade. "Stay with me, old friend,"

Pennywhistle urged. He squeezed Dale's hand hard and blinked his blurring eyes.

Dale took a deep breath and his eyes focused. Pennywhistle had encountered this before in barely conscious dying men, granted final moments of lucidity to make their last wishes known and say goodbye.

"I did what I came for, Colonel. Look after Deborah, Andrew, and Johnny. Tell Andrew I died well."

"Be in no doubt of that."

"I shall miss you, Colonel. Promise me one thing."

"Anything."

"Finish Boney once and for al…" His lips stopped and his eyes turned glassy.

Pennywhistle let go Dale's cold hand and wiped away the tears in his eyes. He wondered what on earth he was going to tell Deborah.

Chapter 16
The Breaking Point

18 June 1815, 4 p.m., ammunition dump behind Mt. St. Jean ridge

Whap! The slap hurt Pennywhistle's cheek, but what hurt even more was the anger and grief behind it.

"You killed my husband! Damn you! You killed my husband!" sobbed Deborah. "I told him we should just go home. I begged him, pleaded with him, but no, he had to follow you one last time. It was like you placed a spell on him, robbed him of his will, and now he lies dead because of it."

"I am so sorry." The pain in Pennywhistle's voice was evident to everyone save Deborah. "I don't know what to say, except I feel that part of me has died with him."

Deborah looked at him contemptuously, then turned and walked away with rapid steps that suggested she could not get out of his sight fast enough.

Deborah's rage shifted to anguish as she looked at Dale's body, laid out in the back of the ammunition wagon. She stroked the corpse's hair, sobbing as she did so. "What am I going to tell Andrew?" she murmured.

Sammie Jo's hand touched Pennywhistle's shoulder. "That wasn't fair. You ain't no more responsible for his death than you are for this battle. You told him to stay in Brussels. His decision to fight was his and his alone, just like it was Deborah's decision to accompany me. He died doing what he set out for, serving alongside a man he admired, and by my reckoning, that ain't a bad way to go."

"I feel very unworthy of that admiration, Sammie Jo. I found a letter in his pocket when I tried to dress his wound; I think it is of the same nature as the one Deborah recited when we met in the rain yesterday. I never got the chance to deliver it."

"Give it to me," Sammie Jo said. "I will deliver it, and talk to her, woman to woman."

"I want her to know that I will take care of her, and Andrew, and Johnny. I will make it my sacred vow—"

"She knows that. Deep down, she already knows that, but right now she is so consumed with bitterness and grief that she can't think straight. Let me deal with her."

He handed Sammie Jo the letter, and she walked over towards the wagon where Deborah stood, weeping.

An ammunition wagon came clattering up, driven by a jubilant Sarah." I found him! I found him," she exclaimed. The wagon ground to a halt next to Pennywhistle. He was surprised at its contents: a pale looking Steven Thynne, minus his lower right leg, but conscious and sipping what, if Thynne had had any say in the matter, was fine brandy.

Pennywhistle reached in and grasped Thynne's hand. "Looks like you won't be doing any dancing for a while, but thank God, you are alive! I trust you will be able to stand the trip to Brussels. We need to get you to a hospital immediately."

"I won't argue with that, "wheezed Thynne, "but now I am damned sorry I missed the Duchess of Richmond's Ball." He smiled wanly. "Sarah heard a story about a remarkable horse doing a remarkable deed and knew it had to be Mandrake. She asked around, located the aid station, and bullied the doctor into releasing me into her care."

Mandrake, tethered to the wagon, snuffled approval.

Sarah came round and confronted Pennywhistle. "Have I your permission to drive the wagon to Brussels?"

"Of course!" Pennywhistle thought quickly. Sometimes the best way to deal with grief was to help another. "As long as you take Deborah with you. You will need a companion and... well... she has lost her husband."

"Oh, no! Oh, I am so sorry."

"Sammie Jo is attempting to console her. Speak to them. I shall have van Dreelin provide water and biscuits for the journey, and I will be sending Private Manners with you as an escort. He is the best of the drifters and fought well at Hougemont."

"Thank you, Sir Thomas! I know just the place in Brussels where my dearest Steven will receive the best care!" Sarah clasped her hands, grateful for the arrangements that Lady Densham had made. She kissed her husband, then walked over to the two women who were speaking in grave tones.

"She is a remarkable woman," croaked Thynne, barely above a whisper. "Strong willed, too. I wouldn't dare die on her. Besides, I am to be a father! A father! What a remarkable turn of events!"

"You had better not die," scolded Pennywhistle with mock severity. "You owe me a dinner at Boodle's. I intend to collect."

"And I would not want to miss the club toasting me, even though I shall be buying their round of drinks."

Thynne's usual bonhomie seemed forced. Something had changed about him, beyond the loss of a leg. The leg seemed symbolic of the amputation of his former life: living from moment to moment, making decisions on the run, and avoiding a settled existence the way a cat avoided water. There was a gravitas about him that Pennywhistle had never sensed before.

Pennywhistle turned to Johnny, who had been patiently standing by his side. "You will go with the women to Brussels. There are many details you can help with, and—"

"No!" exclaimed Johnny. "No!"

"I beg your pardon," said Pennywhistle archly. "I was unaware that you had received a field marshal's baton."

"I'm angry! The *crapauds* killed my stepfather. I want to get back at them. I can't do that in Brussels. But if I stay with you, I know I will get a chance to hurt them. Please, Sir Thomas, give me that chance. Please! Please!"

Pennywhistle took in his earnestness; the cast of his eyes, the determination in his jaw, and the tension in his posture belonged to an adult, not an 11-year-old. The lad was no stranger to war; it was not as if he did not understand what he was asking. In a way, he was a man trapped in a boy's body. Pennywhistle had a lot more confidence about how he would behave under fire than he would in a raw recruit. Johnny had proven brave, adaptable, and resourceful — qualities welcome on the battlefield no matter what the age.

"Very well, Johnny, you may stay. But do not stray from my vision. I already have the death of Dale on my conscience. I do not want to add yours."

"I'm too tough to die!" exclaimed Johnny.

Pennywhistle looked him straight in the eyes. "The invulnerability of youth," he retorted. "Most of the men lying dead here today thought the same thing. Fate has a way of slapping down hubris."

The three women approached, led by Deborah. She held a letter in her hand.

"A few words, Sir Thomas?" asked Deborah in even tones that still contained traces of anger.

"Of course. Would you prefer to speak in private?"

"No, I need to say this so everyone can hear. My late husband wrote something in this letter that reminded me of a truth I had forgotten. We are all a band of brothers... and sisters."

"That is how I see matters, Deborah, and the loss of any member of the band diminishes the whole. I gave your husband my solemn word that you and Andrew Junior will want for nothing, and I will not default on that promise."

"Thank you. I know you are good man, yet I cannot forgive you. You bring honor to the Crown, but you bring death to those who follow you. Perhaps in time I can forgive, but for now... I never wish to speak to you again."

Pennywhistle's expression became a mixture of hurt and resignation. "I cannot blame you. Yet I hope someday you will allow me the chance to win back the affections I have lost."

Perhaps, in time, although I doubt it. Now it is all I can bear to transport my husband to Brussels and give him a decent burial."

"I wish I could attend. Of course I will pay your expenses."

"Thank you, Sir Thomas. Now I must depart. It is a hot day and Brussels is running out of ice."

Pennywhistle nodded; the laws of decay were relentless. In a day or two the present battlefield would reek of a stench that polluted the air for miles in every direction. "You have your story, Deborah, though it is not the one I know you wished to write."

Deborah frowned. "That is true. I have spoken to dozens of soldiers and obtained their accounts. The reporter in me wishes to remain and gather more, but the widow's portion cannot depart this awful place fast enough." She sighed. "I have sought to present the truth, setting aside the persuasiveness of emotions for the conveyance of facts. And yet, because I am a woman and my husband has died, readers will read more than facts in my accounts, because they will know my heart is broken." She bit her lip. "The best service I can render is to report this battle, horrors and all. Doing so will honor my husband, who never spoke anything but the unvarnished truth."

"Tell your readers what kind of man he was," said Sammie Jo earnestly. "I know you serve truth, but let your pain be the ink in your pen. Let your words be..." she struggled to remember the names of the musical forms, "... his eulogy and requiem mass. Give his death a meaning beyond the loss of a single life. Let him represent good NCOs everywhere."

Deborah's dark expression lightened slightly. "My Andrew was always so down to earth and so modest that it never occurred to me that his legacy could inspire others. I shall adopt your suggestion, Sammie Jo."

Deborah, Sarah, Thynne, and their armed escort passed out of Pennywhistle's sight fifteen minutes later. "*Au revoir*," he said quietly.

Grief-stricken as he was, Pennywhistle steeled himself to attend to his duties. The battle still raged, and units needed ammunition. He learned of events through secondhand accounts furnished by officers requesting ammunition. From what he could piece together, Ney had launched a series of furious cavalry assaults on Wellington's left. At least 9,000 riders were involved, and the British had formed 22 squares to fend them off. Disciplined musketry was holding the cavalry at bay, but was worse than useless against French artillery, as each square became a stationary target for cannon fire. The 27th Innskillings, he was informed by one breathless rider, had lost 478 men out of 698, but they remained unbroken.

Another messenger spat in disgust as he relayed his news. Ordered forward to support the King's Dragoon Guards, the 470 men of the Cumberland Hussars, under the command of Lieutenant Colonel von Hacke, had turned their horses in the opposite direction and galloped wildly towards Brussels. They were a volunteer regiment of Germans who spoke no English and had received only a few days' formal training; they were clad in splendid uniforms, but they were soldiers for show, not warriors. This was exactly the sort of unreliability Wellington had had to weigh in his calculations. Most of Wellington's German allies, however, were fighting for all they were worth; Napoleon was very much their enemy.

La Haye Sainte, a walled farmstead three hundred yards in front of Wellington's line, had fallen because its defenders had run out of ammunition. One of the wagons Pennywhistle had sent forward had taken a wrong road and never arrived. Now the farmstead was a dagger pointed at Wellington's heart, and the French would likely use it as a jumping off place for an assault by the Imperial Guard, the finest troops in Europe and Napoleon's last reserve.

During lulls in the fighting, Pennywhistle had ridden forward to scan the field of battle. He'd spotted Wellington several times, accompanied by a stream of aides that grew fewer in number each time they rode past: the fighting was taking a murderous toll on officers, and it was amazing that Wellington remained unscathed. Pennywhistle observed the General personally reorganize and reposition three formations of British squares that had been badly damaged during Ney's cavalry attacks.

No detail was too small for Wellington's practiced eye, and he possessed the sixth sense that brought him to the scene of a crisis just as it reached its tipping point. The calm unflappability with which he resolved those crises gave heart to all those around him. Despite having had less than nine hours sleep over the last three nights, and having been in the saddle since 4 a.m., he radiated the purposeful energy of a man who knew exactly what he was about.

As the day wore on, even the supply dump fell under a pall of heavy smoke. The noises of beating drums, musket and cannon fire, screaming and shouting men, thundering hooves and the whinnying of dying horses gave indications of where the action was hottest. The odors of saltpeter, gun oil, grease, sweat, fear, feces, urine, mud, moldy uniforms, and rye that had been grounded underfoot were thick. Pennywhistle would have given a king's ransom for a breath of fresh sea air.

He was down to his last two wagons when a lieutenant of the 2nd Battalion, 1st Guards Regiment, arrived frantically demanding ammunition. He identified himself as Marcus Aurelias Banner. His regiment had been heavily engaged all day, and they were preparing to defend the right flank of the ridge of Mt. St. Jean against a mounting attack. When he'd left, his men had been down to their last two rounds. Two other messengers had been sent for ammunition, but they had not returned, and he was the regiment's last hope.

It was seven o'clock; seven and a half hours of heavy fighting had exhausted both sides, and each was down to his last reserves. Pennywhistle's job would be done once the wagons departed with Banner, and he would once again be a supernumerary. He was tired of being a spectator; he wanted to be a participant. He also knew from experience that sometimes the smallest of actions at just the right place could prove decisive. He had spent years battling Bonaparte, yet this was the first occasion he had ever occupied the field at the same time as Napoleon. If this was to be the battle that decided the war, he wanted, no, *needed* to be present.

"I'll come myself, Lieutenant." He looked Sammie Jo straight in the eye. "I can't order you to stay here, and even if I could you wouldn't listen. You may accompany me, but I ask you stay out of the line of fire and constrain yourself to using your weapons defensively. And I charge you with looking after Johnny, who has also made his intentions clear."

She nodded.

It was an odd sensation, Pennywhistle reflected, to know one's spouse would be riding into deadly danger. *Yet this must be what wives endure throughout every war,* he mused.

Maxwell surprised him yet again. "I will look out the both of you. And Johnny." Maxwell nodded at Sammie Jo, and she nodded back. There was no friendship in the looks, but there was respect.

Two Dutchmen drove the wagons, while Pennywhistle, Maxwell, and Sammie Jo rode alongside. Johnny sat behind Sammie Jo. Banner summarized the tactical situation for Pennywhistle as the group trotted briskly, trying not to outpace the wagons, which had to navigate around corpses and wounded men, not to mention the many dead and injured horses. The sounds were as horrid as the smells.

The entourage came to a halt a hundred yards behind the 2nd battalion.

The 2nd and 3rd Battalions of the 1st Guards Regiment, 1,600 men, occupied a spur of land shaped like a loaf of bread, three hundred yards north and east of Hougemont, and the same distance west of the *Chausse de Charleroi*. The soldiers of both battalions were lying down, in accordance with Wellington's standard practice. They were easy to see from Pennywhistle's perspective, but almost invisible to any foes advancing directly against them. Because they might have to quickly form square, all were lying four ranks deep, instead of the standard two.

Pennywhistle took out his Ramsden and saw five marching squares headed in their direction, advancing through fields of tall rye. Three more squares waited several hundred yards behind as a reserve. Their bearskin hats and blue overcoats marked them as Napoleon's Imperial Guard, the most renowned infantry in the world. A battalion square consisted of about 750 men, one company per side of the square. Each side was formed of three ranks that could present 180 muskets to discharge at their opponents. While they were not preceded by any skirmishers, each square was accompanied by two guns of horse artillery, and these had opened a deadly fire that had already driven back the British 30th and 73rd Regiments.

Since the guardsmen of the 1st Regiment could not leave their positions, the Dutchmen unloaded the barrels from the wagon and began rolling them forward. Men of each company assisted the Dutchmen in breaking open the barrels and unpacking the ammunition. They had just begun distributing cartridges to the rear rank and file when Pennywhistle realized with horror that the delivery had come too late.

He was witnessing an aspect of Napoleon's Army that had won the French many battles: their speed. The two forward squares of French Imperial Guards were covering ground at a rate that was simply beyond the skills of most infantry. They had already reached rise of ground forward of the spur.

Destination Waterloo

The 3ʳᵈ Battalion of the 1ˢᵗ Guards rose like scarlet spears, shocking the men of the fronting squares, who thought the way forward was clear. The Guards presented a front of 180 men and delivered their two volleys in quick succession. Clouds of smoke rose in the air, and the ground became a bloody carpet of writhing, crawling figures, the wounded struggling to surmount heaps of dead in a vain attempt to get clear.

The 3ʳᵈ gave three cheers and charged with bayonets, driving the French before them. They stopped at a hundred yards to regroup, and then everything went terribly wrong. Someone shouted, "Cavalry!" Torn between dressing the lines and forming square, British soldiers panicked and headed back up toward the ridge in disorder.

The pandemonium left a gap in Wellington's line wide enough for the French to punch through: a golden opportunity— except that fear's miasma was infectious in both directions. The two squares of Imperial Guard that had been savaged by musket fire and cold steel had fallen out of formation. So many of them had died, and so many officers had been killed, that the survivors milled about in confusion or stopped to help fallen comrades.

But the remaining squares were still on the advance. Disaster loomed. Suddenly, Pennywhistle saw a solution — if he acted quickly. He put the spurs to Diable and galloped off.

Confused and astonished, Maxwell and Sammie Jo exchanged baffled looks. Then Sammie Jo shrugged, told Johnny to hold on tight, and spurred her horse after Tom. Maxwell let out a whoop of delight. Action at last! He kicked his horse into a gallop that swiftly overtook Sammie Jo's lumbering mount.

Jacques Gagne's battery near Hougemont was close enough to the Imperial Guard to lend support. His section had fired two shots just before the British Guard opened fire. He had never before seen just how effective coordinated musket fire could be, especially when it came unexpectedly from point black range, directed at a closely massed target. He was shocked by results. He had believed the Imperial Guard was invincible, yet here were two battalions of Napoleon's Own reduced to ineffectiveness. Still, six squares totaling 3,000 men had not yet engaged and looked full of fight. And these battalions included the Old Guard, the elite of the elite. The Emperor always prevailed in tight spots, and Jacques was sure this one would be no different.

Sergent Jean Paul Gagne and his men were engaged in skirmishing with the light companies of the British Coldstream Guards in the fields just east of Hougemont. It was a pointless but necessary activity, not designed to win anything but simply to keep the British occupied. He, too, witnessed the repulse of the two Imperial Guard battalions, and deemed it ominous. Those soldiers were Napoleon's Middle Guard, and they should have been quick to regroup to press their advantage. Perhaps, he reflected grimly, there had been too many new men in their ranks. Even without officers, seasoned *sergents* and *caporals* would have known how to command their units.

He had just killed a British sergeant when he felt a giant fist slam into his chest and shove him backward. He rolled once, then slowly pulled himself to a sitting position. His fingers probed a wound two inches above the left pectoral. It was dangerous and would have been fatal if it had been an inch lower. His extensive experience with wounds told him that with immediate medical attention he would survive; without it, the slow internal bleeding would probably rob him of life within six or seven hours.

He made his choice without hesitation. He would not leave his men rudderless. But he had to find Jacques; he carried a small pouch suspended beneath his right armpit that would be his legacy to his nephew: six small diamonds, taken from a dead friend two days before. Not a fortune, but enough for his nephew to buy the freehold of the family farm and land of his own. His scarred soul rejoiced that one of his last acts would make it possible for his nephew to build something worthwhile and lasting.

The British 52nd Regiment was commanded by a friend of Pennywhistle's, Sir John Colborne. They had both been part of the Spanish campaign in 1812; they were close in age and similar in temperament. Since his commissioning in 1794, Colborne had reached the rank of full colonel solely on merit, not purchasing a single promotion. He had forged the 52nd into the finest light infantry regiment in the British Army and had led it with distinction through the Peninsular War.

Pennywhistle reined in Diable next to a startled Sir John.

"Pennywhistle? What in the blazes are you doing here? Last I heard you were in Vienna with the diplomats."

"Not today, Colonel; I have been on supply detail, but we were too late reaching the 2nd and 3rd Guards." In a few words, he proposed his recommendation.

Colborne smiled. "I had already reached that conclusion and was about to order a right form maneuver."

Such a maneuver would place the 52nd at right angles to the French squares, in a position to pour in deadly enfilade fire.

"You propose to do this entirely on your own hook?" inquired Pennywhistle. "I assume Wellington does not know. Should this go wrong, it is a court-martial offense." Wellington was a commander who permitted small freedom of action to his subordinates, minutely directing every action.

"I would ask permission, but there simply is not time to send a messenger and await a reply."

Pennywhistle surveyed the advancing Imperial Guard squares with his Ramsden. "I estimate their numbers as just over 3,000, Colborne."

"And my own numbers are just over 1,000. I realize it is the reverse ratio of the numbers reckoned necessary for victory, but I shall have the advantage of surprise and an enfilade position. I should welcome your assistance in fixing the location of Number 10 Company to serve as our anchor. You always had a good eye for terrain."

"I should be honored. Do you think the rest of the brigade will rally on us and assist?" The rest of Sir Frederick Adam's Brigade consisted of 580 men of the 2nd Battalion of the 95th Rifles positioned on the 52nd's left, the 180 men of the 3rd Battalion of that same regiment on the 52nd's right, and the 800 men of the 71st, also a light infantry regiment, 200 yards to the rear.

"They cannot rally if we do not begin," replied Colborne. "So let us begin. Good luck to you, Pennywhistle."

"And to you, Colborne." Pennywhistle saluted and galloped off.

Maxwell rode alongside Sammie Jo, judging her to be in greater peril than her husband. He still disliked the vinegar in her personality but had come to realize that her fire, like his, was something that could both burn bad men and provide heat for a good cause.

Sammie Jo kept her promise and pulled up 200 yards to the rear of the British brigade. Her presence was both a puzzlement and an inspiration to the officers nearby, who took turns warning her of the danger and promising to protect her at the hazard of their lives. Sir Frederick Adam rode up and introduced himself. He spoke courteously but firmly, "You should retire to safety, milady. I would not want your death on my conscience."

"I ain't going nowhere, so you better get used to it," was her tart and defiant reply. "I know my way around a battlefield, Sir Frederick, I have Maxwell here, and I brought my shootin' iron. My job is to see to my husband, and not you nor the devil can stop me."

Adam had no idea how to respond to such a fierce statement; he had never encountered a woman who directly rejected his counsel. Despite himself, he admired her courage. He finally shook his head in frustration and sighed in resignation. "Very well, my lady, but I can make no promises for your well-being."

"I don't expect any. I can look after myself just fine."

"I will protect you as well," said Johnny stoutly, placing his hand on the hilt of the short sword he wore at his side. "I have already had a lesson from Mr. Maxwell, and I will slay any Frenchman who comes too close!"

"I feel much safer knowing that" said Sammie Jo with a smile in her voice.

Colborne issued the order for "Right shoulder forward", which was swiftly relayed by drums and bugles. It was command for the left form, a maneuver akin to a wheeling movement. The furthest left-hand company was sent out as a marker, and the rest would turn forty-five degrees and march forward. The terrain afforded the regiment some cover, so unless Napoleon's Imperial Guard was posting scouts, there was the possibility that their appearance would come as a surprise.

Number 9 Company advanced as skirmishers; their job was to distract the attention of the enemy and fix them in position so that number ten company could establish itself. Three of the squares ground to an abrupt halt when Number 9 Company began peppering them with musketry. The skirmishers advanced in pairs, each man covering the other as he reloaded. They fired standing, kneeling, and prone, taking every advantage of the folds of ground.

Pennywhistle calculated angles of maneuver and trajectories of fire, then selected a suitable patch of ground. The lieutenant commanding Number 10 Company was new, and rather than resenting the guidance of an outsider officer, he welcomed Pennywhistle with visible relief.

As he moved about, Pennywhistle overheard some of the men who were murmuring among themselves and pointing. "Why, it's old Bombproofed himself!" For once, he was glad of his nickname, since it appeared to inspire confidence in soldiers who had never met him.

Pennywhistle had the company bugler signal to Colborne that he was ready to receive the rest of the regiment. The 800 remaining men of the remaining Companies completed the rest of the maneuver, moving as swiftly and quietly as they could, forming two lines of four ranks with a front of 200 yards. *Pop Pop Pop!* Number 1 Company opened fire on the nearest French square, joined almost immediately by Number 2 Company.

Even veteran troops can be unmanned by unexpected fire coming from an unthought of direction, and so it was with the French. Shouts of warning and confusion erupted, the formation wavered, losing coherence as men turned to face the source of the musket fire. Colborne did not bother with further volleys; he ordered an advance at a fast pace.

Pennywhistle, like Colborne, rode in advance of his men, encouraging them with his sword. It was a dangerously exposed position, but that was expected of commanders. Field grade officers went mounted because a horse gave them a better view and greater mobility.

The first French square broke all at once, even before Colborne's men reached them, when the line of bayonets was 25 yards distant —

such was the fear of the deadly gashes inflicted by sharp steel. More importantly, the artillerymen accompanying the Imperial Guard abandoned their cannons and fled. Two other squares caught the infection and began a slow retirement, not running, but at a brisk walk that kept them well out of range. They almost certainly would have checked and resumed their offence, but suddenly, the 2nd Battalion of the 95th began to blast the three squares with rifle fire, firing from north of the 52nd and also at a perpendicular angle. The 3rd battalion did the same from the south. The deadly hail of lead frustrated the efforts of French officers to rally their men.

Major General Adam had taken his cue from Colborne and had ordered the 71st to advance. 2,500 men were now on the move, and the tide of red and green swelled to a tsunami that swept all before them.

Two of the three squares of the Old Guard moved up to defend the men of the broken squares, firing volleys to cover the retreat of the Middle Guard instead of exploiting the break in Wellington's line on the ridge of Mt. St. Jean. Unknown to the British, the third square of the Old Guard was protecting their emperor. Napoleon had left his camp stool to march with his soldiers.

Colborne, again on his own initiative, pivoted his lines once again, signaling a right form. Advancing past the walls of La Haye Sainte, he pointed his men straight south, aimed directly at Napoleon's headquarters of Le Caillou. French morale had degenerated so completely that the French at La Haye Saint did nothing, although they could have administered a deadly stab in the back. Indeed, many began evacuating the farmstead, streaming away in headlong retreat.

Pennywhistle saw that Colborne's efforts were going well, brilliantly, in fact. That bothered him. It was too perfect. Sure enough, as soon as he began to worry, something went wrong.

The nine-pounders of Roger's battery had been lending support to the assault of Adam's Brigade, firing canister and shrapnel. They failed to adjust their aim to match the fast advance of their own side. Fragments of shrapnel began to strike the British.

Pennywhistle had gone to the rear of the line, trying to round up and organize stragglers, when one large fragment sheered the top off his hat; an inch lower and it would have been the top of his head. Nonetheless, the kinetic energy was powerful enough to daze him. Pennywhistle slipped from his saddle and landed hard.

60 yards away, five cuirassiers materialized out of the tendrils of smoke like a pack of hungry stray dogs: too few to cause real damage to a British unit, but enough to be a danger to a vulnerable officer. These men were diehards, furious at the collapse of their army and seeking to cause whatever random damage they could out of sheer spite. They saw an officer fall from his horse and began to close on him. Officers were an even fitter target for their revenge than foot soldiers, and the horse he'd been riding would make a fine prize.

Sammie Jo, Johnny mounted behind her, and Maxwell had been watching the battle through spyglasses. They also saw Pennywhistle fall. They were already spurring their horses as fast as they could go when they saw the cuirassiers converging, but they had much more ground to cover to reach Pennywhistle.

Pennywhistle felt groggy, and his vision was blurred at the edges. He staggered slowly to his feet and drew his sword, but his grip seemed wobbly, and the blade felt unnaturally heavy.

Sammie Jo screamed like a demon as she galloped forward. Aiming a long rifle from a saddle while charging was a difficult proposition, but she was as skilled a horsewoman as she was a shooter. She fired

Widowmaker at 120 yards and hit the lead cuirassier squarely between the shoulders. *One down,* she thought, *four to go.*

A captain of the 95th passing close by saw the danger and fired. A second cuirassier fell. A third flew from his saddle, courtesy of a stray round of shrapnel from the same battery that had knocked Pennywhistle from his horse. The remaining two cuirassiers were thundering towards Pennywhistle's position, yelling and waving their blades.

His vision cleared, and he felt strength returning to his limbs. He crouched slightly, bracing himself, and recalled the drill for an infantryman facing a cavalryman. Wait until the rider was very close, then duck under the horse and come up on the side opposite the rider's sword arm. Grab the rider's leg, pull down and sideways.

The horsemen came at him in succession, not together. The first chopped wildly at him, but he stepped aside at the last instant and moved between the legs of the second animal. A hoof clipped his backside, sending him sprawling in the mud. The first horsemen circled back and rode at him. Pennywhistle rolled aside and delivered a glancing blow to the horse's right fetlock.

The second cuirassier aimed his sword squarely at Pennywhistle's throat, but the horse veered aside at the last second because it had only half a rider. Maxwell's sword stroke, delivered from above and behind, had been so filled with angry power that he had literally cut the man in half.

Sammie Jo galloped alongside the first horseman and swung Widowmaker as a club that crashed into the man's jaw. The rider flew from his saddle and hit the ground with a squelchy thud. Before Sammie Jo could halt her horse and finish the job, Johnny leaped from the saddle. He jumped upon the chest of the stunned cavalrymen like a homicidal elf and plunged his sword into the man's heart. The cavalryman's eyes were glassy by the time Sammie Jo reached him.

Johnny captured Diable's reins, while Sammie Jo and Maxwell together hauled Pennywhistle out of the mud. "Thank God, you made it," said Pennywhistle, barely above a whisper, with what seemed to him an agonizing slowness. His head ached and he felt very tired. Sammie Jo examined the top of his head and found a large welt.

"I think you have a concussion. Your battle is done. We need to get you to Brussels," she said with conviction.

Johnny threw his arms around him and hugged him tightly. "I am so glad you are alive."

"Wait, Sammie Jo," Pennywhistle protested, "I still have fight left in me. I must see this battle through to the end." He noticed his vision was blurring again, and his words sounded slightly slurred.

"Your wife is right, Colonel," said Maxwell, with unwonted compassion. "You have done your duty and more. You have been an example to us all, but now it's time to rest on your laurels."

Pennywhistle had not the strength to resist when Maxwell hoisted him onto Diable's back. Seeing how he swayed in the saddle, Sammie Jo mounted up behind him and took the reins. The four slowly trotted back whence they had come.

Pennywhistle felt his consciousness fading, but one of his last sights was of a man in a bicorne hat and grey overcoat on a horse. The horse stood in the middle of the last remaining Imperial Guard square. It was Napoleon, the ogre who had vexed Europe for years, and he was finished. "Now I can die a happy man," Pennywhistle muttered, as he slumped forward into the deepest of sleeps.

To Jacques Gagne's disgust, Fivel's men abandoned their pieces once the cry of "*Le Garde Recule!*" went up. Rumors were rife that the Prussians had arrived on the field, fresh and eager for revenge. His crews ignored his pleas to stay the course. They cut the surviving horses from the traces that bound them to their limbers, then galloped off. Those limited to two feet ran for the rear. Fivel himself was shot dead when he attempted to rally a group of fleeing men. Jacques sat silently weeping beside his remaining gun and wondered how such a noble enterprise had come to such a sad conclusion. His Legion of Honor suddenly seemed a worthless trinket that should be consigned to a dusty attic rather than worn proudly in public.

His uncle, deathly grey, hobbled up, then dropped in a heap at Jacques' feet.

"Oh no, oh no!" sobbed Jacques, pulling his uncle up and bracing his back against the cannon wheel.

"Don't grieve," wheezed his uncle, "I've had a good run. I've seen and done things most men only dream about. I have provided for my men, and now my final duty is to see to you." He reached his shaking hand under his uniform and produced a small velvet pouch which he placed in Jacques' palm. "Open it.'

Jacques did so and his mouth dropped open in astonishment. "Where did you get this?"

"They originally belonged to a Russian Count. A friend looted them in Moscow, but he died recently, without any family. After 15 years of campaigning, I was the closest thing he had to family. Use the diamonds wisely. Show and tell no one. There is a merchant in Charleroi named Monsieur Tallard who can supply you with food, clothing, and transportation for the journey home. His shop is at the sign of the Griffin, hard by the bridge over the River Sambre. A single stone will pay him. Once home, take the remainder of the stones to Monsieur Jacquet in Bayeux; he is a jeweler I know and trust. Just mention my name and you will receive a fair price. You will have enough to live the life of a prosperous farmer." He coughed hard for a few seconds. "Be very careful about whom you trust."

"Right now, the only man I trust is you, Uncle. I so wish Pauline were here to help. She would know what to do."

"I warn you, Jacques, the army is collapsing. Discipline will evaporate, as will supplies. Men will kill for food and shelter. I have seen it before in Russia. You will wonder if your former comrades even belong to the same species."

Jean Paul coughed hard several times. He squeezed Jacques' hand. "Go home and be the good Quaker I could never be. Remember the courage you displayed but consign the cause you fought for to the dustbin of history. The Bourbons will return: make a show of embracing them publicly, no matter how much you despise their characters. Do what I could never do, and forgive those who wronged you. Tell your mother and father I am sorry for the cruel things I said about them. I ask only one favor: name a child or grandchild after me."

"I will, Uncle, and I will never forget you."

"Good... good... good." The light left Jean Paul's eyes, and his hand went limp.

Jacques let go of the dead hand reluctantly. He had never felt so alone.

He took a deep breath. It was 250 kilometers to his home, but he could make it. He believed in himself in a way that no man who had not survived the darkness of battle could understand. He picked himself up and began walking, stopping every so often to fill his haversack from those of the fallen. He knew he could expect no more supplies until he reached Charleroi.

Destination Waterloo

His disgust with the cost of war increased as he walked. The detritus of battle was a horrid thing; he had to thread his way through acres of dead and dying men and horses, enduring their shrieks, moans, and pleas with a forced heartlessness that was the opposite of his compassionate nature. He stepped over a body that had taken the full force of a shrapnel shell. The skin was pock-marked like Swiss cheese, the skull split open; teeth were scattered in every direction, and the force of the explosion had driven three coins and a pen into the flesh of the man's ragged left thigh. The Emperor he had almost worshipped was gone, likely speeding his way to Paris, leaving behind the cost of cleaning up his mistakes.

He never wanted to hear of war again, but he knew he had been irrevocably changed by it. He prayed to the compassionate God that he had nearly forgotten that he would be restored to his former nature, but deep down knew that he would never again be the farm boy who had left Normandy three months before.

Rifle came bounding up to him. He was caked with mud, but Jacques bent down and gave him the strongest embrace he could manage. He would not have to make his journey alone.

He bowed his head, visualized the sign of the Griffin, and resumed walking. He kept that sign in his mind as he plodded forward, but when his stomach growled the wooden placard was replaced by a vision of his mother's face holding out a freshly baked apple pie. The pie smelled wonderful. Even though he knew his mind was playing tricks, the sweet scent drew him forward, his mouth already watering in anticipation of the first delicious bite.

***

Wellington reached his three-story headquarters in the village of Waterloo at 10:30, two and a half hours after Jacques Gagne had started his long walk home. He was weary, sad, and covered in powder grime. He sank into a chair and stared at the floor. His aide, Peter Percy, handed him a list of casualties from among the general officers, and his face darkened as he read the names. Picton, Ponsonby, du Platt, and van Merlin were dead. Uxbridge, Cooke, Kempt, Pack, Grant, Dornberg, Adam, Bijilandt, Kielmansegge, and Halkett were wounded. Nearly every general officer who had directly intervened in a crisis had been struck down. He had campaigned with many of those casualties for years, and their loss affected him deeply. He let out a long yawn of exhaustion, desperate for sleep.

Hesitantly, Percy addressed him. "I hope you don't mind, Your Grace, but I took the liberty of putting Sir Alexander Gordon in your bed. He lost a leg, as you know, and it is not likely that he will last the night."

"You did right, Percy. Just find me a cot." His words came out as a hoarse whisper. "You are my only aide still on his feet." Tears began to stream down his face. "Nothing except a battle lost can be half so melancholy as a battle won. It is terrible to lose so many friends." He sobbed quietly, as his customary reserve crumbled like an ancient wall battered by too many tempests.

"I hope to God, Percy, that I have just fought my last battle."

EPILOGUE

The End of an Era

London, England

Three Months after Waterloo, Pennywhistle lounged in a red leather wing chair, his outstretched legs on a matching footstool, directly in front of a roaring fire in a book-lined study. A cold, autumnal rain pelted the windows. He sipped slowly from a mug of black coffee while perusing a copy of *The Times*. Thynne sat alongside him in a similar chair, his one leg on the floor, his peg leg on his footstool. Thynne had just put down a cup of Darjeeling tea so he could take a bite of a lemon scone.

Countess Margaret Grosvenor had given Pennywhistle the use of her Portland Street townhouse, as she no longer needed it since her marriage to the Earl. Sammie Jo and Sarah had turned the place into a hospital for Pennywhistle to recover from his concussion and Thynne from his amputation. Pennywhistle knew his godmother was prepared to sell the place to him for a song, but he was not sure he'd want to remain in London. The city was home to the best doctors, so he was bound to it until his recovery was complete, but Sammie Jo missed the fresh air, pristine streams, and deep woods of the country, causing him to consider whether to rehabilitate the ancient family residence of Whistlestop on the Scottish border. There she could hike and hunt to her heart's content.

The third convalescent was Maxwell, who had vowed to give up alcohol completely. He had realized that drink started his bouts of rage, rather than soothing them. The withdrawal symptoms of the first week had been horrific: seeing people who were not there, enduring nightmares in the short intervals when he was not in a state of agitated wakefulness, nausea, vomiting, hot and cold sweats, and the recurring sensations that hundreds of spiders were crawling under his skin. He had become violent at times, and it had taken Pennywhistle, Sammie Jo, Thynne, and three servants to hold him down. With Maxwell's permission, they'd finally resorted to a straitjacket.

Sammie Jo and Sarah kept him hydrated with lots of water, lemonade, and orange juice. Twice daily, Sammie Jo served him an herbal tea based on the recipes of her medical mentor, Walks-in-Water. The brew contained a variety of New World herbs designed to quiet cravings as well as promote general healing. She confined him to a bland diet that was rich in fruits and vegetables, banning heavy foods like pork pies and sausages fried in lard. Boiled fish and lean meats became the order of the day, but sweets were permitted because they provided the sugar that had formerly been delivered by alcohol. By the third week, Maxwell's face glowed with the pinkness of health rather than the blotchy ruddiness of the heavy drinker. His eyes sparkled with clarity and welcome, instead of being veined with red and narrowed in suspicion. His mouth seemed more likely to erupt in a smile than a scowl, and his carriage became relaxed and easy instead of resembling a cobra poised to strike.

He had shed twenty pounds, chiefly around the waist and ribs, and had begun a program of vigorous exercise that gave direction to his energies. He raced up and down the stairs of the five-floored establishment ten times a day and adopted the duties of a stevedore whenever heavy packages arrived on the townhouse's loading dock.

Destination Waterloo

His belligerence had been replaced with reflection; he was doing a great deal of soul searching. He had begun attending Methodist meetings, and he had hired a solicitor to locate the illegitimate child he had never seen, as well as the mother. He spent long hours playing with Nicholas, wondering as he did so what his own child was like.

To mark his first month of sobriety, he purchased a puppy, seeing it as a first step on the road to a life guided by love rather than hate. The dog was a Newfoundland, like the dog he had had as a boy. He named the dog Regulus, "little king", and took great delight in training and walking him. The beast soon became a friend of Plymouth, who loved to hitch rides on the dog's back.

Thynne's insouciant optimism did not desert him, even though he went through six prosthetic legs designed by six different makers before he settled on the one that worked best. Learning to walk again was hard, and it took him a month before he dared to negotiate the pavement in front of the townhouse. He extended the length of his walks a little each day and was currently up to a mile: half a mile in the morning and another in the early evening.

The doctor had assured Pennywhistle that his recovery was going as well as could be expected. He had awakened 48 hours after being plucked from the battlefield, a duration of unconsciousness which had caused the doctor much concern. His memory of June 18th was spotty and confused: scattered snippets of events with no apparent relation to each other.

He no longer suffered from headaches and vertigo, but he tired easily, and it was only in the last few days that he could concentrate sufficiently to read anything more demanding than the highlights of the daily newspaper. Sammie Jo read to him in the afternoons from his favorite author, Edward Gibbon, broadening her own education as she did so. She found the Roman Empire a fascinating study, filled with people so unusual that no writer of fiction could have invented them.

Sammie Jo's reading of history sparked an interest in acquiring the formal schooling she had never received, so Tom had hired a tutor at her request. The tutor, Martin Bloomfield, had been educated at Cambridge and had also fought at Waterloo, losing an arm. His health was not good, but his mind was first rate and he loved spreading the benefits of a classical education.

Sammie Jo rode Diable twice daily, continuing to scandalize their neighbors by refusing to ride sidesaddle.

Pennywhistle had always loved to paint, and it became a major part of his therapy. He had previously painted in watercolor; during his convalescence he transitioned to oil and canvas. The still life became a fixture of his practice, featuring flowers, foods, books, and objects bound closely to his daily existence. He found the study and depiction of simple objects relaxing. He also painted portraits of everyone in the townhouse, and as his endurance improved, landscapes. The garden behind the townhouse became a favorite subject, and as he painted, he often struck up conversations with the gardener. Jared Josephs was a genial man who frequently said that working closely with nature was a great boost to his spirits.

One day, Pennywhistle asked Josephs if he could assist, wanting to see for himself if gardening was indeed a tonic for the soul. He found that digging with his fingers and planting his toes in the dirt while coaxing new life from the soil was indeed restorative: Mother Nature proving herself the greatest healer of all.

After seeing so many men go hungry during the Waterloo Campaign, Pennywhistle became particularly enamored with growing foodstuffs. He focused on tomatoes, a New World vegetable that was just beginning to gain popularity in Europe. Checking on the progress of his vines became a daily ritual.

The music room had been closed off since the death of the Earl of Leith ten years before, and the grand piano had been covered by heavy moleskin cloth. One day, on impulse, Pennywhistle removed the cloth and played a few tentative chords remembered from a childhood spent at the side of an indifferent mother who happened to be a master pianist. Pleased with the result, he continued to play, and lessons from years ago came back to him as the keyboard grew more welcoming with each passing note. He found a cache of music in the seat box and decided an hour a day spent mastering its contents would not only improve his manual dexterity but provide a soothing balm for the spirit. The first piece he chose was thoughtful, haunting, and mysterious: Beethoven's Moonlight Sonata; the perfect choice for someone reflecting on what to do with the rest of his life.

Noticing the comfort her husband derived from music, Sammie Jo began to host weekly musical gatherings. She invited local musicians to evenings of supper, discussion, and chamber music. These conversations were entirely about the world of music, not politics or social scandal, and Pennywhistle was gradually drawn out of his shell. Here was ground that would not blow up under him. He listened intently to discussions of new compositions, rising composers, the nuances of variations, and discoveries afforded by improvisation, taking as keen an interest in the distinctions of instrumentation as he formerly had in military armaments.

The week before, Pennywhistle had been penning his letter of resignation when a messenger from the Admiralty arrived with the unexpected news that he had been promoted to full colonel. He suspected Wellington was behind this. Most colonels of marines were naval captains, not marines. The rank was treated as a reward and a sinecure, requiring no duties but furnishing a handsome annual salary.

He had no interest in ever drawing his sword in anger again, and it would be many months before he could wield a blade with anything resembling his old skill. He wondered if he could assist the Royal Marines in another way that did not involve fighting. He had heard rumors that the Marines were about to undergo a massive peacetime reorganization, and he had very definite ideas of what form that should take. Upon reflection, he thought he would like to be an advisor and consultant.

He did find the time to attend the meetings of the Royal Society, of which he was a Fellow. Matters of natural philosophy were much more pleasant to contemplate than military affairs. A discussion of how the Figeater Beetle differed from the Green June Beetle was of more interest to him than arguments about whether Wellington or Bonaparte was the greater general.

The Earl and Margaret called daily, reporting their progress running a charity for Waterloo widows and orphans. Magdalene de Lancey visited often as well. Widowed a week after the battle, she mostly kept company with Sammie Jo and Sarah, who provided much needed comfort.

Private soldiers dropped by from time to time, Waterloo veterans who were down on their luck since leaving the army. They called at the tradesmen's entrance, seeking a meal and a few pence to see them on their way. Pennywhistle made it a point to speak with each veteran at length and hear his story. Not one left without a full stomach and a pocket full of coins. Pennywhistle did not see this as charity but as a delayed payment for services rendered.

Long walks with Sammie Jo had helped rebuild his stamina, and they strengthened the bonds between the two. Much of London was vibrant with promise, but the grinding poverty of certain areas and the bleak faces of their inhabitants troubled him far more than they had before the injury. Having suffered himself, he had heightened sensibilities, and a strong wish to alleviate the suffering of others.

His fame as a man who had been present at both Trafalgar and Waterloo had resulted in a spate of party invitations from the elite of society, but so far, he had declined them all. His memories of both battles were deeply private, shared only with his wife and a few close friends who had also seen battle. The last thing he wanted was to field endless questions about war from effete men or armchair commanders who thought war was some kind of game and could never understand the toll it exacted from a man's soul. However, just that morning his wife had persuaded him to change his policy and accept an invitation to the Duchess of St. Alban's Ball. Sammie Jo loved dancing, and she had argued convincingly that dancing would be beneficial to the recovery of his full coordination. Besides, he'd reflected, seeing her smile as she whirled and twirled always brought him pleasure.

Now Pennywhistle put his mug down and turned toward Thynne, angrily waving his copy of *The Times*. "Did you see this? The Prince Regent has christened the 1st Guards 'The Grenadier Guards' on account of their defeating the Imperial Guard. He has granted them the right to wear bearskins copied from their opponents! Neither the role of Colborne nor the 52nd nor Adam's Brigade is mentioned in this blasted article! Those fellows of the 1st Guards only saw off two squares of Napoleon's eight, yet they are taking credit for the complete defeat of the entire Imperial Guard! That is outrageous!"

"But it's to be expected. The Guards officers come from the Kingdom's most influential families," said Thynne, without any hint of indignation. "Those families want Whitehall to tell a story that glorifies them, even if it's only partly true. They want their moment in the sun, and the publishers of newspapers are determined that their patrons shall have a glorious reputation; they know on which side their bread is buttered. Remember, newspapers are merely the rough drafts of history. The truth will come out eventually, probably years from now, the work of some quiet researcher. I anticipate that this battle will be meat for a great many historians, and that controversies about the battle will become as commonplace as thorns on a rosebush. No sense in getting worked up about it, Tom."

The door opened, and Sammie Jo briskly walked in, her voice bubbling with good cheer. "The rain has stopped and the sun's come out. I thought you boys might want to join me while I take Nicholas out in his perambulator."

Pennywhistle's resentments vanished in an instant.

Nicholas continued to grow and prosper with each passing day. Pennywhistle and Sammie Jo spent so much time with their son that he had begun to question the need for their nanny, Mrs. George. But the woman had worked so hard and earnestly to correct her earlier mistakes that he did not have the heart to discharge her.

"What a splendid idea! Let me grab my hat and we can be off."

When the four reached the front doorsteps, they were surprised to see Maxwell in full dress regalia, holding a bouquet of roses that he had purchased from a passing flower girl. He had just raised his hand to hail a cab.

"Where are you off to?" asked Sammie Jo in surprise. "You haven't been to any parties, but you look like you are on your way to one now."

Maxwell turned to face the four, his expression a mixture of hope and fear. "I just received word from my solicitor that he has found my lost Lenore and my child. They are waiting to meet me at his chambers. I have dressed for the occasion to reassure Lenore that I have shed the mantle of the irresponsible wastrel, and I am bringing roses as a gesture of apology for not fighting for her years ago. The child is a boy, and she has named him Maximillian, after me! It is a most incredible turn of events. I only hope I am worthy of them."

"Of course you will be!" asserted Sammie Jo confidently. "Though when I first met you four months ago, I would have advised them to flee. Your inner demons would have frightened that child out of years of growth and turned Lenore's hair grey. Now I am certain that you will do right by those you want to love. I wish you Godspeed!"

Sammie Jo impulsively swept her arms round his waist and squeezed hard. It was a gesture of real affection that surprised Maxwell. The embrace was the equivalent of receiving a diploma, indicating that he had made sufficient amends and achieved sufficient sobriety that he was ready to rejoin the world. He looked forward to writing a new and happy chapter in his life — and to eating traditional meals that were tastier than his recent fare, even if they were less healthy.

He returned the embrace, realizing that Sammie Jo and company had become what he had never had in childhood: a family that cared enough to fight for him. He determined that Lenore and Maximilian would never again experience the lack of the sense of family that had bedeviled his own childhood.

"Best of luck, old man," said Thynne cheerfully, clapping him on the shoulder.

Pennywhistle shook his hand vigorously. "You will find being a father brings out the best in you."

"Might I hold Nicholas for a moment?" said Maxwell. "Without his unquestioning love, I would never have begun my search."

Sammie Jo handed Nicholas to him, and the infant cooed in delight. Maxwell decided that those tiny sounds were the most sublime music in the world.

The front doors burst open, and Mrs. George leaned her head out the doorway. As soon as she spied them, she began shouting, "Come, oh, do come quickly! Lady Sarah has just gone into labour!"

Thynne's ability to walk suddenly improved tenfold.

***

Village of Kingston, Kent, England.

Deborah Dale had been busy since Waterloo and had turned the energy of grief to writing a book. Countess Grosvenor had reassigned peg-leg Grimsby, the Earl's man, to Deborah, and Grimsby took over the day-to-day running of the Black Robin Inn. Andrew Junior, Johnny, two recently hired journeymen and three women writers kept her press going. Her dispatches had created a sensation in London, coming out at a time when Waterloo mania was sweeping the country.

Deborah wrote from dawn to dusk every day, pausing only for a quick supper and a catnap, then continued writing by candlelight into the long reaches of the night. Her book, *Recollections of Waterloo by a Woman of Perception and Quality*, was ready for publication two months after she had penned the first word.

The first edition sold out within two days, and soon everyone who was anyone was reading it, including the Prince Regent. It was popular because it avoided describing the strategy and tactics of Waterloo and instead focused on the direct actions and feelings of the men who had fought there. Her late husband figured prominently in the narrative. It eased the pain of her grief, knowing that Dales' life, his fidelity, and his courage would be remembered. This was a poor substitute to having Dale alive with her and Andrew, but it was the best she could do.

Writing the book had caused her to reexamine her anger at Thomas Pennywhistle. Deep down, she knew it was misplaced, but she was not quite ready to let go of it. She might consider meeting him and Sammie Jo for tea... in a year or two.

*****

Village of Waterloo, Kingdom of the Netherlands

Hugo van Dreelin's quest to find his soldier son Lucas had been successful, and he struck up a friendship with the village mayor, Monsieur Mansard, the man who had given food to his son. Van Dreelin became Mansard's personal shoulder to cry on, listening over frequent dinners to the horrors of cleaning up the carnage of the battle.

Many of the wounded had endured two nights without any care at all; the doctors of Wellington's army had been utterly overwhelmed. The first night after the battle had been the worst. Most of the survivors were too exhausted and shaken to scour the field for lost comrades; the next morning, friends of the fallen undertook rescue work, acting on an *ad hoc* basis.

The local peasants who'd had their farms and possessions despoiled by the several armies exacted their revenge: prowling the battlefield that first night in search of valuables to be taken from the wounded and dead. The peasants not only did nothing to aid the wounded, they sometimes hurried their passage to the next life.

Many soldiers carried their only wealth on their persons. Watches, jeweled rings, mother-of-pearl lockets, money belts, and pouches of coins were favorite targets. But money could also be made from the sale of gold and silver buttons, gorgets, and epaulettes. Silk sashes fetched a good price, since they could furnish the raw materials for expensive dresses.

Help from Brussels arrived early on the 19th. The mayor of Brussels had requisitioned every horse, driver, wagon, or cart to evacuate the wounded, but it took two full days to move the Anglo-Allied wounded, and an additional three days to move the French. The citizens of Brussels made a magnificent and largely successful effort to turn the entire city into an enormous hospital. British, Prussian and French wounded were treated with equal care and compassion. With the abdication of Napoleon, the French became guests, rather than prisoners of war. As soon as they were well enough to travel, they were sent on their way.

The exact number of dead and wounded was still uncertain, but Mansard told van Dreelin it was in the neighborhood of 43,000. There were also at least 12,000 dead horses. Because of the huge number of dead, disposing of the bodies had proven difficult. The stench of rotting corpses and the armies of rats, mice, insects, and flies had made burial detail an assignment that every sane soldier strove to avoid. Local peasants had been hired to supplement the military men, but they had demanded exorbitant rates to perform those grisly duties. At first, they dug and filled large burial pits, but hot days had accelerated the process of decay. Eventually, the grave diggers bowed to the inevitable and resorted to mass funeral pyres.

Dentists from Brussels descended on the field, eager to extract the teeth from thousands of dead soldiers. For them, Waterloo field was, figuratively speaking, a goldmine. Dentures were nearly always made from the teeth of the dead; collecting teeth from graves was one of the grisly ways that poor folk could earn a few pennies. But teeth scavenged from paupers' graves were of very poor quality. Here were corpses of soldiers: fit, healthy men who had died in their prime. "Waterloo teeth" would soon become a commonplace throughout Europe.

Even three months after the battle, some corpses remained unburied. They had largely been stripped of flesh by crows and carrion eaters. The peasants took the bones and ground them into fertilizer;

the men who had destroyed their crops were now helping to grow new ones.

Waterloo mania was sweeping England. Wealthy tourists were arriving to view the site of Britain's greatest military triumph. The local peasantry prospered by selling them battlefield souvenirs and by serving as guides. The same peasants who had despoiled the wounded and the dead now told stories in which they cast themselves as guardians and saviors of injured British soldiers.

Sergeant Major Edward Cotton, who had fought in the battle, became the most sought after guide. Sergeant Major Owens forged a successful partnership with him, opening a battlefield souvenir shop to which Cotton led visitors after a tour was done. Sergeant Rogers, who had driven one of the ammunition wagons, retired from the army, but instead of purchasing a farm in England he brought his family to Belgium. There he went into business with Cotton and Owens, driving the luxury carriages demanded by tourists who desired to see the battlefield but did not want to suffer inconvenience while doing so.

***

Village of Subles, Normandy, France.

Jacques Gagne reached home in early July, after a two-week journey. Privates Etienne Dupuy and Phillipe Dionne from his unit had found him in Genappe and joined him on his journey. They took comfort in his quiet self-assurance, seeing him as an island of order in a sea of chaos. His companions hailed from farm backgrounds, were only five years his senior, and had no real families to which they could return.

As they walked the long, dusty roads and narrow country lanes, the unique bonds that the trio had forged in battle strengthened to the point that Jacques came to regard Etienne and Phillipe as the brothers he had never had. The trio discussed the apple crop that would need harvesting in autumn, and began hatching plans to open a distillery that would turn those apples into Calvados, the apple brandy for which Normandy was famous. War had aged them but had not killed their youthful ability to dream.

Jacques followed his uncle's instructions, so his small band avoided many of the travails that plagued the masses of servicemen who had been turned loose to fend for themselves.

The proudest day of Jacques' life came when he purchased the freehold of the family farm on behalf of his father. The opportunity to become a landed man was one of the few good things to come out of his short military adventure. The other had been meeting Pauline. Not a day went by that he did not think of her, and yet her memory did not prevent him from planning for marriage a few years down the road. He would have plenty of prospects now that he was a landowner himself, and he would make sure his wise mother approved of the alliance.

He purchased his own orchard of 45 hectares, 111 acres as the English reckoned things, n which grew the three varieties of apple considered most congenial to the making of calvados: *Bisquet*, *Bedan*, and *Petit Joly*. As he explained to his parents, he was a man now, and could no longer go back to living under their roof as a dutiful son; it was time for him to strike out on his own. They fully approved.

He and his two friends managed the orchard with equal parts love and military efficiency.

The farmhouse on his new property would need a lot of work, but building rather than destroying was exactly the tonic the three friends needed. Before they began their labors, he and his friends sat down in some rickety chairs around a dust covered table. Jacques opened an expensive bottle of *Chateau du Breuil* Calvados and poured three glasses. "Soon we will produce our own brand which will put this to shame," said Jacques.

"Perhaps," said Phillipe, "an enterprising veteran will produce a liquor so extraordinary that he shall name it for our fallen commander, who, in spite of how his campaign ended was an extraordinary man."

Rifle came to his side and woofed, so Jacques poured a few milliliters in a bowl and set it at the dog's feet.

He and smiled at his friends and raised his glass in a toast: "To our new life!" He stopped in shock. "*Mon Dieu!* I almost added '*Vive l'Empereur!*' He thought for a moment, smiled, then raised his glass again. "One for all and all for one!"

"One for all and calvados for fun!" shouted Etienne.

"I like that even better!" laughed Jacques. They clinked glasses, and Jacques took his first slow, appreciative sip of the famous brandy, which warmed his tongue rather than burning it, and transformed into a sublime complexity of flavors. He grinned at his friends and ruffled Rifle's fur. He might have lived a lifetime in the past months, but he was still only sixteen years old.

THE END

John Danielski

Author's Notes

Wellington summed up the Battle of Waterloo neatly. "Bonaparte attacked in the old style and was driven off in the old style."

The descriptions of the organizations, tactics, weaponry, and mentality of British, French, and Prussian forces are accurate, though the minor characters representing them are mostly fictional. The names of battery, company, regimental, brigade, and division commanders are rendered accurately.

Location

Though the results of Waterloo were large, the battlefield itself is small, roughly three-square miles. I have walked the battlefield and was struck by how tightly everyone must have been packed: by the battle's end, nearly 170,000 men were fighting in that compact area. The monstrous carnage in such a limited space would have meant that in the hours following the battle's end, it would have been impossible to have taken more than a few steps without treading on either a man or horse that was dead or dying.

By contrast, Gettysburg, the greatest battle of the American Civil War, covered ten square miles. It lasted three days, rather than nine hours, involving roughly the same number of men but generating

8,000 more casualties. Its significance only became clear 18 months after it was fought, while Waterloo's importance was immediately apparent.

The Gettysburg Battlefield today looks much like it did in 1863, though the field now has more than 1,300 statues, monuments, and plaques, as well as 410 cannons. Waterloo has few of the first three and none of the fourth. The field was drastically altered in 1826 when the Mt. St. Jean Ridge was excavated to provide earth for the 40-meter-high Lion Monument that now dominates the field, marking the spot where the hapless Prince of Orange was wounded. Wellington angrily remarked to the King of the Netherlands, Orange's father and the man who had commissioned the monument, "You have destroyed my battlefield."

Waterloo tourism began within weeks of the battle's end. One of the most prominent of the early tourists was the novelist Sir Walter Scott, who visited in late July of 1815. He returned home with a great many battlefield souvenirs, some of which can be seen today at his estate in Abbotsford, Scotland.

Units of Measurement and Napoleon's (disputed) height

It should be noted that although the Metric System was adopted by the French in 1795, French artillery still used inches and pounds for barrel widths and solid shot. Those were slightly different from their English counterparts. As examples, a French 36-pound cannon ball was equivalent to a 32-pound English one, and Napoleon was five feet two in French inches, but in English inches closer to five feet six.

The submarine

The *Nautilus* submarine described in Chapter 1 existed, and I have described its general shape and particulars as best I could; the process was complicated because there are 3 full size models of it displayed in three different museums, and all are slightly different. It is likely the original plans were modified several times. The controls I described are based on conjecture and reflect the limited technology of the times.

Nautilus was designed and tested by the inventor and engineer Robert Fulton on behalf of the French in 1803 and did submerge successfully and sink a test vessel with a torpedo. Napoleon's initial interest in it died for unknown reasons, and the vessel was sold for scrap later in that year. Fulton built what appears to be an improved version for the British Admiralty in 1805, but tests proved abortive and the British cut Fulton loose.

The desertion of the Cumberland Hussars

When the Cumberland Hussars rode into in Brussels, they spent several hours spreading panic, proclaiming that Wellington had been soundly beaten. That panic only abated when the first official messengers arrived from Wellington around 10 pm.

The commander of the Cumberland Hussars, Lieutenant Colonel Adolphus von Hacke, was later arrested, court-martialed, and cashiered from the Army. The men of the regiment were never charged with a crime, and curiously enough they were allowed to add the battle honor of "Waterloo" to their regimental flag before the unit was disbanded in 1816.

The real "Bombproofed"

Captain Charles Diggle, commanding Number 1 Company of the 52nd at Waterloo, was severely wounded in the left temple by canister. Diggle made a miraculous recovery, thanks to a steel plate that a surgeon placed in his head. He kept his shattered skull fragments in a box, along with the canister fragment that had caused the wound, and on his return to London had the steel plate replaced with one of silver. In the center of the plate, engraved in elaborate letters, was the word "Bombproofed." He was ever after known by that sobriquet and lived long enough to become a major general under Queen Victoria.

Source Material for characters based on real people

Pennywhistle is patterned after a real-life Royal Marine hero, Captain Thomas Inch. Jean Paul Gagne is based on a Gascon named Rene Garnier, a veteran who saved Napoleon from a lynching when he was on his way to exile on Elba. Despite his having seen the man only once six years before, Napoleon's remarkable memory allowed him to recall the exact details of Garnier's service.

Sammie Jo's original inspiration was Deborah Sampson Gannett, a woman who disguised herself as a man and served successfully in the Continental Army during the Revolutionary War. She distinguished herself and her true sex was discovered only by accident. She received a government pension in 1804.

Capitaine Julien Fivel did serve at Waterloo and met the fate described in the novel.

Pauline Fourès was an actual camp follower, but of an entirely different kind than the Pauline described in the book. Fourès had smuggled herself to Egypt disguised as a *chasseur* and was the wife of an officer that Napoleon soon reassigned. She became his very public mistress during that campaign. She outlived Napoleon and three husbands. She later made a fortune in the Brazilian timber trade and died in Paris, well into her seventies.

The real Sergeant Major Edward Cotton fought at Waterloo with the 7th Hussars. Upon his retirement from the Army after twenty years of service, he married a woman from near Waterloo, opened an inn, and became a famous tour guide as well as a collector of many Waterloo relics. His hand-drawn and very detailed 1846 map of the battlefield can be viewed at the National Army Museum in London.

Dale, Thynne, Maxwell, the Earl and Countess Grosvenor, and Jacques Gagne are composites of several people, intended to reflect archetypes common to the times.

The descriptions of Wellington and Napoleon are based on details taken from the best and most current biographies about them: Rory Muir's *Wellington: A Path to Glory 1769-1814* and Andrew Robert's *Napoleon: A Life*. Both are highly recommended.

The Duchess of Richmond's Ball

My description of the Duchess of Richmond's Ball differs somewhat from those found in Thackeray's *Vanity Fair* and other novels about the Regency Period, but it is based on sound research. Many novelists based their descriptions on paintings which were made long after the event by artists who had not been present; they are replete with anachronisms and inaccuracies. Historians are not even sure of the actual building in which the ball took place, and accounts of events vary depending on which authority you consult.

Facts and fictions

In an amazing feat of prescience, Wellington commissioned a survey of three spots in Belgium where he might fight Bonaparte more than a year before the great battle of June 18, and the future Waterloo Battlefield was one of them. Although the map made by the Royal

Engineers of the Mt. St. Jean area did go missing, it was only for a day and caused no real problems.

10,000 Saxons were discharged by the Prussian Army after a mutiny and sent home in disgrace, though the castoffs never leagued together to form a criminal organization.

The Prince of Orange's idiotic order at Quatre Bras is accurately described and really did result in the destruction of most of the 69th Regiment.

The battle scenes involving Hougemont are composites of numerous events, but the barring of the gate by McDonnell and the predations of the axe wielding *L'Enforcer, sous lieutenant* Legros, were real.

Something like the incident with the insane women wandering into battle after escaping from an asylum did occur, but it happened in 1944, during Field Marshal Montgomery's Operation Market Garden.

The horse Mandrake is based on the British racehorse Eclipse, who won more than 200 races and was renowned for his size, intelligence, and almost human personality.

The army dog Rifle was real, but he was a pet of the 2nd battalion of the British 95th Regiment, not a French dog. He often accompanied the riflemen into battle, snarling loudly and standing guard over wounded green jackets. He disappeared after Waterloo to the consternation of the battalion. Weeks later, it was discovered that he had survived the battle but had been eaten by hungry Belgians. The British were so angry that they almost came to blows with the Belgians over this.

Yes, there was a five year old girl present at the battle.

The last survivor of Waterloo was Elizabeth Watkins, who died in 1904. As the five year old daughter of a camp follower, she was not a combatant but helped to dress wounds of many men and witnessed the worst parts of the battle.

The question of who beat the Imperial Guard and won the battle for Wellington had long been considered settled, the laurels awarded to the British 1st Foot Guards. I, however, side with the new research of the author Nigel Sale, and consider the credit partially misplaced. The Guardsmen did defeat two of the French Squares, but the other six were defeated by the 52nd Regiment, later assisted by the men of Sir Frederick Adam's Brigade. I invite the reader to read Sale's book and decide for himself.

Destination Waterloo is a work of fiction, and I have taken occasional liberties with the truth in the interest of drama. Historical fiction is about what could have been, might have been, or should have been, sometimes more than what really happened. Novels are entertaining escapism, and historical education is merely an occasional fringe benefit. A novel is a form of theatre and is to reality what a funhouse mirror is to an ordinary one. As an example, Shakespeare created a compelling villain in Richard III, but his character was considerably different from the real person. For those who seek the history beneath the entertainment, I have provided a list of five books to serve as guides to the events of June 18, 1815.

Destination Waterloo

An epitaph written for a soldier killed at Guadalcanal could just as easily apply to any of the dead at Waterloo:

And when he gets to Heaven, to St. Peter he will tell:
'Another soldier reporting, sir. I've served my time in Hell.'

Suggestions for Further Reading

1. ***The Waterloo Companion*** by Mark Adkin.
This coffee table-size book is the best single guide to the battle and the perfect primer on Napoleonic warfare for both the beginner and the aficionado. Lavishly illustrated with plenty of classic paintings and original art, maps, and uniform plates, Adkin provides compact and easily understood explanations of the strategy and tactics of the campaign, the six phases of the battle, the individual commanders, and the weaponry employed. He uses many photographs taken of the modern battlefield by himself, superimposing the movements of individual units upon them. He even includes diagrams showing the exact configurations of the infantry when marching, in line, column, or square. It's an expensive volume, but worth every penny.

2. ***Waterloo: Four Days that Changed Europe's Destiny*** by Tim Clayton.
An excellent, compact, and highly readable pop history of the battle, with a heavy emphasis on human interest stories.

3. ***Waterloo, The Campaign of 1815, Volume Two: From Waterloo to the Restoration of Peace in Europe.*** By John Hussey.

A very detailed, scholarly study of the battle. Sometimes dry and pedantic, this is recommended chiefly for those wanting a deep knowledge of the battle and willing to take the time to explore some of the more obscure controversies associated with it.

4. ***The Lie at the Heart of Waterloo: The Battle's Hidden Last Half Hour*** by Nigel Sale.

A highly controversial but compelling book that posits that the final victory against the Imperial Guard was won not by the British Foot Guards but by the 52nd Regiment. This upsets the traditional view of the battle's conclusion, but the author supports his revolutionary thesis with plenty of sound information. The only weak point is his belief that Wellington engaged in an actual conspiracy to deprive the 52nd of its deserved laurels.

5. ***Waterloo. Four Days, Three Armies, and Three Battles*** By Bernard Cornwell.

A good, quick read that feels like a novel. Not surprising, because Cornwell is the author of the internationally acclaimed Richard Sharpe series set during the Napoleonic Wars.

John Danielski worked his way through university as a living history interpreter at historic Fort Snelling, the birthplace of Minnesota. For four summers, he played a US soldier of 1827; he wore the uniform, performed the drills, demonstrated the volley fire with other interpreters, and even ate the food. A heavy blue wool tailcoat and black shako look smart and snappy, but are pure torture to wear on a boiling summer day.

He has a practical, rather than theoretical, perspective on the weapons of the time. He has fired either replicas or originals of all of the weapons mentioned in his works with live rounds, six-and twelve-pound cannon included. The effect of a 12-pound cannonball on an old Chevy four door must be seen to be believed.

He has a number of marginally useful University degrees, including a *magna cum laude* degree in history from the University of Minnesota. He is a Phi Beta Kappa and holds a black belt in Tae-Kwon-do. He has taught history at both the secondary and university levels and also worked as a newspaper editor.

BLUE WATER SCARLET TIDE

BY

JOHN DANIELSKI

It's the summer of 1814, and Captain Thomas Pennywhistle of the Royal Marines is fighting in a New World war that should never have started, a war where the old rules of engagement do not apply. Here, runaway slaves are your best source of intelligence, treachery is commonplace, and rough justice is the best one can hope to meet—or mete out. The Americans are fiercely determined to defend their new nation and the Great Experiment of the Republic; British Admiral George Cockburn is resolved to exact revenge for the burning of York, and so the war drags on. Thanks to Pennywhistle's ingenuity, observant mind, and military discipline, a British strike force penetrates the critically strategic region of the Chesapeake Bay. But this fight isn't just being waged by soldiers, and the collateral damage to innocents tears at Pennywhistle's heart.

As his past catches up with him, Pennywhistle must decide what is worth fighting for, and what is worth refusing to kill for —especially when he meets his opposite number on the wrong side of a pistol.

PENMORE PRESS
www.penmorepress.com

King's Scarlet

BY

John Danielski

Chivalry comes naturally to Royal Marine captain Thomas Pennywhistle, but in the savage Peninsular War, it's a luxury he can ill afford. Trapped behind enemy lines with vital dispatches for Lord Wellington, Pennywhistle violates orders when he saves a beautiful stranger, setting off a sequence of events that jeopardize his mission. The French launch a massive manhunt to capture him. His Spanish allies prove less than reliable. The woman he rescued has an agenda of her own that might help him along, if it doesn't get them all killed.

A time will come when, outmaneuvered, captured, and stripped of everything, he must stand alone before his enemies. But Pennywhistle is a hard man to kill and too bloody obstinate to concede defeat.

PENMORE PRESS
www.penmorepress.com

Capital's Punishment
by
John Danielski

The White House is in flames, the Capitol a gutted shell. President Madison is in hiding. Organized resistance has collapsed, and British soldiers prowl the streets of Washington.

Two islands of fortitude rise above the sea of chaos—one scarlet, one blue. Royal Marine Captain Thomas Pennywhistle has no wish to see the young American republic destroyed; he must strike a balance between his humanity and his passion for absolute victory. Captain John Tracy of the United States Marines hazards his life on the battlefield, but he must also fight a powerful conspiracy that threatens the country from within.

Pennywhistle and Tracy are forced into an uneasy alliance that will try the resolve of both. Together, they will question the depth of their loyalties as heads and hearts argue for the fate of a nation

PENMORE PRESS
www.penmorepress.com

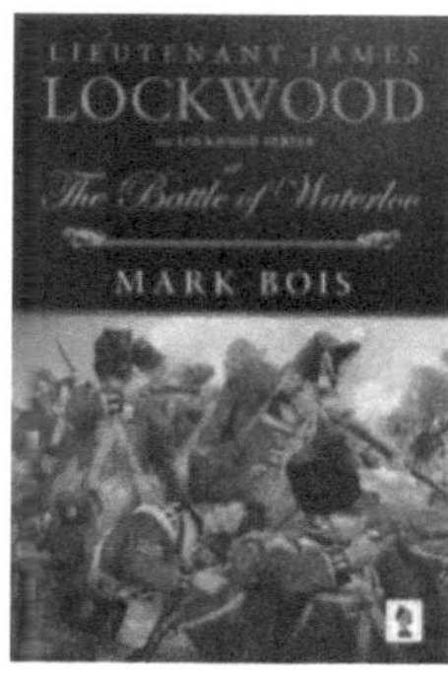

Lieutenant James Lockwood

By

Mark Bois

"Captain Barr desperately wanted to kill Lieutenant Lockwood. He thought constantly of doing so, though he had long since given up any consideration of a formal duel. Lockwood, after all, was a good shot and a fine swordsman; a knife in the back would do. And then Barr dreamt of going back to Ireland, and of taking Brigid Lockwood for his own."

So begins the story of Lieutenant James Lockwood, his wife Brigid, and his deadly rivalry – professional and romantic – with Charles Barr. Lockwood and Barr hold each other's honor hostage, at a time when a man's honor meant more than his life. But can a man as treacherous as Charles Barr be trusted to keep secret the disgrace that could irrevocably ruin Lockwood and his family?

Against a backdrop of famine and uprising in Ireland, and the war between Napoleon and Wellington, showing the famous Inniskilling Regiment in historically accurate detail, here is a romance for the ages, and for all time.

"... Bois' meticulous research and command of historical detail makes this novel a must read. He sets the standard for research and understanding... and the audience will demand more novels from this new author. Historical fiction welcomes Mark Bois with open arms." – Lt. Col. Brad Luebbert, US Army

PENMORE PRESS
www.penmorepress.com

Attache Extraordinaire
by

John Danielski

A real game of Thrones that changed Europe

Lies, intrigue, betrayal: An average day at the Congress of Vienna. Kings, Czars, and Emperors dance a diplomatic minuet what will determine the fate of Europe for a century. Officially, Royal Marine Major Thomas Pennywhistle is the British Naval Attaché. Unofficially, he is on a covert mission to protect the prince Regent. Because the man who murdered his brother is the same one who threatens his prince, Pennywhistle must decide if justice should come by gavel or a gun.

Facing spies, assassins and an impenetrable cliff topped by an impregnable castle, Pennywhistle must confront a ruthless adversary fully as resourceful as he. A serious misstep could explode a conference desperately seeking to repair the damage done by Napoleon. Success will never add to his reputation, while failure

Could smash it forever

PENMORE PRESS
www.penmorepress.com

BELLERAPHON'S CHAMPION

BY

JOHN DANIELSKI

Deep within each man, lies the secret knowledge of whether he is a stalwart or a coward. Three years an un-blooded Royal Marine, 1st Lieutenant Thomas Pennywhistle will finally "meet the lion," protecting HMS *Bellerophon* at the Battle of Trafalgar.

Not only will Pennywhistle be responsible for the lives of 72 marines aboard *Bellerophon* but their direction will fall entirely on his shoulders since his fellow Marine officers consist of a boy, a card shark, and a dying consumptive. If he has what it takes to command, it will take everything he's got.

In the course of battle, he will encounter marvels and terrors; from valiant foes to women performing miracles, from the skill of acrobats to the luck of the ship's cat, from a dead man still full of fight to a coward who has none. He and his marines will meet enemy élan will with trained volleys and disciplined bayonets. Most of all, he will meet himself; discovering just how dark his true nature really is.

Europe will be changed forever by Trafalgar, and so will Pennywhistle.

PENMORE PRESS
www.penmorepress.com

www.ingramcontent.com/pod-product-compliance
Lightning Source LLC
Chambersburg PA
CBHW060726190726
48285CB00001B/84